# Divine Ability Series:
# Ezra's Burden

By
C. R. Ward

**Eloquent Books**

Eloquent Books
An imprint of Strategic Book Group
P.O. Box 333
Durham CT 06422
www.StrategicBookGroup.com

ISBN: 978-1-60911-563-0

# Divine Ability Series:
# Ezra's Burden

*"Work hard and don't suck."*
*C.R.Ward*

# PROLOGUE

The self-proclaimed world's greatest serial killer sat in a bar called Kamikaze nestled in the suburbs of southern West Virginia. His hair was blonde and slicked back and he wore a white shirt with a dark blazer and jeans. He knew the woman he was talking to would be considered very attractive to most people. Every man in the bar had his eye on her from the moment she walked in, but he had caught her eye. Jennifer Parker was dead in that instant; she just didn't know it yet.

The two had found a small corner to get some privacy and the conversation became sexually charged quickly. Just like he knew it would. The woman wore a red miniskirt that hugged her figure so that it looked painted on, topped with matching red heels. Her hair was long and honey blonde. Her hair was styled with hairspray, which he thought odd—most women didn't use hairspray any more. The poor woman was stuck in the eighties.

One glance at her told you what she came to the bar looking for. She wouldn't find it. Not tonight.

"What's your name?" she asked.

"My name is Willie," he said, thinking that was as good a name as any for tonight.

"Mmm. Willie, how about a drink?"

"I'd love one."

Jennifer was already drunk when she walked into the bar and probably high on some other kind of drugs, maybe heroine. He could smell alcohol all over her. How she had managed to get to the bar alone was anyone's guess. The bar wasn't very crowded because it wasn't a weekend or a college night. So the man decided to be patient, to go through the motions. Why rush? He already knew how this night would end for Jennifer.

He reached into his blazer, pulled out a lighter, and flipped it open. He peered through the fire at Jennifer and listened to the flame. The fire spoke to him. It always spoke to him. It was his motivation for almost everything he'd done in life. It was his driving force, his muse.

"Oh God, you have a lighter. Thank you," Jennifer said as she pulled out a pack of cigarettes. "I was dying for a smoke."

After two rounds Jennifer was plastered, but Willie didn't even have a slight buzz. They talked for the rest of the night until they found themselves being ushered out by the bartender.

"Where yo car, Wallie?" Jennifer slurred. She had to lean on Willie to walk. He considered changing his mind about Jennifer. It wouldn't be as fun if she was too drunk to know what was happening to her.

"Right here," Willie said pointing to a dark green Altima. "Why don't you let me take you home?"

"I wuz wondern' why you wuz make'n me wait so long."

A laugh escaped Willie as he thought of what he wanted to do to Jennifer. After an hour and a half of talking to her, he realized how annoying the woman was. She was nothing but a whore with no dreams or ambitions. She would've been suited to be nothing more than a trophy wife and she knew it.

The lights in the bar were off and the parking lot was empty. The bar hadn't been that busy so it didn't take long for the workers to cash out and leave. The bouncers had all left and Willie and Jennifer were alone within forty-five minutes of the bar closing. Willie pressed Jennifer up against his car and leaned in close. He somehow caught the scent of her perfume hidden under all the alcohol. He was rock hard now and wasn't shy about letting her know it.

He ran his hand over her breast and pulled her tighter. Willie opened the back door to the Altima and threw Jennifer inside then climbed on top of her. Jennifer's moans were soft and electric. Even though she was too drunk to talk, she was a passionate lover.

Willie reached down tore Jennifer panties off, and then unbuttoned himself. Curiosity had always been a weakness for Willie. He didn't plan on going this far with the drunken whore but he wanted to know what she felt like. Willie was large and he wasn't gentle. He hammered down on her, giving her all he had. He wanted to make her scream. He reached into his blazer pulled out his lighter and then flicked it on.

He ran the light over her skin. The sudden pain sobered her up a little.

"Wha . . . what are you doin'?"

Willie quickly took his free hand, covered Jennifer's mouth, and touched the flame to her hair. Willie knew he shouldn't do something like this in the car, but it was what the fire wanted. What the fire told him to do. He didn't stop thrusting inside her as Jennifer screamed beholding the end of her hair on fire. Willie wondered if she regretted using all that hairspray.

Willie held Jennifer down as she struggled to put out the fire in her hair. The drugs and alcohol in her system had her caught some where between extreme terror and intense pleasure. Willie wouldn't let her put the fire out. He let her scream as the fire started to scorch parts of her scalp. He reached into another pocket of his blazer and pulled out a small, but sharp knife. Blood from Jennifer's neck sparkled in the light from the fire as it poured onto the back seat like a dam busting into a riverbed.

Willie looked deep into Jennifer's pale blue eyes as the life drained out of her. He couldn't have been happier with her. She was perfect. He could see it in her eyes; Jennifer had reached orgasm as she died. Perfect.

Blood was splattered across the back seat of a dark green Altima outside the empty bar parking lot. Willie sat in the driver's seat and looked at the body in the back seat. Blood was everywhere; the body was mangled and broken, and chunks of flesh barely clung to bone.

Willie knew he had gotten a little carried away. He knew he would. He always did. He had killed enough people to know how it worked for him. He had killed so many people that a normal person would lose track. Not Willie. Every life he had taken was his, and he made sure he kept them with him always.

He started the car, pulled out of the parking lot, and headed to his main objective. This was his last night of warm-ups. Everything that happened now would lead him to his ultimate goal.

It would be easy enough to get rid of the body in his back seat. The car itself was stolen, so Willie was calm and confident. Both the body and the car would be discarded as easily as his false name and appearance. He wouldn't be caught. He couldn't be caught.

He had killed in almost every state in the country and no one ever came close to catching him. He had terrorized towns from coast to coast, all for practice, all to come home. Death was his art, one he had crafted and mastered.

Everything he had done was a prelude. Now he was back in his small, insignificant, backwater town. He crested a mountain and saw two signs. One read: Welcome to Bluefield.

The other sign had pissed him off ever since he first saw it. It was insulting and made him want to gag every time he even thought about it. The sign read:

Bluefield
Birthplace of Dr John F. Nash Jr.
1994 Nobel Prize Winner

He was the best thing to come out of this god-forsaken town. The only comfort he found in the sign was what he imaged it should one day read. He imaged the sign that this town truly deserved: Birthplace of the world's greatest serial killer.

As he came down the other side of the mountain he saw the Frank S. Easley Bridge, the orange lights of Bluefield Avenue and the train tracks that ran underneath it. He saw Bluefield State College campus to his left and a baseball practice field to his right. He flicked open his lighter again and looked out over the town; the fire knew what it wanted. The fire not only spoke to him, but it also showed him the future. It gave him a glimpse into things to come. The message and images were loud and clear. The whole town was already on fire. But nobody knew it yet.

# CHAPTER I

"Lord, thank you for another day, thank you for waking me up in my right mind and for the favor that I walk in because of your love for me." That is the first thing I try to say to myself every morning. That was my prayer.

I woke up with the sun shining through my apartment window and repeated my prayer three times. Not so much as to make sure God heard me as to remind myself that I really meant it.

I stretched out across my king-sized bed and felt the same restlessness flow over me that came every morning. For some reason, as tired as I might be, I never really feel like I can sleep until the sun starts to come up. I looked at the clock and saw 7:30 on the dial.

I forced myself out of bed and began my morning ritual: push-ups until my arms burned, sit- ups until my stomach and back were sore, and three sets of curls with twenty-five pound dumbbells.

After my workout I made my way to the shower and tried to clear my head. I let the warmth of the shower flow over me, taking my time. Showers can wash away more than dirt. Sometimes when I step in, it's as though everything in my life is left on the outside. I washed away my restlessness and my nightmares.

I had to force myself to leave the shower before it turned cold and began to get dressed. As I did, I started to think of all the things that would be involved with my day. None of what was ahead of me was particularly exciting, so I seriously considered getting back into bed. It wasn't an option. I knew that if I did, I would try to stay there for another week.

Today was going to be my first day back at the Bluefield Daily Telegraph. I'm one of only two photographers on staff

1

there, and I hadn't been to work once in the two months since my life was turned upside down. Everyone there knew my story. Hell, everyone in the state of West Virginia seemed to know my story, so nobody at the paper had minded my absence. I don't think anyone there really expected me back at all, but I had to get my mind moving again. I was going crazy staying locked up in here listening to nothing but myself.

I wasn't happy with the idea of having to deal with everyone at work. I knew they all meant well, but who really wants to deal with the stares, the people trying not to stare, and the people who don't know what to say so they just avoid you? I knew it wasn't going to be easy for me, but I never did anything the easy way, despite my nickname.

I dressed in blue jeans, a plain red shirt, and a pair of white and red New Balances. It wasn't my normal work attire; I usually tried to look a bit more professional, but I didn't feel like going all out today. I didn't really need to dress nice for my job anyway. I just took pictures.

I took one quick look at myself in the mirror as I finished brushing my teeth and repeated my prayer. Looking at myself for several seconds, I saw my dark brown skin and the five o'clock shadow of a beard that I had decided to let grow for the time being. I made myself stand to my full height of six foot, two inches, rubbed my hand over my short hair, and took a deep breath.

Again I thought of just getting back in bed, but I knew I needed to get out and face the world. I just wasn't sure if the world wanted to face me right now.

When I was fully ready to go, I had the hardest time leaving my apartment. I was fully dressed, but I couldn't make myself leave, so I walked around for several minutes trying to hype myself up just to walk out the door. I had the feeling that I had forgotten something, but I knew I hadn't. I was just stalling myself on some level, looking for a good enough reason to stay. As I walked around I noticed that even though I've felt like crap, my apartment was still relatively well kept.

I made my way back into my room, ready to give up on my attempt and resigning myself to trying again tomorrow. As soon as I got to my room, my sword collection caught my eye. It wasn't so much of a collection as it was a single Japanese katana that I had hoped would be the beginning of a collection. I had hung it on the wall located at the foot of my bed so that whenever I sat up or just looked down from the bed, I would see it.

Standing in front of the sword made me remember how much it meant to me. I had always been fascinated with Japanese culture, their concepts of honor, the code samurai lived by called Bushido. I ran my hand along the hilt of the sword and rubbed the fabric, admired its black finish and its gold embroidered designs on the hilt and sheath for the katana.

I love swords. I respect them.

Although it was in my room where I spent most of my time over the past eight weeks, I hadn't paid much attention to it. That, if nothing else, spoke volumes as to how severe my mood had been. Swords were ancient symbols of strong, skilled warriors, a reflection of how I imagined myself to be.

The Bible compares the words of the Gospel to a sword, one that could cut down lies, lust, greed, and any other form of evil that may assault you. The Bible says the more of the word you know in your heart, the sharper your sword. Like the sword hanging on my wall, my spiritual sword was sharp and I believed it could cut through anything. I knew that there was no obstacle I couldn't overcome as long as I kept my faith and held to the Gospels in my heart. I just needed to remember to pay attention to it when things got rough.

I finally convinced myself to stop being a bitch-ass, grabbed my Nikon camera and headed out the door.

I walked out onto Pauli Heights parking lot and made my way to my 2005 black Cavalier that I liked to call Dirty Vegas. I named it the day I got it at a police auction. I was told that it was confiscated from some big time drug dealer from Las Vegas who was caught here in West Virginia. A lot of people had passed on the car at the auction because the police found it with about ten pounds of weed and a dead body in the trunk. One could only assume that the owner was trying to hide out in West Virginia after some bad deals went down. I really didn't care who owned it before me because it was in good shape and didn't have many miles on it, which made it a keeper in my book.

It was a bright mid-summer day with hardly a cloud in the sky. After a self-imposed exile, a person forgets how nice something as simple as the sun can feel. My apartment was located in the very back of the complex next to the field of wildflowers outside my living room windows. I took a deep breath, soaked in the scenery, as I unlocked my car door and inhaled the sent of flowers and fresh cut grass before getting in the car.

Suddenly I realized that being cooped up had changed me more than I'd thought. I had never been the stop and smell-the-flowers-type of guy so I couldn't help laughing at myself. Getting out was definitely going to be good for me.

After my brief laugh at myself, my mother's laugh some-how worked its way into my thoughts. I missed her. I wished things had been different between us. I saw her face in my mind smiling at me.

My eyes watered, but no tears fell.

Being emotional just wasn't me. I didn't know how to handle it. I had cried more in the past weeks than I had in the past several years. I took in the scent of flowers again, and the shadow of a bird passing overhead caught my atten-tion. The beauty of the day stopped me from falling into an-other funk. I laughed aloud, harder this time. Emotional just doesn't fit me well. I remembered my swords, both material and spiritual. I was convinced more than ever that getting out would be good for me.

I climbed into Dirty Vegas, pulled out of Pauli Heights and made my way to work, hoping any surprises of the day would be pleasant ones.

# CHAPTER 2

## CAMARA

Camara Johnson had nothing to wear and she was late. She had planned on being at work thirty to forty-five minutes early to give a good first impression for her first day on the job. It wasn't her dream job by far, but she always liked to put one hundred percent of herself into anything she did. Camara thought starting off strong and letting co-workers know what to expect was an important thing for women in the work force.

Camara rumbled through her closet, trying to find the best thing to wear to pull off the look she wanted. The sad thing was that while she felt that she didn't have anything to wear, she knew too well that the problem really was that she had too much. Too many options, too many combinations.

The local weatherman on WVVA news had said that it would be warm today, around eighty, and slightly cloudy. Knowing that should have made it easier, but she was pressed for time and that was making her stressed in mind. Sunny and warm with business professional in her mind equaled some form of skirt. Sometimes Camara hated being a woman—she wished she could just throw on some clothes and head for the door like a man could.

Forty-five minutes later she had decided what to wear and was looking herself over before she left the house. A skirt suit was her choice for the day. It was light tan and came down to midway of her shin, with a matching adjustable band around her waist that made the skirt hug her frame the way she liked. The top of the suit was cut in a v-neck with the collar of a suit but had a white layer underneath. The sleeves were rolled up to just above her elbows, but were loose giving her plenty of room. She hated tight things around her arms. Because of the skirt she chose dark brown, three-inch heels to match.

Camara wasn't made for corporate work. She would much rather sit in a café somewhere with a laptop to finish her book. She hated feeling as though she had to present herself in a certain fashion; she would much rather follow her own personal style.

All in all she was happy with the way the outfit complemented her smooth, dark- brown complexion that she was raised to be very proud of. She took the time to check the shoulder-length braids in her hair as she gave herself one last look.

She was confident. She was ready.

She made her way downstairs where she was instantly hit with the smell of eggs, bacon, sausage, and buttered toast. It was embarrassing that she was almost twenty-five years old and her mother still cooked for her, but she got the feeling that her mother enjoyed it. She swore that when she was forced to move back home almost a month ago, though her mother may have had on the firm "I told you so" face, she was still happy to see her.

She made her way through the living room and, instead of going for the door, she headed for the kitchen. This part of the day was also planned into her schedule; she knew how big her mother was on nutrition. They were living on a fixed income but her mother always insisted on buying as many organic foods as she could for as long as Camara could remember.

Because of her mother, she had become extremely picky with food. She had become picky with almost every aspect of her life, which was something she didn't really like about herself. At one time, she had tried to change this, in efforts to enjoy life, sublimating her standards and principles. It ended just as badly as she should have known it would. Because she wasn't happy with herself, she got mixed up with the wrong crowd, the wrong man. She remembered for a brief moment, how perfect he'd seemed, how she thought that it could work between them. After everything that happened between them, all he ever really gave her was a one-way ticket back to West Virginia, and not even one year after meeting him.

Camara always heard how attaching yourself to the wrong man could turn your world upside down and make you doubt yourself like a child waiting for father's approval. What you don't always hear is that the wrong man doesn't have to be a bad man; he isn't always the drug dealer on the corner. Sometimes it's the nine-to-fivers that just aren't worth anything. Somehow they had both dragged each other down from the beginning.

But, those were thoughts for another time. One of her favorite quotes came to mind: "Optimism can make you look stupid, but cynicism always makes you look cynical." Words of Calum Fisher. To Camara, truer words had rarely been spoken.

Once she reached the bottom of the steps, she was greeted by her mother. Camara's mother was short, but still in good shape for her age. She had always had a strong presence, one you couldn't help but notice when you entered a room. This morning she still had her hair wrapped in the bun she placed it in every night before bed and was still wearing her long silk nightgown that was colored brilliantly like an African dashiki.

"Good morning," her mother said as Camara sat at the table and began to eat.

"Good morning. Did you sleep all right?"

"As well as I ever do. You?"

"Not so great. I'm a little nervous about this job. I don't even really know why it's bothering me so much. I don't even know what I'm going to be doing there."

Camara's mother turned from the stove with a puzzled look. "How did you get the job when you don't even know what the job is?"

Camara inhaled some of her eggs and toast and was now moving to her bacon.

"They hired me as a writer but something went down with their principal photographer. So when they saw I had photography experience on my resume, they offered me more money if I do some photography, too. I know I'm going to be doing some fill in, I just don't know for what."

Camara's mother turned back to her cooking. "So you know what your job is, you just don't know which you'll be doing today."

"Pretty much. They did say something about me going to the Beaver-Graham game tonight so don't let me leave without my camera."

"You're going to wear that to the game?"

Camara finished most of her breakfast and was washing it down with her last sip of juice as she got up from the table to answer her mother.

"No ma'am. I put some extra clothes in the car. I don't want to be at the game in something like this all night. I'm not sure how long I'm going to be there but there's no reason to be walking on the field trying to take pictures in heels. I was thinking about staying for the whole game if it's any good."

"Well, have a good first day. Be careful if you're going to be driving home after the game tonight. You know how the roads can be coming and going from the county."

"I may have been gone for a while, but I still know the roads like the back of my hand. I love you ma."

"I love you, too, baby. And Camara?"

"Ma'am?"

"This is the last time you wolf down my cooking like that, ya hear?"

"Yes, ma'am."

Camara walked down the driveway to her forest green 2004 Saturn and got in. She used to love her car until she moved back home and had to deal with the constant shifting of a manual transmission on West Virginian hills again.

As she drove closer to Bluefield, she began to feel more worried about what her new job would be like. She really didn't get a chance to look around much or meet too many of the people she would be working with. That was always the hardest part about a new job for her, being the new person replacing someone else everybody already liked. Being compared to the one who was there before, and feeling like you had to match up to someone you'd never even met was the absolute worst part of starting a new job.

Camara pulled up to the Bluefield Daily Telegraph fifteen minutes early, which calmed her nerves a bit. She always stressed over being on time. Getting to the paper early gave her a little boost of confidence. The Telegraph was a three-level gray building located across the train tracks from Bluefield State College. Camara looked at the building from her car for a moment. This building would either be a stepping stone or a prison. There was only one way to find out which.

When Camara walked through the second pair of double doors, she saw the receptionist, a woman in her mid-fifties with pale, wrinkled skin, silver hair, and brown reading glasses that were a little too large for her face. Camara remembered the woman's name from the day of her interview—Kim Kohls.

The receptionist tilted her head to look over her large glasses at Camara. A slight smile formed on the edges of her mouth, "Well, look who's back. You must have gotten the job. Today the first day?"

Camara was a little thrown. She thought she picked up a hint of sarcasm in the woman's voice, but she had only met her once and she had always thought it best to reserve judgment of people until she got to know them.

For now, Camara just smiled and said, "I'm as ready as I could be. I'm just glad I got here early. I might have been here earlier, but I didn't know what time the building would be open."

"Oh, I'm always here around this time. I swear, sometimes I feel like I live here," Kim said taking a second to laugh at her own joke. Camara faked a polite laugh.

"Well, I'm glad I made it here when I did. I wanted to look around a little before I get started doing . . . whatever I'm going to be doing."

Mrs. Kolhs leaned back into her seat looking puzzled, "No one told you what you're going to be doing today?"

"I know I'm going to be writing, but beyond that I think I might have some other duties. They were a little vague on what those duties were. Something with photography, I think."

"Oh, that's right I had almost forgot about Ezra," Mrs. Kolhs said with a solemn face. Camara thought she sensed Mrs, Kolhs drifting off into a sad place for a moment.

"Who is Ezra?"

Mrs. Kohls snapped back to reality by Camara's question.

"Oh, he's just one of your co-workers. You'll meet him sooner or later, if at all," Kim said as she laughed at herself again. "Did anyone give you the tour?"

Camara was a little put off at the dismissal of her question. Sometimes withholding judgment on people proved more difficult than it should be. Some people just made it hard.

Again she smiled, half laughed at Mrs. Kohls and said, "No, not really. They didn't really have time to show me around. Everyone seemed busy trying to cover that fire that broke out in Bluefield that day. My interview went by pretty fast."

"Well, we can't have you coming in on your first day without knowing the lay of the land, can we? Hold on, darlin'. I can't leave the front desk, but I can get you someone to show you around. Hold on." Mrs. Kohls got up from her desk and went into the room directly behind her.

After about a minute or so, Mrs. Kohls came back with a man Camara thought couldn't be more than a couple of years older than her. He was about 5'9" with short neat, sandy-blonde hair and wore a dark yellow shirt with brown khakis, shiny brown shoes, a brown tie, and a million-dollar smile.

Camara noticed a refined quality about him, something about the way he carried himself said he was a confident and well-educated man. Camara thought she would like him right away, but if there was one thing that leaving West Virginia for college had taught her, it was to reserve judgment on people who gave both good and bad first impressions. Leopards may not be able to change their spots, but Camara knew a few that could camouflage them.

Mrs. Kohls walked over to Camara and extended her hand in Camara's direction. "Nate," she said, "this is our newest hire. She'll be our new writer."

Camara decided to take some initiative since it was obvious that Mrs. Kohls didn't remember her name. She extended a hand to her appointed tour guide and introduced herself.

Camara made sure her handshake was firm, looked straight into brownish-green eyes and said, "Nice to meet you. My name is Camara." She noticed that his shake was firm but gentle. Camara always thought you can tell a lot about a person by their hands.

"Nice to meet you too, Camara. My name is Nathan Goodman, but just call me Nate," he said.

Mrs. Kohls interrupted, saying, "Well, I leave you in good hands, Camara. Nate will take good care of you. I would show you around myself, but like I said, I can't leave the desk. And I have some paperwork I need to do. They like to throw all the busy work my way." Kim laughed at her own brand of humor again. She made her way to her desk.

Nate and Camara both laughed politely at Mrs. Kohls' little joke. Nate gestured for Camara to follow him through a doorway on the left of the door leading into the business office.

"Thank you, Mrs. Kohls," Camara said as they were leaving the lobby.

"Kim."

"Ma'am?"

"Just call me Kim. Mrs. Kohls was my mother."

"Well, thank you, Kim."

As Nate opened the door for Camara, she realized she hadn't noticed it before. The last time she was here she used the elevator that was directly on the right after entering the second double doors of the building. Nate was leading her to a stairwell leading to the second floor of the building. As they walked up the steps Nate said, "So this your first day, huh?"

"Yeah."

"You nervous?"

"A little, but not really. I'll just need some time to get used to my surroundings."

"Well, that shouldn't take long. This isn't a very big building. There isn't really a lot to see. Didn't anyone show you around after your interview? They usually do that."

"No, I don't think anyone really had time to. All I really got to see was the front desk, the elevator, and the room where they asked me a bunch of questions and made me take a written test."

"Ha, I forgot about that essay they made you writers do. I bet that sucked. Don't worry too much about Kim, by the way, she's harmless. More goofy than anything else."

Camara managed a small laugh and a slight smile as they reached the second floor. Then, they entered what looked like the break room. Three small tables sat in the center of the room with a coffee machine, two snack machines, a sink, and several kitchen cabinets. There was also a small refrigerator along with several trash cans.

"As you can probably tell, this is the break room. There's not much to it, just make sure you don't eat anything out of the vending machines. They don't change the food out often enough so you just don't know when you're going to get something that's close to its expiration date."

"Noted," Camara said as she turned her attention to a door directly in front of her. "What's through there?"

"That's where they handle the money. Some nice people, but you beat everyone here so you'll have to meet them later."

Nate then led Camara through another door adjacent the one they had just entered. Through the door was yet another stairwell leading upward. Nate took the stairs, continuing to talk to Camara.

"So do you think that you're going to like it here?"

"I've had a fair first impression of everything, so it's looking good so far. What do you do, Nate?"

"Ads," Nate replied as he reached the top of the staircase and opened the door for her. "I'm actually one of the sales reps for the paper. I spend most of my day going out and trying to get local businesses to advertise in the paper. I'm only here for about two or three hours a day on average. The majority of my day is spent out in the field. I'm just an early bird."

As Camara passed through the door Nate held open, she recognized the main newsroom. Her interview was held in the meeting room to her far right. There was a row of offices to the left. Computers were on every desk and the writers had their own spaces. There were no cubicals, which Camara hadn't expected when she saw the newsroom on the day of her interview. Nate walked through the door in a straight line continuing his tour.

"This is where you'll likely be doing the majority of your work, I'd say. Off to your right is where Nancy Hasley sits. She writes the obituaries. She's the only one who pretty much has something new to write about every day no matter what. I think she's off today though."

Camara smirked and raised an eyebrow at Nate's sense of humor; she wondered what he would be like in a more social setting. She didn't bother to tell him she already knew Nancy.

"Right in front of where you'll be sitting are the sports writers. To the left is where Ann Cornwell sits. She does the personal ads. The center pillar looking thing here is where the computer mainframes are. Try to stay out of there because if you so much as walk by it and something breaks, people will start pointing the finger at you."

Camara followed Nate around the other side of the room where all the graphic designers and the sales reps sat. Next, he took Camara back to the corner of the office and took her to the area on the left where the darkrooms were. Once they finished there, Nate led her back into the main newsroom.

"Well, that pretty much concludes the tour, Camara. Only printing room is left. There are a couple of other things I could show you, but why spoil the mystery? If you keep coming in early, you should feel free to explore the building as much as you want. There aren't many locked doors around here, and it's pretty much an open door policy so you know . . . feel free."

Camara thanked Nate for showing her around as he made his way to the elevator on the far right of the newsroom.

Once Nate hit the down button on the elevator, Camara began to look around again, taking in her surroundings. She figured she had a couple of minutes to look around some more before her new co-workers started to come in. She walked around the circular newsroom one more time, making sure not to touch anything.

The day had started off well. She was confident that she could handle anything that was thrown at her, and, for the first time, she was truly optimistic about being back in West Virginia. She might be all right after all.

# CHAPTER 3

## EZRA

I took my time getting to the paper. I thought several times about calling my boss first but I didn't want to hear her try to talk me out of coming in. I already knew the routine with her. I pulled into the parking lot after grabbing a quick bite to eat from the Hardee's across the street. I sat in my car for a good five minutes, finishing my breakfast.

I scooped up my camera, slung it around my neck, and headed for the double door entrance. I had to force myself to stay calm and remember that this wasn't my first day on the job. I had been working here for three years. I knew these people. There was no reason to be nervous about coming back.

As I walked through the double doors, I saw Kim Kohls busy with some paper work, so busy that she didn't even notice me. The bad thing about Kim was that she pretty much had a one-track mind. Once she got her mind set on something, she really couldn't do anything else, which wasn't a good quality for someone in charge of greeting people entering your business.

Kim kept her nose buried in her work for several seconds before I decided to just say hello. I didn't mean to, but I startled her. She dropped her pen and jumped back when she heard my voice. You could tell she was a little embarrassed, but that was overshadowed by the shock on her face.

"Ezra, you scared the bejeezus out of me. If you were a snake, you woulda bit me," she said as she put one hand over her chest and removed her glasses with the other.

"Hey Kim, how have you been?" I said with a smile. Kim's sense of humor was pure old school—a little goofy but honest. Not matter how you felt about her, you had to admit that she was always herself. She didn't know how to be any other way.

She moved from behind her desk and gave me a hug. "How are you? Did you tell anyone that you would be here today? I sure as heck didn't know."

"No," I said as she backed away from me, giving me some distance and looking as if she had done something wrong. I think she remembered that I wasn't a huggy-touchy type of guy with most people. I didn't want to make her feel uncomfortable so I answered her question in more detail. "I thought it might be better if I just popped up. I didn't want Lois trying to talk me out of coming back. I thought it best to just talk to her in person."

Kim, like a lot of people I knew, tended to wear her emotions and thoughts on her sleeve. It was easy to tell that she didn't think that was a good idea for me to just show up like this. It was all over her face. I tried to pretend I didn't notice and didn't give her a chance to cover it up by saying something stupid.

"So, is Lois here yet?" I asked as I made my way to the stairs to the left of the lobby behind Kim's desk.

"Oh, most everyone got here about thirty minutes ago. She should be up there somewhere," she said as she made her way back around her desk. She was still carrying the same worried expression, badly hidden behind a smile.

"Thanks," I said and hustled up the steps to the door leading to the main newsroom. I really didn't want to deal with everyone, but I knew I would have to when I decided to come in today. I just didn't think I was prepared to handle it because I was forced to deal with so much already. I really had no idea what to say to anyone.

"Such a dummy," I said to myself under my breath. This wasn't like me. I decided to just deal with crossing the proverbial bridges when I got to them and opened the door to the newsroom. I'm not sure why, but I was surprised that everyone was busy and didn't seem to notice me. It was a little embarrassing. I really thought that when I entered the room, it would be like a spotlight shining down on me like I was center stage on a Broadway play.

I walked straight ahead to the production department where I would find the office of Lois Thompson, the head of that department. Everyone seemed to have a lot going on. I walked past the writers' desks and they all seemed to be preoccupied with their work. I thought I saw a new face, a new writer sitting beside Will Anchor. I just kept heading to Lois's office though. I wasn't really in the mood to be nosey. There must have been some hot news going on in Bluefield because I had never seen the newsroom this busy.

Now that I thought about it, I really had no idea what had been going on outside of my apartment. I hadn't really kept in contact with anyone and I didn't so much as touch my TV. I didn't really care what was going on. I was still too wrapped up in my own problems.

I tried not to think about it and walked to Lois Thompson's office in the far corner of the room. The designers were probably the most stressed people working at the paper due to the deadlines and timetables they had to work with on a daily basis.

As I got closer to Lois's office, I saw the door was open, so I went right in without knocking. I thought for a second that I should stop and say something to the people I passed on my way, but no one seemed to pay me any attention and I wasn't in the mood to start any small talk.

Lois was on the phone when I entered her office and was busy frantically writing some notes down. Everything about how she was moving, holding herself slumped over her desk, the mess her office was in, everything screamed foul mood with too much to do and too many people to check on. Folders were everywhere and notes covered her computer. File cabinets that would normally be organized were flung open; the contents of the cabinets covered an area of the floor near the corner of the office and around Lois's desk. Maybe calling first would have been a good idea.

Lois finished her phone call and was about to move to her computer when she noticed me standing in front of her desk. When she saw me, she stopped dead in her tracks.

"Ezra!" she said in earnest surprise.

I caught a slight smile starting to take shape at the corner of her lips, which I was instantly grateful for. I wasn't sure how she would react to my popping in after seeing how much she had going on.

She got up from the assortment of unorganized papers and clutter that was threatening to take over her office and came to hug me. I was a little surprised at myself because I actually didn't mind.

Lois was a good ten years older than me and nine inches shorter. She had jet black hair that was starting to gray in small areas and she refused to color it out. She was a good twenty or thirty pounds overweight for her 5'4" frame and prematurely wrinkling skin. Lois was a good boss. She had a way of knowing what tone to take with a person, and she had a warm smile with comforting eyes. Sometimes, even though we were completely different, she was more of a friend to me than a boss.

"How have you been, Ezra?" she said, as she took a step back to give me space.

"I'm good," I said rubbing the back of my neck feeling a little awkward. I thought the best thing to do was to just brush over everything and hope she wouldn't push too hard for now.

"I would rather not talk about me right now—if that's possible. What's going on around here? Why's everyone so busy?"

I could tell she was a little annoyed at how quickly I had changed the subject, but she didn't seem to want to push the issue now. She relented and answered my question even though she must have had several of her own.

"They're thinking of canceling the Beaver-Graham game tonight," Lois said with a sigh as she shifted her weight and folded her arms.

"That's tonight? Who could cancel the game? That's one of the biggest high school football rivalries in the state! Why?"

"The mayor, that's who. And she's not the only one. A lot has been going on lately, Ezra. There's been a string of accidents in Bluefield over the last several weeks."

"What type of accidents?" I asked without really wanting to know. I had a feeling I knew where this was going and it was starting to turn my stomach in knots.

"Fires," Lois said without blinking. "There have been several fires. Mostly people's homes going up in minutes, but that's not all. There have been several missing children reported. Several rapes and murders. All happening in the past few weeks. It's crazy. This much news doesn't happen in a year in Bluefield let alone several weeks."

Lois's words made my throat feel dry and my pulse quicken. I felt concern for the people who had been through so much but I was also pissed off.

Lois must have caught on to how I was feeling and quickly resumed the conversation. "Some people are scared, and they just want to be careful. I think canceling the game would be a good idea, but too many people have rallied against it."

"So the game's on for tonight then?"

"Yep," Lois said with a hint of disappointment. I could tell she really didn't think the game was a good idea, but I wasn't really willing to talk about it much more.

"Well, if the game is tonight, at least I can get to work. I really think it would do me some good."

"Are you sure you're ready to be out around that many people?" Lois asked me evenly. I hated to admit it to her that I wasn't really sure if I was ready. So I didn't.

"I need to get moving, Lois. Doing nothing is killing me. Besides you know Mark sucks at doing sports photography. All his pics just come out blurry or he chops off people's heads and what not."

"Mark quit," Lois said, rubbing her hand through her dark hair and making her way back around her desk.

"Why did he quit?" I asked.

"Because he was about to get fired. He never would have made it as long as he did around here if not for you. No insult to you, Ezra, but your job isn't really that hard. Why he couldn't be at any given place on time and take a decent picture is beyond me."

"When did he quit?" I asked, starting to get a little angry.

"A little over a week ago. I know you and him were close, but face it, Ezra, that man was just lazy."

"He did okay work. He wasn't the best, but he did all right. What were you going to do about the game tonight if I hadn't come back?"

"We hired someone. I didn't know when you were coming back, but I knew I needed someone for this, so I hired a new photographer."

"What?" I shouted without even thinking. I was already aggravated that she had practically forced a friend of mine to quit; now she was telling me that I had been replaced too. "Why would you hire a new photographer without even getting in touch with me? I understand you would have needed someone for the big games and stuff but you could have easily just hired some freelancer!" I said defensively. I don't know why, but I felt attacked. Just one minute ago she'd acted as if she was concerned about me, but the next minute, she told me I had been replaced.

"It's not what you think, Ezra, calm down," she said, looking me straight in my eye empathetically but firmly.

"That's bullcrap!" I screamed at her. I was beginning to lose control. I really couldn't think. I didn't know what I was saying. I only knew that I was angry and feeling challenged and being told what to do. It wasn't helping me one bit. "Are you really telling me you just hired someone else to do my job? This is all I have right now, Lois! How could you just—"

"Now wait one minute!" she yelled cutting me off. I had forgotten what it was like to be put in my place. The world didn't revolve around me; Lois must have thought it was time for me to remember that.

"This is my office and you will not use that tone with me here or any where else." She managed to keep her tone even and authoritative as she continued. "Yes, Ezra, I did hire another photographer, but I hired her to replace Mark, not you. I would have used a freelancer, but Jim Rhodes moved three weeks ago and I needed another writer. When an applicant came in who could do both, we scooped her up. You still have your job if you want it. Since you're here, I was about to ask you to go take some pictures at the game tonight."

I tried to interrupt her right there. I wanted to tell her why I was mad, she just didn't understand. She wasn't getting it. Before I could get anything in, she shot me a look that shut me up.

"I was still going to ask you to go, but I wanted you to meet the new girl there. She has a good resume but not a lot of experience with sporting events. However, I already told her that she would be going tonight. After tonight she'll mostly be doing fill- in writing and the stuff Mark used to do for us. I don't have a problem with you going, too. You don't even have to talk to her if you really don't want to, but she'll be there. Okay?"

Lois had a way of pausing after she finished talking that gave you just enough time to think about how stupid you are for arguing with her in the first place. She would hold her ground firmly while looking at you, almost daring you to say something. I may have been acting irrational, but I still knew when to keep quiet.

I didn't say anything, just kept quiet and avoided her eyes. I was already too ashamed of myself to look at her. I didn't even really pay attention to everything she had just said.

"You don't need to be here for the rest of the day. Just go to the game tonight and when you come to turn in your photos, we'll talk about this then." She looked at me, her arms folded.

I raised my eyes to hers. I could feel the anger inside me boiling up again. She was basically telling me to leave! I exhaled deeply through my nose and began to grind my teeth at being discarded like trash. I didn't have anything to say to her that could possibly help so I turned to leave her office. I wasn't so much angry as embarrassed, but that still didn't help.

Once I was at the door, Lois called to me.

"Ezra, I know you've been though a lot lately, and I'm not going to tell you that you need more time, but that little outburst wasn't like you. If you're really set on going to the game tonight you need to make sure you're okay. If you ever want to talk— I mean really talk, let me know."

As she finished, my anger still boiled inside me, but not as strong. I was too worked up to talk, and after embarrassing myself the way I had, I wasn't sure how I would be able to talk to her on the level she wanted. I didn't know when I would be ready.

Not really knowing what to say, I walked out of the office and made my way to the door. Now more than before I didn't want to stop and talk to anyone. I wasn't sure how loud I had been, but I knew that people outside of Lois's office heard some, if not all, of what I had said. The door was wide open and this was not exactly a big newsroom.

I avoided everyone staring at me but could feel them watching as I reached the door and made my way out of the building. I thought Kim tried to say something to me but I ignored her too. I paced to the parking lot, then hopped in Dirty Vegas and took the avenue heading toward Princeton.

I was at work for all of eight minutes before my boss sent me home. All things considered, it wasn't the best way to start the day.

As I was driving on Highway 460, approaching closer to Pauli Heights, I realized how much I didn't want to go home. The whole point of me going back to work today was to avoid being at my place. I was tired of being there, and I wasn't ready to go back so soon to sit around and do nothing.

Instead of taking my turnoff to Blue Prince road, I drove on into Princeton and headed for the Princeton Health and Fitness Center. I was still wound tight and feeling anxious after my talk with Lois. A workout would be as good a way as any to work off some frustration.

It didn't take me long to get to the fitness center, and when I got there, I wondered why I hadn't done this sooner. I liked working out. Besides photography and reading, it was probably my favorite thing to do. I love the feeling of pushing myself. I loved the results the hard work gave me. My body was sculpted just the way I wanted, lean and muscular without being bulky or stiff. Nothing takes me away from my stress like working out.

In addition to being stressed and angry, I also felt stupid. I started to think about what Lois had said to me and the more I did, the more I realized I had been out of line. I would definitely owe her an apology tomorrow.

I grabbed workout clothes and shoes that I kept in my trunk and headed for the entrance. The fitness center was probably the best place in this area of Mercer County to work out. It was kind of pricey at forty dollars a month but for the equipment they had and the set up of the place, I thought it was worth it. I walked into the lobby of the center and scanned my membership badge on my keychain at the front desk.

I was about to reach the locker rooms to change when I heard a familiar voice coming from one of the studio workout rooms. I couldn't believe that I had been so wrapped up in myself that I had forgotten that one of my best friends taught an aerobics class there.

Looking in on the class, I saw that they were just finishing up and gathering their things to leave. The workout room was spacious with mirrors on three of the four walls. The lights were still dim to give the nightclub atmosphere for the Zumba class that just finished. I scanned the room and saw Tamra Knick, or T, as I liked to call her. She was in the far corner of the room, taking her long brownish blonde hair out of a ponytail and running her fingers through it. I waited until the room cleared and watched T after she rolled up the sleeves of her shirt, and sifted through her backpack to pull out some papers.

I inched closer to her. She must have heard my footsteps because she turned and beamed at me before I got half-way across the room. I stopped dead in my tracks when she saw me. I made it look like my effort to sneak up on her had been fouled with a defeated look on my face and a snap of my fingers.

"Crap! You caught me!" I exclaimed.

I peered into Tamra's cool, greenish-brown eyes that sparkled whenever she smiled. She ran to meet me with a hug. I laughed at her a little as she squeezed me as hard as she could; I had forgotten how strong she was.

She backed off, held me at arms length, and looked up at me, as if trying to think of what to say. Finally, she reared back and punched me in my left arm with her right fist.

"What the hell is wrong with you?" she yelled. "I've been worried about you! You can't answer the phone or answer the door or reply to a damn text?!"

"I'm sorry," I said. "I had a hard time dealing with things."

T shifted her weight to one side and folded her arms.

"How long are you going to be here?" she asked as several people started to file into the aerobics room.

"For a while. I was planning on working out for about an hour or two."

"Well, this is my last Zumba class coming in now. It should only last about an hour. Can you meet me in the pool later?"

"Sounds good. I think I got some trunks in my car."

"Okay. I've got to get the class over with so I'll meet you there. Don't run off on me."

"I'll wait for you. Promise."

I left T to begin her class, then got my swim trunks out of my car to put them in my locker. After I changed clothes I went to the second floor to the workout area. I spent about fifty minutes or so, worked as many different muscle groups as I could, then went back to the locker rooms to shower up for the pool.

I had always liked the pool at the center because it was only about five feet deep on either end. I had always had a fear of drowning despite being a good swimmer. Because the pool was shallow, I could do more laps without really having to worry about getting tired. I knew my body and working out for the first time after so long would have me sore in the morning, so I decided to get into the smaller heated pool. I welcomed the warmth of the water, swam over to the heater to wait for T to join me.

I had waited for about ten minutes when T walked in the pool toward me with natural elegance in every step. She was wearing a pale blue two-piece swimsuit with her hair already wet and thrown over one shoulder. I watched her dive into the pool on the opposite end and swim under the water. T had always been a graceful woman, at home in the water. She made swimming look effortless, like she was just as home in the water as a dolphin.

She surfaced beside me, leaned against the pool's heaters, and pulled her hair back over her head.

"Hi," she said, her green eyes capturing mine. "How're you doing, handsome? I don't think I've ever seen you around here before."

I laughed at her corny come-on line.

"I don't really get out here much. You?"

"Oh, I'm here all the time. I love working out. Can't you tell?" she said, putting the palms of her hands on the edge of the pool and pulling herself up. She flexed her triceps and abs.

She dropped back into the pool, and our guffaws could be heard clear across the pool. T and I had been friends since college and we had always been flirty, but never done anything to take our relationship past a friendship level.

"It's good to see you, T. You really have no idea," I said to her with a smile.

"Yeah, well I'm just happy to know you're still alive. I really did try to get in touch with you. A lot."

"I'm sorry. I really am. I just had to get through some stuff alone. I just wasn't ready to talk."

"Don't worry about it. You know how I am, so I can't blame you. I'm not even so much mad at you as worried. Besides, I've been going crazy without you to talk to. You wouldn't believe the drama I've been through lately."

"You! Having drama in your life? I don't believe it," I said sarcastically

"Shut up," T said as she hit me in my arm. "I'm serious. I can't help it if drama follows me around. It's not my fault, Ezra. It really isn't."

T was a good friend. Sometimes too good for some people. For one reason or another the drama of her friends always ended up her own, kind of like me. I'd tried numerous times to get her to cut several people out of her life, but she had a hard time letting go of people once she cared about them, again, kind of like me.

"I know," I said. "Who was it this time?"

"Ha. A better question would be who isn't it? Tiffany got kicked out of her apartment and has been staying with me for a week now. Charles has been calling me like every freakin' night complaining about his girlfriend and telling me he's in love with me and shit. He's dating my friend, and he won't stop hitting on me! I would tell Melissa he's doing it, but you know as well as I do that she won't believe me. She'll just take his side like the idiot she can be sometimes. I don't even know if I want to get started in on Conner."

"I thought you dropped that guy a couple of months ago? Why are you still talking to him?"

"Because I'm horny, and he's the best option I have right now."

"I thought you said he was bad in that department."

"Yeah," T said, pausing. "But I'm horny and he's the best option I have right now." We laughed again.

T gazed at me slightly and a narrow smile edged her lips. We didn't say anything to each other for a moment as we both enjoyed the silence. I took a deep breath, stretched, and let the warmth of the water wash over me.

"You got plans tonight?" I asked, feeling my bones and joints pop. I could feel the tension in my muscles releasing.

"Conner."

"Really?"

"Yes, really."

"You sure that's a good idea?"

"No. I'm just tired of sleeping alone at night. Conner's not that bad a guy if he knows his limits."

"You could do better ya know?"

"How's Eva doing?"

"Oh, that's not fair!"

"How many times did I tell you that girl was crazy? It took you what? Two and half years to let that go?" T said pointing a finger in my face and chuckling.

"All right! All right!" I said throwing both my hands up in surrender. "You're right. I'll admit it. But you're still going to have to say uncle."

"What?" T said, puzzled. I started dousing her face with water before she could get another word out. She tried to splash back but I had the element of surprise and wasn't letting up.

"Say it. Say it!" I said to her.

"Never!" Next thing I knew T was under the water, grabbing one of my legs and forcing me under. One of the things that made it easy for T and me to hang out was that we both liked to compete. We play fought for a little longer than necessary because neither one of us wanted to lose. The fight only ended when we were both too tired to keep going. When we were through, we both were on opposite sides of the pool laughing at our own silliness.

"You give up yet?" I asked through labored breath.

"Hell no!" T replied with the same labored breathing as me. "Wanna call a truce though?"

"Sure. Truce it is. What time is it?" I asked T because she was in a better position to see the large clock mounted on the wall of the pool hall.

"Looks like it's about three fifteen. You got somewhere to be?"

"Yeah. Gotta go to the game."

"You working?" T asked, swimming over to my side of the pool.

"Yeah. Today is my first day back. I almost wish I hadn't gone in today at all."

"Why? What happened?"

"I don't want to go into it right now. You wanna come to the game with me? I could use the company."

T gave me an annoyed look. She didn't like me being short with her and she wouldn't put up with it. To avoid an argument later, I coughed up more details.

"They hired another photographer."

"Really? Well, that's good, right? I remember you saying that the paper was growing and that you were wanting some help because that Mark guy sucked at his job."

"Yeah, well, they fired Mark. They were hiring my replacement."

"Didn't you just say you were working tonight?"

"Yeah."

"So. You can't be too replaced if they want you to go to the game and take pictures tonight."

"I guess you're right," I said. I didn't expect her to really understand how I felt because I didn't understand it myself. I didn't want to go into it so I gave the abridged version.

"They hired a rookie, and they want me to go and show them how I do things—which is complete bull because I know Lois and there's no way she would let someone on staff if she didn't think they could handle any work she might throw at them. She told me she was sending me to help the new guy, but I know she's just sending me to make me feel better. I was so mad I didn't even hear the bulk of what she was saying, which isn't like me. You know I don't get mad that often."

"So, why go if you feel that bad about it?"

"I don't know . . . curious. I guess. I want to know what this guy looks like. I'd feel better if you came with me though."

"Sorry, Easy," T said calling me by my nickname. "Conner, remember?"

I raised an eyebrow in T's direction.

"I know. I can't help it," she said.

"Whatever. I still think you can do better. I gotta go. I'll hit you up later in the week," I said, climbing out of the pool. "You getting out?"

"Not yet. I think I'm going to hop in the big pool and swim some laps," T said following me out.

"It was good seeing you, sweetie. Don't be a stranger." She put her arms around my waist and gave me a tight hug.

"Never. Luv ya much, T."

"Luv ya much, Easy."

In a way, I would rather stay with T instead of going to the game. I needed to pour my heart out to someone. T was one of the few people I would even attempt to do something like that with. Now wasn't the time though, and I really was curious to know what the new guy was going to be like.

I left the fitness center after changing clothes and drove back to my apartment so I could shower, change for the game, and grab a bite to eat. Seeing T had been a big help. She'd always been a breath of fresh air to me, and I couldn't remember who I used to talk to before I met her.

By the time I got to my apartment, got ready and cooked some lemon chicken, it was a quarter to six which wasn't good. The game would be packed. Something told me I'd be walking close to half a mile or more just to get to Mitchell Stadium.

I made sure I had a full battery in my camera and made my way to Dirty Vegas. I wondered what I would say to my new co-worker when I met him.

# CHAPTER 4

## CAMARA

*Well, that went by fast.* Camara thought as she went walking across the parking lot of the Telegraph. It had only seemed like minutes since she first arrived at work, but it had already been eight hours. After that man had caused a scene, the day just flew by. Camara wondered what the deal was with all the tension she felt while he was in the newsroom. Lois had mentioned that he would be at the Beaver-Graham game with her tonight. She was a little worried about working with him, but Lois assured her it would be all right. She had a lot of questions, but she knew the answers were none of her business.

Camara tried to push it from her mind and focus on the rest of her day. She hopped in her car but had no destination in mind. She didn't bother driving all the way back to Welch only to come back for the Beaver-Graham game an hour later.

She thought about calling her friends or her mother, but she wasn't really in the mood to talk. She decided to get a bite to eat after changing her clothes. She wanted to be comfortable for the game so she had packed a simple pair of jeans, tennis shoes, and a brown shirt. She also had a light jacket just in case it got colder.

One of the bad things about Bluefield was that there weren't many things to do to pass the time. She still had a solid hour before the game started after she ate and changed. She decided to head to Bluefield City Park, a short walk from Mitchell Stadium.

Camara remembered coming to this park when she was a child and playing with her friends and her mother. Her father had even managed to bring her here once or twice. This park had always been a source of good memories for her. Maybe one day she would come and read a book by the shallow creek that ran through the park.

She pulled into the parking lot of the football stadium, and walked to the park. She let the memories of her childhood wash over her, happy to see that the park had gotten an update. All of the slides and jungle gyms were new and some of the basketball goals had a fresh coat of paint and new chain nets.

Camara walked deeper into the park, sat on a small bridge that overlooked the creek, and listened to the water. *It was the perfect game day*. Camara looked up at the rolling hills surrounding the park. She hadn't been away long, but she had forgotten how beautiful West Virginia could be. The trees, a vibrant green, seemed to dance in the wind against the clear blue sky. The air was crisp and thick with the smell of freshly cut grass. It wouldn't be long before the trees would start to explode into shades of red and orange, and hues of yellow and brown.

Being in the park was a nice way to find some mental relief. She hadn't talked to anyone about how she really felt about being back home. Not even her mother. She had been keeping everything bottled up inside. Camara hoped that finding a job and staying busy would be enough to keep the past buried and behind her. Hopefully she would soon have her credit card debt behind her as well.

Thinking about the debt she was buried under made her think about how she had acquired it. She thought about ex—Tarquan. She thought about how he had promised her the world and had given her everything she wanted, for a time. She thought about his smile, why she had loved him and the day she knew it would never work between them.

She had lost too much of herself when she was with Tarquan. He had changed her forever and there was no going back. She was stuck being the person he had made her.

Camara was grateful that the park and the stadium were so close together. She could hear the sound of the high school bands warming up. She had been so lost in her own thoughts that she didn't notice the time.

Camara stood and walked across the park into Mitchell Stadium's parking lot. She knew there was still time before the kick-off because the parking lot was only half full. She felt good about not having to rush.

After one quick stop by her car to get her camera, Camara walked up the ramps to the stadium. She hoped she would get there before the man she was supposed to be working with. She wasn't sure what to think about him or how she should even approach him, or if she should approach him at all.

She moved up the home side of the field, waved the badge Lois had given her at the security guard, and then walked into the stadium. Camara considered the irony of finding herself there. She remembered how much she had hated Bluefield when she was in high school. There were a lot of females she hated here from Bluefield. Camara could remember all the fights she used to get into. There was never any love between Bluefield and her old school, Mount View.

Tonight's Bluefield-Graham game had always been big because the two schools shared the stadium. During the year, one team would play a home game here while the other would play away. They usually alternated who dressed in home gear every year. There was even a trophy that the winner would take home for bragging rights.

Memories of high school danced through her mind as she took several pictures of the growing crowd and of both teams warming up. Camara decided to climb to the top of the stands on the Graham side so she could take a picture of the whole field and capture the Bluefield crowd during kick off.

The stadium was full in no time as people filed in wearing their team colors. The town had gone all out this year. Posters, spirit towels, and banners were everywhere. A woman, Kim Lee, sang the national anthem. Just as she finished a small fireworks display went off and skydivers landed in the field with a parachute that had both the Bluefield Beavers logo, a profile view of an angry cartoon beaver, and the

Graham G-men logo, a yellow sheriff's badge. The skydivers got the crowd even more animated as anticipation for the kickoff built to a fever pitch.

Bluefield had won the toss and the coach decided to kick first. Bluefield and Graham lined up, and the Bluefield kicker got the game started as three jets blew over the field and drove the game into high gear.

Camara wondered how Bluefield had gotten the money to make the game this big of a production. She was impressed by how smoothly everything was going. She even found herself getting a little excited and she wasn't from either school.

She checked her camera, saw that she had filled her memory card, and reached into her pocket to grab another. She scanned the action from the top of the Graham side and had taken several shots of the action when she spotted the man who had caused the scene at work today on the field taking pictures. She used her camera as binoculars to watch him for a few seconds. He didn't seem like the same person. He had a smile on his face, and a few people came up and talked to him. Camara's curiosity was getting to her so she decided to go introduce herself. She wanted to know what he was like.

She carefully climbed down from the stands before realizing she hadn't bothered to ask anyone his name. Lois might have mentioned it, but she couldn't remember. She had wanted to ask earlier but everyone was so tense after he left that she hadn't bothered.

She flashed her badge to the guard so he would let her onto the field. She had kept her eye on her new co-worker and was relived to see that he was cute, nice build, too.

Camara walked behind him and tapped him on the shoulder. As he turned around, she took a picture as soon as he faced her. She looked at the picture through the viewfinder; he didn't look shocked in the picture. He even managed a slight smile that curled the edge of his lips. Not bad.

"Um . . . can I help you?" he said looking confused.

"You work at the paper right?" Camara said smiling.

"Yeah," he said, sounding even more confused.

"Well, so do I."

"You're the new photographer Lois hired?"

"Yep."

"You?" he asked looking at Camara as though she was speaking a foreign language.

"You look surprised. Didn't you know I was going to be here?"

"I'm sorry. I was just expecting a guy."

"Well, sorry to disappoint you."

"Oh, I'm not disappointed. My name is Ezra," he said showing off a perfect smile, exposing perfectly straight white teeth.

"My name is Camara," she said as the hometeam scored and the crowd screamed, drowning her out. They probably should have caught that on film, but Ezra's attention was on her, and she didn't want to shy away from it just yet. He was too cute.

"Your name is Camera?" he asked, and then leaned in closer to hear over the crowd. Camara didn't recognize his cologne, but it was pleasant, masculine.

"No." She waited a brief second until the crowd calmed. "My name is Cam-a-ra." She carefully articulated each syllable.

"Camara. That's a nice name." he smiled again.

She smiled back at him. She wasn't sure what it was but something made her want to know more about him. Today was turning into a pretty good day. She didn't think she would hate her job after all. If nothing else, she might make a friend or two.

# CHAPTER 5

The roar of the crowd went through me like a shockwave as both sides of the stadium cheered their teams off the field for halftime. The game had been going by fast and I was surprised to find myself having a good time. It turned out to be a high-scoring, exciting game. Both teams were playing their butts off, and I was also enjoying my new co-worker's company.

We had already gotten enough pictures for the paper. If we hadn't spent so much time talking, we might have gotten even more shots. I really didn't plan to stay for the whole game, but I couldn't tear myself away.

The crowd was competing for spots at the concession stands while Camara and I were still on the field. We didn't even try to fight through the vultures. Instead, we stood on the fifty-yard line and let everyone else fight for hotdogs.

"How long have you been into photography?" I asked her.

"It's always been an interest of mine, I guess. I used to be a real ham when I was a kid. I loved being in pictures. Somewhere along the way I started wanting to be behind the camera instead of in front of it. You?"

"Pretty much the same. My granddad use to have this old Polaroid camera, you know, the one you use to have to shake and wait? He used to let me play with the thing all the time. I even took it apart once and put it back together."

"Really. Boy genius, huh?" Camara said.

"Not really. I said I put it back together. Not that I got it working again."

"Oh, so just the curious one?"

"Bingo."

"So, where'd you learn about photography?" Camara asked me as we started to pace up and down the field.

"Books mostly. I wanted to go to an art institute in Georgia for it but it never worked out for me. You go to college anywhere?"

"Kentucky University. I majored in philosophy and creative writing with a minor in photography. Best and worst five and a half years of my life. Did you do college at all?"

"I'm a proud member of the Thundering Herd, baby," I said pounding my chest.

Camara looked away from me and laughed slightly.

"What's so funny?"

"Nothing, you just sound so proud that you went to Marshall. It's kinda cute. What was your major?"

"Social work with a minor in music. Don't ask me how but, I finished in four years, a lot of people I know didn't. Photography was always just a hobby that I wound up making into a living. Why I'm not doing something with my degree, I really don't know."

"Hey, at least you finished," Camara said and for the first time didn't look at me when she spoke. I could tell that, for some reason, school was a soft spot for her, but she played it off and I didn't push.

It was so crowded at the stadium that the bands were just now getting set up to run though their routines for the halftime show. The horns were just warming up as the Beavers band was first to take the field.

"Follow me," I had to practically scream in Camara's ear to be heard over the band.

I walked off the field to the Beaver side and made my way up the bleachers to the press box; I knew it would be quieter there. I also wanted to get a few overhead shots of the band's formations just in case Lois wanted to use them later.

Camara and I stood near the press box and watched the halftime show. From this high in the stadium we could see just how packed the stadium was. I imaged most of these people came out to get their minds off of the horrors that had been going on in Bluefield lately. If you looked at the people at the game, you would never know their neighborhoods had been terrorized, murders were happening at an alarming rate, and the game had almost been cancelled.

I pushed the thoughts away as Camara and I made our way back to the field as the halftime show was wrapping up. The teams came out just as pumped after halftime as they did when the game started. I had Camara walk with me around to the Graham side so we could get the Beaver fans' reactions. Camara and I talked about our hobbies, music, favorite sports. Conversation between us was easy and relaxing. She was interesting and always seemed to have at least something to say about everything. It was already dark and the game was all but over before we even knew it. It started to look like the Beavers' were going to pull it out this year. I headed to the visitors' entrance. My car was parked all the way on Maryland Avenue off Stadium Drive and I wanted o avoid the traffic if possible.

"I think I might bounce a little early. It might take two hours to get out of here if we wait," I said to Camara over the roar of the Beaver fans. There were two minutes left in the game, and the Beavers had Graham by a touchdown. Graham had the ball on the Beavers' forty-five yard line. No one else was about to leave but us. We had got so wrapped in our conversation that the game was just background noise.

"I guess I should do the same. My car is all the way on the other end. I've got to make it all the way to the park."

"I'm still a little deeper out than you. Want me to walk with you?"

"Oh my God!" a woman beside Camara and me screamed.

The woman seemed frantic for what seemed like no reason at all. It took the sound of the explosion coming from a house on Stadium Drive to make me realize what had happened. She must have seen the fire before everyone else. The explosion boomed so loudly it stopped everything in the stadium. The crowd stopped cheering and the teams stopped playing as clouds of fire shot high into the night sky.

I didn't stop to think about what I was doing; my legs were on autopilot. I ran down the visitors' ramp and across the parking lot. I couldn't believe what I was seeing. Why now? Why here? Most everyone else was stock still as I ran along Stadium Drive at full sprint.

I didn't stop until I was in front of the house. I stood across the street and watched the blaze start to claim the woods behind the house as well as the homes on either side. Dark embers of charred material fell caking the ground with ash as the fire spread. I could hear the pounding in my chest as I stared into the fire and a wave of memories flooded my thoughts. The fire had me in a trance that I only came out of when Camara placed her hand on my shoulder.

"Ezra, are you okay?" she asked through slightly labored breath.

I looked at her, and then back into the flame. I might have been impressed that Camara was able to keep up with me as I ran, but the fire had me reliving my own private hell. Camara and I were the first in front of the house from the stadium, and other people were just catching up. The next thing I knew, I was shaken to my core by what I saw coming from the house. A person came stumbling out of the home completely on fire. I couldn't tell if it was a man or a woman, but I could see the pain echoed through every move. The arms flared frantically trying to put out burning flesh. Smoke rose from the white-hot flames, as the person on fire fanned both hands toward their throat in a desperate plea for air. I couldn't comprehend how a person could have survived the explosion let alone be able to walk out of the house.

I was paralyzed. So was everyone else. No one ran to aid the person or try to put out the flames. The heat coming from the body was so intense, the flame so fierce, that it would have been impossible to get close enough to help without setting yourself on fire. Everyone knew it was too late. The flaming figure staggered in my direction with one hand extended, mouth frozen in a silent scream, lungs futilely searching for oxygen only for it to be claimed by the fire. The figure burned and fell to its knees in the middle of the street right in front of Camara and me.

I took two steps back from the horror unfolding in front of me. I was able to tell from this close that it was a woman and my heart went out to her. It would have been a mercy if she had died instantly. Her eyes caught mine and in that moment, I felt she looked through me, cutting me in half. I've never felt so helpless.

Then the woman fell backward, chunks of meat dripping off her body, exposing the bone underneath. The smell of burning flesh invaded my nostrils causing me to gag.

I looked at Camara and saw the tears running down her cheeks. She had both hands over her mouth. Her body was trembling and her hands were shaking. She finally looked back at me.

"Welcome back to Bluefield," I said.

"What?" she asked hands still over her mouth.

Then I looked away from her, and back at the hell in front of me. I did the only thing I could think to do. I took a picture.

# CHAPTER 6

## CAMARA

*Did he just take a picture? I can't believe he just took a freakin' picture!* Camara was sure none of the other people around had noticed but she was right beside Ezra and he had definitely just taken a picture. He looked just as shaken as she felt but he had managed to do what was farthest from her mind. He took a freaking picture!

She wanted to hit him at first, but the look on his face poured out the empathy he felt. He stood still, unblinking, at the fire as if he hadn't realized he'd just had the audacity to capture it on film.

The sounds of sirens in the distance pulled Camara out of herself as fire trucks and ambulances made their way to the scene. Still she didn't know how to react. A woman had just died not ten feet away from her. What was she supposed to do? What was she supposed to say?

Camara heard sirens of the police, firemen and ambulances as they all pulled up at about the same time. Some started putting out the fire in the middle of the street; the woman's body looked like nothing more than a charred heap against the pavement. Other firemen made their way to the two houses on either side of the one that exploded. The home that was the source of the fire was too far gone so they focused on stopping the blaze from spreading.

Camara stood beside Ezra, waiting, hoping he would offer some answers when a weird feeling came over her. The people on the street and sidewalks were glaring in her direction. She thought they were all looking at her, whispering under their breath. Then, she began to realize, everyone was looking past her at Ezra. If Ezra noticed at all, he didn't acknowledge anyone.

Camara stepped back as the ambulance workers hastened to the body in the middle of the street, and the police pushed back the crowd. Camara was about to say something to Ezra regarding the people's stares when a police officer marched up to him. The officer was a white man who looked to be in his late thirties. *Chief of police,* Camara thought when she looked more closely at his uniform. The officer had deep brown eyes and dark hair. He looked to be in good shape and carried himself in a controlled manner even under these circumstances. Camara could see how he could be intimidating to most people.

"Ezra Walker!" the officer screamed. "Why am I not surprised to see you here? Come with me. Now!"

"I don't need this right now, Ray," Ezra said standing his ground while being confronted by the officer.

"I didn't ask you what you needed, Walker, I told you to come with me," the officer said, now mere inches from Ezra's face.

"This is how you're going to come at me? This is how you're going to come at me when there's a dead woman on the street, and in front of all these people?" Ezra said more calmly.

"What are you doing here, Ezra?" the officer said. His face was red and the anger and tension he felt showed on his face, veins popping up on his forehead and neck. Camara couldn't understand what this was about. Why was the officer fixated on Ezra at a time like this? Everything was happening so fast.

"Not now, Ray," Ezra said.

"Chief Wilson to you, damnit! I'm not going to take your smug attitude, Walker." The officer got closer to Ezra and said something so low that if Camara had not been beside them she wouldn't have heard. "If I find out you had anything to do with this, I swear before God and all that's holy . . ."

Ezra leaned in closer to Officer Wilson in return. Ezra said something too low for Camara to hear this time. Then he pointed to the fire and the gathering crowd. More people were gathering from the stadium. Camara tried to draw her attention away from Ezra and Officer Wilson. She started to become very uncomfortable. She couldn't stand to look at the smoldering corpse in front of her, or the fire that was still out of control. Just about everyone else was looking right at Ezra and Officer Wilson.

After several very tense seconds, Ezra pulled back from Officer Wilson and gently put his hand on Camara's back, leading her in the direction of the stadium. Camara looked back at Chief Wilson as Ezra ushered her down the street. Chief Wilson's anger was written all over his face, yet he said nothing to Ezra as he walked away. Instead he turned his attention to the crowd and began barking orders at the policemen under his command.

Tension and paranoia spread as more and more people crammed themselves onto the street. The cacophony of the people rose as everyone became more and more panicked. No one knew what was going on. People were scared, but they were all drawn to the scene like moths to a flame. Officer Wilson would have a hell of a time getting the crowd under control and convincing everyone to go home.

Camara was surprised as Ezra grabbed her hand and fought his way through the crowd. She was sure they were the only ones moving away from the fire. Everyone stared at Ezra when he passed. Again Ezra seemed oblivious to everyone around him.

Once they cleared the crowd and were well into Mitchell Stadium's parking lot, Ezra finally spoke.

"Your car is close to the park, right?" He said and looked at her with the same kind eyes she had looked into all evening.

"What? Oh, yeah, I'm all the way by the park," Camara said. She wasn't really sure how to react to Ezra. He acted like they had just left the game and everything was normal. He didn't show one sign of being mad at Officer Wilson for getting in his face; he didn't ever look back as more sirens wailed in the background and the crowd grew louder.

"All the firetrucks and ambulances are going to be coming from the other side of Stadium so it's going to be a lot easier for us to get out of here if we hit College Avenue from the park."

"Okay." It was the only respond Camara could muster.

"Can you give me a ride to my car? We'll have to loop around to get to it. I would have taken you there and driven you to yours, but like I said, that would take forever. I'm all the way on Cherry Street."

Camara nodded her head. "Okay," she said, trying not to give away how shaken she was. Why was he acting so blasé about the situation?

They arrived at her car and got in. Camara tried to put on her seat belt but her hand was shaking as she tried to fasten it. As soon as she had a second to relax, the image of the burning woman kept flashing in her mind. She could still smell the burning flesh and she felt like she was going to lose it. Her breathing started to get labored as she looked through the windshield of her car. The crowd was starting to become more and more riled up. People were starting to throw things. Everything was happening so damn fast.

Camara's eyes watered but no tears fell.

"Don't feel bad. What just happened wouldn't be a easy thing for anyone to handle," Ezra said calmly.

Camara tried to catch her breath and turned to look at Ezra. He wasn't looking back at her but rather at the fire and the crowd ahead.

There was something she had to know. Something she had to ask. "How are you so . . . calm?"

Ezra broke his gaze from the fire and looked into the night sky away from Camara. For the first time he seemed really affected by what was happening. "If you've seen one fire, then you've seen them all." He said in a very matter of fact way. Then left it at that.

*Are you fucking serious?* Camara thought but didn't bother to push. Instead she took another moment to compose herself. She started the car and edged out of the parking lot.

As Camara pulled out she took one last look down Stadium Drive and saw another much smaller, explosion than the first come from the same house. The crowd showed no sign of letting up. Neither did the fire.

# CHAPTER 7

*Well . . . that was fun.* My day had been a rollercoaster, one that had me more than ready to get off. When dramatic things happen, I tend to go on autopilot. Most people mistake what looks like calmness for grave disinterest, as if I don't care about what's happening. That couldn't be further from the truth.

Camara dropped me off at my car, and we said our goodbyes. She looked pretty shaken when she was driving, but she was holding it together. I would've gotten her number to make sure she had gotten home okay, but that didn't seem appropriate.

I popped in my favorite Cold Play CD to avoided spending too much time with my thoughts on the way home. I did my best to block out the images of the burning corpse. I pulled off 460 and hit Blue Prince Road to my apartment. All the lights were off as I threw my keys on my stereo and walked in the living room. I was about to reach for the light when I noticed something on my couch. I looked at the shadow for several seconds trying to figure out what it was. My mind had to be playing tricks on me. Who the hell would be in my apartment?

I resisted my first impulse to run over and pound on whoever had broke into my place. When it comes to the fight or flight response, I'm more on the fight end of things. I tend to try and smash whatever scares me. That put me in a very bad position once so I try to resist the urge long enough to sort things out. Before I could get a word out, the figure turned on the lamp I had beside the couch.

"I coulda killed you seven times by now." A familiar voice teased me as the light flickered on.

"You would've tried," I said to my younger brother as he got up from the couch. I was relieved to see it was him. I didn't admit to him how much his little surprise had scared me. The last thing I needed was a surprise like this.

"What up?" my brother said as he came over to give me a hug.

"What are you doing here, Zeus?" I asked.

"I can't come see my big brother?" he said, even though big brother only describes me in age. He was a good inch or two taller than me and all muscle. His athletic build would have been right at home on the football field as somebody's running back.

"How the hell did you get in my apartment?"

"Living in Baltimore teaches you a thing or two. Where you been? I've been waiting here forever."

"The Beaver-Graham game was tonight."

"Forgot about that. You know P-town is my heart. Don't think I ever went to the Beaver-Graham game. How was it?"

"I'll tell you later. Want something to drink?" I said making my way to the refrigerator.

"That's all right. I already got a drink and made myself some food."

"I'm glad you made yourself at home."

"We family. I knew you wouldn't mind."

I grabbed a Bud Light and sat down at my table. I was happy that my brother was here. I was going to need someone to talk to.

Zeus also got a beer out of the refrigerator and sat across from me at the table.

"Didn't see these. You know, if you would have answered your phone or something, then I wouldn't have had to break into your place like this. I can understand wanting some space, but I thought you done killed yourself in here or something. I was getting worried."

"You know me better than that. Killing yourself is a weak man's way out. I ain't weak," I said taking a sip of my beer.

"That isn't completely true. You should meet some of the people I run into at work. One thing I've learned is that when left alone to your own demons, there's little a person couldn't be driven to. It's not good to spend so much time alone."

My brother is a bounty hunter. It's the only job he's ever held. He spent most of his adult life in Baltimore where his mother was born and raised. We didn't start to get close until he was around eight or nine when his mother would bring him and our older sister Isis to visit our dad. From about age nine to thirteen his mom dropped him and Isis off with our dad and left them here. It was in those four years that we bonded most.

Growing up in the streets of Baltimore was rough on him. His life would be a lot different if his mom hadn't gotten involved with a bounty hunter when he was thirteen. That man had taken Zeus under his wing and the old man even let Zeus start going on assignments with his team, The Pack, when Zeus was only fourteen.

Zeus never told me much about his work until recently when the old man died and left him in charge of The Pack. Zeus was in charge of the strike team now, at the age of twenty-four. He took his responsibility seriously. He even tried to get me to join, but my problem with guns would make it hard to stay alive in his line of work.

"Even if you don't want to talk about your feelings, it's still good to talk," he said while leaning back in his chair.

"Fine. You want to talk? I'll talk."

I didn't talk about what he probably expected me to. I simply told him about my day. I spent the next fifteen minutes telling him about what I did at work. Told him about how I acted in Lois's office, about working out my frustrations at the fitness center, and about talking to T. I told him about going to the game and I ended up talking about Camara more than I planned. Then I told him about the explosion at the end of the game.

I told him about the fire and the woman who came out of the house after it exploded. I even mentioned all the stares I got at the game before and during the fire.

When I was finished, Zeus sat up in his chair and looked off into space.

"Shit," he said. "He's moving a lot faster than I thought."

"What are you talking about?" I asked.

He looked at me after leaning back in his seat, rubbed his head, and proceeded to give me some really bad news.

"I wanted to come check on you, but I'm also here looking for a bounty. This is different from most runaways I bring in. This dude is real big-time shit. The old man was chasing this guy since I was like sixteen.

"I'm not even sure if I should be telling you this, but I think you're indirectly involved, so I'm letting you know. This guy is a serial killer of the highest order. A real deranged lunatic. And he's good, Ezra. So good most people in the circles I work in don't even think he exists."

"What? How am I involved with a serial killer?" I said as calmly as I could. Zeus wasn't the type of person to make stuff up or say things lightly.

"We don't have to go right into the heavy shit. Why don't you tell me more about that chick with the braids? You gonna smash that?"

"Are you serious?" I said, getting a little annoyed.

"I'm just worried, your taste can be a little shady. I don't even wanna get started on Eva," Zeus said taking another sip of his drink.

He put his beer down and struck a more serious tone.

"This guy picks off suburban neighborhoods. The old man had a figure, a guess at how many people this guy's killed. By now the number should be upwards of six hundred."

"Six hundred!" I said almost choking on my beer. "How does one man kill six hundred people?"

Zeus locked eyes with me, "Like I said, that's a guess, it could be less, but that's exactly what I'm dealing with, Ezra. I'm telling you this guy is no joke. He doesn't make mistakes. He has no pattern, no set group of people he goes after. He's a crazy random killer. I tried to get inside the guy's head and damn near went crazy. It wears enough on me just trying to track the bastard.

"The only thing that's really consistent is that, for whatever reason, he won't hurt kids, and for him, a 'kid' is anyone age five and under. He'll burn things from time to time too, but not always.

"Think about how easy it is to do stuff like this in a small town like Bluefield. Things like this don't happen all the time in areas like this, and when it does, the local authorities just aren't ready to handle it. The most cops around here have to deal with is drunken domestic violence, busting the drug dealer of the month, and hanging out at whatever club is open because it's likely to get shot up. I'm going to keep the detectives out my mouth because you know they ain't doing a damn thing most of the time. How often do you think they have to detect anything around here? I bet they get their fair share but not like the big city guys.

"This is like Michael Jordan in his prime playing high school kids. That's why he's never been caught. That and the fact that there's no proof of what the guy really looks like."

"Wait a minute, wait a minute," I couldn't listen to this another second. My brother had never been a liar so I was inclined to believe everything he was telling me, but it was hard. It sounded like he was describing some suburban legend, not a real person. "You mean to tell me you don't even know what the guy looks like?"

"I've seen the guy face-to-face a few times, Ezra. Every single time I saw him he looked different. I know that sounds crazy, but I kid you not. This guy can make himself look like a completely different person. First time I saw him he was a white guy with blonde hair, the next he was a black guy. Once I would've sworn the motherfucker was Asian. That's how the old man named him. 'AKA'— that's what he called him. The bastard even started using the name for himself."

"Could you please stop cursing so much? And that doesn't make any sense. How can someone look so different every time you see him?"

"I don't know if he's just really good with makeup or if he's just got the money to have a lot of plastic surgery. Could be both. Either way, he's really good with blending in. Like I said, I only seen him a handful of times, and every time I almost died for it. And I'll try to watch my mouth, preacher man."

"Don't call me that."

"Your life will be better when you accept it."

"Whatever. Get to the point. What does this have to do with me? How am I involved?" I asked impatiently.

Zeus took a deep breath. Whenever Zeus had to pause to say something, that something was usually intense. I tried to brace myself to be hit like the coyote from the roadrunner cartoons.

"I reviewed the case files. I checked and double checked. Looked through everything the old man came up with, and I'm sure AKA is here in Bluefield. Sometimes no pattern is a pattern. He may not think so, but he leaves his mark if not any evidence. I think that he killed your mom."

And the anvil drops.

There was silence between us. I took a moment to collect my thoughts. Right when I was about to say something, Zeus's phone rang. It cut through the silence, startling us both.

"Text message," he said. "I gotta go. Need to follow up on this lead. We'll finish this tomorrow. There's more to this you need to know, but it can wait for now."

"You're really going to leave me with that? Just drop a bombshell and roll out?"

"This is important. I have to leave. This is all guesswork. If you would tell me something about that day, maybe—"

"No! I don't . . . I don't want to talk about it."

"What did I just say about keeping stuff bottled up?"

"Drop it, Zeus."

"I read the files. You didn't even give a statement to the police. You were there, Ezra, what happened? If you just—"

"I said drop it!" I pounded the table with my fist. He didn't get it. Nobody did.

We sat in silence, which felt like forever to me. I wasn't mad at Zeus, but my anger was being channeled in his direction.

"I'm just trying to help, Ezra. Your mom was like a mom to me, too. You're not the only one hurt by what happened to her."

"You going to come back here tonight and stay?" I asked.

Zeus let out a small sigh then said, "I got a hotel. I'll hit you up tomorrow."

"Why are you going to spend money on a hotel when you could just stay here?"

"No thanks. I would but when was the last time you cleaned this place? It's all musty in here and shit, smells like BO and ass crack. Change your sheets. Open a window. Fuck."

I shrugged off Zeus's joke as he went to leave. I wasn't in the mood to wisecrack.

"One more thing. You haven't been reading the paper have you?" Zeus asked looking back at me from the door.

"No. Why?"

"I kept a copy from two months ago. I think you need to read it. It might answer some of the questions you've got."

"I'll check it out in the morning."

"Just don't forget. I'll see you tomorrow."

"Zeus?"

"Yeah?"

"Do you know anything about the fires breaking out in Bluefield?"

"Maybe. We'll talk about that later, too. Promise."

I didn't feel like calling Zeus out as he left. I would bet one month's pay that the late night "tip" he just got was really a booty call. It didn't really bother me that he left. I wanted to take my time and think about the info he had given me; I wanted to get some perspective.

I went into my spare room and grabbed my electric guitar. Behind my apartment complex is an empty parking lot were a Hills store used to be. I hopped in Dirty Vegas and headed there so I could play my guitar without waking any of my neighbors.

I plugged into my car, fired up the amps in the back, and played some Hendrix. I didn't do this much because it was murder on the battery, but it was good to let loose from time to time. I let myself get lost in rifts and tried not to think about the fact that there very well could be a serial killer in Bluefield.

I had spent a lot of time trying to figure out why someone would do what they did to my mother. Now to find out that it may have all been random, just some sick bastard getting his rocks off. I wasn't sure how to feel about what Zeus had told me. I just had more questions. If this guy was so good why, would he be in Bluefield? Would he come after me? Is he still in Bluefield? If so, who could he be? Was there really no pattern? Was he responsible for the fire after the game tonight?

Zeus wasn't telling me something, I knew him too well for him to completely hide anything from me. I couldn't put my finger on it yet, but I knew he would spill it sooner or later.

The more I thought, the more my head hurt. I let myself get lost in Hendrix. I poured my frustrations into the guitar and in return it filled the parking lot with a therapeutic melody. I forgot about everything—time had no meaning to me when my guitar was in my hands. Reality drowned away to be replaced by electric chords from the depths of my soul. I rocked out in the empty parking lot and let the night get lost in a purple haze.

# CHAPTER 8

## CAMARA

Camara was walking on the longest road on God's green earth. She had been walking for what now felt like her entire life, and it was unbelievably hot. The sun was beaming down on her and she could barely see because of all the sweat dripping down over her eyes.

Every step was getting harder. She felt weighed down by something. She didn't have any bags, but she still felt weighed down. She couldn't remember why she had worn the long white sundress. It was for some occasion. She was supposed to take her place somewhere or maybe meet someone. She couldn't remember why she had worn it.

Camara walked and walked until she finally reached the end of the road. She had at last reached the ocean, and it was beautiful. The sun was just setting on the horizon creating gorgeous shades of blues, purples, orange and reds. Camara couldn't remember seeing a more peaceful sight in her life.

She wanted to reach the water, but she couldn't find a way down to it. She was standing on a road and held a railing that stretched out across the beach. From where she stood, she could look down to the beach but it seemed too far to possibly reach. She would have jumped over the railing but she knew she would just get her dress dirty. The beach was breathtaking and the water looked refreshing and relaxing, but it hardly seemed worth the possible pain if she sprained her ankle.

Camara was still hot. The heat was starting to burn her back. Her head was hot from her braids. She was looking at a sunset but could feel heat blistering her back.

She turned around and saw a powerful storm coming her way. Purple lightning was striking the ground on either side of the road. The storm seemed to scorch the sky and shake the ground on either side. The air crackled with static electricity and pricked her skin like a thousand needles all poking her at once. She couldn't take her eyes off the purple lighting.

The sound of thunder blasted in her ears louder than anything she had heard before. She grabbed her ears, looked up, and couldn't believe what she was seeing. A pair of talons like an eagle's was ripping a hole in the sky. The claws were huge and covered in blood that dripped and saturated the ground in liquid crimson. They cut the air from the center and spread outward creating a hole big enough for a single eye to look through.

The eye was huge and glowed bright—the color of fire; it looked right at Camara. It looked right through her. It penetrated her very being. Even though she was fully clothed, the eye's gaze made her feel naked and exposed.

Camara was waiting for someone, but who? She didn't know how but she knew the person coming would save her. She knew when he arrived they would run down to the ocean and drift off into the sea together. Where was he? Why couldn't she see him? He had to be there. Where was he? She had worn the dress to meet someone, hadn't she?

Thunder cracked again and the tear in the sky opened wider as one of the claws reached out to grab Camara in a hail of lightning that shook the ground. Horrifying screams filled the air, screams of pain and agony that called out to Camara's soul welcoming her among them.

Where was he? Who was he? He should be here by now. She was meeting someone. He would save her, but where was he?

"You are mine," said the thundering voice from the creature in the sky. The voice was haunting and malicious; it drained every ounce of hope from Camara. She knew she was about to die.

The road Camara had walked on began to crumble and break. The purple lightning struck the ground around her with more intensity. The huge claw encompassed her.

No one was coming to save her.

Darkness began to surround her, and the last image in Camara's mind was of the beach and the beautiful sunset. She thought of the drop down to the sandy beach and how good the water would have felt if she had made it to the ocean. It didn't seem as far a drop now that she thought about it. Camara closed her eyes and wished she had found the strength to jump.

# CHAPTER 9

## CAMARA

She woke violently from her dream and had to gasp for air. Camara was sitting up in her bed with both hands close to her chest trying to catch a breath. She tried to calm down and started to rub the beads of sweat from her face.

It took her a moment to realize she was in her bedroom. She had the dream again, and it had never seemed more real. She had the same dream during college, but it had only been flashes in her mind, never this clear. She could never remember all of it.

She would remember walking, a storm of some kind, and a malevolent voice calling out to her. That had been all there was to it. Until now.

Camara's heart was beating hard in her chest—so hard she could feel it in her hands and head. She began to take deep calming breaths and forced herself to focus on one spot in her room.

When her heart at last settled in her chest, she moved to put her feet on the floor and sit on the edge of the bed. She rubbed her hand through her hair and tried to collect her thoughts. She must have been acting forcefully in her sleep because the wrap she put on her hair was gone. The braids she had in were frizzy, and she could feel that a couple of them would have to be redone.

Sleep wasn't an option right now; she was too anxious. The thought of putting her head back on her pillow to sleep literally made her feel sick. Camara got up, reached for another wrap to tie down her hair until she felt like fixing it, and then put on a huge white Georgetown shirt that once belonged to her older brother.

Her big brother Tony had been her hero. Hardly a day went by when she didn't think about how wrong and unfair it was that he was taken from her. He was strong, smart and Camara looked up to him more than anyone. She was only thirteen when he went off to college and got himself killed.

The digital clock next to Camara's bed read 3:30 a.m. She seriously doubted that she would make it back to sleep tonight. She was too wound up. She went downstairs to fix herself some tea and maybe get into one of the several books she'd started, but couldn't seem to finish. When she got to the kitchen she was surprised to see her mother awake and sitting at the table.

"Well, you're up early for getting in so late," her mother said without looking up from the cup of tea she was sipping.

Camara's mother was sitting at the kitchen table looking as if she had been waiting for Camara to join her. It made Camara wonder just how loud she had been in her sleep.

"You're up early, too," Camara said as she grabbed a cup from the cabinet and poured herself some of the tea her mother had made. "I couldn't sleep. Bad dream."

"I heard."

"What was I saying?" Camara asked taking a seat across from her mother.

"Nothing that made any sense. I was sleep when you got home so if you don't plan on going back to bed, why don't you tell me how your first day at work went?" Allison Johnson said between sips of tea. Allison had always been sharp and quick to pick up things, especially with her family. Her friends had named her "Alley Cat" for a reason. Camara could remember her mother telling her how she had never really understood the connection, but had grown to like the name regardless.

"I don't even know where to start," Camara said half snickering.

"The beginning is always a good place to start a story. Why don't you try there?"

Camara took a deep breath and inhaled the aroma of the fresh jasmine tea in her cup before taking a small sip. Her mother had made it just the way she liked it. Just a little sugar and a lot of honey, perfect.

Camara took her time and told her mother all about her mediocre day and her daunting night.

She knew her mother would pick up on it so she decided to tell her about the dream to fill in the gaps of silence. Somehow it was easier to talk about that than the fire. That surprised Camara because she hadn't been able to say a word about her dreams since she started having them.

The Alley Cat sat back in her chair and listened to her daughter intently. She didn't interrupt, didn't ask any questions; she just sat and listened. When she was sure Camara had finished, she got up from the table and said, "Come in the living room with me, Camie."

Camara was a little annoyed that her mother hadn't bothered to comment on anything she just said, but still got up to follow. One thing she always admired about her mother was how well she had aged. Camara's mother moved just as gracefully and strong now in her late sixties as she ever did in her younger days. She had been forty-three when Camara was born. She used to call Camara her "miracle baby" because she thought she was too old to have any more children.

There were several blankets folded up on the couch so Camara and her mother sat on opposite ends of the couch and rolled themselves up nicely. Camara was a little curious to hear what, it anything, her mom would say about her story. They sat in the living room for several seconds, sipping tea and getting comfortable. Camara was just about to give up hope on her mother saying anything and was just about to start on something random when the wise old Alley Cat finally spoke, "Quite a day you had."

Camara gave a small scoff at her mother's understatement.

"I'm sorry for those people and I'm sorry you had to see what you saw tonight. I can only imagine how terrible that was. I might have a hard time sleeping just hearing you talk about it."

"Sorry," Camara said taking the time to sniff her tea before taking another sip. "I tried not to talk much about that part."

"Well, you did. You might not have said as much about that as you did other things, but you said plenty, missy."

"Sorry I . . ."

"No. It's good that you did. It's good to express how you feel about things like that. It's good to get things out. There's a lot more you need to get out, isn't there, Camie?"

Camara's only response was a deep sigh that seemed to drain the energy from her body and remind her how tired she was. She had just started working and getting settled in McDowell County, and she already felt like she needed a vacation from her life.

"I don't think I want to talk about that right this second. Let's deal with one emotional trauma at a time please," Camara said. The irony of her own growing emotional baggage still being locked away was almost too much. *If I had as much money in the bank as feeling inside me, all my problems would be solved.* She thought.

"I never asked why you had to move back home, did I, Camie?" Alley Cat said, her words pulling Camara out of herself.

"No, ma'am," Camara said clearing her throat. She didn't want the conversation to go this route yet. She was just feeling better about her dream; she didn't need her mother digging up skeletons now.

"I'm not going to ask you either. You know why?"

"No, ma'am," Camara said.

"Because you're a grown woman. You have to decide things for yourself. You have to take care of yourself. I'm an old lady and I won't be around forever. If you want my advice, you know where to find me. I'm right here, and I'm always willing to put a little something in your ear if you want it."

"Yes, ma'am." Camara was twenty-four years old and her mommy could still make her feel like a little girl even while telling her she was a grown woman. It was one of the things that Camara liked about their talks. They always took her

back to happier times; a simpler time, that Camara sometimes wished she could have back.

"And about that dream."

"Ma'am?" Camara asked with a raised eyebrow.

The Alley Cat looked her daughter deep in the eye. "Stop
running and take a faith leap. God will be there to catch you
if no one else is."

# CHAPTER 10

The sun was shining through the window on the second floor apartment of the Econo Lodge and woke the occupant in room 7F. The man in room 7F sprang out of bed as soon as the sunbeams hit his face. He had waited two days for this and he was about to pop with excitement.

He couldn't have slept more than five hours, but he was very energetic. He had plenty of spring in his step as he sauntered to the shower. He turned the water up as hot as it would go and loved it. He let the water run over his body and the steam quickly filled the bathroom. He loved the heat, the burning sensation drizzling down his body from head to toe. The slight blistering of his skin was perfect. The heat was intoxicating. The burning was nirvana.

He didn't exit the shower until the water ran warm. He let himself air dry. He didn't want to ruin the sensation his skin was feeling by rubbing it with a towel. While drying, he thought about how he wanted to look today. How tall would he be? What color hair, eyes?

The thought of the list of things on his agenda for today had him giddy as a schoolgirl. He looked at himself in the mirror and decided on blue eyes and dark brown hair. He decided to go with his natural height of 6'0".

He wore his favorite shirt, red short-sleeve shirt with black trim and a black skull with two spoons shaped like crossbones underneath it. The shirt read "Cereal Killer" across the bottom. Tattered blue jeans and grass-stained Nikes completed his attire for the day. He scooped up the large red and white cooler with its precious cargo inside and managed to maintain his euphoric mood as he headed out the door.

Today was going to be a good day. He was going to announce his presence to the town of Bluefield. How would they react? How would they change? He couldn't wait for the town's response.

He locked the door to his hotel room and made his way down to the parking lot. The man from 7F got in a dark brown sedan and turned left on Cumberland Road. He knew he had no reason to, but he was being very careful. It was impossible for him to get caught. He even took the time to strap his cargo into the passenger seat, which he thought was fucking hilarious.

He could not stop himself from giggling as he looked at the cooler and thought about what was inside. How would Bluefield react? *What oh, what would they do when they find out they always knew? Oh, what will they do?* The man from 7F thought.

The brown sedan made its way down Cumberland Road, onto Bland Street, and then hit College Avenue until reaching the Bluefield City Park. The car made its way around the circular layout of the park and stopped at a shelter toward the back.

The man from room 7F parked on the side of the road, stepped out of the car and walked to Pavilion #2 where he knew a family had reserved the space for a family reunion later that afternoon. He shook the cooler just for the pleasure of hearing its contents, and then placed it on the center table.

The family would arrive soon so he really wouldn't be able to enjoy his "dropoff" the way he wanted. He wanted to see the reactions on their faces, but he had a schedule. Routes to plan. Targets to pick. People to stalk. He pulled out a black magic marker and wrote the word "SODA" on both sides of the cooler. Then he wrote a little message to Mr. Champion on the bottom.

*What will they do?* The man from 7F thought. *What will they do?*

# CHAPTER 11

## CAMARA

Life went smoothly in the Johnson household. Since Camara and her mother had a heart-to-heart early Saturday morning, things had gotten better between them. It was almost like Camara had never left. Almost.

Alley Cat had even managed to drag Camara to church on Sunday. Camara was sure she hadn't been to church herself since after her first semester at Kentucky. She didn't really want to admit it, but she really enjoyed the service. She had never been a very big church person. Her mother always tried to get her to go as a child, but if her father didn't have to go, Camara never really understand why she had to.

Even though Camara enjoyed the service, she honestly didn't understand all of it. She just didn't understand some of the things church folk did. The pastor's message was about Jonah and the whale. It was about God's power to forgive and how people should, too, how people are always given a chance to make things right, like the people Jonah was sent to talk to. Camara could relate to the people Jonah talked to; she had a lot that needed forgiven herself.

Camara didn't bother to redo the braids in her hair after her nightmare had ruined them. She went with the natural look and styled her dark brown hair into a crinkly afro.

Once she had her hair the way she liked it, she dressed in a brown patterned blouse with a matching brown blazer, tan slacks and a thin white belt. The outfit was topped off with white three-inch heels making Camara 5'10".

Camara wasn't sure how she felt about going to work that Monday. She knew she would be asked about the fire. Will Anchor had written the article about what happened after the game. Camara was grateful she didn't have to. She wasn't sure she could after witnessing it first hand the way she did.

The images of that night were still fresh in her mind and she would give almost anything to get them out.

She was a little excited to see Ezra though. Maybe more curious than anything; but still she wanted to see him. She really enjoyed his company. She also wondered how he was handling what they had seen. How was he reacting? She wondered if Ezra had any nightmares over the weekend.

"Well, good morning!" Camara heard as she entered the lobby of the Daily Telegraph.

"Hello, Miss Kohls. How are you doing?" Camara said, smiling at the receptionist.

"It's Kim. Just Kim, dear. Miss Kohls was my mamma," Kim said and laughed at herself a little.

"Is Miss Kim okay then?" Camara asked jokingly.

"That'll work," Kim said with a shrug of her shoulders. "Ready for another day?"

"Ready as can be. I'll see you later, Miss Kim," Camara said while making her way to the staircase.

When Camara stepped into the main newsroom, she was surprise to see it was full and busy. Everyone was already there working. Camara checked her watch and was sure she was a solid five minutes early. *Did I miss something?* Camara thought as she strolled to her desk.

She didn't even have time to sit at her desk and get organized when a tall slender woman walked over to her. She wore a navy blue suit jacket trimmed in black with matching blouse, skirt and shoes. The woman wore her height proudly and confidence emanated from her every movement. "Camara Johnson, I need you to come with me, dear," the woman said, gesturing for Camara to follow.

Camara was a little confused. The woman was maybe 6'0" without her high heels. Camara thought she was the tallest woman working at the paper. The woman had light brown hair and chestnut eyes, the same color as Camara's. She was tanned, looked to be in her mid-thirties and in very good shape. There was an exotic look about her that you didn't find too often in West Virginia.

"Um, okay," was all Camara could manage to say to the woman as she turned and motioned for her to follow. *Great! I've been on the job one day and I already did something to piss someone off.* Camara followed the woman to a corner office to the right of the newsroom.

It wasn't a big office, but then again, it wasn't a big newsroom. Camara took a quick glance around the office. There were plenty of pictures of a man that Camara could only assume was the woman's husband. There were also pictures of a handsome baby boy that looked no more than three. The baby had his father's eyes and nose, and his mother's mouth and jaw. The office was bright and colorful with flower decorations and several figurines of lighthouses. On the desk was a nameplate which read Melissa Cervantes-Editor-in-Chief.

*Damn it!* Camara took a seat in front of the desk. *This can't be good.*

"Why did you want to work here, Miss Johnson?" Melissa Cervantes asked while leaning back in her chair. She folded her arms ready to listen intently to Camara's answer.

*How the hell am I supposed to answer that?* Camara was concerned by the way Melissa Cervantes had addressed her as "Miss Johnson." That meant this wasn't going to be a friendly buddy-buddy type of talk. This was all business. But, what business?

Camara took a deep breath, then began. "Well I guess-" she barely got the words out before being cut off.

"I missed your initial interview because I was out of town and Lois seemed to like you enough to sneak you by without my approval. The only reason she was able to do that is because of how short-handed we've been lately. You're already through the systems so I can't do anything, except make sure Lois can't do something like that again. I think it's only fair that I tell you that I'm not impressed."

*What the hell, I've been here one freakin' day!* Camara did her best not to show any emotion. She straightened her posture and locked into Mrs. Cervante's eyes. She had to remind herself to breathe steadily to keep the dam of anger from busting inside her. She sat patiently and let Mrs. Cervantes finish.

"Do you have any idea how many reporters I know who would do anything to witness what you did on Friday night? Do you know what type of opportunity that is for a writer? Frankly I think your lack of interest in covering the story is appalling. I certainly wouldn't have hired someone with such a blatant disrespect for his or her craft."

Camara could feel the dam of anger rising already and it looked as if it might rain. The flood was coming; Mrs. Cervantes showed no sign of letting up.

"If Will wasn't so good at his job, this would be a lot more serious. Even though he wasn't there until after the fact he did an excellent job depicting the night's events. However, as good as he is, I can't help but think that you could have done better having been there. To put it bluntly, I'm a little shocked that a woman of your ethnicity wouldn't welcome the opportunity to prove herself."

The lightning was brewing in the distance. Camara could feel it. Get ready to open the floodgates.

"I would have thought a woman of color with your particular appearance and choice of . . . hair style would be a little more ambitious."

Annnd . . . thunder crack!

"Excuse me?" Camara said affronted. She made no attempt to hide how insulted she felt.

"I was simply trying to say—" Mrs. Cervantes started before being cut off by Camara.

"I believe I know exactly what you were just trying to say, Mrs. Cervantes. I'll have you know I really don't appreciate it." Camara spoke and never left Mrs. Cervantes's eyes as she did. She made sure not to do anything stereotypical like waving her finger or shaking her head back and forth or cocking it to one side. She was going to express exactly how she felt as articulately as possible then leave this office. Mrs. Cervantes was going to take her seriously.

"You weren't here for my interview so you don't know why I applied for this job or what it means to me to have it. It's true that my degrees from Kentucky University aren't in journalism. They were actually for philosophy and creative writing with a minor in photography, but I assure you I'm more than qualified for this job.

"Yes, I was hesitant to write that article because this is all very new to me. Excuse me if after seeing a person burn to death right in front of me that my first thought that occurs to me is not one of personal career advancement.

"In all realness, ma'am, I would hope that I would never become so jaded to the tragic circumstances of others that I look at them as a stepping stone to better my own life. The people you know who take joy and excitement in disastrous events are nothing more than vultures, and I'll gladly tell them to their faces as clearly as I'm saying it to you.

"Unless my clothes are outside of some dress code I wasn't made aware of my hair styling doesn't meet with some type of ordinance, then I think it better for us both not to discuss them in the future. Now that we're done here, when I exit this office, should I leave the building or go back to my desk?"

Camara couldn't help but smile slightly at Mrs. Cervantes's reaction though she suppressed it as much as she could. As Camara spoke, Mrs. Cervantes leaned back further into her chair and her eyes narrowed. The color bloomed on Mrs. Cervantes's cheeks and Camara could almost imagine steam coming out of her nose and ears.

Camara kept her face even and waited for Mrs. Cervantes to respond. Camara wasn't sure what Cervantes was expecting but it was clear that she hadn't given it to her.

"You're young, Camara. I'm only trying to help you understand the business you're in," Mrs. Cervantes said through a forced smile.

*Oh, now I'm "Camara" and not "Miss Johnson," you smarmy bitch?* It took some control but Camara kept the words in her mind and caught them there before they found their way to her mouth. *Thank God mom made me go to church yesterday. Lord, give me the strength.*

"Well, Mrs. Cervantes, I appreciate the concern. If there's not anything else ma'am, front door or desk?" Camara said raising an eyebrow.

"Oh, you're going back to your desk, Camara. Before you're finished working here you're going to understand what you say means to be a real journalist. Tragic circumstances are not career builders but opportunities to expose the truth. Think about the people who were there that night or the people who heard about it since. Now imagine these people terrified as rumors fly about what happened, then picture people having nowhere to go to find out what really happened. Picture them having nowhere to turn to find the truth.

"That is what a real journalist does, Camara. We find the truth. We give people the facts. To be a reporter is to commit to the truth. I want you to think about that. Are you here to just get by and sit at your desk and look cute, or are you here to work?

"There should be write-ups on your desk. Try to have them done by three, would you? Also if there are any further developments on the explosion from Friday, I fully expect *you* to follow up on them," Mrs. Cervantes said.

"Yes, ma'am." Camara felt too angry to respond any other way. She rose from her chair and made her way to the door.

"Camara," Mrs. Cervantes said just as Camara was outside the door.

"Ma'am?" Camara said unable to hold in the, what next, tone that escaped her.

"Call me, Melissa."

Camara tried to hide her confused look. She wasn't expecting that.

"All right then, Melissa," Camara said and exited the office.

*What the hell was that about?* Camara could have sworn she saw a smile form on the corners of Melissa's mouth in contrast to the venom in her eyes. What was she supposed to take from that? The more Cervantes talked, that more pissed Camara had felt. The worst thing was that Mrs. Cervantes, or rather "Melissa," was right. Journalism was supposed to be about the truth. Camara hated being wrong and after the attitude she had, she was a little embarrassed which only made her more angry.

Camara was trying to focus on her work when she saw Ezra walk into the photography lab at the far end of the newsroom. He hadn't looked her way. He hadn't looked at anyone when he came into the newsroom. Camara had had such a good time with him Friday at the game that she forgot the awkwardness that surrounded the newsroom the last time he was there. It made her even more curious about what was going on with him. What was he really like? Ezra seemed to be one person that morning, and then a completely different person that evening. Which was the real him?

Camara looked at the write-ups on her desk and didn't think that it would take her more than two or three hours to finish them all. It would actually take longer. She had to admit Melissa's pep-talk had, in fact, motivated her. She didn't want to give her a single reason to say anything pompous, so she put her all into the write-ups. Camara read and reread what she wrote. Good wasn't good enough anymore, it had to be perfect.

She had finished everything but the proof when Nancy Hasley sat down beside her. Nancy was about 5'5", slightly overweight, had light brown skin and thick bifocal glasses. Seeing her was a pleasant surprise.

"Nanny!" Camara screamed and jumped out of her seat to give her "Nanny" a hug.

"Camie! Hey, sugah! When did you start working here?" Nancy Hasley asked, beaming from ear to ear. When things were pretty bad between Camara's parents, Nancy had been there through most of it.

"Today is only my second day. I thought you were on vacation. Momma hadn't said anything about you still being here. I didn't know until some people around the office mentioned your name."

"Well, you know how your mother can be. It probably just slipped her mind. What do they have you doing?" Nanny asked while placing her things on her desk.

"Well, of course, they realized how talented I am; so they wanted me to take over and run the whole paper, but I decided I would just dabble in some writing and occasionally moonlight in photography."

"Thank you for holding back, Miss Johnson. Your sacrifice is our job security. What made you be so kind?"

Camara folded her arms and shifted her weight. "I didn't want everyone in constant fear of being outshined so I thought it best to try a little kindness, you know, take a back seat. Just for now, of course."

"Of course."

Nanny and Camara shared a good laugh.

They talked briefly, and then admitted they had to get to work before they missed their deadlines. Camara was almost finished when Ezra sat on the edge of her desk and flopped down some blown-up copies of Friday's house fire.

"When did I take this?" Ezra said looking genuinely confused.

Camara laughed a little. The look on his face was priceless. Did he really not remember?

"It looks like you took it as soon as you got there. When do you think you took it?" Camara asked smiling.

Ezra sighed deeply and rubbed his hand over his head. Camara thought that maybe she had been a little out of line and was starting to feel a little embarrassed. Then Ezra made eye contact with her again and said, "Looks like I took it after a person just burned to death in front of me. I'm not sure what I was thinking, but I'm glad I took it. Look here."

Ezra pointed to a spot in the picture just behind the house. Camara hadn't noticed it at first. Everyone was too focused on the woman running out of the house to notice, but there it was as plain as day. There was a figure in the background.

Toward the back of the house where the forest was, they're stood a lone silhouette. You couldn't make out any real defining features, but you could tell it was a man.

"Oh, my God!" Camara said. "What do you think this means?"

"Nothing right now. We don't have any proof for anything, but if I were a betting man—"

Camara looked up at Ezra with a smirk. "You would bet this is our pyromaniac?"

"Great minds think alike," Ezra said with a dangerously charming smile.

Camara had to look away from him for a second to gain her composure. His smile had sent a jolt through her that she wasn't ready for. She cleared her throat as quietly and covertly as she could.

"So what are you going to do with this?" she finally asked, forcing herself to look at him.

"I'm not sure. At this point it could mean nothing or it could mean everything. I think I might take it to—" Ezra was cut off by his own phone ringing.

Camara waited as Ezra checked his phone and read the text. It seemed to be a long one and the more he scrolled down it, the more agitated he became.

"That was from my brother. They just found something interesting at Bluefield City Park."

# CHAPTER 12

## EZRA

Camara and I jumped into Dirty Vegas and drove to Bluefield City Park. The park wasn't far from Mitchell Stadium or the house that burned just two days ago. Zeus didn't give me too much information in the text, but it was a safe bet that this had something to do with the fires. I needed to know more. It would probably be healthier for me if I'd let this go, but if half of what Zeus told me was true, I was going to be involved whether I liked it or not.

"What made you want to come with me? I didn't think you were covering stories like this," I asked Camara as we hit Stadium Drive.

"I wasn't. I had a little talk with Melissa this morning. She told me to handle anything that might be related to the fire that happened Friday. You did say this might be related, right?"

"Maybe," I said.

"Well, even if it isn't, it got me out of the office."

"So, Melissa showed you her charming side already?"

"If that's what you call it. What's up with her? Is she like that to everybody?" Camara still looked ticked off by whatever Melissa had said to her.

"Believe it or not she's just trying to help you. Did you cry?"

"What?" Camara turned to me looking slightly shocked.

"Did you cry when she was talking to you? Well . . . then again, if you had cried she probably would have fired you, so I can assume you didn't."

Camara turned away from me and looked confused.

"Stick with us for a couple of months," I said, "You'll see what I'm talking about. You might even like Melissa when it's all said and done."

72

"I highly doubt that," Camara said dryly.

It didn't take long for us to pass the spot of the house fire. The house was completely destroyed and both the neighboring house and forest were scorched. Camara and I were both quiet as we passed.

We pulled into the park and saw a swarm of police cars parked helter skelter in the parking lots and grass fields. We couldn't drive too far into the park because the police had most everything taped off. I sent Zeus a text telling him to meet us at the basketball courts. We were going to need him if we wanted to get a closer look at what happened. It took Zeus five minutes to walk the distance of the park. He was all decked out in a gray jacket, matching slacks, and a dark red shirt—ever the professional.

"Glad you could make it to the party," Zeus said while pulling me into a bear hug.

"Thanks for the invite," I replied.

"Who's this?" Zeus asked, turning his attention to Camara while putting on his best smile.

"I'm Camara Johnson. I work at the paper," she said, extending her hand.

"Zeus. Zeus Champion." Zeus shook Camara's hand and checked her out in his own subtle way, which wasn't very subtle at all. Camara didn't look very impressed by him.

A little bit of tension filled the air, and I couldn't be sure where it was coming from, so I tried to move the conversation on.

"What's going on? You were pretty vague in your message," I said, as the three of us walked in the direction of the police cars.

"Well, you know about the fire Friday night," Zeus began. "Once they got the fire out, they still didn't find all the bodies of the family." Zeus reached in his breast pocket, pulled out a small notepad and started reading.

"The woman who ran out of the house was Carla Douglas. She was thirty-two and lived in the house with her husband Samuel Douglas, thirty-five, and their two children Michael and John. Michael was only eight, John was six. They weren't able to find the boys' bodies. They found the husband in the house with his skull bashed in. We asked around about the two boys. None of the victims' friends or family had them, so we assumed that the boys were in the house, but we never found then. It looks like our guy was in the house for a while before it blew up. They also think that Mrs. Douglas was raped, but I find that very unlikely."

"Why? You said the guy was in the house for a while, right?" I interrupted.

"Yeah," Zeus said, "but if this is who I think it is, then rape isn't in his MO."

"Why do you think a killer wouldn't be capable of rape?" Camara asked.

"That's not how he gets off, darlin'. The killing gets his mojo going, pussy not so much."

We walked deeper into the park. Zeus stopped us before we got too close to the taped off areas.

"So, do you take pictures too or are you here to cover the story?" Zeus asked Camara harshly.

"I'm actually capable of both, but for now I'm covering the story," Camara replied evenly.

"Well, why don't you try to pry a statement out of one of the cops. I need to speak with Ezra in private—if you don't mind," Zeus said with a overly polite smile.

"That's fine," Camara said with venom in her eyes. She walked toward the police officers. I could tell she didn't like the tone my brother had used to dismiss her. Zeus had that way with women. They either instantly loved him or hated him. I was starting to think Camara would end up choosing the latter.

Once Camara was a good enough distance away, Zeus started up.

"Why the hell did you bring her with you?" he said looking irritated.

"What's wrong with her? Don't tell me you hooked up with her before."

"Hell no! I've never seen that chick before in my life. Girl's shooting darts at me though. If you had any ideas, don't waste your time on her. She's probably a lesbian."

"So, now if a girl isn't interested in you, she has to be gay? Are you serious?"

"That's just how it goes, bro. Don't hate me' cause you ain't me."

"Can we get back to business, please?" I asked, for answers. "What's going on here? What did they find? I thought you said this guy doesn't have MO?"

Zeus took a deep breath. At the moment he looked like the weight of the world had been resting on his shoulders for way too long.

"He doesn't. He very well could've raped that woman. I don't want to give any reason for that to be in the papers. The press can be nothing more than a pack of vultures, and I didn't want to give too many details around her. They found little John and Michael's heads in a cooler down on pavilion number two. That's what this is about. A family had rented the pavilion for a family reunion and some kids stumbled on the heads. The cooler must have been there a good hour before anyone thought to look inside it. There was a message on the bottom of the cooler that only a few people would understand or consider as anything but a sick joke."

Zeus had my interest. I was racking my brain as he spoke, trying to fill in the pieces for myself. "What did it say?"

"Youngblood," Zeus said with a grim expression.

"Two little kids heads found in a cooler with the word 'Youngblood' written on the bottom. That sounds like a sick joke to me. What type of meaning does that have for you?" I asked, puzzled.

"'Youngblood' was my name when I first started with The Pack in Baltimore. It's what the old man used to call me. Everybody who would know that is dead now—except for one person."

"AKA?" I asked, catching my brother's eye.

Zeus returned my glance, and I could see the muscle clench in his jaw.

"This isn't your fault, Zeus. You can't blame yourself for what a psycho does," I said placing a hand on his shoulder.

"That's the thing—he's not a psycho," Zeus said, slapping my hand away. "He's a damn pyromaniac, murdering, genius son-of-a-bitch! He's smart and good at not getting caught. He knows when to attack and he knows when to run. He doesn't do the stupid shit like most of the people The Pack and I go after. He's in a different league and he knows it. He's always one step ahead of me, and he keeps getting better. This is how I know it's him. He does something like this to me every time. All I need is a reason to justify bringing The Pack to West Virginia, and I can get him this time. I know it!"

"In my book, if you get off on killing, then you're a psycho. I don't care how smart he is. He's getting off with fire and what not. To me, that screams psycho," I said through a half smile.

"Why do you always act like shit doesn't bother you? Stop making jokes. This guy probably killed your mom, Ezra, doesn't that piss you off?" Zeus asked.

"I don't want to talk about my mother, Zeus. We don't know for certain if it was this guy anyway." I felt the funk coming back on. I was doing well, but now I was being hit with the sudden urge to curl up in the fetal position.

"Well, if you tell me some of what you saw that night, I might be able to put some pieces together. He probably—"

"Not now, Zeus," I said cutting him off.

"Fine. That's really all I got for you. I just wanted you to know by telling you in person that I'm one hundred percent sure AKA is in Bluefield. If I don't get some back up and find him soon, things will get worse. We've only seen the beginning of the killing," Zeus said. "It's already going to be too late for some people. More are going to die before this is over, Ezra."

We stood in silence for several seconds. I knew better than to try to reason with Zeus when he got this angry so I snapped a few pictures of the cops in the area where the heads had been found. I took a couple of shots of Camara talking to a few of the police officers. It looked like she was throwing on the charm and it wouldn't surprise me if she ended up knowing more about what was happing than she was supposed to. I wondered what would end up in the paper tomorrow.

"Did you read the paper I left for you?" Zeus asked.

"No. I was going to, but I feel asleep. Why's it so important?"

Zeus reached into his breast pocket and pulled out a folded up article from the paper and handed it to me. "Read it," he said. "Now."

I opened up the clipping, which was from the front page of the Bluefield Daily Telegraph dated a little over two months ago. I read the headlines, reached the dates and couldn't believe what I was seeing. I couldn't believe this had been in the paper. I couldn't believe I didn't know about it. I felt the same type of hurt and betrayal that I'd felt standing in Lois's office my first day back.

Everything made more sense now. Why no one spoke to me when I went back to work. Why police chief Wilson had been in my face and everyone had looked at me the way they did after the fire. There was a spotlight shining on me and now I knew why.

"Where's the rest of it?" I asked in the most neutral tone I could manage.

"You should have all of it at your apartment. I'm sorry I didn't just tell you but I thought it would be better if you read it for yourself. I figured you wouldn't have bothered to look at the paper when you went MIA on everybody. What are you going to do about it?"

"What can I do?" I asked, shrugging my shoulders.

"You can quit. You can get another job. Put that social work degree to work for you. It's not like you have a lot of reasons to stay in West Virginia."

"I'll think about it. I might just give them a chance to tell me how they feel first. See how long it takes for one of them to say something about it. Some people owe me an explanation. I want to be sure who my friends are before I burn any bridges. What are you going to do?"

"AKA won't hit the same side of town twice in a row. He likes to spice things up. Likes to do something different almost every time. I'll wait a couple of weeks for a trail to show itself. North side, east end, the west, or south side, I just need to wait for him to show me which way his game is being played this time. I need to wait for the next murder."

# CHAPTER 13

I couldn't wait. It was killing me to just sit around and pass the time while waiting for someone else to die. It had been a week since the two little boys' heads were found in the park, and nothing else had happened. Zeus had been in positions like this before so he was a little more adjusted to the downtime. It was easy for him to distract himself. It wasn't so easy for me.

It took five days of going to work acting oblivious to the article written about me before Lois finally said something to me about it. We had a long heart-to-heart and she seemed to give me the general consensus of the newsroom. I was hitting an even split so far with half the people believing the article and the other half not. It was probably better that way. That way I had a good feel for who my real friends were.

I couldn't stand the thought of sitting back and doing nothing anymore. I had to at least try something, but I had no idea what. Somehow I found myself for the second night walking the streets of the upper north side of Bluefield. I'm still not sure what was making me do it. I knew how bad it would be if anyone recognized me out here at 3:30 in the morning. I knew what type of assumptions it would create, but I didn't care.

North side was one of only two sides of town not to be hit with a fire yet and that got me thinking. I checked the papers and caught up on all the news that I had missed the past two months and found some interesting facts.

Most of the fires happened to the south of town, six in all, and that was the affluent side of town. All rapes that had been reported were on the north side and east end, what people might classify as the poorer sections. There had been ten cases of rape between the north and east end of Bluefield in the span of four months. The police didn't think the rapes and fires were connected. They didn't consider all those crimes could have been committed by the same person. It was hard to believe that a white person who could move around unnoticed on south side would go unnoticed on north or east, same for a black guy walking around the sidewalks on south side. It just didn't make sense for the same person to be able to move so easily through both. What should that be telling the police? I talked to Zeus about my suspicions and he looked at me like I didn't tell him a single thing he didn't already know. "Let it go, Ezra. This is my fight and I'll handle it. You don't want to be involved any more than you already are. Trust me."

My brother's warning echoed in my head as I walked the streets hearing nothing but the hum of the streetlights. Zeus probably knew what he was talking about. He was probably right, but I couldn't let it go. Not until I did something.

I already knew that what I was currently doing was very stupid. Here I was creeping on the streets of north side wearing a pair of jeans and a hoody with an already dubious reputation. Being recognized this time of night alone might get me thrown in jail for all I knew.

Still I felt I had to be here. As nervous as I was, it made me feel better on some level. I felt like I was doing something. I didn't know how bad or good it was, but it was something. I walked up and down the hills and alleyways on the "wrong side of the tracks" as some people like to call the north side.

The railroad that separated north side from the rest of Bluefield was a big part of the town's glory days. Those days are long gone and the town is now a shell of its former self. There were too many vacated, run down buildings that were in the way of the town expansion and kept people looking at mirrors to a shattered past. I wondered how the town would be different if those beat down relics weren't there.

I stayed on the north side and walked the tracks for a while before I reached Bluefield State's campus. My mind kept rerunning all the facts I learned from the papers I read as I walked. The streets were quiet and I felt a slight breeze rolling off the mountains, rustling the trees. The only other sounds I noticed were the occasional barks of dogs in the neighborhood. If one of them attacked, all I had to protect myself with was a large knife I kept at the small of my back. I was trained to use it just like I was trained to use swords. My dad had taught my brothers, sisters and me how to fight. He had taught me how to handle myself, but I knew my dad would disapprove of me being on the streets. I already knew what Zeus would say about me only having a knife with me.

I walked by Mahood, one of the buildings on the college campus. I was just about to call it a night when I heard a scream echo off the buildings. It was faint but definitely a woman's scream. Someone was hurt, but I couldn't tell exactly where the scream came from. I crouched low and crept in the direction of my best guess. My heart thumped and my breath deepened. My walks on northside were meant to be therapeutic, a way for me to release some tension and clear my head. I didn't really expect to come across anything. This was stupid. What was I doing here?

Bluefield State is a historically black school, which was why it was located on the north side of town. They had to carve out the mountain and build the entire campus on a slope; this caused the roads to be narrow. Concrete walls ran up and down the campus, holding back different sections of mountain. I made full use of those walls as I edged to the area where I thought the scream had originated.

My heart pounded so loud I thought anyone around would be able to hear it. I was anxious, excited and terrified all at once. My body just moved on its own, even as the thoughts of how crazy this was hammered in my mind. What was going on? What was I about to stumble upon?

No answers came to me. It didn't matter. The scream was probably nothing. Could be college kids goofing off on campus, but I had to know. I waited and listened. I started to think that I had heard it in my head. Maybe I was just being paranoid.

Again I heard the scream—louder this time. Bluefield State's gym was a three-level structure that sat separate from the mountain. It had an upper level where the actual gym was and two lower levels. From the walkway of the upper level, there was a solid hundred foot drop to the ground. I crept silently to the gym's upper level entries and glanced over the railing. The scream came from the gym's ground level, where the gym and the mountain were parallel with each other creating a narrow breezeway. It was dark; all I could make out were shadows. Something violent was happening. I wasn't willing to make my presence known so I ran as fast as I could off the upper level and down the far side of the building to get a closer look at what was happening. The whole time I ran, my mind was flooded with possibilities. What if I had misread the situation? I could be nothing more than a peeping tom, interrupting two lovers. I'd come this far. I had to be sure.

I pulled my knife and stopped to gain my composure on the far side of the building. I edged myself over to the corner and peered into the darkness. I stopped and listened, crouching low trying hard to slip around the corner. The only lights came from the streetlights far above; even from this close I could only make out shapes.

The two figures were close together and moving violently back and forth in the dark. As my eyes adjusted to the darkness I could tell now that one of the shadows was a woman. Her hands were moving frantically trying to push the other larger shadow away from her. She groaned and grunted as the larger shadow did its best to hold her into position, clawing at her mouth to keep her quiet. Whoever this guy was, he was huge. Well over six feet. I saw him strike the woman several times in the face and stomach.

I couldn't bring myself to turn away. I couldn't bring myself to do anything. My heart was pounding; I could feel it in my ears now. What was I supposed to do? Why didn't I bring my cell phone with me? How stupid! My whole body was shaking except for the hand clasped tightly to my knife.

I could hear the woman's voice now, barely a hoarse whisper. She couldn't scream for help anymore. I heard her voice rasping in a futile effort to get her attacker off her. Whoever she was, she was tough.

It had only been seconds since I arrived but I already felt disgusted with myself. Why wasn't I doing something? Why wasn't I helping? Everything was happening so fast. I looked down at the blade in my right hand and my reflection looked back at me. I knew what I had to do. God help me. Why did I put myself in a position like this? Why was I hesitating?

Then I heard it. A quick and sudden snap. The snap hit my ears from the darkness like someone breaking a tree branch. The sound bounced off the corner of the alley way and hit my heart, sinking all hope I felt for the girl. It was a sound that I'm sure would haunt me for the rest of my life. I looked up and saw the man holding the woman against the wall, her body now limp. Her neck had snapped. He'd killed her! I just stood by while someone was killed!

Stupid! Stupid! I waited too long. Couldn't have been more than fifteen seconds. I was right there, and I was still too late.

The man had the woman's body against the wall and continued thrusting in and out of her even after she was dead. It looked like he enjoyed the sex more with her dead but kept beating her like he was upset the fight was over.

Every ounce of hesitation and fear left me to be replaced with focus and anger. I couldn't sit back and keep watching this! I wasn't going to just leave with my tail between my legs either! I used everything I had to sprint the distance between the Goliath and me. My muscles tensed and blood rushed in my veins as I surged into the darkness. He didn't hear me coming until I was half way there, but he still had time to drop the girl, and pull up his pants to face me before I reached him. He was quick.

I led with my right, trying to bury the knife deep into his chest to the hilt. He was too fast for me even though I had caught him off guard. He caught me at the wrist with one hand and lifted me off the ground by the chest with the other. Then he slammed me into the wall where the girl had died only seconds before. His hands were massive and strong. I wasn't sure if I could break his hold. He had me pinned. Some light was coming from above, but I still couldn't see his face. Suddenly he had me in the same position the woman had been in. I was seeing what she had seen as she died.

The Goliath felt as if he were made of steel. He was stronger than me, much stronger. He still had my right arm pinned with his left and was using his right forearm to choke the life out of me. He leaned in close and lifted me up to get a look at my face. The pressure on my throat increased as he lifted me; I was already starting to get light headed, my vision was blurring.

"Ezra?" I heard come from the killer in a deep growl. This psycho knew my name! He knew, or at least recognized me!

He was shocked to see me, which gave me the opening I needed to bring one of my legs up and catch him with a knee square in the jaw. He let me go and stumbled back a few steps. I took the time to catch a breath and put my knife back in its holster on my back. I ran in fast and angry. I wasn't thinking. I was running off pure emotion, something I was always taught not to do in a fight. I had to fight smart if I was going to survive this. I doubted the Goliath would hesitate to leave my cold lifeless body in this alley to be found alongside the girl. It took me a second to get my energy. I was closer to being choked than I realized. I didn't think he had any weapons; he would've had them out while raping the girl. Maybe I could get him easier if he thought my knife was no longer on me. Maybe I could regain the element of surprise.

I lunged at him and he threw a powerful right hook that would have crushed my face if it had connected. He was the angry one now. He threw a series of punches my way and I bobbed and weaved around them. He was strong and quick but not very agile. His arms seemed like they should have been longer than they were for someone his height. Every blow he threw that didn't land gave me more confidence. I couldn't help but test the guy as my fighting instincts kicked in. I was getting myself prepped to go on the offensive. I controlled my breathing and danced on my toes. It was pitch black in the alley, so I could barely see the Goliath. His heavy breathing gave him away. He huffed with every punch. His steps grew clumsy with every haymaker he tried to deliver.

The girl he had killed put him through the ringer as she struggled. He probably killed her when he did because he was getting tired of fighting her. Her futile efforts for survival were making my own fight to stay alive possible.

I watched his movement as best I could. Our brawl could have been in a better place, the alley was narrow, the ground uneven. My agility was my upper hand. It might have been all that was keeping me alive.

I faked a punch up high to his jaw then punched down and stuck with my left fist where his right knee should have been. Instead I hit something hard, something that wasn't flesh and bone. Pain shot through my hand. Something wasn't right about this guy.

He reached out with both hands and lifted me like a father picking up his five-year-old son, but I was ready for him this time. I reached for my knife then slammed it deep into his shoulder. He dropped me instantly but not before he delivered a haymaker to my jaw in desperation. I saw it coming and managed to roll far enough away from the blow not to be caught with its full force. If I would've taken it full on, he could've knocked me unconscious, then game over.

He didn't scream or yell out in pain. He didn't say anything. The Goliath grabbed his shoulder and growled like an angry wolf. How crazy was this guy?

I put the knife back in its case after being rocked by his punch and saw the Goliath start to run away. He was fast but not fast enough to lose me. I shook off the effects of his blow and gave chase. There was something weird about the way he was moving when he ran. Something acquired in the stride of his steps. Still he was quick as hell.

The Goliath vaulted up one of the concrete walls of the campus and scurried up the shrub-filled slope. I ran after him not fully knowing what I was going to do if I caught him. I wasn't about to just let him get away, but what was I going to do? I couldn't just kill him. Could I? Should I?

I lost sight of him for only a moment when he jumped over another wall. I wasn't far behind him, and when I got over the wall, I saw him sliding down the guardrail of a steep staircase. I mounted the guardrail, sliding down not far after him. I concentrated on keeping my balance and using the time to catch my second wind.

I almost tripped from the forward momentum as I hit the ground in a run and turned on the jets to gain any ground I might have lost. I heard the sound of a train motoring by and used the noise of its engines like war drums, the bumping of the locomotive fueling my legs. I pushed myself harder, fighting the lactic acid building in my muscles. I ignored the pain and fear. I forgot the stupidity of my own actions and threw the consequences out the window. Nothing was on my mind but my goal. I was chasing a murderer. Pain didn't matter. Fatigue didn't matter. This bastard wasn't going to lose me.

We were running through a level parking lot and I started to gain some ground. I could feel sweat running down my face and back. I was almost on him now. I would have him on the next straight way we hit. I could feel it.

He mounted another foothill then he was running along part of the Frank S. Easley bridge. I wasn't far behind him when I heard an unexpected boom and felt something nick my left shoulder. Two more pops echoed through the night, and then two whistling sounds flew by. Both sounded only inches from my head. I jumped and took cover behind the concrete wall that protected pedestrians from traffic on the bridge.

I had nowhere to go, no way to attack him. There was no direction for me to run that he wouldn't be able to pick me off with his pistol. I couldn't jump off the bridge if I wanted to due to the large fence on my side of the bridge. Where the hell did he get that gun? Did he have it the whole time? Why didn't he shoot me earlier if he had it on him?

I tried to steady my breath so I could hear him walking toward me but I could only hear the sound of the train rumbling under the bridge.

"That smell. I just love that smell." I heard a malicious voice scream from the other side of the bridge.

I looked over my concrete barrier to find out where the guy was and why he hadn't jumped over the small wall to shoot me. When I peered over the barrier, the man was standing on the opposite wall that dropped off to the railroad below. I still couldn't see details of his face. It was covered in shadow but I could swear I saw a grin. A killing grin.

"I'll be seeing more of you, Ezra," he said, looking right at me. I was able to hear more clearly this time since the train had almost passed.

"That smell." I looked on as the man fell backward in a free fall off the bridge and kept that same malevolent smile on his face. "Fresh youngblood!" he screamed disappearing over the edge.

I jumped over the wall that had separated us and looked over the edge. I saw the train, loaded up with coal, passing under the bridge. The last car had just passed; I wouldn't be able to follow. He had gotten away. My anger was only surpassed by the revelation of the killer's words. He called me "Fresh youngblood."

It was really him.

I had just met AKA.

# CHAPTER 14

**EZRA**

It only took Zeus ten minutes to get to my place. It seemed as if I had just gotten home when my brother's boisterous knocking threatened to break my door to splinters.

"I'm coming! Stop before you wake my neighbors!" I barked. It was almost 5 a.m. and the last thing I needed was for someone to file a complaint on me with the landlord.

I opened the door and instantly regretted it. Zeus burst in, grabbed me by the shirt with both hands, and slammed me against the wall. He came in so hard that the door had swung open then shut itself from the momentum.

"What the fuck is wrong with you!" he screamed and slammed me against the wall again. "You idiot! Do you have any idea what you just did! He's going to come after you harder now. You just drew a fucking target on your chest! I told you to stay out of it!"

"Let me go, Zeus!" I shot back at him, "And stop cursing."

"Why did you do it? What are you trying to prove?"

I locked eyes with him. "Let. Me. Go," I said to him without blinking.

"Dammit, Ezra!" Zeus shouted then let me fall to the floor.

I stayed quiet and let the silence speak as Zeus paced back and forth in my living room. I went to the refrigerator, grabbed a beer, and sat it at the table waiting for him to calm down.

"Where's your laptop? Do you have internet in here?" Zeus asked.

"In my guest room. The password is 'dragonfly.'" I said evenly.

Zeus disappeared into my guestroom without saying another word. I didn't bother him while he did whatever he was doing. My mind was busy rewinding what had happened. I tried to relive what happened forwards and backwards. Every detail, every sight and sound left me with a weird feeling. Some things just weren't adding up. I was hoping Zeus would be able to connect some of the dots for me when he calmed down.

It didn't take me long to patch up my shoulder. A Band-Aid was all I needed. It was barely a flesh wound, but it made me think about how dangerous it was running after a murderer. I don't know what I was thinking being out there, but I was sure my vigilante days were over.

Ten minutes after he entered, Zeus came out of my guest room, but he didn't look any less angry. He sat down at the table across from me and didn't look up. His jaw was clenched, and he kept opening and closing his right hand.

"Tell me what happened," he said. "I want every detail you remember. Don't leave out anything. Every smell. Every sound. No matter how unimportant it might seem to you. I need to know everything you can tell me."

It took an hour to tell him what I had experienced. I'm not sure if it was how dramatic the experience was or just the fact that I had been constantly playing it in my head since it happened, but I managed to tell Zeus everything. I could tell he was concentrating on my every word. He was taking everything in. I did my best to paint a picture for him as clearly as I could.

When I finished giving him the facts, I went into how I felt about everything. I told him how guilty I felt about letting the girl die. I confided in Zeus in a way I never had before. He was the only person I thought would be able to understand. I asked how I was supposed to live with what happened. I asked him what I should do.

"I'm sorry I slammed you against the wall," he said, "You don't understand what you've done though. He's going to come after you now. He'll probably do it just to get to me, but he'll still do it, and there's nothing I can do about it. There're a lot of ways for him to track you down, but I was able to stop some of them using your computer."

"What are you talking about?" I asked.

"There are several ways for someone to find all types of private information on the web if you know where to look. I did what I could myself but I'm no computer genius, so I made a call to a guy in The Pack. No one will be able to find you on the web in the next hour or so. I just hope it's enough time. You do not want that freak showing up here."

"I should be able to handle myself. He didn't seem that tough," I said.

Zeus leaned forward in his seat and stared me down like I just said something completely stupid.

"First of all, Ezra, you caught him by surprise. I can guarantee that won't happen again. The fact that you ran into him at all is hard to believe. I've been chasing him for years, and I've never accidentally run up on him once. Second, he was wearing stilts to make himself taller. That's why he couldn't touch you when you fought and that's why you were able to keep up with him so easy when he ran. Next time count on both of those being the opposite of what they were tonight. Third, you're not dead. The only reason you're still alive is because he wants to play with you some more. He had a gun, right? He thinks you're interesting. You're in over your head now."

Stilts. I didn't think about that. That's why his running looked awkward, and his lateral movement when we fought was so off. "I thought you said I was already in deep?" I asked.

"You were just in deep before. Now you're in deep shit over your head."

"That's reassuring. Thanks," I said getting up from the table.

"Just keeping it honest," Zeus said grabbing the beer and taking a sip.

I let out a deep sigh and rubbed my eyes. "Maybe the police will find something to lead to him. I'll give a statement tomorrow," I said.

"You'll do what?" Zeus asked with a shocked expression.

"You can't really be thinking about going to the cops."

"Why wouldn't I? I saw a murder. Why wouldn't I tell the cops about it? I should have called them before coming back here and calling you. I would have gone straight to the police if I had been thinking straight. I just wanted to get out of there," I said.

"Are you really that oblivious to what people around you think? Ezra, this is a small town and you're not the people's favorite right now. It won't matter what you say to the police, you'll still be a suspect. I know how unfair that seems, but that's your reality right now. I can only image how you must feel knowing that your reputation with the whole town can be torn apart with one newspaper article, but that's how things are with people. It takes them forever to love you and only a second to hate you."

"So what am I supposed to do when I see news reports about that girl's murder? You just want me to play dumb?"

"Play dumb, fool. I want you to act fucking retarded," Zeus said emphatically. "Did anybody see you on north side? Did you leave any blood on the scene or clothes? Is there anyway that anyone would be able to tell you were there unless you told them?"

I took a second and replayed the night in my head again and considered each of Zeus's questions. I was punched in the jaw pretty hard, but I was sure I didn't bleed. No teeth were missing. I got nicked by a bullet but it was barely as scratch.

"I doubt it. No one should know I was there. I'm not sure though with that forensic stuff they have now. I'm not sure what they can find," I admitted.

"Long as you didn't leave anything major behind don't worry about it. The real world isn't like what you see on CSI. Forensic work is a whole lot of long hours and inconclusive evidence at best. It works but it's not like TV, trust me," Zeus said. I didn't doubt him.

"As long as you didn't bleed at the scene you're okay. I'm sure a lot of people spit in that alley. Won't be enough to link you to the scene."

I walked to the counter where I had laid my knife and picked it up.

"Didn't you tell me you didn't have any DNA for this guy on file?" I asked Zeus.

"Yeah, that's right. We got nothing. No hair samples. No prints. No DNA. No nothing. The bastard has been perfect for years. He's a fucking ghost. The FBI, the CIA, none of the big guys even believe he exist," Zeus said to me while rubbing tired eyes. "Why you askn'?"

I unsheathed my knife from its case and looked at the dry crimson DNA that covered it. The knife that probably saved my life when I buried it into AKA.

"You want some?"

# CHAPTER 15

## CAMARA

Camara walked into the Applebee's in Bluefield, Virginia, and looked for her best friend. She'd just gotten back in town from house hunting in North Carolina, and Camara couldn't wait to see her. Camara looked around the restaurant again but still didn't see who she was looking for, so she had the hostess give her a table for two with a good view of the door.

She ordered her drink and used her time waiting to remember all the trouble she and her friend Michonne Snow used to get into when they were kids. Whether playing jokes on their older brother, detention for talking too much in class or skipping class all together, Michonne was always right there with her. Michonne had lived across the street from Camara until they both left for college. They had been through a lot together and nobody knew Camara better than Michonne.

Not five minutes after Camara arrived, Michonne walked in. Camara recognized her by her caramel-colored skin and long hair that she had let grow down to the center of her back.

"Snowflake!" Camara screamed, unable to hide her excitement.

"Camie!" Michonne screamed back with a beaming smile.

Camara sprang from the table and ran to hug her friend.

"It's so good to see you," Camara said taking a step back to look at Michonne from top to bottom.

"I know. It's good to see you, too. I've been going crazy without you to talk to. What happened, girl? All of a sudden your phone didn't work, your e-mail address was nonexistent, and your Facebook and Myspace were both deleted. I thought you died or something; I was really worried about you. I didn't have your mom's number anymore or anything,"

Michonne said still smiling, clearly happier to see Camara than upset at being out of touch for so long.

"That's a long story," Camara admitted, shaking her head and looking down trying to put on her most pitiful face. "I don't want to talk about it just yet." She poked out her bottom lip like a five-year-old child. Then she looked up at Michonne, smiled, and the two shared a laugh.

"You're silly," Michonne said.

"I know. We're sitting over here, come on. Catch me up with you first then I'll fill you in on the details of my sad life."

Michonne and Camara sat across from each other and immediately started talking as if they had last talked yesterday instead of over two months ago.

"I'm not even sure where to start. I've been wanting to tell you so much, but now that I'm with you none of that crap really seems that important," Michonne said.

"A wise old Alley Cat once told me that when that happens to just start at the beginning. I've got no where to go so I'm all ears," Camara said crossing her legs and leaning forward in her chair, eager to hear Michonne's stories. Camara just knew whatever was going on with Michonne couldn't have been worse than what was going on with her.

"The beginning," Michonne said. "That's easier said then done." Michonne paused briefly, trying to find the right words. "Well . . . I'm engaged."

"What? That's great, right?" Camara said, smiling.

"Right," Michonne said, unenthusiastically.

Camara looked at her friend, confused. She had known Michonne too long and too well not to know there was more. Camara was about to force the answers out of her when the waiter appeared and asked if they were ready to order. Camara went for the salmon with steamed vegetables, and Michonne elected to have the three cheese chicken penne. The waiter took their orders, then brought back a sweet tea for Camara and water with lemon for Michonne.

When it was clear that the waiter wouldn't be back for several minutes, Camara started the conversation back up.

"Why aren't you happy to be getting married?" Camara asked.

"I am happy, Camie. I am. It's just . . ." Michonne paused again, struggling to find the right words to express her feelings. "It's just sometimes Adam looks at me like he doesn't see me, you know? Like he sees what he 'thinks' I will be rather than what I really am. Does that make sense?"

"A little."

"It's that and the fact that he's white. I don't care he's white; its just, his parents were fine with him 'dating' a black girl, but then they switched up on me as soon as they found out he was 'marrying' one."

"How does your family feel about him?" Camara asked.

"Oh, my mom and dad love Adam. He's treated me better than any man I ever dated. Adam talks to my dad all the time, and my mom is just in love with him."

"Well, if he's good enough for your family, then you should be good enough for his."

"That's the thing. I got along great with his parents up until Adam asked me to marry him. I just don't think his mom wants half-black babies running around. I think his dad will be okay with a little time, but his mom is poison and she keeps getting in Adam's head."

"Pop out a couple of mixed babies. Once that woman sees how cute they are, she'll be singing a different tone. They're from a different generation—just give it time. Now let me see it," Camara commanded.

Michonne rolled her eyes feigning ignorance, knowing full well what Camara expected to see. "What? What are you talking about? See what?" Michonne said.

"Bitch, you know what I'm talking about," Camara said beckoning Michonne with her fingers.

"Bam!" Michonne finally said, and lifted her hand over the table extending it to Camara.

Camara looked at the ring and was surprised she hadn't noticed it right away. It was so beautiful it took her breath away. If she and Michonne weren't such good friends, she would've clubbed her upside the head and run out with the damn thing. Camara took Michonne's hand and looked closer at the ring to inspect every detail. It was an elegant two-and-a-half carat, princess-cut, premiere diamond set in a twenty-four-karat white gold waterfall mounting with quarter-carat baguettes running down either side.

"Damn! What did you say Adam does again?"

"He's a pharmacist. You knew that."

"Yeah, but judging from this rock on your hand, I'd say he was filling out a few prescriptions on the street," Camara said jokingly.

"He told me he saved up for three years to get this ring."

"I thought the two of you have only been dating for three years?"

Michonne smiled and fought to hold back a giddy laugh. "He said he started saving after our first date. He knew he wanted to marry me then and had been saving ever since."

"That's sweet. A little corny and weird, but still sweet," Camara said, smiling.

"I know," Michonne said unable to control herself. "Isn't it great?"

"Okay, now I'm a little confused. You apparently love the cornball, so what was with the doom and gloom a second ago?"

"I told you, Camie, his parents. His whole freaking family."

"You're not marrying his family."

"Yes, I am. You just can't come between a man and his mother and expect everything to just work itself out. That's like if a man came between me and my daddy. It just wouldn't work, and family is very important to both Adam and me. I don't know what do," Michonne admitted sheepishly.

"Do you love him?"

"Most of the time."

"Do you want to marry him?"

"I'm wearing the ring."

Camara chuckled and sat up in her chair. "Girl, if someone presented me with a rock like that, please believe, I would take it. Why you're wearing the ring wasn't the question."

"Yes. I want to marry him," Michonne said laughing.

"Then get married."

"Wait a minute," Michonne said suddenly. "How did we end up staying on my drama when you're the one who fell off the face of the earth? Seriously, what happened to you?"

"What's taking the food so long?" Camara asked looking in the direction of the kitchen.

"Don't even try to change the subject. Spill it," Michonne said not trying to hide her irritation.

Camara let out a deep sigh and relented to Michonne's iron will. She knew she couldn't put it off any longer. She paused for a second, trying to take her own advice and start at the beginning.

"Well, you remember me telling you about Tarquan, right?"

"I knew it! I knew it had something to do with him. He just seemed too perfect from the get go. What'd he do?"

"Well, thanks for sharing your concern with me while we were dating," Camara said sarcastically.

"You wouldn't have believed me if I told you. So what'd he do?" Michonne asked more enthusiastically this time.

"Could you not sound so excited?" Camara said not trying to conceal the hurt in her voice.

Michonne looked genuinely remorseful for her outburst.

Camara accepted her friend's silent apology and continued her story.

"I told you about Tarquan and how perfect he was. He was always around, very attentive and considerate. He did a lot to take care of me and he challenged me mentally. He was also fine as hell."

"He was okay," Michonne interrupted. "He was too big a guy for my taste. I like my men slim and slender. All that muscle just scares me."

"I know how you like'em. I've seen pictures of Adam. Poor boy's a toothpick, bless his heart," Camara said as they both got a laugh from her joke.

"I've heard the 'too good' before," Michonne said, "where's the 'to be true' part? That's what I wanna know."

"Did I ever tell you what Tarquan did for a living?" Camara asked.

"If you did, I don't remember."

"He runs his own business. Two actually. He runs a small advertising firm and a growing construction company both out of Kentucky."

"He runs them both himself?" Michonne asked, clearly impressed.

"Yep. He's the big boss at both of them. Real legit work."

"Looks like you caught yourself a baller," Michonne said now resting her cheek into her left palm that was propped up on the table. "I'm not sure I'm seeing the problem here, Camie. I think you're going to have to break it down for me." Michonne's expression darkened, confusion etched into her features.

"Think about it, Michonne. The guy owns and runs two businesses yet he was always available. He could always drop everything to do whatever I want. He never went on any business trips. He never answered his phone when we were together. The damn thing never even rang when were together."

"You think he was lying the whole time about the business thing?" Michonne asked.

"No, they're real. He took me to the main offices for both. You can find his designs all over Kentucky and the web if you know where to look."

"So maybe he just has really good right-hand men that do the bulk of the real work while he just calls the shots."

"That's what I thought," Camara admitted. "The problem was the type of people that would come around every once and a while. The type of guys you wouldn't expect someone like Tarquan to hang around or be associated with. You know how nosy I can be, right? Well . . . I ended up seeing some things that I shouldn't have."

"Things like what?" Michonne said, sipping her water, caught on Camara's every word.

Camara hesitated. She hadn't told anyone the whole story of her sojourn back in Bluefield. Camara looked at Michonne who was on the edge of her seat waiting for her to continue. Camara took a breath and revealed more detail.

"Money," Camara said evenly.

Michonne looked disappointed. "Money? You saw money. What? You said the guy owns like two successful businesses, and you left because you saw money? You've completely lost me now," Michonne said in a irritated tone.

"You don't understand," Camara started but stopped as the waiter approached their table with their food. He placed the salmon in front of Camara and the penne in front of Michonne. He asked if everything looked okay and went on to his next table.

"What's wrong with the guy having cash? Lots of wealthy people prefer a money clip to a bankcard. I'm sorry, Camie, I'm just not seeing the problem here," Michonne said through bites of her penne.

"The cash wasn't the problem. It was where it came from that bothered me."

"You knew what he did for a living, so why did that bother you? Why didn't you just ask him where it all came from if you had suspicions? Why not just ask to see the books? You two were dating for long enough to make that okay, right?" Michonne managed to say through a mouthful.

"You know I'm nosy, right?" Camara said sliding a piece of salmon into her mouth.

"What did you do?"

"I kind of went on the Internet and researched his companies. If you know how, you can find most businesses' potential earning power. Especially for public traded companies like Tarquan's. Nothing concrete, you know, just estimates. I went through and crunched some numbers, and the cash I was seeing floating around didn't match the income I later found that his companies were reporting. The money in his bank accounts lined up okay but all the cash around was off the radar."

"Wait a minute, wait a minute!" Michonne shrieked, interrupting Camara.

"Did he let you look at his bank accounts? Camie, I was kidding about the look at his books thing, you know," Michonne said, and Camara could feel her friend eye balling her as she looked down at her salmon.

"He didn't exactly know I looked at his accounts," Camara admitted avoiding Michonne's disapproving stare.

"Oooooo," Michonne let out in one breath. "How did you do that without him knowing?"

"It wasn't as hard as you might think," Camara said, starting in on her steamed vegetables. "Tarquan is a organized person. Very methodical. It was easy once I knew where to look."

"Still I'm too much of a coward to even attempt something like that," Michonne admitted. "That's very illegal, by the way."

"Well, the money alone wasn't what did it for me. I was pushed to that extreme. I started to get glimpses of his temper."

"Did he hit you?" Michonne asked in horror. "See, that's why I don't mess with them big guys. I like to know I can chop a man in the throat and run if I need to."

"No, he never hit me," Camara said smothering her laughter. "It was more in the way he treated other people. Then he would look at me sometimes. He could be intimidating, and he knew it. He tried to intimidate me, but I wouldn't let him most of the time. Sometimes I thought he liked me because he saw me as some type of challenge."

"What set you off then? What made you come running back to Bluefield and go MIA on your friends?"

Michonne's questions were making her re-live events that she would have gladly never thought of again. Camara placed a hand over her eyes to shield her impending tears from view. Michonne reached out, gently took Camara's hand in hers, and held it firmly. Camara was unprepared for the emotional jolt as the flash of her own blood- stained hands invaded her mind. She hadn't realized how much she let down her guard around Michonne.

"Can we . . . can we just change the subject for a little while?" Camara asked weakly.

"Sure can," Michonne said with a reaffirming smile. "We can talk about anything you like. You don't need to tell me all this now, or at all if you don't want."

Camara held onto Michonne's hand and searched for a less stressful, but still interesting topic.

"I will tell you. It's just . . . talking about it makes it worse, makes it more real. I promise I will talk to you about it; just not this second," Camara said, wiping her eyes.

"Well, I'm going to hold you to that promise," Michonne said with a gentle smile.

"My job isn't as bad as I thought it would be," Camara finally said.

Michonne groaned under her breath. "Be careful about that, girl. Next thing you know you'll get comfortable, and your excursion to Bluefield will turn into a self- imposed five-year exile. You know the field is like quicksand. Easy to get sucked in, damn near impossible to get out," Michonne said, joking, but the truth in the joke got both a laugh and a smile out of Camara.

"Don't worry, I've got a plan. I won't be working here that long. I hope," Camara said as the size of her debt skipped across her mind.

"I hope not," Michonne said, digging into her penne again. "What's so good about the paper these days? Why you start-ing to like it?"

Camara took a huge bite of the salmon to consider how best to answer that. The murders she had to cover were ter-rible, but there were good sides to the job. One of the main reason's the paper had been bearable was because of Ezra.

They had talked quite a bit over the past week, and Camara couldn't help but like him. He was interesting if nothing else. One of the things that attracted her to him was the fact that he was so different from Tarquan and every other guy she had been attracted to in the past. Camara wondered what that said about her state of mind.

"The people are all mostly nice, and I'm finding that I enjoy the work more than I thought I would. Only one person really got on my bad side so far, and that was the editor-in-chief, Mrs. Cervantes."

"How did you make enemies with the boss already?" Michonne asked, taking a sip of her water.

"I don't know. I didn't do anything. She's just a bitch as far as I can tell."

"Any cuties working there?" Michonne asked.

"I don't know if I'm ready for another relationship now. All this Tarquan drama just went down several months ago."

"That's not what I asked you," Michonne said, staring Camara down. "But I can assume that a few cuties are there because you wouldn't have to tell yourself that you're not ready for a relationship if there weren't. So spill it. Describe."

Camara smiled. She didn't want to make it seem like she had a schoolgirl crush on a co-worker so soon.

"This one guy who showed me around named Nate was pretty hot, but I'm sure he's married," Camara started in order to divert suspicion. Then, as casually as she could while sipping her tea, "This guy named Ezra is kinda cute, too."

Michonne's eyes grew large with shock as if Camara had just calmly announced the end of the world.

"Ezra Walker, he still works there?!" Michonne blurted out. She leaned in close to Camara and said something softly to avoid wondering ears. Michonne's words may have been soft but to Camara they sounded like booms from a cannon. "You know he killed his mother, right?" Michonne said all at once with deadly serious eyes.

Camara nearly spit her tea all over Michonne's face. "He what?" Camara said though her own coughs, struggling to catch her breath.

"He's really still working there?" Michonne asked in an almost whisper; every word rumbling in Camara's ears.

"Yeah," Camara said. "What are you talking about?"

"Are you being serious with me right now? Are you sure it's Ezra? Ezra Walker?"

"We worked together yesterday, so yes I'm sure. And how many Ezras do you know walking around in Bluefield? Yes, Ezra Walker. What the hell do you mean he killed his mother?" Camara demanded.

"Camie, it was all in the paper, and then all over News Channel 6 and News 59. You couldn't have missed . . ." Michonne paused in thought and snapped her fingers as if she just cracked out some mystery. "That's right. You didn't get back in town until all that hype started to settle down, and that was around the time I left. You really don't know."

"Know what?"

"Did you ever meet him before you started to work at the paper?" Michonne asked. "How well do you know Ezra?"

"No, I just met the guy a couple of weeks ago. How well do 'you' know him?" Camara shot back.

"Not well. He's not from the county, and he's a little older than us."

"Well, I knew that much."

"All I personally know about him is what I've heard, okay? I'm not an expert on the guy, but all this was in the news."

Camara was listening as best she could but her mind was in overdrive. Questions were coming to her faster that Michonne was giving details. Camara started to feel impatient.

"If it was on the news, then why isn't he in jail?" Camara inquired.

"No evidence. They didn't have any witness who saw anything incriminating enough to prosecute. They didn't even have enough on him to bring him in for questioning as far as I know."

"They didn't bring him in for questioning, but you think it was him? That doesn't make sense," Camara said, now rubbing her temple with her right hand.

"They say Ezra and his mother didn't get along real well. Nothing serious really, but not many people can say they ever saw the two of them out together. They were never really around each other, ya know? That's not that weird in and of itself, but I also hear there was some drama between Ezra and his mom and dad. Some money drama, you know? That and everyone apparently loved his mother. No one would have had a reason to do what was done to her. Ezra was the only one they could find with anything resembling a motive, something to do with money I think. Only no proof. The motive itself was largely hearsay, so they had nothing to charge him with."

It was Camara who was on the edge of her seat, "How did she die?"

"In a fire," Michonne said evenly.

"Shit," Camara said under her breath, remembering the people's reaction to Ezra at the fire near the stadium a couple of weeks ago.

"Yeah, then Ezra just disappears, and then all this stuff starts happening all over the city. I was gone, so this part is all third party hearsay also, but they say that's when all the fires started breaking out, when Ezra went under the radar. Not to mention all the stuff happening on north side and east end that isn't being reported as much as the well- to-do people's houses burning down. A woman gets raped on north side, and nobody says anything, but let a rich white man's house burn down on south side! Oh, God!"

Camara was in total shock, her heart threatening to jump out her chest. All the signs were there now that she thought about it. No one had said anything to her. She wasn't sure what to think. Camara had always thought herself a good judge of character, but Tarquan had given her plenty of reason to doubt herself. The man she had worked with certainly didn't seem capable of murder, and it was clear not everyone thought he was, unlike Michonne. He wouldn't have been allowed back at the paper if that was the case. Lois wouldn't want Camara to work with Ezra if she thought he was a killer. Would she?

More importantly, if there was an incriminating article about him in the paper why did he go back to work there? Why knowingly put himself in that position?

"My advice is to stay as far away as you can from Ezra Walker, Camie," Michonne said pointing her fork at Camara.

"Uh huh." It was all Camara could say as she picked at her salmon. Of course, she wasn't sure if she could avoid him now. She had to figure him out. She had to know the truth about Ezra Walker.

****

The rest of Camara's dinner flew by. She and Michonne finally found some lighter topics to discuss, and as they left, Camara made sure that Michonne would be able to get in touch with her later. Camara was going to go straight home but her curiosity got the best of her. Her mind worked in overtime to find the fastest way to get the answers she wanted.

Then it hit her. Craft Memorial Library. That would be her best bet. She drove her Saturn to downtown Bluefield, entered the library and headed straight for the newspaper archives. The library was a two-level building nestled in the heart of downtown Bluefield. Rows of books lined the shelves on the left once you entered and a lounge area for reading and computers was on the right. Toward the back, next to the books was where Camara began her search. It took her a little over an hour to find the article she was looking for since she didn't have an exact date. The article, written by a man named "Jim Rhodes," was short but damaging to Ezra's reputation all the same. Camara tried to remember being introduced to a reporter by that name, but was sure that he must have left before she started working at the paper.

Camara looked through both subsequent and previous newspapers and there wasn't one mention of Ezra in any of them except for the one she found by Jim Rhodes. Camara thought that was strange. There wasn't a single follow-up article in any paper from back then until today. The article wasn't even very well-written. Camara wondered how Rhodes got Mrs. Cervantes's seal of approval.

Camara read then reread the article. She couldn't take her eyes off it.

*Residents of southeast Bluefield, W. Va. remain in shock today as one of their own died in a housefire. People lined up and down the street watching in horror as firefighters tried to put out the last of the embers that continued to flicker in the smoldering home of Sherri Walker.*

*Once the fire was completely out and firefighters were clear to search the premises, they found what was left of the victim. Miss Walker's charred body was found in her, bedroom covered with ceiling debris.*

*Firefighter Rush Gooden said, "It looks like she was pinned down by the debris from the overhead ceiling boards. The smoke from the fire choked her as she burned to death. It also appears she was decapitated by more falling debris. The poor woman never made it out of bed."*

*The initial investigation for the cause of the fire were not conclusive. According to firefighters' reports, the flame put off a blue hue despite the absence of propane or gas heaters in the home.*

*"Normally, with most fires like that, it's easy to find the cause of the incident," Gooden said. "It's usually a gas leak, whether accidental or purposeful. This house, however, was electrically heated, and the signs we saw didn't match the signs we found or the ones reported."*

*Also frustrating, was the lack of information the police received from Miss Walker's only son, Ezra Walker. Several neighbors of Miss Walker reported her son going into the house moments before the fire started.*

*Jonah Collins, Miss Walker's neighbor for 12 years, said, "Ezra comes to visit his mother every weekend, so I didn't think nothing of it when he showed up and walked inside the house. I had just finished cutting my grass, ya see, and was putting my lawnmower into my shed when he pulled up. He waved hello to me, and I waved back real normal like. Thought nothing of it."*

Collins said that he went inside his house about the same time Walker went into his mother's house. *"Next thing I know, I'm sittin' in my favorite chair, and I look out the window. I looked across the street, and the whole dang house was on fire. It couldn't have been much more than ten minutes when he went in 'cause that's how long it took me to warm up my dinner,"* Collins said.

*Further questions were raised about what Walker was doing in the house prior to the fire. Another neighbor, Selita Lockheart said,* "I saw the fire as I was washing dishes in my kitchen. I grabbed my cell phone and immediately called 911 and ran across the street. By that time I wasn't the only one on the street gawking at the fire. I knew Sherri was in the house, or at least I thought she was, and then I saw Ezra's car parked outside. Sherri was my best friend, and I was terrified at the thought of what could have happened to her."

"Then I got excited when I saw Ezra walking out from the back of the house toward the street. I thought he must have gotten his mother out or maybe she wasn't in the house at all. But, then Ezra walked past everyone with this blank face and didn't say a word.

"I mean he was walking like nothing had happened and sat on the hood of his car. All of us were freaking out, but no one really knew what to say to him. We asked about his mother. We tried to get him to talk, but he didn't say a word. His face was so . . . indifferent."

*Police reported that Walker refused to give a statement the day of the fire. One firefighter reported Walker staring off into space and whispering to himself. As the firefighter investigation went on, it began to look more towards arson. Ezra Walker quickly became the prime suspect to Police Chief Ray Wilson.*

"We don't have enough to prosecute anyone at this time, but we will be watching suspects closely for the foreseeable *future until everything is investigated thoroughly," Police Chief Ray Wilson said. "Currently the only one who knows what transpired in the home before the fire is Mr. Walker, but he is reluctant to give a statement at this time."*

*Upon further interviewing of Miss Walker's neighbors, Officer Wilson reported several close friends of the victim saying that Walker and his mother had been arguing over the past several weeks about some money that Miss Walker had recently come into. There were also several reports of a strain on the Walkers' relationship due to the recent acquisition of money.*

*One neighbor reported seeing Walker storm out of the house several times the previous week. No official statements on these matters were made.*

*A service will be conducted for Sherri Walker, 51, tomorrow at noon.*

\*\*\*\*

Camara read the article three times, and then read the obituary written by Nancy twice before she looked at her watch and saw that it was nearly nine o'clock. It was time for the library to close and Camara realized that that she and the clerk were the only two in the library. Camara made sure to mark the exact place she'd found the article in case she wanted to look more closely into the skeletons in Ezra's closet.

She felt a little dirty and deceptive for looking into Ezra's past this closely when they'd just meet, but she was so damn curious, and she wasn't about to be caught by surprise again. She wanted to know what she would be getting herself into by working with him. She also had to admit that the mystery of Ezra intrigued her now more than ever. There seemed to be two different Ezra Walkers—the Ezra some people thought could have committed matricide, and then the one she had gotten to know briefly over the past couple of weeks. The Ezra she knew just didn't seem capable of such a thing.

Camara left the library lost in her thoughts. Reading the new accounts really didn't help. Now she had more questions and even fewer answers. Camara wished she wasn't so nosy. She started her car, pulled out from the library, then quickly hit the avenue to start her trip back to the county. Camara was so lost in her thoughts she didn't notice she had been followed since leaving the restaurant.

# CHAPTER 16

The man from 7F couldn't believe what he was seeing. He couldn't believe the level of ignorance the people in this town had. Were they all retarded? He sat in his dark brown sedan and looked out over Bluefield City Park where people were mocking his masterpiece. They were vomiting over his art and laughing in his face.

The people of this town should be hiding in their homes, afraid to come out in daylight, and yet here they were walking around like the inconsequential little shits he always knew them to be. It made him sick.

To add insult to injury, there had been almost no mention of his latest work. He would have to repay Mr. Walker for almost ruining that for him. He had already tried to find his address, but Zeus had already had his damn Pack cover his brother's tracks. It didn't matter. It was better that way really. He would find him one way or another and in his own time.

The man from 7F had been content to just toy with Ezra, but now he had to die, and in grand fashion. He already had it planned. Ezra just had to be found. He could just follow him from work, but that would be too easy. His god would deliver Ezra to him. He was sure of it.

For now the man from 7F focused his attention on more pressing matters. A black woman dead in the alleyway of Bluefield State College didn't raise much fuss in the white areas of town. It was deplorable to him that people valued skin color so much. The right skin tone in the right part of a town counted for so much.

Skin color was just a means to an end for him. A way for him to move freely where and when he wanted. He wondered what type of storms would rise up if a white woman had been found dead and raped on the north side of Bluefield, on the wrong side of the tracks. White, black, yellow or brown it made no difference to him. They were just colors he used to paint on the canvas of death. Death was his art, and his art was his life. And flame, the flame was his inspiration. His muse. His god.

The man from 7f flicked his Zippo lighter on and off in his hand and watched the flame dance for him until he snapped the lighter shut ending the flame's life. The Zippo was silver with blue lines on the side. It also had a quote from Schiele, his favorite German expressionist. The quote read: "Everything is dead while it lives."

He opened the lighter giving birth to the flame and then killed it again. And again. He enjoyed birthing the flame almost as much as he enjoyed killing it. Fire was ruthless and unrelenting, unprejudiced and no respecter of person, the way the man from room 7F thought of himself.

This town didn't respect fire. This town didn't respect him.

Two white children around the age of ten scampered over to the creek that cut through the park not far from the brown sedan. The two children scampered and splashed around the water. He held up the lighter and flickered the flame to life. He held it up so that it danced between the two children as if it were playing with them. Then he shut the top of the lighter snuffing out the flame once again. After a quick survey of the area, the man from 7F got out of his sedan and calmly walked toward the creek were the two children played.

The flame had spoken. His colors were chosen. The canvas was set.

# CHAPTER 17

## CAMARA

Time passed quickly for Camara over the past week. She spent most of her days avoiding Mrs. Cervantes from fear that she would grab her keyboard and smash it across the woman's face. Camara wasn't normally a violent person, but there was something about the way Mrs. Cervantes looked at her that pushed her buttons.

Thankfully, she found Mrs. Cervantes easy enough to ignore, and she wished it were as easy to get away from her Nanny. Camara loved Nancy and thought it would be fun working beside her. That was until she realized that it would be almost impossible to get any work done around her. At first Camara liked talking to Nancy until everything that came out of her mouth was some type of gossip. Camara had to wonder what Nanny said about her when she wasn't around.

Normally Camara just listened, but today she decided she should ask some questions that were eating at her. Nancy gossiped so much Camara might as well get some information she really wanted. She waited until she and Nancy were alone in the breakroom before she started in on her.

"How long have you been working here, Nanny?" Camara asked while picking at the chicken salad she had brought for lunch.

"I've been here about two years now. It's a good job. Nice pace, easy, always something to do. Makes you feel old, though. I've written a lot of friends' obituaries. I've even written my own a couple of times for when I kick the bucket," Nancy said with a chuckle.

"Isn't that a little morbid?" Camara asked taken aback. Nancy never seemed the doom and gloom type who would write her own obituary.

"Just don't want anyone messing it up. I'm making a career of writing other people's so why not write my own? Still can't get it right, though."

"You ever wish you got married, Nanny?" Camara asked.

"Not really. What brought that on?"

"Just you talking about writing you own obituary. I don't know. Do you ever regret not getting married?"

"Yes and no. Sometimes." Nancy seemed to answer as truthfully as she could. "I was too wild to settle down when I was younger. Always causing some trouble. I'm too wild now."

Camara let out a laugh. "You? Wild? Oh, shut up! What're you into, Nanny?"

"It's better you don't know," Nanny insisted with an impish grin. "I don't want to be a bad influence on you."

"What if I'm about to get into some tomfoolery myself and need some advice from an old maverick?" Camara asked, putting on her most mischievous smile.

"Oh, lordy, what did you do?"

"Nothing. I didn't do anything," Camara said, biting a piece of her cereal bar she brought along with her salad. "Yet," she added to tug on her Nancy's curiosity.

"Ok, tell me," Nanny said. "Come on, spill it. You've had that same look on your face since you were five. Every time you were up to something your mother always knew to whoop you before you even got started. Come on, girl, cough it up."

Camara laughed and tried to look embarrassed, playing it up a little. Then, she went for the kill.

"What do you know about Ezra?" she asked without making eye contact.

"Do you have eyes for the paper's own Mr. Walker?" Nancy asked, fluttering her eyes.

Camara giggled like a girl and bit her bottom lip. Camara didn't like acting like this, but it was easy to be this way with someone who had changed her diapers. It was true she was starting to like Ezra, but she also wanted to get an honest straightforward answer. Camara knew that if Nancy thought her heart was invested in the opinion she gave about Ezra, then she would put aside any gossip or hearsay and offer up what she believed to be the truth. For all her talk, Nancy was a good judge of people; you just had to know how to get her to admit the facts rather than tell a story.

Nancy took her time giving her opinion. Camara could tell she was wading through everyone else's opinion she had heard to find her own. Camara waited quietly for Nancy to find the truth.

Finally Nancy said, "I like Ezra. I think you would be good for him now. I think he could use a good woman like you in his life. There's a lot of talk going on about that boy. I don't buy into any of it. Which is why you haven't heard me say much of anything about him before; I don't perpetuate lies." Nancy ended her speech with a proud nod. "Everything I say about people is Gospel truth. Unlike some people who I won't get started in on."

Camara wasn't quite ready for that response, but she managed to mask her shock with a look of pleasant surprise. She expected Nancy to start in on Ezra. Nancy speaking kindly about him could only mean one thing. She really liked Ezra.

"What kind of talk?" Camara asked, faking ignorance. If anything, all those "whoop'ns" she got as a kid taught her how to play dumb and look innocent.

"If you don't know, then you don't need to. It's all a load of crap any way you look at it. People can just be stupid sometimes."

Again not the answer Camara expected. Nancy not coughing up some kind of details about someone? Unheard of! She couldn't believe that this was the same woman that she had sat beside and had explained just about everyone at the paper's life story. It was a little surprising that she had to mention Ezra first to get Nanny to start in on him now that she thought about it.

Then Camara's heart skipped a beat as Ezra walked into the breakroom.

"Well! Speak of the devil!" Nancy said to Camara's horror.

"Hey, Nancy. Were you two talking about me?" Ezra said as he went to the counter to start a cup of coffee. "Which was it—the good or the bad?"

"Only the good, sweetie," Nanny said, getting up from the table and shooting a wink in Camara's direction while Ezra's back was turned. "Well, I'm back to work. I have to stop being lazy. A lot of dead people to write about."

"Take it easy, Nancy," Ezra said as Nancy exited the break room. "You don't have to get back, too?" Ezra asked, turning from the brewing coffee to Camara.

"No. I'm pretty much done with everything I need to do for a while. I can afford to be lazy a little."

"Don't let Melissa hear you say that. How are you two getting along?"

"I don't really have anything to say about Mrs. Cervantes," Camara remarked, rolling her eyes.

"Sorry, didn't mean to touch a sore spot."

"It's not that big of a deal; don't worry about it. What're you doing down here? You break'n too?"

"Not really. I take the pictures, remember? There's not really much for me to do here once I get the pictures in. I just float around and check in with Lois from time to time until she tells me to go somewhere."

"Do you like your job? I mean, you seem really talented. You could do well at just about any newspaper, so why stay in Bluefield?" Camara asked. She turn to face Ezra and crossed her legs showing interest in his answer.

"I like it here okay. As for why I don't leave, I guess I just can't really find a good reason to. I'm stuck in the blackhole of Bluefield. What can I say?"

"I hear you," Camara said and looked away knowing all to well what he meant. She had known too many people that fell in that same blackhole and lost sight of their dreams or escaped to chase their goals only to be sucked back in.

"What are you doing in the Field, if you don't mind my asking?" Ezra asked and drew Camara's eyes to his. Ezra had a way of looking at you that made it unmistakable when his attention was focused on you. He would look right at you, without staring, with his very kind brown eyes. You could tell he was listening rather that waiting for his chance to speak. Camara had noticed it the day she introduced herself to him. The same chill ran down her spine and fluttered her heart then as it was now. *What is it about him? Why is he different?*

"No, I don't mind. It's just life, you know. Catch a couple of hard knocks then you have to come home to regroup," Camara said, forcing herself to keep Ezra's gaze.

"I heard that. How are you doing being back? You going crazy in the county yet?" Ezra said as he walked over to the table and sat across from Camara.

"You have no idea. I'm so bored. There's just nothing to do here. There's a really nice movie theater in McDowell, but it's so easy to get a bootleg in the county there's almost no reason to go. I really miss Kentucky. There was always something going on."

"There's stuff to do in the Field. You just have to know where to look. Where to go," Ezra said tilting his head back with a slight grin. Camara noticed how he had a way of moving that echoed the truth. His body language rang confidence, but it wasn't cocky like the men Camara was used to dealing with.

"Stuff like what? Go to the Mountaineer? One of the clubs that keep getting shot up and closed?" Camara challenged, folding her arms.

Ezra laughed at that and Camara felt a small amount of satisfaction. She liked his laugh. It sounded genuine. She doubted that he could fake a laugh if he tried.

"If that's the type of fun you're looking to have then you would be disappointed. There's other ways to have fun though," Ezra said showing off his perfectly straight white teeth. Camara thought he must have worn braces when he was younger. He had to. Nobody was born with a smile that gorgeous.

"Like what?" Camara asked.

"We're in West Virginia. It really is 'Wild and Wonderful,' if you didn't know."

"I thought it was 'Open For Business.'"

"Naw, that was stupid. Wild and Wonderful. You just have to know where to look," Ezra said getting up to pour his coffee.

"Why don't you show me then?" Camara said surprised by the way her question had come out. It was more suggestive then she intended.

Ezra looked back at her and looked slightly flustered. She could tell he wasn't expecting her question.

"I could do that."

"Good. When should I pick you up, Ezra?" Camara said, liking the sound of his name rolling off her lips.

He poured a cup of coffee and replied with his back to Camara, "So you're picking me up, are you?"

"I asked you so I think it's only right. What day is good for you? This Friday? Saturday? I never have anything to do so either is good for me."

Ezra turned around with his coffee looking confident and composed. This time it was Camara's turn to be flustered, her heart skipping a beat when he said, "Neither." And took a sip of his coffee.

"Oh," Camara said, feeling a little embarrassed and very rejected.

"But Monday is perfect. I've already made plans for this weekend. How's Monday for you?" he said, flashing the pearly whites again.

"Oh," Camara said relief washing over her. Ezra had a playful way of sending her emotions on a rollercoaster, and she wasn't sure she needed that in her life right now. She wondered if he knew what he was doing to her.

"Monday's fine," Camara said. "What are we doing?"

"I'll let that be a surprise."

"Where can I pick you up?"

"You're serious about that, aren't you?"

"Why wouldn't I be? I asked you out, right?"

"In that case, we can leave after work on Monday. You can just bring me back to my car here. I don't want to have you running around all over the place with gas being so expensive."

"That works. Can I get a little hint of what we're doing?"

"It wouldn't be a surprise if I did," he said, making his way to the door leading back to the newsroom.

"Back on the clock?" Camara asked.

"Bout to see what Lois has for me. I doubt I'll be here at all tomorrow. I might not see you again until Monday, so don't forget," Ezra said with his dangerous smirk this time, exuding self-confidence from his eyes.

Camara censored the jolt she felt and said, "I asked you. So *you* don't forget. I want my surprise, too." Camara shot back a flirty look of her own and hoped it had the same effect on him as his did on her.

"Monday," Ezra said.

"Monday," Camara replied.

Then he was through the door and Camara could breathe normally again.

****

Camara couldn't resist going to Mercer Mall after work. She needed to try and find something for her date with Ezra on Monday. She stayed until the mall closed but still couldn't find what she was looking for. She had always liked surprises but hated being unprepared. She wished Ezra had given her a clue about what he had in mind.

Camara decided to surf the web for a while when she got home. She could probably express ship something and have it by Saturday. When limited in options, online shopping was always a good way to go.

As she drove to Welch, Camara wondered if her date with Ezra was a good idea. He was a co-worker, and it hadn't been too long ago that she had discovered that most of Bluefield thought he was capable of murder. She had spent so much time building him up in her mind that finding out about his dubious reputation made her even more curious.

It was dark as Camara traveled the twisted roads with her high beams on, but she still almost didn't see the man standing on the side of the road waving his hands until it was almost too late. The man was coming from the left side of the road into Camara's lane. She swerved to miss him, nearly grazing the guardrail and flying off the mountain in the process. Camara slowed down and looked in her rear view mirror while trying to make sense of what just happened. Who would be out on these mountain roads at night? There were no streetlights. It was pitch black on the roads to the county; what the hell were they doing? Did they need help?

It didn't make sense for someone to be in the middle of the road unless there was some kind of trouble. She thought about stopping but she hadn't reached Kimball or Kyle yet, let alone Welch, and her cell didn't work in this part of the county.

Camara was looking in her rearview and almost plowed into the blockade across the road. Three cars were lined across both lanes. Camara downshifted hard, swerved and slammed the breaks. She stopped with plenty of space between her and the other cars that blocked the road. The blockade scared the hell out of her; she needed time to compose herself. She felt like her heart had lodged itself in her throat. She couldn't swallow. She couldn't get a breath.

She didn't have time to calm down before someone pulled open the driver side door and pulled her into the darkness of the mountain road. Camara wanted to fight but she was still too disoriented; she let her body go limp and tried to get her mind to catch up with what was happening.

Camara tried to take in the cold night air and to focus on any sounds around her. She heard the footsteps of several people, three men, Camara guessed. She also focused on the hands that were dragging her into the middle of the street. They weren't big but they were strong. Camara thought that she could get away from him if she recovered her breathing fast enough, but she needed a plan first. There were already too many people to run from. What the hell was this about?

"Hurry up, rookie. We're on a schedule." Camara heard a deep voice say from somewhere in the dark.

"I'm comin'. This bitch nearly hit me," the one that dragged Camara from her car said. His voice didn't sound very mature. Camara guessed he was around seventeen, nineteen at most. What was this, some kind of high school prank? Camara was sure she could get away from the punk dragging her, but what about the others? Where they armed? How many were there? What did they want?

The boy threw Camara to her knees in the middle of the street as the other men gathered around her. They all kept their distance but had Camara surrounded like they were waiting for someone. The only light came from the three cars that were used to block the road. The lights burned holes in Camara's eyes forcing her to look away.

Camara could hear a lone figure approaching from the cars. The pace was slow and rhythmic, like someone taking a stroll in a park. The figure halted right in front of her and placed a gentle hand on her face forcing her to look up. Camara's eyes weren't adjusted to the mix of dark shadow and blinding light. She couldn't make out any features of the face.

The man's hands were large but soft like he had never known a day of manual labor. He ran his hand across her hair, then her cheeks. His touch was familiar to Camara. A finger brushed across her lips, then down her neck finding its way to her shoulders, her breast. The man touched her like a long lost lover. His touch was passionate and sensual, full of confidence and devoid of hesitation. Camara still couldn't make out the man's face, but she knew who it was. She knew what this was about. What she didn't know was if she would leave the cold mountain road alive.

Suddenly the gentle hand became a hammer and collided across the side of Camara's face.

"Tarquan," Camara said spitting blood to the ground.

"That's Snap to you now. Get up, bitch." Her ex-lover's, voice was cold. Nothing remained of the affection they once shared.

She rose slowly, doing her best not to show how the punch had rocked her. She caught her breath and focused on staying calm. *I can still get away anytime I want.* Camara reminded herself. She wasn't nearly as confident as she wanted to be. She didn't know if she was going to leave alive, but none of these bastards would touch her again. She would make sure of that much.

"What's this about, Tarquan? I left you in Kentucky for a reason. I thought you had good enough sense to know when a relationship is over. Why are you here?" Camara commanded. She stood strong, not backing down from Tarquan, secure in her bravado.

"You know why we're here," another familiar voice shot out of the darkness. Someone stepped forward.

"I wasn't talking to you, Dyson," Camara said, looking over at Tarquan's right hand man. He was bigger then she remembered. The scary thing about Dyson was he was every bit as smart as he was huge—not a person to be underestimated.

"I know why you're here, Dyson. Still the tin soldier taking orders and not asking questions I see."

"You don't get to call me that anymore. The name's Dice. We want our money. Give it all back, and you go back home and don't see us again."

Camara turned and faced Tarquan. "Money! What money? What kind of lies have you been telling your toy soldiers now, Tarquan?" Camara turned back to Dice, venom lacing her every word. "I can see something like this from the other idiots around him to buy this shit, but not you. I expected better of you, 'Dice.' I thought you were smarter."

"Rookie, check her car," Tarquan said nonchalantly as if he were asking someone to do something as simple as look for his keys.

The rookie went over to her Saturn and began his search. Camara didn't bother to protest. She knew she would get no mercy with Tarquan. Not anymore.

The rookie searched the car for only a minute or so. Tension saturated the air as everyone waited for the rookie to return. Tarquan's face was still covered in shadow. Camara stared at him as he paced back and forth. He wouldn't return her gaze. Why was that? Camara's blood began to boil. What the fuck was Tarquan doing? What did he want?

Camara's mind was flooded with questions. Then the rookie walked in front of her and dropped something on the ground. Camara looked and saw a wad of money wrapped in a rubber band at her feet. The wad had to be about two grand.

"What the hell! What game are you playing, Tarquan? Is this how you got all your little toy soldiers to follow you here? I didn't take shit from you and you know it!" Camara barked with anger, kicking the money in Tarquan's direction.

Tarquan advanced on Camara and she stood her ground. She fully expected the hammer to rain down on her again, but Tarquan stopped only inches from her face, both hands in his pockets.

"You know what you did, Camie." His voice was cold as ice, but his eyes burned with fire as he spoke. "Don't fool yourself into thinking you're so special that I would waste my time coming to this crackerjack state just to see your chicken-leg ass. You know me better than that and my men do, too. You've got something that belongs to me and I want it back. Maybe you spent it. Maybe you used it to help your mother—I really don't give a damn. Out of respect for the love I once had for you, I'll let you leave here tonight. I'll give you six months to give back what's mine. I think that's only fair. I hear you could work it off in Princeton. Might catch a fair price with the rednecks on Mercer Street. If I don't get back what's mine in six months, all of it, I'll just kill your mother and consider the debt paid. I'm not—"

Tarquan's words were cut short by a soft click that rang out into the night, rooting everyone in place like the surrounding mountain trees. Cold hard steel was pressed against the bottom of Tarquan's chin and Camara watched the anger and confidence in his eyes transform to pure fear. Camara finally got a clear look at Tarquan's face. She saw his clean-cut hair and trimmed beard, his honey-colored skin. She had surprised him. Scared him. Camara knew that indignity was worse than losing every cent he had.

Camara pressed her 9mm Glock against his head and enjoyed the power she had over him. All of Tarquan's soldiers were slow to react and unprepared for Camara pulling out a gun. A couple of them started to fumble for their own weapons, but Camara spoke before any of them could do anything.

"Don't even think about it or you all lose your money train! Tell them to throw their pieces on the ground beside me or I blow your fucking head off," Camara demanded.

Camara watched Tarquan's eyes gain their resolve after the initial shock. He stared her down. Camara could read his silent dare. He was calling her bluff.

"You don't have it in you," Tarquan said, confidently. Camara kept the gun in its upward angle and tilted it to the side of Tarquan's face. Then she squeezed the trigger.

The explosion from the gun made all the men jump, and Tarquan yelled out in pain as a gash opened up on the side of his face from the bullet. Blood ran down Tarquan's face, and he cursed loudly in pain. Camara grabbed him by the crotch, hard, and put the gun in his face again.

"I said throw the guns over to me! Now!" Camara screamed.

The toy soldiers threw their guns over as they were commanded and held their places. Camara could feel all of their eyes on her waiting for her to make a mistake. They were all still, like lions waiting for their chance to pounce. They wouldn't find one.

"Damn girl! Now I remember why I liked you. I'll let you leave here tonight because I already said I would, but this isn't going to end well for you now."

With a gun pointed in his face and a hand crushing his balls, Tarquan still managed to sound smug. It was hard for Camara to remember what she ever saw in him. It made her skin crawl that she ever let him touch her.

"Don't get in my face again, Tarquan. If you come near my mother, I'll fucking kill you."

"Six months," Tarquan said through a sinister smile that sent chills running down Camara's spine.

"I'm going to leave here now, and I don't want you or your cronies to follow me."

"I gave you my word and my word is my bond. Six months." His voice was ice cold again. "But this isn't going to end well for you now. This could've been easy, Camara."

Camara turned on her heels and walked to her car. She didn't bother to look at any of the lapdogs that Tarquan brought with him. As soon as she got to her car, a shot was fired from behind her. She raised her gun and pointed in the direction the blast had come and saw the rookie that had taken her out of her car on the ground, covered in his own blood.

Tarquan stood, gun in hand, staring directly at her. He must have had the gun on him the whole time.

"It's important to frisk people, gentlemen. I hope you all remember that for future reference."

Camara jumped in her car and got back on the road once Tarquan signaled the roadblock clear. One thing she knew about Tarquan was that he was a man of his word—least in front of his boys. She knew he would let her go if he said so, but it also meant that Camara could very well only have six months to live. She drove by the blockade, then looked back into the rear view mirror as Tarquan's toy soldiers threw the rookie's body over the guardrails and down the mountain. The body may never be found, lost in the brush of the mountainside. As she drove, she struggled to comprehend what had just happened. They had been following her. They knew when she was on the road to Welch. They knew the road she would be traveling on and were able to block it off. This was planned. A single horrifying thought rippled through her mind as she drove.

*They know where I live.*

# CHAPTER 18

I revved the engine of my ATV and rolled effortlessly over the rocky mountain trail, watching trees whiz by. I was kicking in into high gear, moving faster than I ever had before over the trail I had taken countless times. As fast as I went, I still had a hard time keeping up with T. She was a pro at ATV riding if there ever was one. I was getting pretty good, but I still found myself eating her dust every time we rode together.

It took T months to convince me to go four-wheeling with her. It had always seemed like a very redneck thing to me. I had to admit it, though, I fell in love with it after the first time. Now, one weekend a month, T and I headed to McDowell County and rode the Hatfield and McCoy Trail.

ATV riding had been growing in popularity for the past several years in West Virginia, and now that I had actually tried it, I was all too willing to jump on the bandwagon. The sport has gotten so big that it's becoming a top source of revenue for the state. You can even find the governor strapping up and coming down to the county to ride from time to time.

T and I set out at six that morning because we wanted to ride the trail a little farther than we normally did. We usually stayed in the county, but the trail went clear into Kentucky and as far as Ohio. T and I were eager to do some exploring.

Once we were in Kentucky, we set up camp. We had never gone on an overnight trip before, and it was a welcome change. It felt good to get away from Bluefield and the accusing stares and gossip.

T had packed a tent large enough for the two of us to share. I don't think she wanted to sleep in a tent by herself anymore than I did. She had on a blue shirt with the fitness center logo and a pair of Dallas Maverick basketball shorts. I was rock'n a pair of gray sweats, and I had skipped the shirt since it was pretty warm in the tent.

We had gotten comfortable when T finally asked me a question I knew she had been dying to ask all day.

"So, where are you gonna take that girl for your first date?"

"I've got a couple of ideas. I'm still mulling it over."

"Just don't do anything stupid like bringing her out here. This isn't good first date material," T said as she lay beside me. Her emerald green eyes sparkled though uncontrolled sandy blonde hair.

"I think she might be the type of girl who would like something like this. But you're right. This isn't first date stuff. What do you think I should do? I promised her something wild or wonderful."

"Wild or wonderful? Did you really say that?"

"Yes. Where do you think I should take her?"

"Dinner and a movie are always good for a first date. Movie first to lighten it up between you two, then dinner to talk about the movie. Get to know each other."

"I want something more than that. Something about her seems special. I'm not sure what. It's . . . I don't know."

"That's what dates are for, Easy. You see something in someone and you find out what it is and if you want to know more," T said sitting up, stretching out her arms. She rolled up her sleeves and opened a can of beans.

"A little late to be eating, don't you think?" I asked, sitting up myself.

"Not tired. So I'm eating. We'll burn it off in the morning anyway."

I got a little hungry myself and fixed some ramen noodles on a little battery powered stove we brought.

"It's good to hear you talk about another girl besides Eva. I didn't think you would ever let that girl go. You're a lot better off without her craziness following you around."

"Now if you could just get rid of Conner your life could be more sane, too," I said through a mouth full of noodles.

"Conner's not that bad."

"If you say so. You're just keeping him around for sex. One day you're going to realize what a chump he is. Then it will be too late 'cause you'll have feelings for him."

"I'm not going to get any feelings for him. I just can't stand to sleep alone every night. Tired of hugging a damn oversized stuffed animal or pillows to go to sleep. I don't want a relationship now anyway. I just want a nice friend with benefits that will be honest with me. If he wants to start dating someone, he'll just tell me. I don't care. Just don't be doing me while you're doing somebody else. No feelings, no attachments, no fights, just good sex. Is that too much to ask for?"

"I guess not. I offered though."

T looked at me through her hair and raised an eyebrow.

"Oh, shut up. That's the reason Eva went crazy, you know. If you would've just given the girl some, she might have been okay. What girl has to break up with a guy because he *won't* have sex with her?"

"Eva had issues. That wasn't all my fault. I was in a transitional stage. I'm trying to wait until I'm married before I have sex again. Sex equals drama."

"Uh-huh. Good luck with that. That just proves my point. I turn you down 'cause I know you. You would've fallen in love with me, and then our friendship would've been over. You've been in the friend zone for seven years, buddy. Deal with it," T said with a laugh.

"Didn't say you were wrong to say no. It's a good thing you did actually. Just saying I offered."

"I would've been more tempted if you looked like you do now back then. You got some muscles on you now," T said leaning over and punching my bare chest.

"Oh, if I had been working out then you would'a said yes?" I asked in amusement.

"I said I would've been more tempted. You were like a toothpick two and a half years ago. I would've hurt you."

"You wouldn't have hurt me then, and you couldn't hurt me now," I said confidently.

T turned a slight shade of red and brushed her hair to one side with her hand. She avoided looking at me for a second then said, "You're still too nice. I'm only attracted to ass-holes, remember? Sorry."

"No worries. That was a one-time offer anyway. You're in the friend zone, homie. Deal with it," I said finishing up my noodles as T put her beans down.

"So what do you know about this girl anyway? Why do you think she's so special?"

"I honestly don't know a lot. We just had a couple of really good conversations. It's was effortless being around her, ya know?"

"Just make sure you keep the spark alive. You gotta make her heart jump a few times or you'll end up in the zone."

"The friend zone," T and I said in unison.

"That wouldn't be so bad. I could be friends with her if nothing else."

"You need somebody, Ezra. You're a good man. You shouldn't have to go it alone. A relationship fits you."

"I guess you're right."

"You at least need to get laid," T said, smiling at me.

I grabbed my pillow and hit T in the head with it. "Shut up."

T grabbed her pillow and war broke out in the tent. T and I beat each other senseless with our pillows and wrestled. The battle didn't last long because we were both tired from riding the trail, but T managed to pin me on my back. She won but she cheated. She knew where I was ticklish.

"I win." T proclaimed her victory, pinning down my arms and sitting on my stomach.

"I let you," I said through labored breath that matched T's. We had managed to work up a little sweat.

T released me from her death grip and lay beside me. She was sweaty and her shoulder length hair was all over the place, but T still managed to look pretty.

"You ready to go back to reality tomorrow?" T asked, brushing her hair from her face.

"Not even close."

She looked solemn suddenly and then turned away.

"What's wrong?" I asked, wondering if our friendly flirting had struck a nerve.

"You're one of my best friends, Ezra. You're my most stable friend. You're my rock. I love you much, Easy."

"I love you much, too, T," I said. Love you much was my way of expressing my feelings to family and close friends, something that T had picked up on. T was as close as they come so this wasn't the first time we had said it to each other.

Tamra was a good friend, and I did love her. As much as we flirted and were attracted to each other, we both knew it would never last between us. A relationship would ruin the friendship. High quality friendships are few and far between and not worth ruining for physical attraction. It was a silent understanding between us.

"Promise you won't ever fall in love with me, Ezra."

"Only if you promise me the same," I said smiling, trying to joke. "You're not really my type anyway. Too pale."

"You're a good man, Ezra," T said to me looking deeply into my eyes. "Do you feel good about this girl? You think there's something there?"

"Maybe," I said a little confused.

"You think she's a good girl? You know what I mean, a keeper?"

"She could be. Why are you asking me this?"

"I don't want to see you get hurt. You need a good girl. Not a girl like me. That's why I want you to promise not to fall in love with me. A girl like me would break your heart."

# CHAPTER 19

I kept myself as busy as possible Monday. I tried not to think too much about my date with Camara, but I was excited. I'd forgotten how fun it was experiencing someone new. I tried to keep my mind looking forward to possible beginnings instead of all the sudden endings I had gone through over the past few months. If nothing else, I needed the distraction.

The murder at Bluefield State was still fresh in my head. I missed most of the initial reports thanks to my camping trip with T. I got an unpleasant reminder as soon as I got back in Bluefield. The news of the girl's death struck a real nerve in the community, especially the black community. The girl's name was Isabelle Sparks. She was a freshman in her first semester at Bluefield State and was studying nursing. Her family was from Florida and had sent her to West Virginia because they thought it would be safer. She had a full academic scholarship; nothing but potential and a bright future should've been waiting for Isabelle. A life full of promise, snuffed out before it could really get started.

As soon as I heard all this, I felt sick to my stomach. I felt guilty for not doing more to help Isabelle. I hated myself for watching her die. Zeus was waiting for me when I got back to give me the news himself. He said he wanted to be there when I heard so I wouldn't do anything stupid like go to the police, which I probably would have if he hadn't been there to stop me. I still didn't understand why it was stupid, but I trusted Zeus. I knew he had my best interest at heart.

I was waiting in my car in the Telegraph's parking lot when Camara pulled up at a quarter to five. Right on time. She parked her car beside mine, and I hopped in. She was wearing a short-sleeve, yellow cotton shirt with white pants and matching yellow and white earrings and bracelet. Her hair was straight tonight. It covered one side of her face like a waterfall, which was a different, but a very nice look. She had also highlighted the ends of her hair amber brown. It was a touch I wasn't expecting, but I liked it all the same. I couldn't tell what perfume she was wearing, but whatever it was smelled fantastic.

I had on a black button-up shirt with dark blue Qruel jeans. I thought we complimented each other well enough for the night I had planned.

"Was I late?" she asked.

"No. I was early. 'Never let someone wait for you.' Something my father always told me. It kinda stuck with me. I like the new look."

"Really, you like it? I don't know why but I wanted to try something different."

"I like it," I said. "You ready to have a good time?"

"Where are we off to?"

"Still a surprise. Hope you're hungry."

"I could eat."

"Then, I'll be the navigator."

"Mysterious to the end, huh?"

"Please. I'm an open book."

Camara laughed. "If you're an open book, then I haven't been able to find the Rosetta stone yet."

"I'm not as hard to read as hieroglyphics. Trust me."

Camara pulled out of the parking lot and stopped before hitting Bluefield Avenue.

"Which way am I turning, Mister Navigator?" Camara asked with what I took for genuine excitement.

"Make a right. We're going into Virginia."

**** 

"I can't believe you remembered I loved seafood. I only mentioned it once," Camara said as we sat in the Mayflower restaurant in Bluefield, Virginia.

I'd been here a few times before and they always took care of me here. No one would stare at me. The Mayflower was probably the best and closest place to get quality seafood in the area. It was a little pricey, but I wasn't worried about it. I thought Camara might be worth it. I was looking forward to her proving me right.

The atmosphere of the place was perfect—dimly lit with a chandelier over every table. Each table also had a fine silk tablecloth with a small flower arrangement illuminated by a single candle. The plush designs in the carpeting had always reminded me of a classy French restaurant.

"I honestly didn't know there was a Mayflower around here."

"It's been here for years."

"Well, I was stuck in the county for most of my life, so getting out to restaurants up in Bluefield just didn't happen very often. Occasions to go out to restaurants at all were few and far between. If we did make it out this way, it was to the Ryan's or Shoney's all you can eat."

"I still can't believe you're from the Patch," I said sipping my water.

"And why's that?"

"No offense or anything. It's just most of the people I know from McDowell County don't really act like you. The way you talk. The way you dress. You know. You just seem a little different."

"Oh, I know what you mean. I get that a lot actually from people who know what McDowell is like. People tend to stereotype McDowell, and I really can't blame them sometimes. The Patch really isn't that bad, but I was all too happy to get out all the same," Camara said, rubbing her finger over her own glass of water. "Being different got me into quite a few fights when I was younger."

"A playground brawler, huh?"

"Undefeated."

"What caused all the scraps?"

"Jealousy. My mother used to send me to stay with my uncle in California every summer. He was a doctor and didn't have any kids himself, so he would spoil the hell out of me and my brother. I would come back with clothes from all these designer stores, using slang and singing songs that wouldn't reach West Virginia for like two months. Being privileged in that way got me hated on. People thought my life was like that all the time, but I was in the same boat as everyone else during the school year. No better off really. What about you, Mr. Walker?"

"What about me? I was born and raised in the Field."

"I wouldn't have guessed you were from here. You have a sophistication about you that isn't found from black men in Bluefield too often."

"Now, you're the first to tell me anything like that."

"Really? I have a hard time believing that."

Camara locked eyes with me and a spark flew in my chest. How did she do that to me?

"You said your dad taught you to never be late. What else did he teach you?"

"My dad was into a lot of things. He gave me a guitar when I was eight. I never put that thing down. He gave me a katana, too."

"Your dad gave you a sword when you were eight?" Camara said with a raised eyebrow.

"Yep. I couldn't touch the thing until I was eighteen though. He was real selective with which one of us he taught what."

"You have siblings besides Zeus?"

"I have an older sister named Isis and a younger brother and sister both still in high school."

"That's a lot of kids."

"We don't all have the same mother."

"Poppa was a rolling stone?" she asked.

"Bingo."

Camara and I were so into our conversation that we almost didn't notice the waiter standing by our table. I think he had been there for a couple of seconds, waiting for us to look up. We took out our menus and looked at them for the first time since we sat down.

It took me a second to convince Camara to get whatever she wanted. Price didn't matter tonight. She ended up going for the lobster dinner, and I ordered up the catfish. The food was worth the trip to Virginia, and best of all, Camara approved.

After dinner, we went to a club in Princeton called The Room Upstairs on Mercer street. My friend Allen and I played guitar together from time to time, and I knew he was going to be there. The Room Upstairs usually hosted several open mike nights, but tonight, Allen was going to have his entire jazz band with him. I took a chance with this one, and it paid off. We didn't talk about it beforehand, but it turned out Camara loved jazz music almost as much as I did.

The club was small but had enough room for a small dance floor. The dim lighting inside made for an intimate setting. Despite its size, gaining a sense of privacy was easy. Everyone sat at small tables as if they were on their own private islands. The slight scent of incense burning throughout the club mixed with the jazz making for a perfect atmosphere. Most people were just fine staying in their seats and listening to the band play, but not Camara.

We weren't in the club ten minutes before she pulled me up and ushered me to the dance floor. Allen was on lead guitar and when he saw me on the floor, he kicked it up into overdrive. Even when we played together, Allen had a way of making me want to move. I could never figure out how anyone could manage to stay still while he was playing. Most people didn't.

The rest of the band followed Allen's lead. First the drums picked up and then the horns. You could feel the instruments' vibrations through the floor and walls. The air was caked with sweat and incense. No rehearsals or practices could teach them the song they played. It was pure heart and soul, pure jazz. The whole place was rocking, and Camara and I were in the center of it. At one point, the entire club backed off and watched us swing and sashay our way back and forth on the dance floor. All eyes were on us. Center stage was our stage. Camara and I got lost in each other, and I loved every second of it. I think Camara was a little surprised to see that I could more than hold my own on the dance floor.

When we finally stopped, we were both covered in sweat and breathing heavily. All the onlookers in the club clapped and cheered their approval of our exhibition. Allen had slowed things down again so everyone else could join in. He had the band play some slow, grinding jazz music. It didn't matter who you were or if I you were born with two left feet, everyone could grind.

Camara and I made our way to the corner of the dance floor. No one was watching us anymore, but I wouldn't have cared if they were. She pressed herself against me. It was hot and the air was getting thick, but I didn't want to let her go. Her hands cascaded down my shoulders. My hands found their way to her hips and pulled her in closer. The room was crowded, but nobody mattered to me but Camara. As we danced, her eyes would occasionally catch mine. Her gaze was deep and passionate. She was everything I needed, everything I had been missing. She quickly became the calm in the center of the storm my life had become. It normally would've bothered me a little how fast things were moving, but I didn't care. I was tired of over thinking everything. This felt right, and I wasn't about to fight it.

Elegant fingers explored my abs as Camara leaned into me and said, "Tonight was perfect. You're dangerous."

"What do you mean? Dangerous how?"

"The way you move. I knew you could dance."

"And how's that?" I asked, grinning.

"A girl can always tell, Mr. Walker. You're definitely dangerous."

I placed my hand on her cheek. She looked nervous, almost jumpy at my touch. I thought she was going to pull away from me. Then, she turned around, and we danced with her back to me. She pressed herself close to me, and I wrapped my arms around her. I leaned down slightly and placed my face near hers. Camara's skin was soft and welcoming. I could get lost in her touch. From this close, I could smell her perfume over the musk and sweat that saturated the air.

Camara reached back with one hand and rubbed the side of my head continuing to move in time with the music. She then looked back into my eyes and gave me the sweetest kiss. It was soft and tender, yet powerful. It felt like more than a kiss—it felt like a beginning. A chill shot down my spine that both scared and excited me.

Camara turned around and leaned into me resting her head on my shoulder. We held each other and didn't say a word. There was no need for words at that moment. It was perfect.

# CHAPTER 20

## CAMARA

True to his word, Ezra got Camara home before one a.m. She didn't know how it was possible that it was already one. The night went by so fast. Camara opened the door as quietly as she could and inched her way through the living room. She didn't want to wake the Alley Cat. She tiptoed her way to her room, but before she could make it to the steps, a familiar voice cut through the darkness.

"So how was your date?" Camara could feel her mother smiling as she heard her voice coming from the kitchen.

"Why are you sitting in the dark? Don't you ever sleep?"

"The dark helps me put things in perspective. And I take power naps throughout the day, so I don't need to sleep much, just like any cat."

Camara was in too good a mood to get in a battle of wits with her mother. She turned on the lights, sat down at the table, and thought of a way to change the subject.

"Why didn't you tell me Nancy Hasley still worked at the paper?"

Alley Cat made a face at the mentioning of Nancy's name, as if she'd caught a whiff of something foul. It surprised Camara. Nancy and her mother had been best friends since before she was born.

"I don't want to talk about her," Camara's mother said catching an attitude.

"Why? Didn't you know she was working there still?" Camara asked, puzzled.

"I'm not going to talk about her, Camara. I don't keep up with what Nancy does all the time."

Camara was still in a good mood so she didn't bother to push the subject like she would any other time. This battle would have to be fought another night. She was on too much of a high to let something like this bring her down.

"What were you trying to put in perspective?" she asked quickly to change the subject again.

"I was thinking about your father."

"What about him?" Camara asked, rubbing her hand through her sweaty hair. She had pretty much sweated out the effects of the straight iron she used to get her hair to lay flat. Her natural frizz was starting to come back.

"I've thought it over, and I'm convinced that I killed him. He's dead because of me."

"What!?" Camara said eyes full of shock. "Mom, daddy had a heart attack."

"Yes, he did."

Camara didn't feel like dealing with all this cryptic talk. She didn't have the patience to deal with this right now. She was finally on a high after feeling like her life was going all to hell for the past several months. She wasn't ready to let the feeling go. She almost got up from the table and left right then, but she knew her mother would be hurt if she did.

Camara didn't know what to say so she waited for her mother to explain herself. She couldn't think of a way to ask that wouldn't come out rude, so she waited in awkward silence until her mother spoke.

"You know how your father was."

"I know," Camara said merely agreeing with the statement. Camara had made peace with what her father was a long time ago. It took her a long time to let go of the anger she felt for him. There was no need to dwell on it now that he was gone.

"I just got sick of it, Camara. I got sick of the lies. I got sick of the drinking. I got tired of sharing a house with someone who had grown so far apart from me. And, most importantly, I got impatient with him for never going to church with me. It wasn't so much that he wouldn't go, but he wouldn't even try! His lack of faith influenced you and Tony, and I let that happen. I couldn't take it any more. So I stopped praying for him. I just couldn't do it any more. I stopped praying for him and three months later, the man was dead. It makes me wonder what would have happened if I hadn't given up on him. Maybe if I hadn't, things would have gotten better."

Camara couldn't believe what she was hearing. It was all total nonsense. She would never say that to her mother though. Faith was important to her mother, but Camara's faith had never been that strong. As much as her mother loved and tried to protect her, Camara had seen too much as a child to put much stock in the "All-knowing." Too many of her prayers had gone unanswered.

"It's not your fault, mom. You put up with him for a lot longer than most could. Longer than you should have."

The Alley Cat looked off into space. It made Camara sad to know that they loved each other so much but couldn't help each other. It was a sad and lonely feeling, one that Ezra had helped her forget.

Camara didn't have the faith her mother did, she believed in herself. She would get herself out of her mess, and her mother would have to do the same.

"How was your date?" Alley Cat asked. Camara sensed she wanted something enjoyable to think about.

Camara quickly replayed her night to herself. Her smile came back. Only one word could describe the evening.

"Wonderful."

# CHAPTER 21

The hours between one and three o'clock in the morning were the man from 7F's favorite time. There was almost limitless potential for mayhem at this time. This was the time of lust, the time of death. The devil's hour.

He had always hated fishing. Ever since he was a child and his father made his pitiful attempts to bond with him between beatings. It was boring and a complete waste of time. The only chance for excitement was when a fish was stupid enough to take the bait, and there wasn't much pay off. He thought that if fishing was more like this he and his father might have gotten along.

The man from 7F was crouched in the shadows, staring at a BB&T ATM in Princeton. Several cars had rolled up and had been allowed to move on. Nothing was impressive about them. Small fish. Guppies. Easily caught but then just thrown back.

Just as the man was about to give up and try another ATM, a big fish arrived. A black Escalade pulled up to the bank. He donned his mask and placed the silencer on his .9mm with gloved hands. The bad thing about fishing was that you had to wait for the fish to come to you even when you could see them right in front of you. They could be right there and you had to wait. It was maddening. This was much better. Much more proactive.

This was the best part of hunting. The build up. The approach.

The man in the car was too wrapped up in what he was doing to look up until it was too late. There was a silent shot, and the ATM's camera shattered. Another shot fired into the driver's head. The only regret he felt was that it was over so quickly. Next time, he might use a knife to liven things up.

The cutting sensation would add variety, and variety was the spice of life after all.

The man from 7F calmly threw the driver to the ground of the bank parking lot and wiped away most of the blood. He got in the car and saw that he'd hit the jackpot. The driver had taken out six hundred dollars. Two a.m. in Princeton with six hundred dollars. The only logical place to go now was Southern Exposure.

He walked into the strip club and took a corner seat. He was confident in the look he had chosen. There was no doubt in his mind that he could hold a long conversation with anyone here and none of them would be able to recognize him in the morning.

He waited and watched unimpressive dancers take their turns on the pole. None of them were worth his time. He thought about cutting his losses, simply shooting everyone in the club, and then leaving. He considered torching the place to resurrect his savior once again—to give birth to fire on a grand scale and to sacrifice his enemies to the flame was his ultimate glory. However, that honor was going to be reserved for Walker. But he was growing bored. He needed a target.

He would have jumped the gun and carried out his plan if a worthy target hadn't mounted the stage. She wore a red and black plaid miniskirt with a tight short sleeve button up and black heels. Her breasts were perfect, not too small but not too large. Her waist was narrow, and her legs were long and slender, just the right thickness. Even through the multi-colored strobe light, you could tell her shoulder-length hair was jet black. Her stage music was Metallica and she moved every bit as fast and violently as the music she picked.

The man from 7F got up from his seat and walked to the bar. Every man had his eyes glued to the stage, throwing their hard earned dollars to the spinning beauty.

"Who is that on the stage?" he asked, sounding as awe-struck as the idiots in the club.

"That's Onyx," the bartender said. "Something special, ain't she?"

"I'd like to have some private time with her. Do you think you can make that happen?"

"Get in line, buddy. You ain't the only one," he said, pointing to Onyx's flock of onlookers.

Three hundred dollars worth of crisp twenty dollar bills found their way into the bartender's tip jar.

"Can you make it happen?"

The bartender pulled the jar behind the bar and gave it a quick count.

"I'll see what I can do."

\*\*\*\*

The man from 7F could be very charming when he wanted to be. After three private lap dances and several drinks, it was easy to get Onyx in his car once the club closed. With any woman, all that was needed was the right conversation. The right intentions, or in this case the right preserved intentions. Most women often misread his intent for charm or mystery. As soon as Onyx looked him in the eyes, he had her.

It didn't take long to get the stripper to the hotel room either. He was, however, surprised that he actually liked the woman. She seemed very intelligent and witty— not the type of girl who should be working at a strip club. After only an hour and a half of talking to her, it was clear that she belonged in a college library somewhere. She was a diamond in the rough.

She had changed into her street clothes and looked just as sexy as she did on stage. Her outfit consisted of nothing more than tattered jeans and a tight T-shirt.

As soon as they entered the room, they were all over each other.

He lifted her up off the ground and pressed himself against her. He ripped at her clothes until she had no secrets from him. He considered actually just having sex with her. He was aroused by her and not just as a potential kill. He wanted her, but that wasn't why he'd brought her here.

"What's your name?" he asked.

Onyx licked her lips and ran her tongue over her teeth. "Does it matter?"

"You want to know mine?"

The stripper ran a hand down his chest and grabbed his crotch. She smiled when she felt the size of his erection.

"Tonight your name is, 'big daddy.' Why don't we let the lion out of his cage?" she said as she worked to release his pants while still pinned to the wall.

"My name is Calvin Bridges."

"That's interesting," she said, stroking him.

"Also known as John Grayson."

"Ok."

"Also known as Sean Greenwood and Grant Harper."

"Sure."

"Also known as Patrick Collins. Also known as Stuart Young. Also known as Steven Sisk. Also known as Howard Jordan."

He entered the woman violently, thrusting himself in her as far and as hard as he could. She moaned, on the edge of pleasure and pain, transfixed between the two. He put both hands around her neck and began to squeeze, using every ounce of force he had.

He stared into her eyes and enjoyed the shock on her face as she realized what was happening to her. He looked deep into her eyes to find the fire within her. The spark of life burned bright as the will to live flared up in her soul. Then the spark started to fade from her eyes. He leaned in close and whispered, "You can call me AKA. All the people that know me best do."

\*\*\*\*

AKA took his time cleaning up after himself. He got a little carried away, but didn't feel the need to rush. He organized all the major pieces of Onyx and placed them on one of the beds in the hotel room. He wondered why he always had to cut his victims in so many pieces when killing his way; it made the cover-up work such a pain. Then he grabbed a can of gasoline with his gloved hands and soaked the sheets and floor.

He had a small flare rigged to a timer, which he also placed on the bed. He had thought ahead and had placed all his clothes in the opposite corner of the room, away from all the slashing and cutting that had been done. Blood was everywhere in the hotel room but he didn't have a drop on his clothing.

He washed the blood from his skin then checked his disguise before leaving the room. His sandy blonde hair. His green eyes. It was all still perfect. As he knew it would be.

AKA used Onyx's cell phone to call a cab, then calmly walked outside after placing a do not disturb sign on the door. Once he was in the cab he gently pressed a button that detonated the small bomb he placed in the car he had stolen earlier that night.

His only regret was that he wouldn't be able to see the fires in the hotel room or the car being engulfed. All things considered, tonight was a good night. But AKA was still bored. Killing individuals only went so far with him. He needed to keep things interesting. He pulled out his lighter in the back of the cab and flicked the flame to life. He stared into its flickering magnificence and listened.

It was time to blow up something big.

# CHAPTER 22

It felt weird not seeing Camara all day after our date. Lois had sent me a text with my field assignments for today, so I didn't have time to go by the paper. I doubted Camara would have been there anyway.

There were two murders last night and Melissa insisted that Camara follow up on them. I was a little concerned about her looking into the killings because of how outlandish they sounded. Stuff like this just didn't happen in Princeton. A man killed and his car stolen at an ATM. A woman's body found chopped to pieces in what was left of a burned hotel room. Stuff like that wasn't supposed to happen around here.

I was grateful in more ways than one for my date with Camara last night. Besides having a great time, I also had an alibi. Plenty of people saw me at the Room Upstairs last night, so I shouldn't have people thinking I was involved with the murders.

All of my assignments for the paper were done by five o'clock. I emailed all the pictures needed for today to Lois. I called Camara when I was done. She was on her way to meet one of her friends from the Patch. I was a little disappointed that I wouldn't see her today but thought that might be a good thing. It was not good to smother each other after the first date. I still couldn't believe I went, let alone, had such a great time.

I drove Dirty Vegas down Bluefield Avenue until I reached the Wade Center. I used to volunteer there regularly until a freight train hit my life a few months back. My mom pleaded with me to volunteer there for weeks with no success. She finally bribed me with one hundred dollars to get me in the door. She bet me that if I could come back afterward and

145

honestly tell her I didn't like it, I could keep the money. Needless to say, she got her money back.

The Wade Center was an after-school program for kids in Bluefield. Most of the kids who went there didn't have fathers in their lives and my mother thought I would be a good role model for some of them.

"Those kids need a positive male role model in their lives to look up to. A mother can take you far, but only a man can teach a boy how to be a man." I can still hear my mother's words, as clear as if she had said them yesterday.

I wasn't sure how the kids at the Center would greet me after being gone so long. I didn't know how bad my reputation would be. I hadn't talked to any of the other volunteers either, so God only knew how this was going to go. The only way to find out was to go inside. I threw caution to the wind and entered the center completely unprepared for what awaited me inside.

"Easy!" I heard several kids shout in unison as soon as I walked into the computer lab where they did their homework. I burst out into my widest smile as all the kids who remembered me ran to greet me.

I ran around the center for a few minutes playing with the kids before Megan Green forced me to act my age and make the kids finish their homework. Megan had been managing the center for almost two years. In those two years, she had devoted a lot of her time and energy to the kids here. She was also a big reason the Center was able to get the grants it needed to stay open.

It took us several minutes to calm everyone down. Before we got the kids started back on their work, one of my three favorite kids came up to hug me. You're not supposed to have favorites in this kind of volunteer work, but I couldn't help it. Janice Green was the sweetest, most adorable, seven-year-old girl I'd ever met. She had light bronze skin and green eyes. Her hair was long, naturally light brown and dark at the roots. It was held back with little teddy-bear barettes and today she was decked out in a Dora the Explorer tee shirt.

"Where have you been?" little Jani demanded while tapping her foot and placing her little fists on her hips.

I knelt down on one knee to get as close to eye level as I could with her and tried to charm the seven-year-old-grown woman.

"Did you miss me?"

"Maybe," she said rolling her eyes at me.

"Aww. Well, I missed you."

"So."

"So, didn't you miss me back?"

"Hummp!" Jani grunted then stomped her way back to her seat in the computer lab.

Two words described the little girl. Too grown.

Megan walked up behind me and tapped me on the shoulder motioning for me to follow her outside into the hallway. Megan was a very attractive black woman, but she always toned it down when she was working with the kids. She had on her glasses and her hair was pulled back in a tight ponytail. She always wore tennis shoes and jeans to the center. In a lot of ways she looked like a librarian. She appeared much older than she really was, much more refined than her years should allow.

"I think my daughter has a crush on you," she said once we were in the hall.

"She only likes me because I'm taller than the other boys. How have you been, Megan?"

"I'm good, Ezra. I haven't seen you around here for awhile. You didn't have to stay away you know. The kids did miss you, despite how Jani acts."

"I'm sorry. The way people have been reacting to me around town—that is, the way they've been looking at me—I wasn't sure how welcome I would be here."

"Ten-year-olds don't read the paper, Ezra."

"Yeah, but their parents do."

"Are you good? Really?"

"I'm good. Promise. How are things going in the life of a strong black single mom?"

"You know me. I live here. Can't stop, won't stop. These kids are my life."

"Where are my two little ninjas?" I asked.

Megan looked up and instantly made me feel like crap. She had on the pity look like I'd missed something. She looked as though she had something to tell me that everyone already knew, but I was the last to get the memo. I could tell she was cursing her luck about having to be the one to break the news to me.

"What?" I said slightly hunching my shoulders ready for her words to hit me like a sledgehammer in the chest. "What happened?"

"Nick Cooper and Charles Dwight have been missing for a week now," Megan said, and each syllable was a ton of weight assaulting me all at once.

"What happened? Did they run away or something?" I asked the question, but I already knew the answer.

"No. They went missing from Bluefield Park. They were there in the middle of the day and nobody saw anything. No witnesses, no trace of what happened to them. Just gone."

Nick and Charles were good kids, smart kids. I knew they wouldn't have run away. If they were missing for this long, it had to be serious. I was trying to wrap my head around what Megan was telling me when I heard an unwelcome voice in the hallway.

"Ezra Walker!" I heard my name grunted followed by thundering footsteps.

"Officer Wilson, it's a pleasure to see you again. Will you be sticking around to help the children with their math?"

"Come with me. Now!" Officer Wilson said motioning for me to follow. He turned on his heel and walked outside. It annoyed me that he didn't bother looking back to make sure I was following. How did he know I was here?

Megan looked concerned. I'm sure she didn't understand why the chief of police was in the Wade Center demanding an audience with me. I smiled at her and offered as much re-assurance as I could, but truthfully I really didn't know what this was about either. I started getting a headache as soon as I stepped outside. I really didn't want to deal with this. Not now.

Officer Wilson was standing on the steps when I got outside. He stood impatiently like I had kept him waiting for an hour rather than ten seconds. He scanned the street and across the concrete basketball courts outside the Wade Center. His face was already red from holding in anger.

"Where were you last night, Walker?" he asked curtly.

"I was with a friend. Had a great time. If I knew you were lonely, I would've given you a call and invited you along. The more the merrier you know."

He turned around and got in my face just as close as he had been at the Beaver-Graham game bombing. His cheeks were scarlet and I thought the vein in his forehead was in danger of bursting.

"Do you think I'm a goddamn joke, Walker? Do you honestly think that I won't pull out my gun right now and blow your fucking brains out if I knew it would save lives? I'm just not going to risk my career or my freedom on you. Yet."

Wilson was barreling down on me. His voice was hard and serious. He stared at me with an intensity I wasn't ready for, but I didn't back down.

"I don't have any proof, yet. I don't have any evidence, but more than enough suspicion. All roads point to you. I don't know if you've snapped or what, but I've come here to promise you one thing: Whoever is doing this will mess up. And when that mistake is made, if I find out I'm right about you, if I find that it was you who killed those people, that you took those boys and you still have the fucking balls to set foot in this center, you would be better off to take a knife and cut your wrists than to let me get my hands on you. Do you understand me?"

I didn't have a response for Officer Wilson, so I didn't offer one. I was sure that my silence pissed him off more than anything I could have said. He must have felt that he'd gotten his point across because he left without saying anything else.

As he turned to leave, I saw him nod at two men in a silver Impala across the street. I recognized the two from a photo shoot I did for the Bluefield Police Academy months ago. One guy was a new recruit to the force, the other a veteran of about ten years.

It didn't take me long to put two and two together. This was how he knew I was at the Wade Center—Chief Wilson had assigned me my very own babysitters.

# CHAPTER 23

## CAMARA

Camara was spending more time working off the clock than she wanted. It had only been a week since the murders in Princeton and she had become engrossed with them. What type of person could do things like that and keep the frame of mind needed to not be caught? Whoever did this had to be one very smooth operator.

Camara didn't expect any evidence to turn up at the hotel since most of the floor that the fire was on was scorched. There wasn't any evidence at the ATM scene either. No fingerprints, no DNA, no nothing. The guy didn't even step in the blood left on the ground by the victim. The most frustrating thing was the hotel security videos. Whoever this guy was—he'd done his homework. He hadn't even once looked at any of the cameras. Not a single angle of any of the cameras offered a good view of his face. His ethnicity and build were about all the videos offered.

Out of nowhere, Camara became an investigative reporter, and she wasn't sure if she liked it. She was starting to feel the blackhole of West Virginia threatening to suck her in. She could think of plenty of reasons to not like her job, but the mystery had her now. Focusing on the scandals of Bluefield got her mind off her own problems and it was a welcome escape.

Camara drove along Blue Prince Road smiling as she approached Ezra's apartment. They had been talking steadily back and forth since their date on Monday, but hadn't had much time to see each other. Today was the championship game for the semi-pro baseball team, the Princeton Devil Rays. Camara wasn't much of a baseball fan, but Ezra had asked her to go and she wasn't about to turn him down after the night they had had.

As she walked to the door of the apartment, a frightening thought ran though her mind: Was she putting Ezra in danger by spending time with him? Tarquan would stick to his word, that she was sure. It was just the type of man he was. But, she had time and she was going to enjoy it with a more pleasant distraction than following the trail of a homicidal maniac.

Ezra came to the door after several knocks. He wore a black wife-beater, blue jeans and his million dollar smile.

"Am I too early?" Camara took a quick survey of Ezra's muscles as she asked and didn't bother to hide it.

"No, no, come in. I just need to get on a shirt and brush my teeth. Then we're good to go."

Ezra stepped aside and let Camara in. As soon as she set foot in the apartment, she was impressed. It wasn't very big, but with one glance, it was possible to get a feel for the type of man Ezra was. Several paintings, drawings and photographs covered the walls and were arranged neatly around the walls. Each looked like it had been put up with care and their positions in the apartment given thought. There was a chest set off to the side with a large bookshelf behind it. Someone was a veracious reader.

"Make yourself at home. I'll just be a second," Ezra said as he went to the bathroom.

Camara took a closer look around Ezra's apartment. The more she looked, the more she liked what she saw. It was clean and organized. Everything was where it seemed it should be. It looked like Ezra put a lot of thought into the design of his home. She wanted to be nosier but confined herself to the living room. She ran her finger across the books on the shelf finding a very diverse collection including books by Eric Jerome Dickey, James Patterson, Jim Butcher, Christopher Golden, Stephen King, and Zane. He also had all seven Harry Potter books and several other authors Camara didn't even recognize.

Ezra came into the living room wearing a purple shirt with black and white lettering. The shirt read:


Divine Ability
Conduit of Strength
What's yours?


"What's Divine Ability?" Camara asked having never seen the term used on a shirt before.

"Something my dad talks about all the time. I just put it on a shirt and designed some patterns around it."

"You designed that?"

"Yeah. It's kind of corny I guess, but I like it."

"No, I think it looks nice on you," Camara said as she ran her hands gently across the embroidered letters and designs.

"It fits you. What does it mean?"

"It's kind of silly."

Camara hit Ezra in the chest with her fist then looked up in his eyes.

"Stop play'n and tell me. If it was that silly, you wouldn't have worn it."

"Okay. Okay. Jezz," Ezra said as he grabbed a light jacket from his closet. "My dad always felt that we all had a divine ability. The best way to describe it would be like a God-given talent. We all have something that God arms us with that helps us in our personal relationship with him and in the spirit realm, and with our fellow man in the soulish realm."

"Okay," Camara said not trying to hide her confusion.

Ezra chuckled. "Come on. I'll explain it on the way."

Camara rode with Ezra in his car as they made their way to Hunnicutt Sports Complex for the baseball game and Ezra continued his explanation.

"Divine ability describes the talents God gives you. Like some people can touch people with singing. Some people are powerful intercessors. Even things simple as ushering people into the right seats can be a divine ability."

"I don't get it but it still makes a little sense, I guess. So 'Conduit of Strength' means . . . what exactly?"

"My dad never spent much time with me or my brothers or sisters when we were coming up, but he swore up and down he knew us better than we knew ourselves. It used to bother me a lot that he would say that when he was never around, but I had to admit he was right about us most of the time. He used to tell me that my faith was so strong that when things got bad, my faith would strengthen the people around me. God was my rock. I would be everyone else's rock to show them how powerful God was in my life, and so they would allow God to be their rock. Does that make any sense?"

"No," Camara said admitting the truth.

"It's hard to explain, easier to show. You should come to church with me one Sunday. It'll help me explain."

"I'd like that," Camara said.

She took time to mull over the concepts Ezra was speaking about, but it all sounded Greek to her. She gave up for the time being and turned her attention to the stack of CDs in Ezra's center compartment.

"Do you mind?" Camara asked pointing to the CDs.

"Help yourself."

Camara looked through all them and wasn't surprised by the diversity she found. Ezra had everything from Gnarles Barkley to Jill Scott. She thumped through tracks by Floetry, John Mayor, Jimmy Hendrix, Fallout Boy, U2, Common, and Kanye West. There were even some oldies that Alley Cat would get into like Smoky Robinson, The Temptations, and Marvin Gaye.

"You like a lot of different stuff."

"I like to keep it fresh. What do you listen to?"

"Some of what you've got here actually. Don't think I've heard a lot of Fallout Boy or the Gorillaz. Who is Flobot?"

"Pop it in. You might like it."

Hunnicutt Sports Complex wasn't far from Ezra's apartment so it only took about fifteen minutes to get there. The Hunnicutt Stadium was a little bigger than Mitchell Stadium in Bluefield and it looked a little newer, too. Once inside, Camara let Ezra roam around to take some pre-game pictures while she got some drinks and hotdogs. Then she tried to find some good seats that would allow them so see the majority of the action. The place was packed before the opening pitch. The sun was setting in beautiful rays of orange, reds and purples that blended in with the fading blue sky. The complex's lights were already on before the game started.

Camara climbed up into the stands and found a good seat. Ezra had wanted to stay for the whole game, so Camara made herself comfortable. She made sure to catch Ezra's eye to let him know where she was sitting. She watched as Ezra caught the opening pitch on film and made his way to the stands after snapping off several pictures of the action that followed.

Camara felt a light breeze starting to set in. It was starting to look like Ezra was the smart one for bring his jacket. She wouldn't ask, but she wondered if he would let her wear it.

Ezra was halfway up the stands when Camara heard a boom that sounded like a crack of thunder from somewhere in the stadium, but there wasn't a cloud in the sky. The cold breeze was suddenly the last thing on Camara's mind as all hell started to break loose.

# CHAPTER 24

## EZRA

I looked to my left and couldn't believe my eyes. Two people had been tossed into the air by an explosion, fire and smoke flashing between them. The blast had rocked the stands and caused several people to fall into the twisted support beams under the bleachers. I moved to go see if I could help someone when another thunder crack went off behind me.

Fans were starting to realize what was happening, and everyone started to panic. I heard several screams and saw people pointing to the sky above the baseball field. Several black dots were in the sky. The dots peaked over the field and started to descend towards the stands. I counted at least eight with a glance before I realized what they were.

"GRENADES!" someone screamed.

Now everyone was in full panic. They pushed and shoved and tried to escape the danger raining down on them. I turned to find Camara. To my relief, she was already running toward me. She grabbed my arm and tried to pull me with her off the bleachers.

"Let's go! What are you doing!?" she said with fear in her eyes.

"No! We're good here!" I said and reached out for her, stopping her momentum.

I picked her up then forced her down on the bleachers before she could protest. I threw myself on top of her to shield her from any shrapnel and prayed that I had judged the trajectory of the grenades right.

I heard two explosions before I went deaf. A high-pitched squeal or buzzing had replaced my sense of hearing. I told myself to stay calm and my hearing would come back. I looked down at Camara and she seemed to be okay.

"Are you hurt?" I asked her.

She answered me, but I couldn't hear a thing she said. The buzzing in my ears was starting to subside a little, so I asked her again wondering if she heard me the first time.

"Stop screaming." I heard her say this time.

I pulled myself off her and helped her up. She didn't look like she was cut or hit with anything in the blast. I looked around at the Hunnicutt Sport Complex. It resembled a battlefield more than a baseball field. Several people had missing limbs and were in need of serious medical attention. I counted at least two people that looked as if it may be too late for them. It all happened so fast. From what I saw, it looked like there had been at least four explosions, but I couldn't be sure.

"I think you just saved my life," Camara said while my back was to her as I continued to survey the carnage.

"Which way were you about to run?" I asked looking back at her.

Camara pointed to a hole in the stands where several people had been hit with a direct blast and fell through to the ground.

"It's a good thing I stopped you then. You're okay right? You've got blood on you."

"I don't think it's mine," Camara said giving me a concerned look which prompted me to look myself over.

I had been so busy looking around at everyone else I hadn't bothered to look at myself. My ears were still ringing and my head was throbbing. I had cuts down my left side. One or two that might need stitches. My left leg had also been cut up pretty good. As I started to realize how hurt I was, my vision began to blur. I was losing more blood than I thought. My adrenaline rush was fading. I started falling to my right when Camara caught me. I thought she would lower me to the ground, but she supported the bulk of my weight and ushered me off the stands. She was a lot stronger than I realized.

Princeton Hospital was less than a two-minute drive from the sports complex and ambulances quickly pulled up with their sirens screaming. I must have looked really bad because I didn't have to wait in line to be looked at.

I was relieved to know my injuries looked worse than they really were. I had lost some blood, but nothing serious. I would have to stay in bed for a while and likely have a headache in the morning, but that was about it. I was given a few stitches then told I could go. Under normal circumstances, I might have been asked to stay but there were people in need of more serious help. I was more than happy to get out of the way.

"Well, aren't you just dramatic?" Camara came over and said to me after I had been stitched up.

"What do you mean?" I asked.

"You just wanted to see if I would be worried about you, so you went and got yourself hurt."

Camara leaned toward me and gently rubbed her hand over my bandaged head. Her hand went down my cheek, and she pulled me into her and kissed me on the cheek.

"You saved my life," she said with her brow tenderly resting on mine.

"Maybe."

She backed up from me slightly. Just enough for me to see her eyes.

"You saved my life," she said again placing a hand on mine. Our eyes stayed locked on each other's. "Let me show you how grateful I am. Tonight."

The woman was aggressive. It was a little intimidating, but I couldn't lie. I kinda liked it. I looked into her brown eyes and had to look away. She had caught me off guard with that and I was a little embarrassed. Girls usually responded like this to Zeus, not me. I wasn't sure how to react to aggressive women.

I started to respond when the two men standing behind her caught my attention. My headache came back as I realized it was Ren and Stimpy. That's what I had decided to call the two cops that Officer Wilson had assigned to follow me for about a week now.

"Hello, Ezra." Camara and I both jumped somewhat as Chief Wilson himself appeared out of nowhere. He had on a pair of jeans and a Princeton Devil Rays shirt. He had his son, Taylor, with him. If I remember right, he was about ten years old and was the spitting image of his father. They had on matching clothes that made them look like an all-American father and son expecting a fun day of baseball and hotdogs. That wasn't what they got today. "You look pretty banged up, Ezra. Are you okay?"

I narrowed my eyes and didn't respond to Officer Wilson's false concern. I didn't have anything to say to him. I didn't want to give him the satisfaction.

"Since you're here, Officer Wilson, perhaps you'd like to answer some questions for the paper," Camara said moving in between Wilson and me. She even pulled out a little hand held recorder.

Wilson glanced down at her and looked smug as ever. He gave her a condescending smile that might have prompted me to hit him if I was in a better condition and his son wasn't around.

"As you can see, Miss Johnson, I have more important matters to attend to," Officer Wilson said as he looked past Camara and at me again. He didn't say anything else as he and his son walked off. Other on duty officers were pulling up, but Wilson would have his hands full for a while. I wasn't sure why, but his son looked back at me and smiled and waved. I hadn't noticed it at first, but the kid looked like he really was concerned if I was okay. Whatever Chief Wilson's opinion of me was, he must have been keeping it to himself. He looked like a good kid, a smart kid. Seeing him made me remember how Ray used to be a pretty good guy. He had always been nice to me until several months ago. I still didn't know what bug had crawled up his butt.

I took a deep breath and didn't let Ray Wilson get to me. My head was pounding and drowsiness from the medicine was settling in. I needed to sleep. Ren and Stimpy stared me down again and my headache tapered off into my right eye socket in the form of a twitch.

"Are you okay?" Camara asked, seeing the anguish build on my face. After Wilson, it was good to hear the genuine concern in her voice. "I could call someone back over here if you need me to."

"No, I just need to get some rest," I said as I moved to get out of the ambulance. Camara shepherded me through the parking lot as I reached in my pocket and handed her the keys. "You should probably drive Dirty Vegas. I'm a little wobbly walking, don't think I wanna try driving."

Camara took the keys from me and looked up at me, puzzled, "Drive what?"

# CHAPTER 25

## CAMARA

It was dark when Camara pulled into Pauli Heights Apartments. She parked "Dirty Vegas" in its regular spot and helped Ezra inside his apartment. As soon as they got inside, Ezra threw himself on his couch and started rubbing his head.

"How are you feeling?" Camara asked.

"Not too bad actually. I don't know what they gave me for the pain, but whatever it was, it's working."

"You want me to turn on the TV?"

"No. I'd rather not deal with the noise."

"You look tired."

"That's because I am. I don't wanna fall asleep though. My mind is still in overdrive. None of this makes much sense to me. Why would someone blow up Hunnicutt? There's no way one person could have chucked all those grenades, no way someone could have thrown them that far either. They crossed the length of the field to get to the stands. What's the point of all that?"

"You're not Sherlock Holmes. Stop stressing yourself. Personally, I'm just happy you're okay," Camara said.

Ezra smiled and looked away from her. He seemed so confident most of the time, but Camara's smile still made him look shy. She liked that about him. He was a lot different than the men Camara had been used to. One of the best things about Ezra was that he was so fine, but somehow he didn't even know it.

Ezra got up off the couch and went into his room. "I'll be right back. Need to get out of these torn-up clothes."

As he went into his room, Camara noticed how dirty her own clothes were. Ezra had protected her from most of the

161

debris, but she still had a light film of dirt on her and smelled like smoke. She went to Ezra's door and knocked lightly.

"Ezra."

"Yeah?"

"Would you mind if I took a shower? I feel filthy in these clothes, too."

"Sure. Do you need something to change into?"

"If you have something. Yeah."

"Hold on."

Camara waited patiently by the door and heard Ezra shifting through his closet. She wanted to go into his room but she fought back the temptation.

When Ezra came to the door, he was holding a pair of green sweatpants that said Thundering Herd down one leg in white letters. He also had a pink shirt. Ezra had taken off his shirt and Camara quickly took in the details of his muscles before locking onto his eyes.

"This stuff should fit."

Camara looked at the clothes he brought and raised an eyebrow. "You into pink?"

Ezra chuckled. "I designed this shirt for my older sister. Don't ask me how, but I ended up with more than one of them," he said handing them to Camara.

Camara held up the shirt and read:

Divine Ability
Healer
What's yours?

"Well, this one doesn't require as much explanation. So your sister's a healer?"

"That's a long story. She doesn't like to talk about it much. Take your time in there. I don't think I'll take a shower tonight because of the stitches. I'll wash up in the morning. You can stay the night if you think it's too late to drive back to the Patch. You take the bed, I'll hit up the couch."

"Okay." Camara said and smiled at Ezra. She hung the clothes he'd given her over one arm and placed the opposite hand on Ezra's chest. He was a little shy to her touch and she could feel him somewhat pull away. She kissed him softly on the lips then looked into his eyes. "Thank you for saving me," she said grinning up at him.

"You don't have to keep saying that, you know."

"You don't have to be scared of me, you know?"

"Who said I was scared?"

Camara giggled as she turned around and headed for the bathroom and shut the door. She undressed and got in the shower and was pleased to see how clean it was. Not just the shower, but the whole bathroom. She did what Ezra said and took her time in the shower. A part of her hoped Ezra would join her, but she knew he wouldn't. Camara had messed around and gotten a crush on a goody-goody. She thought about the fact that several years ago she would've thought a guy like Ezra was soft and not given him the time of day. *Guess I'm growing up.*

Camara doubted he would come in his own bathroom while she was there unless invited, and then persuaded. The more time Camara spent around him, the harder it was for her to picture him hurting anyone, let alone killing his own mother.

While she was drying off, she gave her own mother a call to let her know where she was. Alley Cat was relieved that she was okay, but Camara could feel her eyes rolling on the other end of the phone when she mentioned where she was staying. Her mother didn't go into a speech, which Camara was thankful for.

She exited the bathroom wearing the clothes Ezra gave her. She didn't bother to put her bra back on and decided to go straight to bed. She had thought it over and didn't think tonight would be a good night to throw herself on Ezra, even though she wanted to. Plus all the adrenaline from earlier today had worn off. She was crashing fast.

She found Ezra on his couch fighting sleep. He wore a pair of cotton pajama pants with no shirt or socks. She looked at him for a moment and almost started to feel guilty that she was even in his life. She wasn't sure what type of danger she was putting him in by being around him, by developing feelings for him. It was too fast, too soon to feel this way about a man.

Her mind flashed to Tarquan and his toy soldiers. She wondered if he was responsible for the bombing. She didn't put it past him, but it didn't seem like his style. Unless he was losing it. Unless he finally was living up to his sire name and had truly snapped.

Camara looked at Ezra and a smile edged its way across her lips. She didn't feel like sleeping alone tonight when she didn't have to, so she went into the bedroom and grabbed two pillows and a blanket.

"Ezra. Ezra," Camara said tapping him on the head.

"Hump." Ezra grunted as his eyes opened slightly. "You ain't leaving, are ya?"

Camara chortled to herself. When Ezra was tired, his voice took on a little more of a southern accent. It was adorable. Camara eased her way behind him.

"Come here, Ezra."

"What?" Ezra turned and asked through heavy eyes.

Camara laid on the couch under Ezra then turned him on his back. She made herself comfortable on the pillows she brought, placed her arms around Ezra, and rested his head on her chest. Then she threw the blanket over them.

"I might not be able to stay awake now," he said sounding even more like a country boy.

"That's the plan, buster," she said and kissed him on the forehead. "That's the plan."

# CHAPTER 26

## EZRA

I sprung awake from the pounding on my door and was instantly irritated. It felt like ants were dancing on my temples, as I pulled myself up from the couch. Camara also awoke as the pounding continued.

"Who is it?" I shouted, hoping that whoever it was would just go away.

"It's me. Hurry up and let me in. We need to talk." I heard my brother's voice from the other side of the door.

I adjusted my bandages and looked back at Camara. She looked beautiful even half sleep and rubbing the eye crust from her eyes. It made me feel good that she had decided to stay. It was hard to feel bad around her, period.

I went to the door and looked at the clock on my wall. It was three in the morning. I had no idea what Zeus had to say to me at this time of night: I just knew that it had better be good.

I opened the door and Zeus stood in my hallway wearing black from head to toe. He even had on a light trench coat that caused him to look like nothing more than a huge black silhouette.

"Dang, Morpheus," I said.

Zeus laughed and showed bright teeth in an almost sinister smile. "Do you really want to know how deep the rabbit hole goes, Neo?" he asked and let himself in.

He entered the living room where Camara stood on her toes stretching her arms out over her head. If Zeus was surprised to see her in my apartment, he didn't show it.

"Miss Johnson," he said and smiled, acknowledging her presence.

"Mr. Champion," she replied.

"Zeus and I need to talk. You can take the bed. We'll just be outside, okay."

Camara yawned and stretched again. "That's fine. I'm not going anywhere," she said as she walked back to my bedroom. "Just don't be afraid to join me when you're done."

I motioned for Zeus to follow me back outside. Once in the hallway we sat on the wooden steps that led to the next level of apartments.

"Why didn't you stop me from coming in, if you had that girl in there?" he asked.

"You didn't give me a chance."

"She is fine, by the way. Got a fatty and a nice rack on her. You hit the jackpot."

"Do you mind?" I said irritated. My brother wasn't helping my headache.

"I really hope you hit that. She's pretty much throwing it at you. You did smash that, right?"

"I don't want to discuss that with you now."

Zeus sighed and rolled his eyes. "You are a disappointment. You bored her to death talking about DA or some shit, didn't you? Just smut that bitch out."

"Just tell me why you're here at three in the morning, please."

Zeus hung his head slightly. He looked like he just put a weight on his shoulders. One only he knew about. "I went to Hunnicutt. Looked at the damage."

"How bad was it? I was so discombobulated, I don't really remember."

"There won't be any games played there for some time. Three people died and twenty-four injured. In retrospect, it wasn't as bad as it could've been. Only a couple of bleachers were destroyed, but the grenades were put in key places, which is why I'm surprised that so few people got hurt. If those explosives had been any bigger . . ." Zeus said hanging his head as though a memory came to his mind that would better off be long forgotten. "What do you remember?" he asked.

"Not much. I heard two booms, then looked in the sky above the field and saw grenades raining down. There's no way one guy could have chucked those bombs."

Zeus was sitting on the step above where I sat and looked down at me. I didn't return his gaze but I could feel it. "When did I say AKA was working alone?"

I looked at his serious face and my headache returned. I didn't need to hear this crap right now.

"So, this did have something to do with me being there?" I asked.

"Not likely."

"I thought you just said—"

"I said AK isn't working alone," Zeus interrupted. "I didn't say this was an attack against you, personally."

"What makes you think it wasn't?" I asked.

"First, whatever you saw falling onto the stadium wasn't grenades. They were just distractions. You might not have been thinking about it, but there is a huge net that separates the crowd from the baseball field at Hunnicutt. Those things were distractions whatever they were. All the damage came from under the bleachers. The stands exploded upward and outward, not inward."

I had forgotten about the net at Hunnicutt. It was there and always had been. I felt stupid for overlooking something that obvious.

"So what does that mean?" I asked.

"That means, that whoever set the blast to go off, didn't have a specific target. They just wanted to cause a panic and blow shit up. If AKA was after you, he would have got you. That's just how he works. If he's random, he's random. If he has a target, he has a target. That's how it works with him. So far at least."

"I don't get it. Why would he do that?"

"Cause he's getting bored. He's not getting the attention he wants. You haven't seen a lot of this stuff on the news, have you?"

"No. Not a lot."

"That's because I've been working hard to keep it quiet."

"Why?" I asked getting more and more confused by Zeus's methods.

"I wanted to agitate him. You don't get it, Ezra, this guy doesn't make mistakes often, if at all. I need to piss him off so he makes mistakes, and refusing him his spotlight, is the best way to do that. Chasing a serial killer is a lot like following breadcrumbs. I need the bastard to drop some breadcrumbs. Do you know what I've been doing the past couple of weeks?"

"Hunching some girls around town?" I said offering my honest opinion.

"Well, yeah, but I've also been doing fieldwork. You know, real detective shit. I've scouted just about every hotel in Princeton and Bluefield. I've checked out most car dealers for recent cash purchases. Went through files and info on the victims, looking for possible connections. There aren't any, by the way. I've been busting my ass on this."

I could tell by the way Zeus talked that he was a little offended that I thought he wasn't doing anything. I started to apologize, but he stopped me before I could get a word out, like he knew what I was going to say and was already forgiving me.

"Do you think he'll go after our brother or sisters?"

Zeus sighed deeply like the question drained him. "I doubt it," he said after a brief pause. "I hardly talk to Isis, she's been pissed at me since our mom died. I've talked to Val, like what, ten times since she was born. I'm not sure I would recognize Israel if I saw him, it's been so long. How old are Val and Israel now anyway?"

"Val's seventeen and Israel is fifteen."

"See, I didn't even know that. AK won't go after them. It wouldn't hurt me enough if he did."

"You know, if I suddenly wasn't your favorite brother, I wouldn't mind."

"Sorry. Too late," he said and we both laughed at a joke that shouldn't have been funny.

"What do we do now?" I asked.

Zeus pulled himself up from the steps and I followed suit. "We don't do any thing. I've got somewhere to be and you need to go in your apartment and lose your virginity," he said wiping the dust off he had gathered from the steps.

"I'm not a virgin."

"As long as it's been since you got some, believe me, you classify as a born-again virgin."

"Whatever. You look tired, you gonna make it where you going?"

"Hell yeah, I'm gonna make it. You ain't hiding behind me. Go pop your cherry."

"Just because I don't need to have sex every day doesn't mean—"

"I don't wanna hear it," Zeus said interrupting me. "If you want the girl to think you're gay, that's your business."

I rolled my eyes and didn't press the issue. Zeus gave me a hug before he left, and I went back into my apartment, when something Zeus said echoed in my mind. He said that he needed AKA to drop some breadcrumbs. I forgot to ask if he had found any.

# CHAPTER 27

## CAMARA

Camara lay on Ezra's bed and doubted that he would come in. She hadn't heard him come back in the apartment, yet. She was curious about what Zeus had to tell Ezra at this time of night, but wasn't about to spy on them. She wasn't that nosey.

She became tired of waiting for something that likely wouldn't happen and was about to go to sleep, when her cell phone rang. She picked it up without looking.

"Hello," she said expecting to hear her mother on the other end.

"Are you okay?"

Camara sprung up in the bed recognizing the sound of the voice. "Snap!"

"Aww, you don't call me Tarquan no more."

"Didn't you tell me not to?" Camara felt herself getting angry and tried to keep her voice down.

"Doesn't mean I don't like hearing you say it."

"You really have snapped. Why are you calling me? How did you get this number?"

"Don't worry. This isn't about my money. That's not why I'm calling."

"I don't have your damn money. How the hell did you plant that shit in my car? I don't know what type of game you're playing, Snap, but it isn't funny."

"You don't hear me laughing. I just wanted to make sure your new man was treating you right. He looks soft. Fool looks like SpongeBob. Maybe I should have some of my boys tough'n him up for you."

Camara could feel Snap's cold, calculating, arrogant face bearing down on her as if he was in the room. It sent a chill down her spine.

"Was that you? Did you blow up Hunnicutt?" she said with all her anger catching in her throat, still trying to keep quiet.

"Don't worry, I'll give SpongeBob six months, too. See what type of love jones you catch in that time."

"I hate you," Camara said into the phone meaning it with everything she had. "What do you want from me?"

"You should already know. You'll soon find out," Snap said then hung up.

Camara was so mad she couldn't stand it. A tear rolled down her cheek and she tried to gain her composure as she heard Ezra come back into the apartment.

He came to the doorway and asked, "Are you okay?"

"I'm fine," Camara lied. "I'll be better, if you come in the bed with me." Camara looked at him, letting him know what she wanted. What she needed.

It was dark so she couldn't see his face, but she heard a deep sigh come from his core. "There's things we need to talk about first." Ezra said. "Sleep in here tonight, please. We'll talk in the morning. Okay."

"Okay," Camara said trying to hide the sting of rejection she felt.

Ezra gently shut the door and when it closed, Camara threw herself back on the bed. *One man was too damn rotten and the other was too damn nice.* Life wasn't fair.

Camara stared up into the darkness of the ceiling and wondered how long Ezra was in the apartment before he shut the door. Had he heard any of her conversation?

# CHAPTER 28

Glorious. Absolutely glorious. There was no way the people of this town could deny him now. Everything would finally start to move faster now. He had already secured locations for up to five different safe houses with dozens of routes to get to each.

He was ready.

He went back to room 7F one last time. Just to pour his energy into the room. Let his spirit resonate in the atmosphere for the next dimwit to feel. He wondered if anyone would realize that for a time this was the epicenter of all the fires and butchery that plagued this pathetic town for weeks.

He checked out of his hotel room and packed up what little he had left and moved to the car, which would have to be replaced soon. He felt invigorated like a basketball player after a good game. He couldn't wait to see his "stats" in the paper. How many injured? How many killed?

It didn't take long to get to his new home, his new epicenter on Union Street. His new day-to-day disguise was a caramel complexioned African-American. Not much was needed for this ruse. Only some simple skin pigmentation, a shorter cut of his natural hair and the hue of his own eye color. A few artificial tattoos rounded out the look nicely.

Some of the neighbors had even come over to introduce themselves. It was easy enough to make them think he was who they wanted him to be. The house was small, two bedrooms, which was more than he really needed. The cops would be checking the hotels soon. New home owners will catch red flags from the police, too, but he was confident that he would have time before he would have to move again.

Everything was in the house and in the process of being organized into the things he would have to take with him as opposed to things he could discard if he needed to leave in a hurry. Then the unexpected happened. The doorbell rang.

The killer put a knife in his hand, a Glock in the back of his pants, and went to the door. He peeped through the door as a wicked smile formed on his mouth. He tucked his shirt over the gun and held on to the knife behind the door, so it wouldn't be seen.

"What's up, shortie?" he said and let the words come out naturally.

"Hello, um my name's Ashley. I live two houses up the street," said a young black girl, no more than eighteen. She was a little overweight and wore glasses, but had a nice rack, which judging by her top, she didn't seem shy about showing off.

"What's up, Ashley? Your momma know you over a stranger's house late at night?"

"I'm grown enough to be where I want, when I want," she said doing her best grown woman impression.

"And what do you want here, Ashley?" he said looking her body over. His gaze resting on the youthful, perky breasts on display.

"Just wanted to let you know where to find me. I've been watching you. Now you can watch back."

"And what if I ain't interested in just watch'n?"

"Then you know where and when to find me," the teenager said licking her lips. Then she turned and walked away. She stopped when she got on the sidewalk and turned. "Hey, what's your name?"

"Larnell Odom," he said with out hesitation. It was as good a name as any.

"Be seeing you, Larnell," the girl said before walking off for good this time.

Larnell was excited. Everything always fell into place for him. Everything always turned out perfect. He pulled his lighter out of his pocket and watched his god dance for him. It was all about patience now.

He wondered how long he should wait before killing little Ashley.

# CHAPTER 29

???

Little Miss Ashley had Larnell's adrenaline pumping with enthusiasm. She was a superb example of how easy things were here. People ran to him like lambs to the slaughter. They wanted to die. Thinking about the people in this town sent chills up and down his spine. He got goosebumps thinking about his grand exit. He knew it would be glorious. He just had to be patient.

It was five in the morning as Larnell drove to his storage garage in Bramwell. He had been waiting for things to progress to this stage. Now things were going to really get fun. The bombing of Hunnicutt Sports Complex should have been the last straw for those idiots of Mercer County. There would be more searching now. People would be more vigilant, too.

Not that he was scared of them. The main reason for his change in methods was that fire was his favorite way to kill and terrorize. He didn't want it to lose its luster. He didn't want it to become routine.

He got to the storage building, opened the pad lock, and raised the metal door. A smile formed on the edge of Larnell's lips as he flipped the switch to turn on a single light in the garage. The red and yellow cab he bought sat perfectly in its spot, just as he left it. He went through the trouble of creating a dummy cab company and even painted the logo and designs on the cab himself.

Larnell walked around the cab and admired every inch of it. He wondered how many people would die in the back seat before this method would have to be discarded. His cab. His death machine.

# CHAPTER 30

### EZRA

I needed to get out of Bluefield for a couple of days after the Hunnicutt bombing. I packed enough stuff for a weekend and headed to the capital of West Virginia to visit my older sister. Isis and I talk regularly but I hadn't seen her for months. Everything going on in the Field, was as good an excuse as any to make the almost two-hour trip to Charleston.

One day after the bombing, the town was already engrossed in the story. It was only speculation on their part, but the media started to point the finger at local gangs in the neighborhood. Gangs in Bluefield now-a-days weren't much to speak of, nothing like they were in the mid-nineties. Even when things were at their worst in places like Tiffany Manor, things never got to this level of terrorism.

The media had it all wrong and I couldn't really blame them. The thought that one man could terrorize a whole town like this wouldn't have crossed my mind if not for Zeus. The media had also blown the lid open on just about every murder, rape, kidnapping, and fire that occurred in the last three months. I think Camara had a hand in that. They started trying to track down all the victim's family members to interview them. That's when I decided to take a quick sabbatical from the Field. I talked to Lois about it and she understood.

It was dark by the time I got to MacCorkle Avenue where Isis owned and lived out of a nice-sized tattoo shop. That building was her pride and joy, and I was proud of her for accomplishing her dream. I can't think of anyone else I knew who would go after a goal the way Isis did. She did a lot of hustling to get what she had, and be where she was.

I pulled up to the tattoo shop and read the sign I designed for her. *Isis Ink,* the sign said in red and black lettering. The shop was closed for the night, but the door was open. All

I had to carry was one medium-sized duffle bag that read, Promise Fighting. I didn't want to be gone too long. Being absent from the Field too long now would raise even more eyebrows. I knew Wilson was still having me followed. I could only imagine what he thought of my trip, but I didn't care.

I didn't bother to turn on the light, as I walked in the shop and locked the door behind me. I had been here to help Isis with most of the initial set up of the shop, so I knew the layout. I went to the door in the back of the shop and climbed the steps that led to Isis's apartment.

I knocked twice on the door to announce my presence, then went in.

"Isis. Where you at, girl?" I said with a smile already on my face.

I walked down the hallway leading to the main bedroom and was caught by surprise from behind me.

"Aaaaahhh!" I heard a scream just as someone jumped on my back and wrapped their arms and legs around me. I wasn't ready for the sudden weight, and we both crashed to the ground.

I heard a familiar laugh and turned behind me to see my big sister. She really caught me by surprise. She's usually not this wired up.

"You're happy to see me, aren't you?" I said sitting up to give her a hug.

"You have no idea," she said.

We both laughed and joked around for a bit. It was fun to act silly around Isis. She had a way of making me feel like we were little kids again even though our childhoods weren't that great.

Once we stopped acting like we were seven years old again, I placed my duffle bag in her spare bedroom.

It was good to see Isis. She had on a pair of shorts and a black sports bra. She had cut her hair almost bald a few years ago in an attempt to go "all natural" and it had grown back out. Her hair was now in dozens of little twists that ran backward. Her skin was a shade or two darker than mine, and I noticed she had added a few new tattoos. She had a few patterns running down her left leg, and it looked like she had tatted her waist just below the belly button.

"Were you about to work out or something?" I asked.

"Yep. P90X. Just got finished. I was about to jump in the shower, when I heard Dirty Vegas pull up. You hungry?"

"Yeah, now that you mention it. I haven't eaten anything since last night."

"I've got some food for you in the microwave and there's some leftovers in the refrigerator. I'm stink'n like a hog monkey. I really need to shower."

"I can smell, and I agree with you. When did you start working out?" I asked. "You never liked to workout before."

"I was getting lazy and getting fat," Isis said patting her freshly formed four pack. I found her statement hard to believe because Isis had always been skinny as a rail. She's my big sister, but only in age. She's five-five and had never weighed more than a buck twenty. I shot her a look, signaling my disbelief that she was getting "fat."

"Okay, okay I wasn't getting fat, but I was really out of shape. It didn't take me long to get back into a routine. I'm not trying to get buff, just cut, you know."

"Let me see what you got," I said like I had doubted her progress.

Any doubts I had, false or otherwise, were quickly shut down as Isis went into full flexing positions like she was a professional bodybuilder. She winced up her face and grunted like a mini She-Hulk. She had made progress, and in a short time. After several seconds, neither of us could hold a straight face and we burst out laughing. I was impressed by Isis. She looked like she stepped out of the pages of a Marvel comic book, just without the oversized breasts.

"And I'm not on anything either. I'm all natural," she said with a wink, obviously proud of herself.

"Never doubted you."

"I'm going to hop in the shower, help yourself. I'll be right out."

While Isis was gone, I raided her cabinets and refrigerator. She had several dishes that looked like she had cooked herself. Indian recipes that she must have gotten from her college friends. I helped myself and downed most of the food before Isis finally joined me at the table. She had on an orange Virginia Tech shirt with maroon VT shorts.

Isis made her own plate and we talked, laughed, and just had a good time. She showed me the new decorations she had in her apartment, which I had somehow missed. I'm usually very observant, but my hunger must've given me tunnel vision. She had painted the walls a medium mauve—a big improvement on the bright yellow that was there when she moved in. There were also several African and Indian style statues and paintings throughout the apartment. The fashion and layout of Isis's apartment was very much her, but it was also a homage to the friends she had meet from different parts of the world while in college.

We didn't talk about the bombing at Hunnicutt or the killings happening in Bluefield lately. She tried to bring it up once, but I could tell she thought better of it. She could see that I didn't want to discuss it before the words left her mouth. That was one of the many things Isis was good at. She was a seer.

"You talk to dad lately?" she asked more to keep the conversation going than anything.

"He hasn't called me. I haven't called him," I said curtly.

"Well, you should. At least check to make sure he's alive, once in a while. Just swallow your pride and call him. I know you want to."

"And, what makes you think that?"

Isis pointed to my duffle bag.

"You're carrying a Promise Fighting bag. What does that tell you?"

"That it was the only bag I had to carry my stuff in."

"You and dad were real close at one point, Ezra. What happened?"

I didn't have an answer for that, so I didn't offer one. Things got complicated between my dad and me, before my mom died and had gotten worse after her death. I hadn't talked to anyone about it, and I knew Isis was concerned. Zeus was too, but he wouldn't drill me about it.

"At least go talk to the man, Ezra. It could do you some good. Maybe put some things in perspective," Isis said implying that she knew why I was here, why I was getting away, without having to be told. I hate it when she does that.

I avoided her gaze and my eyes were drawn to a pair of nunchucks on the wall above the stereo system at the far end of her living room. They were the solid metal type that could screw together. If I didn't know what they were, I would just think it was a metal cylinder hanging on the wall.

"You keep them? I thought you hated those things. You told dad you wanted a sword and wouldn't touch the them," I said laughing, remembering when dad had given her the nunchucks when we were kids.

"After he explained his reasoning for why he gave them to me, I didn't mind as much. I still wanted a sword and was pissed when he gave you one instead."

That was one of the things that never really made sense to me. Dad gave all of us weapons when we were young. Each of us got a different one. I would have to ask him about that one day.

"You ever wonder why dad tried to make us all ninjas when we were little?" I asked.

Isis smiled at me the way she does when she knows something I don't. I hated it when she did that, too.

"No. He told me. If you go see him, he might tell you too."

# CHAPTER 31

## CAMARA

Camara was excited to go to work today. She couldn't believe it, but she was. This job had started to turn into more than she had ever imagined. The bombing of Hunnicutt Sports Complex was on News Channel 6 and had attracted more attention to the other crimes happening in Bluefield. Thanks to her investigation!

Once the news broke about a possible link of the crimes to the bombing, people started to come forward. Several women reported being raped, and cold murders cases that had been closed were being reopened. Camara couldn't believe it. She was making a difference. All the nights of reading through old newspapers and countless interviews were finally paying off.

Suddenly, the news was a big thing in Bluefield. Camara felt like there was a spotlight on everything she wrote. Everyone was reading the paper. The Bluefield Daily Telegraph had never sold more papers. Camara felt a little overwhelmed because Mrs. Cervantes wouldn't let her drop the story even if she wanted to. Once things got this big, she had expected to be brushed aside, but Cervantes words were fresh in her ear: "You started it. You're going to finish it or quit."

Quitting wasn't an option right now, so Camara did her best investigative reporter act and hit the streets. Over the next couple of days, she drove the streets of Princeton and Bluefield. She interviewed as many of the people who were at the Hunnicutt bombing as possible. She talked with every rape victim over the last three to four months that would talk to her again. She hated bothering them but she wanted to be sure she hadn't missed any important details.

This was all new to her, and she didn't really know what to do. Mrs. Cervantes had pretty much thrown her out on her own. *This is your job now. Get it done.* Camara thought. She had compiled a lot of information over the past two days, more than she thought possible. Thankfully, she was organized. Her desk was covered with notes and scribbles of ideas. She was trying to connect the dots with everything that had been happening but was starting to doubt there were any connections to be found. Everything seemed so random. There had to be a link; Camara could feel it.

Ezra had come to Camara's mind several times. He had told her that he would be visiting his sister in Charleston for a few days and wanted to know if she could cover for him. She liked that he wasn't always available for some reason. She liked that he didn't crowd her or push himself on her like most men. She couldn't afford to think about him all the time; she didn't need to be thinking about him at all. For now she had her job and some days that was more than enough.

Someone had contacted Camara and said they had documented proof that the bombings, murders and rapes were connected. Camara had major doubts that the tip would pay off, but she still decided to follow up on it. Up until now, she just had the town talking about her suspicions, but now she needed some proof or she would be laughed out of town.

The contact had wanted to meet her at the old parking center on Bluefield Avenue. Camara wasn't scared, but she knew it wasn't smart to go by herself, so she asked Nate Goodman to go with her. Luckily, he was available and more than happy to tag along.

"You think this is going to pan out to be much of anything?" Nate asked as Camara pulled up to the parking center.

"Probably not, but I should at least follow up. If you ask me, this whole thing is crazy. This stuff is suppose to happen in big cities, not Bluefield, West Virginia. When I took this job, I thought I would be writing about Bluegrass concerts and an occasional DUI."

"You would've been several months ago. I don't know what's happening to this town," Nate said. He was starting to feel nervous, his eyes constantly darting back and forth checking the parking lot. Camara started to think it might have been better to just come by herself.

Camara pulled into a space and they got out of the car. They walked side by side in the dark towards the parking center. Camara was focusing on her breathing, making sure it was calm and steady. Her hands moved to the small of her back to check her Glock. She didn't expect anything to happen, but she wasn't going to be unprepared. She also adjusted her jacket and ran a hand through her braids so Nate wouldn't be suspicious that she was packing.

It was dark on the street. This section of Bluefield Avenue wasn't very well lit, but it was even darker in the parking center. Camara wasn't sure, but if she had to guess, she would say the center must've been built in the seventies. It was a pale, baby blue color and several sections were rusting away. There weren't many lights in the center, and even fewer that worked. This space was never made with the intention of being used at night. Nobody parks here anymore. The only reason it had been maintained at all was for the flea market sales held here on Fridays and Saturdays in the summer months.

Camara now thought that it was a really good idea that she switched her heels out for some tennis shoes. She had on her most comfortable jeans and a jacket with a black And 1 shirt that belonged to her brother underneath.

As they walked farther into the parking center, Nate looked more and more nervous. His breathing was becoming ragged and his movements were stiff and jagged. Camara was starting to worry about him. She could tell he was sweating and thought that if she could see his face in the dark, it would be blood red.

Camara pulled out two small flashlights from her jacket pocket and handed one to Nate.

"Are you going to be okay?" she asked.

"Yeah. Yeah, I'm fine. How far into this thing do you have to go to meet this guy?"

"Third floor."

Thanks to the flashlights Camara saw the look of horror that exploded onto Nate's face. "Third floor! Are you crazy? You're not really going that far up there, are you?"

"Keep your voice down!" Camara said signaling Nate to hush. "Not much choice. I'm not sure if it was okay that I brought someone with me or not, so no more outbursts. The voice didn't say come alone. Just come with me to the second floor, I'll take it from there."

Nate looked a little relieved. Camara couldn't help wonder how Ezra would react in this situation. Nate had turned out to be a decent friend, but he was proving himself to be a bit of a chicken shit in a crunch. That was good though. It's always a good thing to know what people are capable of, how they react when the pressure's on. She doubted she would ask Nate to help with things like this in the future.

They reached the apex of the second floor and Nate hung back. If needed, he was in the perfect position to either run to Camara's aid or run like hell out of the parking center. Camara questioned which he would do if the choice had to be made.

Camara placed her gun in her right jacket pocket and had the flashlight in her left. The center was empty and drafty and she was already starting to get annoyed. She wanted this over with. *Ten minutes.* If no one showed up in ten minutes, she was leaving no matter what. Damn the story. This was probably someone's idea of a joke, anyway.

It didn't take three minutes before she heard a voice call out to her from the darkest corner of the complex.

"Camara Johnson?" a cold mechanical voice echoed across the center.

Camara turned her flashlight in the direction the voice had come from. As she did, she saw a person in a long trench coat and hat, like you see in old school detective movies. She couldn't tell if the person was standing up straight or slouching over. The voice was being masked with some type of device that made it impossible to tell if the person was male or female, and the coat also hid the figure of the person.

Camara didn't like this. She felt exposed. Her informant had total anonymity, which meant either they didn't trust her or they had something to hide.

"You already know who I am. You called me here, remember?" Camara said. Her voice was strong and steady. She was sure there wasn't a hint of fear in her words and she was proud of that.

"Are you alone?" the electronic voice asked. There was nothing to give off what the person was thinking. No body language. No emotion. Nothing. There was only a cold, electronic impartiality.

Camara decided to go with her gut and answered the question truthfully.

"No. I'm not," Camara said as if the answer to the question was obvious and didn't need to be asked.

A faint cackle came from the informant in the corner that Camara took to be a laugh. Camara keep her light on the person in the corner and listened. She didn't interrupt and wouldn't, unless she needed to.

"Very good, Miss Johnson. Your answer to that question just set the stage for our meeting and any that may be forthcoming. Although, I must admit that I hope the occasions for us to meet like this prove to be few and far between.

"I can tell this situation is making you uncomfortable, so I'll make this quick. Allow me to start off by thanking you for your coming and thanking you for your honesty. Honesty is important between co-workers, don't you agree? Until this madman is caught, I think it would behoove the town of Bluefield if we become co-workers. This man needs to be caught or he will move to another town, just like this one, and continue his senseless slaughter of innocents.

"The first way to stop him is to prove his existence to the people. You see Miss Johnson, this man is like the devil incarnate. The greatest trick the devil ever played on mankind was for him to make man think he didn't exist. Even though, they see the devil's work, they still choose to deny his existence. The same will happen here, unless people are provided with proof. This killer does exist, Miss Johnson, and it's time people knew as I, and now you, know."

The person in the corner reached into their coat to pull out something. Camara was on edge listening to every word. Just about every word spoken raised questions. Camara was more confused now than she was before. She felt like she knew less now than before this 'meeting' began. Her right hand was ready for whatever was about to be pulled out by the informant, and her left kept the light steady. Her eyes didn't leave the informant.

Then the figure pulled out a large brown envelope from their coat and held it up for Camara to see.

"You told me the truth, Miss Johnson, so I'll return the courtesy. Do not let anyone read this right away. Do not put the findings here into tomorrow's paper. Keep this for your eyes only until certain events occur. You'll know when to release this information. If you believe nothing I say, believe what I tell you now. I will contact you again in the same manner as I did this time." the electronic voice echoed again through the complex before kneeling down and sliding the package over to Camara. "Be careful what, and who you trust, Miss Johnson."

Camara followed the package with her flashlight as it stopped at her feet. When she raised her light back to the corner where her informant had stood, no one was there. Camara searched the area with her light, but saw no one.

Camara picked up the package placed it inside her jacket, and zipped it up concealing it. She reached Nate, by this time his face was cherry red, and he was drenched in his own sweat.

"What happened? I could only hear some scary robot voice. What did it say? Did it give you anything?" Nate asked with nervous anticipation and excitement.

"Yea, but none of it made any sense to me," Camara said honestly enough.

"Well, did they give you anything? Any proof?" Nate asked again, as they got into the car.

"Didn't give me anything," Camara said as she pulled onto the avenue. "I think this was a wild goose chase."

# CHAPTER 32

## CAMARA

Camara wasn't sure how she felt about lying to Nate about the information she had been given. He had, in a sense, stuck his neck out for her. After seeing him sweat like a hog, she felt he was probably entitled to know something. But Camara wasn't ready to share. Not until she understood what she had, anyway.

Once she got home, she opened the envelope. The information inside blew her mind. She couldn't believe it, she didn't want to. It didn't seem possible for someone to have this much information on the killer. Names of missing people, rape victims, murdered people. There were times and dates—just an impossible amount of information—about the killer's patterns and movements over the past several years.

Camara got on her mother's computer and confirmed as much of the information as she could, which wasn't much. She had never been good at internet research. Some people just had a knack for that type of thing, but she definitely wasn't one of them. She wasn't sure what she was supposed to do. This stuff couldn't just be put in the paper without validation, and for some reason, she didn't want to take it to the Bluefield Police. This just seemed too big for the local authorities. Something had to be done with this information though, but who could it be given to?

Thinking about it was starting to give Camara a migraine. It reminded her why she didn't want a career in journalism. She never wanted to be Lois Lane—there was never a Superman around in the real world when you needed him. This was too much responsibility for her.

In the morning, Camara organized everything into a folder and left it at home while she went to work. She thought about telling Mrs. Cervantes about the package but was hesitant.

When Camara sat down at her desk at the Telegraph, she found a letter addressed to her. Her name was handwritten on the outside and the rest of the letter was typed. The first thing she thought was that it might be some type of assignment from Cervantes or maybe something from Ezra, but the handwriting looked wrong.

She put her things down and read the note, but immediately wished she hadn't. She wished she hadn't noticed it at all. Camara didn't have to go chasing the killer anymore. The killer just found her.

# CHAPTER 33

## CAMARA

Camara didn't have any choice other than to take this to Cervantes. She rushed into the editor's office with urgency written on her face.

"Is there something I can do for you, Miss Johnson?" Mrs. Cervantes asked, her annoyance evident in every word. "This had better be good for you to barge into my office that way."

"This was on my desk," was the only explanation Camara offered as she presented the letter to her boss.

Mrs. Cervantes snatched the letter from Camara's hand but held her tongue. Camara knew there would be trouble if Cervantes felt what she read wasn't worth her while, but she knew that wouldn't be the case. Mrs. Cervantes read the whole letter before looking up at Camara again.

"This was on your desk?"

"Yes," Camara answered knowing that she had already told her that.

"When did you get here?"

"Walked in the door about five minutes ago."

Mrs. Cervantes looked at the letter again and rose from her seat. "Stay right here. I'll be back," she said without looking at Camara as she exited the office.

It didn't take ten minutes for Mrs. Cervantes to round up Lois Thompson, head of the production department, and Kim Kohls from the front desk. Mrs. Cervantes also brought in a man named Jack Napier and a woman named Travonne Berry. Jack was the paper's managing editor. He was a reasonably attractive man in his early forties and appeared to be in good shape. His hair was blond and slightly graying at the temples. Travonne was the news editor. She was a woman who looked like she had just hit her thirties but was still turning heads. She had long red hair and bright green eyes. Camara had remembered seeing all of them around the office before, but she didn't know exactly what their jobs were. They introduced themselves to Camara and asked her to address them by their first names. Camara liked them both almost instantly.

Once Mrs. Cervantes assembled everyone, she shut the door, and took her seat at her desk. It was clear to Camara as everyone stood in the small office, that none of them had a clue what this was about. Everyone waited for the announcement, hoping to hear a good explanation for this impromptu meeting. Mrs. Kohls was the oldest, so no one minded giving her the only other seat in the office.

Camara stood against the far wall opposite Mrs. Cervantes's desk and listened to her start to explain. She began in an overly dramatic fashion as Camara knew she would.

"We have a very important decision to make, ladies and gentlemen, and it may very well affect the town, the state, or possibly the entire nation." It took all of Camara's strength to avoid rolling her eyes at Mrs. Cervantes's opening statement. She didn't know how many impulses like that she could suppress.

Mrs. Cervantes held the letter in front of her, told everyone what it was and where it came from, as far as she knew anyway, then began to read the letter aloud.

*To whomever is investigating the recent arsons, rapes, kidnappings and murders in the Mercer County area, allow me to make your job less difficult. You see, I am all of these rolled into one. I am your fire starter. I am your taker of innocents. I am you abductor of children. I am your killer. I am AKA, for I have many names. This letter is my "coming out" announcement. My grand reveal. Too long have I lived in the shadows with no one to admire my work, with no one as my equal. So I've decided to come home and make my presence known. To prove I am everything I say I am, you can find the bodies of Nick Cooper and*

*Charles Dwight at the bottom of Jimmy Lewis Lake in Nemours, West Virginia. If this letter is not printed in tomorrow's edition of the Telegraph, in its entirety, I will set fire to twenty houses in Bluefield the following night and give birth to my god in a way none in this pathetic town has ever seen. The killings may continue after that or they may not. It's up to this pathetic town to decide.*

When she was finished reading, she fell silent giving the words time to resonate in the room. Kim looked to be on the verge of tears. Travonne looked in shock and Jack's face was tight and stern. His jaw was clenched and his hands were curled into sledgehammers. Camara thought he was seconds away from punching a hole in the wall.

When Mrs. Cervantes was sure the words had sunk in with everyone, she began to speak. As she spoke, she looked at and only addressed Kim. She folded the note neatly and carefully, holding it up for Kim to see before asking: "Who delivered this? Who put this on Camara's desk?"

Kim was fighting the tears back but quickly losing the battle.

"I did," she said weakly. Kim started to sob more openly after catching everyone's attention with her answer. We waited for her to regain her composure so she could offer some type of explanation. "A nice little African-American girl came to the paper. She was already here when I got here this morning. She said she was Camara's niece and had a letter that she had to deliver from her mother. I didn't pay her much attention. I just took the note and placed it on Camara's desk. It had her name on it after all. I didn't think nothing of it."

Mrs. Cervantes looked at Kim like she was crazy then asked, "Jesus, Kim, why are you crying? Nobody's accusing you of anything."

"This is going to be all my fault. If I would've just been paying attention, I could maybe point the girl out and help the police catch the killer. Now, people are going to die and it's all my fault." Kim started to weep again.

Mrs. Cervantes sighed deeply. "Kim, take the rest of the day off."

"Oh my God, you're firing me. I knew it! Oh, God! I'm so sorry!"

It took Mrs. Cervantes five minutes to convince Kim that she wasn't fired and that nobody blamed her. Once Kim had finally left the office, Travonne and Jack still hadn't said a word. There was a long pause before Mrs. Cervantes finally broke the silence.

"I brought the two of you in here because I want your opinions. I know this is a shock, but we don't have much time. We need to do something, now. If this is going to run in tomorrow's paper, the decision to do it needs to be made now. What do you think, Jack?" Mrs. Cervantes said as she faced her managing editor.

"Don't print it," Jack said through gritted teeth.

"What?" Travonne said suddenly snapping out of the haze she was in. "Didn't you hear what it said? He's going to kill more people if we don't print it."

"Weren't you listening to what it said? He's going to kill people whether we print it or not. Why give in to him? We need to try and find that girl who delivered this and make her talk. We don't even know if this is real. It could be a sick high school joke for all we know."

"What about the children he said were at the bottom of Jimmy Lewis Lake? What are we going to do about that, Jack?"

"We give the information to the police and have them search the lake. If they find the bodies, then we'll know there's some truth to the letter."

"What the hell is wrong with you?" Travonne said. It was obvious her emotions were starting to get to her. "How can you be so cold? These are children we're talking about. More people could die."

"I know who we're talking about. I'm just saying, that if they find something, then we know the letter has some truth to it. That's all I said." Jack raised his hands in a defensive jester. "We can't print something this big without knowing if it's real. It's just not a good idea. It's down right irresponsible."

"There's no way the police can organize a search of the lake before the deadline to make print for tomorrow," Mrs. Cervantes said cutting in on the conversation. "Another reason I brought everyone in here was because any backlash from this will fall on us. This could only hurt Jack and Travonne on a professional level, but everyone in Bluefield will point the finger at Camara and me."

"Me?" Camara said. Up until this point, she was happy to just stand off to the side and listen to the bigwigs talk their talk. She really didn't expect to be drawn into this. "Why would people point the finger at me?"

Mrs. Cervantes looked Camara squarely in the eye and said, "Well, dear, because if we print this story you're going to write it. Saying 'Take it to print, but I don't want to write it' is the same as saying 'I quit' as far as I'm concerned."

"Well, if that's true, Mrs. Cervantes, then I think it should be my decision if the story goes to print or not. The letter was on my desk so I should have a say so on what happens with it." Camara wasn't sure how that would go over with Mrs. Cervantes. After a few tense seconds and a stare-down competition, Mrs. Cervantes leaned back into her chair. How Camara had won was beyond her.

"Very well, Miss Johnson. What do you think we should do?"

Camara could feel Jack and Travonne's eyes on her. She had their full attention as well as Mrs. Cervantes's. She did her best to ignore both Jack and Travonne, and chose to focus her answer completely in Mrs. Cervantes's direction.

"There are too many mistakes in the letter. I didn't catch them at first, but I picked up on some things when you were reading it. First it says 'To whoever is investigating,' but as we all see, it was addressed to me and everyone knows I'm the one investigating them.

"Second, they say that they 'are coming home' by being in Bluefield, and then they say this is their 'grand reveal.' Well, an announcement in the paper doesn't seem too grand to me. It's more like an introduction. Third, the way it's written. The hints. They seem deliberate to me. Especially after hearing it read aloud. I think this bastard is planning to set fire to Bluefield tomorrow night if we print this or not. This fucker just wants everyone to know about it first.

"I think we should have the police search the lake and then start trying to figure out how to stop these fires from happening. I'm not going to tell you how to run this paper, Mrs. Cervantes, but I don't think we should print the letter."

Mrs. Cervantes's office was quiet for what Camara thought felt like forever. She wasn't sure how what she said had been taken, but she was sure Travonne thought she was full of it, so she did her best to avoid her gaze.

Again it was Mrs. Cervantes who broke the silence. "Camara."

"Yes, Mrs. Cervantes."

"I'm not going to tell you again to call me Melissa. Now, get this letter to the police. It's evidence."

# CHAPTER 34

## EZRA

I love being around my sister. I wish Isis and I had more time together, but one of us was always caught up in something. We had a lot of fun in Charleston even though the bulk of our time was spent just talking.

We worked out together which was something new for us to do together. We went to the arcade and even wrestled a little, like we used to when we were kids. I used to think she always won our wrestling matches because she was older and bigger than me at the time. I've got a good six inches on her, but she was still about to flip me over her shoulder. Still hurt, too.

I listened to Erika Badu on the trip back to Bluefield. Seeing Isis was good, but I knew I had to stop running from my problems sooner or later. I was still having nightmares about what happened to the girl at Bluefield State. I was worried about little Nick Cooper and Charles Dwight, and my mother was never far from my mind no matter what I did.

I decided to take my sister up on her advice and go visit someone I had been avoiding. I was sure I hadn't seen or talked to him since my mom's funeral. I was going to stop by my apartment first, but instead cut down Mercer Street. I pulled up at Promise Fighting Dojo and sat in my car for several minutes. I had no idea what to say once I saw him. I hadn't called him in so long, but he hadn't called me either. I guess that made us even.

I thought about calling Camara or T. I wanted to check in with Zeus and see if he had dug up anything. Then I heard Isis in my head telling me to stop being a punk and just go in the freaking dojo.

There was no reason for me to stay here all day. Just a quick in and out to make sure the old man was still alive. Besides, how much could have happened in Bluefield since I'd been gone?

# CHAPTER 35

**EZRA**

I walked into the empty lobby of the Promise Fighting dojo and it was like walking through a time portal. Memories of my childhood came rushing back. This dojo opened when I was three and I couldn't remember how many afternoons I spent here.

Several ancient weapons were proudly displayed high enough on the walls of the dojo to be out of reach of the kids, but low enough for them all to take notice. I walked around looking at all of the trophies and mementos won by students. The sound of kids laughing drew my attention to the practice floor.

I peeked though the doorway leading to the practice floor. The dojo instructor looked like he was at the end of a lesson. I stood out of sight and listened.

"Never underestimate any opponent. Never take anything for granted when you're in a fight. Never hold back." The familiar words coming from the instructor made me feel ten all over again.

"This speech is getting old, Sensei Promise," one of the female students in the class rose to her feet and said. "It's always the same."

"Just because it's old doesn't mean it doesn't still apply," Promise said. I could tell he was trying to be polite, holding his tongue at the disrespect.

"Old people always say that. Especially people that are older than color TV," the little girl said to get a laugh from her classmates.

"You're right. I'm old," Promise said with a smile on his face. "I'm not going to try and argue that. I remember when color TVs came out, I remember when calculators came out,

198

and I also remember when your mother used to sell it on the corner for a quarter."

The poor girl must be new to the dojo. Anyone who had been around Promise long enough would have known that was coming. Once the class finished laughing at the girl, Promise finished his speech and dismissed the class.

Promise went into his office. I followed as soon as the class left and the dojo was empty. I almost made it to the door and knocked, but before I could, it burst open and my world was turned upside down, literally. I flew upside down across the dojo. I managed to center myself just enough to gain some control and avoid landing on my head.

I spun around. Promise came barreling at me with every bit of his six foot five, two hundred and fifty pound frame. Promise had trained in almost every fighting style on the planet and had even managed to master a few of them. He was quick and agile for his size. Most wouldn't expect this type of speed from a man his size, but I knew better.

Several blows from his large quick hands came at me with the force and precision of guided missiles. One strike narrowly missed me and created a crater in the plaster wall. I wasn't scared or worried; we had done this dance before. I used my lateral movement, stayed on my heels and blocked or dodged every blow. I was glad that I went to see Isis this past weekend. If I hadn't been sparing with her, I might not have been ready for this and one of Promise's atomic bombs might have connected.

I did a shaky back flip to give myself some space and to prepare to go on the offensive. When I righted myself, Promise was already at a wall on the far side of the dojo. He picked up two kendo sticks and threw one my way. I smiled and caught the kendo stick in mid-air and readied myself for the impending charge. Kendo sticks were a type of wooden sword used in training for combat with real swords. They weren't deadly like real swords, but they still stung like hell. I would spend just as much time in this dojo practicing with these things as any wanna-be-hoop star did on the court with a basketball.

As fast as Promise was, he was no match for me with a kendo stick—hadn't been since I was sixteen. Our stick's clashed with a thunderous echo. It didn't take me long to exploit Promise's weakness in his guard and land a blow to his chest and hand that disarmed him. A final blow to his leg landed him flat on his back.

We were both sweating and breathing hard, me a little more than Promise, which was a little embarrassing since he had just cracked his fifties. The fight lasted about thirty seconds from beginning to end. I stood over Promise and pointed the kendo stick at him. "Hey, dad, I think I won," I said trying to hide just how tired I was.

Promised smiled and laughed. "Damn! Shouldn't have given you the kendo stick."

I couldn't fight back my smile and took the next best thing to a compliment from my dad. "Nope. You shouldn't have."

# CHAPTER 36

"You're out of shape," was the first thing my dad said to me as I helped pull him off the floor.

"I still won," I said reminding him of the fact that he was the one flat on his back not ten seconds ago.

"You're still out of shape and you wouldn't have won if I hadn't brought out those damn sticks. I forgot how good you were with those things. What are you doing here?"

"Just wanted to make sure you were still alive. Haven't talked to you in a while," I said as I followed my dad into his office. "What's with the impromptu sparing match?"

"I had a dream. I knew you would be coming today. You need the practice."

"If you knew I was coming, then why ask what I was doing here?"

"I said I knew you were coming, not why you were coming. There's a difference, Ezra."

"Did your dream tell you to try and give me a concussion?" I asked as I put down the kendo stick and sat in the main office with my dad. His office was spacious and had a huge window looking out into the main entrance. On the walls were Nunchucks Sai's, Sherikin, more commonly known as throwing stars, and other weapons used in martial arts. There were also several pictures of Zeus, Isis, Israel, Val, and myself on the wall. All the pictures were taken when we were younger—happier. A time before we realized that each one of us having different moms, besides Zeus and Isis, was a weird thing. Promise was a good man overall, depending on who you asked. Women were his only real weakness, and for some reason, he never realized his weakness affected more people than just himself, until it was too late.

"As a matter of fact, yes. My dream did tell me to start a fight with you. You need to be sharp. You need to brush up on your swordplay. I'm one hundred percent sure you'll need your fighting skills soon. I saw it in my dream and you know my dreams always come true." My father spoke with utmost confidence. He hadn't told me much about his dreams over the years, but every one he had ever told me did, in fact, come true. I never liked it when he dreamed.

"Well, thanks, I guess. But if you don't mind, I'd rather not get the details."

"Fine by me," he said as he propped his feet up on his desk. "So tell me what brings you here? Isis finally got to you?"

"Maybe."

"It doesn't matter, it's good to see you. I haven't heard from you since the funeral. How are you holding up?"

I'm not sure why but getting into a sparing match with my dad made it easier to open up. I told him how I felt. How lonely I got sometimes. What happened between Eva and me, why we broke up. It was hard to explain how I felt that I was putting more into Eva than I was getting out. Eva was great, but as much as I was able to help her; she couldn't help me. I couldn't grow if I was with her. I regretted staying with her for as long as I did; all I really did was make things worse when we finally split. I said a little about Camara but stayed vague about her. I learned a long time ago not to completely trust my dad's advice when it came to women. I told dad about Zeus and his hunt for a serial killer in the Bluefield-Princeton area. I left out the part about the killer being fixated on me because of what happened at Bluefield State.

He didn't interrupt me and only asked questions that kept me on track and got more details out of me. When I was finished, he took his feet off his desk and sat upright in his chair.

"You're a good man, Ezra. A lot better man than me, I'm proud to say. You're handling all this a lot better than I would. I respect that. I know we've grown apart since you've gotten older, but I want to make sure you know I love you and I'm proud of you. You're a rock. That's your divine ability. You stand strong on who you are and what you believe in. You can lift people's spirits even when you feel like shit yourself. Your faith has always impressed me son.

"But you can't always do it alone. Don't try to be your own rock."

As big and scary as my dad could still be, he could also be just as soft sometimes. It almost made me feel bad for avoiding him for so long.

"I want you to pick up your training," he said in a more serious tone.

"I've been meaning to work out more if that's what you mean," I said slightly confused with his sudden seriousness.

"There was a reason I attacked you back there."

"I know, you told me. Your dream, right?"

Promise leaned in close and zeroed in on my eyes. He had my full attention and he wasn't about to let go. "In my dream you were fighting in a field of fire. You were bloody and broken. You couldn't fight back anymore. Then whoever you were fighting killed you and left your body to burn. All I had to bury were ashes. You got beat because you got stupid, you got angry. You're not Zeus. Don't try to fight like him. Cage and focus your anger or it'll kill you. All of my dreams have come true. Please, don't let this one."

# CHAPTER 37

### EZRA

I left the dojo an hour after I arrived and got into Dirty Vegas. Seeing dad went pretty well after all. We managed to talk about a lot without talking much at all. I was a little unnerved about his dream. Truthfully, it scared the crap out of me, but I wasn't going to let him know that. Still, I was a little mad. I could've sworn I asked him not to give me the details of his dream.

I got in Dirty Vegas and made my way to Pauli Heights. On the way I made a phone call that I should have made a couple of days ago. The phone rang a couple of times before Camara picked up.

"Hello, stranger. I was starting to think you forgot about me." I heard her sweet voice say and my mood instantly lightened. I didn't realize how much I'd missed the sound of her voice.

"How could I forget you?"

"I was asking myself the same question." I could almost feel her smiling on the other end.

"What are you doing today?" I asked.

"A lot. I don't want to talk about it over the phone though. I'll be done by two hopefully."

"I was thinking we should do something today."

"That's possible. What did you have in mind? I had my wonderful date. I'm ready for my wild one."

My heart jerked a little when she had said that. Something about the way her silky voice used a suggestive tone had me twisted.

"Good then, I have just the thing in mind."

"Do you now?"

"Yes, I do. Can you meet me at my place at four?"

"Yeah, I can do that. What's the plan? Can a girl get some heads up this time?"

"If I told you, it wouldn't be a surprise."

"Give me a hint," she said. She had a way of sounding sexy on the phone. I couldn't help wonder why I hadn't noticed before, maybe I was just paying more attention. She had the type of voice that makes a man hand over his whole wallet if he's not careful. I almost ended up telling her exactly what I had planned, but caught myself.

"You'll find out soon. I want you to be surprised. I've been wanting to do this with you for a while now. I think you'll like it."

"Ok, now you really have to give me a hint. Come on, just a hint, Ezra. Please."

I liked hearing my name roll off her tongue. "You're going to want to wear a swimsuit. That's all I'm giving you."

Camara let out a sigh of disappointment. "You would've had to tell me that anyway, buster."

"I know. See you at four?" I said masking as much excitement as I could.

"I can't wait," Camara said.

"Four o'clock."

"I'll be there."

# CHAPTER 38

## CAMARA

Camara wished she could've stayed on the phone with Ezra longer. She was on Route 120 on her way to Jimmy Lewis Lake. Route 120 leads through Wolfe, West Virginia, and into Pocahontas. It was a serene and enjoyable drive. The road was covered with trees on both sides and ran parallel to a small creek. The sun broke through the trees and rays of golden light dotted the road. It was a two-lane road with some turns you could speed through and others you had to take your time to get past safely. Camara liked the road because it kept her mind active and focused on what she was doing.

It wouldn't have been long before her cell signal went out this deep into Appalachia, so she had gotten off the phone with Ezra at just the right time. From Bluefield it only took fifteen minutes to get to the Valley in Nemours. The area was quiet and beautiful. Camara could see how people would think this was a nice place to live. She wondered what they would think if the bodies of little Nick Cooper and Charles Dwight were found in their peaceful setting.

By the time Camara got to the lake, police had the place sectioned off and divers were already in the water. Camara was impressed by how fast the search for the bodies had been organized.

She parked her Saturn on the gravel path leading to the lake and walked over to the police blockade. She spotted a friend and waved him over. She waited for Jeff Newman to walk over and talk to her. Jeff was a sergeant on the Bluefield Police force. Camara had met him the day at the park when the heads of two murder victims, Michael and John Douglas, were found in a cooler in Bluefield City Park. He didn't give Camara much information about what happened there that day, but Camara hadn't really asked him to. She asked him a couple of questions, but once she realized that he was attracted to her, she mostly flirted with him. She thought it would be a good idea to butter him up, just in case he was in a position to help her later. Seeing him on the scene had given her some gratification that she could be a shameless flirt.

"You made it here quickly, Miss Johnson," Jeff said. He was in full uniform. His demeanor told others that he was proud of his rank on the police force. He was a little taller than Camara, about five eleven and well built. He had blonde hair cut in a short military style, piercing blue eyes and chiseled features, a strong jaw line and cheekbones. Camara thought he looked young for a sergeant and was much more handsome than any policeman she had ever seen, *He resembles a slightly younger Daniel Craig*, Camara thought after seeing him a second time. She wondered what drove him to work as a small town police sergeant when he could be walking a runway in Paris somewhere.

"I couldn't miss the party when I invited everyone here," Camara said and put on her most flirtatious smile. "I'm surprised you were able to get this together so fast."

"It wasn't my doing. Thank Chief Wilson. He's really upset about this. Really lit a fire under everybody, gave a speech and everything a day or two ago. Gave another one just before the divers set up. Thanks for calling me on this though."

"Thanks for giving my your number so I could call," Camara said folding her arms. She wanted to make sure Jeff noticed that she didn't have a camera or any type of recorder on her. She didn't want him to have a reason to hesitate to talk to her. "Have you heard anything from the people that live near by? Anyone saying anything?"

"We haven't needed to talk to them yet," Jeff said.

"What? Why not?"

Jeff looked around to see if anyone was listening before he spoke. Jeff was very professional and wasn't about to talk to just any reporter drilling him with questions. Camara liked how it made her felt that she had gotten him to warm up enough to talk to her in only one meeting and a phone call.

"Well, we've already found the bodies," Jeff said with a sad expression. Camara thought that he looked like he was hoping not to find anything in the lake.

Camara's eyes were wide with shock. She didn't expect them to find anything either. That fact that they had found the bodies, and so fast, made Camara doubt her judgment to not run the letter from the killer.

"If you've found the bodies, why are people still in the water?" Camara finally managed to say.

Camara stayed quiet while Jeff gave her the details. "I said we found bodies. Not that they were the boys you said we would find. Five divers entered the lake at the same time. The lake isn't that big, so they were going to swim in clockwise circles and work their way to the center. The thing is, as soon as all five divers got in the water, they all found a different body. The total count now is eight and we think that one of them might be Nick Cooper, but we're not sure. The body was badly beaten."

Camara ran her hand through her hair and couldn't believe what she was hearing.

"What makes you think that body was Nick Cooper then?" Camara asked.

"There was a note sealed in a bag. The bag was inside the boy's mouth and his mouth was sewn shut," Jeff said with disgust in his voice.

Camara touched Jeff's shoulder slightly to draw his eyes to hers. "Do you think you can get me a copy of that note? Or at least write down what it says for me?"

Jeff smiled at Camara then looked around at his other officers. Camara could feel the wheel of fortune spinning. She hoped she would come up lucky.

"I'll see what I can do. But, no promises," Jeff said and walked off.

Camara needed to know what the letter said. An overwhelming feeling of guilt was coming over her as she realized that Bluefield might be set to burn tomorrow night. She felt as though she had just lit the fuse herself.

# CHAPTER 39

## EZRA

It wasn't smart of me to be planning a wild date without actually making sure I was able to pull it off. I gave T a call right after I hung up with Camara. I had something specific in mind and needed help to make it happen. I told T my plan and she told me she would see what she could do. I knew she would come through. She always does.

The anticipation of seeing Camara had me more excited than I had been in months. As soon as I put the key in the door, I heard a familiar voice from behind me. It was the last person I was ready to deal with. The voice alone almost ruined my good mood.

"Somebody looks awfully happy. You must have a date," I heard my ex-girlfriend's voice come from the steps leading to the second floor of my apartment. I didn't bother to turn and look at her. I should have just walked inside my apartment, but I knew if I didn't acknowledge her, she might never go away.

I rubbed my eyes and let out a deep sigh. "What are you doing here, Eva?"

"I have something important to talk to you about. You can tell me about your date first—if you like though," she said. Her voice used to sound warm and seductive, now it just made my skin crawl.

I finally turned to look at her. She was standing on the steps wearing five-inch heels and black tights with a long turquoise top that hugged her upper body and came down on her like a miniskirt. The shirt was also sleeveless and cut in a v-neck that would guide any man's eyes to her proudly displayed breasts. Her hair was shorter than last time I saw her, and was also dyed a honey brown. The outfit was so tight

210

on her it showcased every dangerous curve. I knew my lack of expression pissed her off, but I didn't care.

"What do you want?" I asked again.

"You haven't missed me, Easy?" she said walking toward me in slow sultry steps, her hips swaying like she was on a Paris runway.

"Now that you're here, I miss you being gone if that's what you mean." Eva had one of the best bodies I'd ever seen in or outside of any magazine. I was unbelievably attracted to her from the second I laid eyes on her—what man wouldn't be? I thought she was the sexiest girl I'd ever meet. That was up until I really got to know her. Now I wanted to throw a paper bag over her.

I could tell that my remark hurt her a little. She was starting to realize she really didn't have the same place in my heart that she used to.

"Who is that girl you been going out with?" Eva managed to ask as though she had a right to know. "Are you fucking her?"

"I don't have time for you, Eva. You don't even have a reason to be here," I said as a turned toward my apartment.

"After everything we went through together, you really feel like I don't have a reason to be here?"

"No."

"Why, Ezra? What did I do that was so bad?"

"You were cheating on me!"

"You were cheating on me first!"

"That's a lie. I never touched another woman when we were together."

"You may not have cheated physically, but you cheated all the same."

"What are you talking about?"

"Your friend. That white girl. T!"

"Oh, here we go. What, Eva? What about T?"

"I shared everything with you, Ezra. Everything! I told you things that I would never tell any one. I confided in you, but you never opened up to me. You were all too willing to run to your friend Tamra and tell her all your little secrets."

"I met Tamra long before I meet you, Eva."

"That still doesn't give you the right to always but her first. I was dating you— not her. I'm the one in love with you. Why did you let her in where you wouldn't let me?"

"If you loved me, you wouldn't have cheated on me."

"You're a self-righteous prick, Ezra, you know that? Not everyone is as perfect as you. God knows I tried, but I just couldn't measure up to the holy Ezra Walker."

"Stop. Just stop. You're embarrassing yourself. What's wrong with you?"

"Me? What's wrong with you? Think about it, Ezra, just think about it. I told you what I was like before we started dating. I told you! I quit doing a lot of things, I gave up a lot of shit to make you happy. I started going to church with you, I started praying with you, I was willing to give up sex until I was married to you. All I wanted was for you to *really* open up to me, but you couldn't, could you?"

"Why would you do that to me? You turned my world upside down, made me change, fall in love with you, and then locked me out. What the fuck?"

"You don't understand. As much as you say you changed, you never got it. You were holding on to me for your changes, you were losing yourself in me and I didn't want that to happen."

"Bullshit, Ezra! Bullshit!"

"It wasn't about giving up weed or clubbing or sex. It was about spiritual growth, about being a better person. Everything you did, you did for me. That's not the right reason to change your life. We couldn't grow together."

"You mean you couldn't grow when you were busy helping me, right?"

"That's not what I said."

"But it's what you meant. I know you well enough to read between the lines."

"Eva, I don't . . . I don't know what else to tell you."

"Are. You. Fucking. Her?"

"No, I'm not."

"You going to?"

"Why are you doing this? Why are you here? Really?"

"What's wrong with me? Why don't you want me? What is it? Look at me. Every other nigger in this town wants me, why not you? Why wouldn't you have sex with me?"

"It's not all about the physical, Eva, there's more to a relationship than that. You're sexy as hell, but sex alone can't keep a relationship going. I know you tried, but you tried for the wrong reasons. I don't believe in a wife being a better half. You have to be complete with or without your wife. You have to be two complete wholes that complement each other. Being with me you were never going to be your own whole and I wasn't going to grow any more. It wouldn't have worked in the long term."

"So, I'm a bad person."

"I didn't say that."

"A nice ass and perky tits are all I have to offer you."

"I didn't say that either."

"Yes, you did! Yes, you fucking did! I'm a trophy at best. Is that right, Ezra?"

"You're putting words in my mouth."

"I should just fucking kill myself. Is that what you want?" Eva said with tears flowing from her eyes. She was losing it and I didn't know how to help her. Her emotions had taken over and she was only hearing what she wanted to hear no matter what I said.

I couldn't help her. I couldn't get through to her with reason so I started to lose my temper. I knew I shouldn't have, but I couldn't help it. "See Eva, it's that crap right there, that's what made me sick of you." This was maddening. I had too much going on.

I just wanted her to go away, I didn't need any of this now. "You always have to have things your way. You always have to have control. Trying to keep someone around by making them feel sorry for you is childish. You've pulled this death threat stuff before and I'm sick of it. Grow up, Eva!"

"Then help me, Ezra. Stop acting like your own shit doesn't stink! Just because you're not sex-crazed like most guys doesn't make you a fucking saint. You're not perfect! Why do you expect every one else to be? That's why you didn't get along with your own mother! If I kill myself, it will be on your head just like your mom's death was! Can you live with that, Ezra?"

I almost sprung forward and punched her in the face for that. I think the only reason I didn't was because it hurt me more than made me angry. Lies sting. The truth hurts to the core.

I turned and opened the door to my apartment. "Go home, Eva," I said as I started to shut the door.

"Damn you! You really don't care about me enough to even act mad. You're telling me to commit suicide! Is that what you want? You think I won't do it?"

I used to feel bad about how Eva was now. She had been a little unhinged ever since we broke up. I never really thought I could have that effect on a person. My not handling things with her better was something I thought I would regret for a long time, but I honestly didn't care any more. Just like some things can't be undone, some things can't be unsaid. "You've made that threat before, Eva, but you're still here, aren't you?" I said without looking back at her as I walked into my apartment. Then I shut the door.

\*\*\*\*

I wasn't going to let Eva ruin the day I had planned, but she did force images into my mind that I would rather not think about before a date. I thought about my relationship with Eva and how it all went sour. I thought about Nick Cooper and Charles Dwight, the two boys from the Wade Center. I hadn't heard any news on them. I prayed they were all right, but I wasn't too optimistic.

I thought about Isabelle Sparks, the girl from Bluefield State that I couldn't help. The guilt I felt about letting Isabelle die was almost unbearable some times. It wouldn't have been as bad if I didn't know her name or what she had looked like. There had been a memorial service for her at Bluefield State and her funeral was a couple of weeks ago. I thought about going, but chickened out.

Eva had really gotten to me and I hated her for it. I focused on the day I had planned and called T to make sure my wild date was ready. Everything was all set like I knew it would be. T always comes through when I need her to.

"Are you sure about this, Ezra?" T asked on the other line of the phone. "How do you know she's even into stuff like this?"

"Just taking a shot in the dark. You don't think she'll like it?"

"Well, it's not for everybody."

"She'll like it."

"If you say so, just pull a Will Smith in *Hitch*."

I burst out in a laugh remembering the scene T was talking about. "That's why I got you pulling double duty for me."

"What are you doing to get ready?"

"Trying to get Eva's craziness out of my head."

"Eva? Why are you thinking about that psycho?"

I realized I shouldn't have brought Eva up when talking to Tamra. She wouldn't let it go until I gave her the whole story so I bit down and got ready to swallow another speech. "She paid me a visit just now. It was the same as it's been since we broke up. She looked good, acted crazy."

"What did she do?"

I could tell from her voice that T was already getting angry and I hadn't even told her what had happened. "I don't really want to talk about it. Can't you just go over her place and take care of her for me?"

"Are you serious?" T said and made it sound more like she was trying to get confirmation rather than making a sarcastic remark.

There was a pause of silence on the phone, but then I finally told her no.

"Are you sure? I know where she lives and I promise it would never come back to you. I could make it look like an accident. I've been waiting for you to ask me, I've got it all planned out."

I paused again, trying to figure out if she was serious. Thankfully before I could say anything T burst out laughing. I love T, but she scares me sometimes.

"You were just kidding, right?" I asked and T continued to laugh.

"Of course," she said off handedly. "Text me when you're done with your date so I can pick my stuff up. Luv ya much," T said then hung up. I've got to remember not to mention Eva around her again. T wouldn't really try to have Eva killed but she would try to pound her face in.

I had time before Camara would get to my place so I did some exercises and took a shower. I put on a plain white tee with my blue and white swim trunks and made myself some chicken alfredo.

Just as I finished my meal, I heard a knock at the door and went to open it. I hoped it wasn't Zeus showing up with bad news or Eva coming back to aggravate me some more. I opened the door and there stood Camara grinning at me with one hand on her hip. She had on sandals, short blue jean shorts with a white see-thru tank top which revealed the straps of her blue swimsuit. She carried a pink and white bebe bag that looked big enough to hold a change of clothes. Her hair was down and crinkly like she just took it out of braids. She was beautiful from head to toe.

"I hope I'm dressed right."

"That's perfect. You ready?"

"I'm always ready to get wild, Ezra," she said. "Where are we going?"

"Be patient," I said. "It's still a surprise."

# CHAPTER 40

Camara and I hopped in Dirty Vegas and headed down 460 until we hit 77 going towards Wytheville. I could tell Camara still had no idea where we were going and I loved the idea of completely surprising her. I didn't give her much time to wonder where we were going because I kept the conversation going, which wasn't hard to do. Camara and I could talk about anything. She was the most mentally stimulating woman I had been around in a long time. Being with her made the trip go by quicker than it ever had before.

"What was it like going to Marshall?" Camara asked me as we exited the East River Mountain Tunnel.

"It was college life, you know. I had a hard time adjusting at first, my first semester was pretty rough, but I got through it. Even managed to finish in four years."

"You finished in four years straight? You're the only person I know who can say that."

"What can I say? I was determined. It was easy once you got that freaking Marshall Plan out the way."

"What would you say was the best part?"

"The people, hands down. I met a lot of people. Still keep in touch with a few of them. I think above all that's what college is all about. In life it's all about who you know. Where you can go in life is often based on who you meet in college for a lot of people."

"That's how I feel—or felt."

"What changed your point of view?"

"The big stinking pile of debt I got myself in. I just had to go out of state like a dummy. Should've stayed in West Virginia."

I didn't say anything to that although I understood what she was talking about. I knew too many people who were desperate to get out of West Virginia and ended up over their heads financially.

"Where are we going?" Camara asked.

I shook my head to let Camara know that we still had a little more traveling to do.

"I told you a bit about my family last time. What about yours? Do you have any brothers or sisters?"

"I had a brother," Camara said with just a hint of sadness in her voice. "He was murdered a long time ago."

"I'm sorry," I said wishing I hadn't asked.

"It's okay. Like I said it was a long time ago. I couldn't accept it for a long time, but it was his own fault. He put himself in a bad position for a stupid reason. I looked up to him more than anyone, more than my mother or my dad. I thought he was perfect. It crushed my world to find out how senselessly he died. It's awful how the death of someone you love can put you in such a bad place for such a long time," Camara said and looked out the window as though she was staring down the road to her past.

I kept my mouth shut as her words brought up my own painful recent experiences with death.

We moved the conversation on to lighter topics. There was a lot to know about Camara and I couldn't get enough. One thing that surprised me was how much she was able to get me to talk. I've always been more of a listener, but Camara was easy to open up to. I couldn't imagine anyone not being able to talk to her.

It wasn't long before we got to the surprise I had waiting for us. Camara's eyes grew wide and her beaming smile signaled her approval. We pulled into Claytor Lake and two jet skis were waiting with our names on them.

"You have jet skis?" she asked as she climbed out of the car and ran over to the jet skis parked just off the bank of the lake.

"Let's just say I still have a few friends in Bluefield," I said and tried to make a mental note that I owed T about five favors now.

I went to the trunk of my car and pulled out two lifejackets. "You know how to drive one of these?"

"Oh yeah! When I went to LA to visit my uncle we used to do this all the time. I just never thought there was a place around here to do stuff like this. Throw me the lifejacket," she said grinning from ear to ear.

Camara was excited. She start bouncing up and down like a little girl as she tried to put on her lifejacket. She could barely keep still long enough to put it on right.

Claytor Lake was a huge man-made lake built in 1939. The valley was flooded and a dam was built to provide hydroelectric power to this region of the Appalachians. Some people say that if you were to scuba dive to the bottom you would see remnants of old houses that were in the valley when it was flooded.

It was partly cloudy today and the rays of sun shining on the lake made it look like it was covered with thousands of crystals. The water was clearer than I had ever seen it before. A slight constant breeze caused the trees to dance as their shadows swayed across the crystal-covered lake. Only the sounds of an eagle overhead accompanied the rushing leaves and gentle waves hitting the sand.

Usually the lake is crawling with college students, mostly from Radford University or locals living around the lake, but today Camara and I had the whole lake to ourselves. It was our private racetrack. Camara's body was athletic and toned and definitely not all for show. She had real muscle that gave her the ability to have complete control over her jet ski. We pushed the skis hard and long, making sure to explore almost every inch of the lake. It blew Camara's mind that some sections of the lake had sand on them. A manmade beach at a manmade lake.

We danced around the lake on our jet skis until the sun started to fall below the tree cover. With the sun down, the air would cool very fast, so Camara and I called it a day. We made our way back to the car and anchored the jet skis. I sent T a text letting her know that we finished, and we toweled off and climbed in the car.

"I can't believe there's a place to go jet skiing this close to West Virginia and there's a beach. A beach! Who knew?" Camara said sounding truly amazed. "This was perfect, Ezra."

"I'm glad you approve. You hungry?"

"Starving."

"Well, you got two choices. We can either go out to eat or you can come back to my place and let me cook for you."

"You cook?" Camara said with a raised eyebrow.

"I've been known to throw down in the kitchen from time to time," I said chin up feeling fully confident in my cooking skills.

"Huh oh, this I gotta see."

I pulled out from the lake and got back on 81 South. Camara and I talked the whole way back to Princeton. I couldn't remember the last time I had so much fun. I had such a good time I almost forgot that two police officers were still following me as we left Claytor Lake. Almost.

# CHAPTER 41

## CAMARA

Camara thought she might be falling for Ezra. The past seventy-two hours had been some of the worst of her life, but Ezra had managed to make her forget it all. She didn't think about anyone or anything while she was with him.

They pulled up to Pauli Heights apartment just as the sun gave way to a three- quarter moon over the Appalachian Mountains. It was so beautiful Camara wished she had her camera with her. Once in the apartment, Camara plopped back on the couch and stretched out her limbs.

"That was perfect," she said feeling that was an under-statement. "What are we going to do next time?"

"In all honesty, I'm not sure. I'm making this up as I go if you haven't figured that out by now."

"Really? And here I was thinking you were a regular Casanova."

"I didn't say I wasn't. I'm sure Casanova had to ad lib once in a while."

"I still can't believe there's a beach on that lake."

"You still hungry?"

"Still starving."

"Good. Let me hop in the shower then I'll fix us something. I don't like to cook when I smell like a lake," Ezra said as he made his way to the bathroom.

Before he could disappear into the hallway Camara called out, "Hey!"

Ezra stopped dead in his tracks and turned to look at Camara now sitting up on the couch. Camara ran her hand through her hair and tilted her head down in a coy jester. A mischievous grin formed across her lips as her eyes found their way to Ezra's.

"Do you want some company?" she said feeling just a hint of apprehension for being so aggressive.

Ezra smiled and looked away from her. Camara could tell he was actually mulling it over. She had a good idea what the answer might be, but she wanted to test him anyway.

"Not yet," Ezra said then locked eyes with Camara.

"Okay," she said without avoiding his gaze or giving off a hint of embarrassment. Camara was a woman who went after what she wanted and she wasn't ashamed of it. "You don't make it easy to back down, you know."

Ezra took off his shirt and showed off his muscles. Camara thought he had one of the most well defined set of abs she had ever seen. His frame wasn't bulky but was still very muscular. His chest and arms looked like they were cut from marble.

"I never said I wanted you to back down," he said as he turned to walk down the hall then into the bathroom.

It took Camara a moment to catch her breath. *This is so fucking backwards.* Camara thought to herself with a deep sigh.

Once she heard the shower start up, Camara looked for the TV. She needed something to divert her attention before she went into the bathroom and really put Ezra to the test. She opened Ezra's entertainment center and found a PlayStation 3. Camara didn't know Ezra had one. He didn't seem like the type. He hadn't mentioned video games even once like most guys do. She looked through his stack of games and picked one that she had been wanting to play—God of War.

Camara had just put the game in and made herself comfortable when she heard her phone ring. She checked the phone to find she had three missed call, two voicemails, and a text message.

Her calls were from Alley Cat, Michonne, and Nate. Camara's mother just wanted to know where she was and Nate had called to tell Camara about the findings at Jimmy Lewis Lake. Camara already knew all the grim details of the scene and didn't need to be reminded now.

When she checked the text, she realized that it came from a blocked number. The text read: I hope my money was at that lake.

Camara stared at the text for several seconds. Being with Ezra had worked too well. Being with him was a dream; the text was a wake up call. She had been dancing in the clouds for the later part of the day. Reading the text felt like a punch to the gut.

# CHAPTER 42

*What the hell is wrong with me?* I thought as warm water from the shower rained over me. The main reason I never had sex with Eva was because I was trying to live my life right and not make the same mistakes my father had made. But when I really think about it, I realized it had a lot to do with me being unable to find anything mentally stimulating about her. She was just a body to me. Better to look at than talk to. I felt bad about that on several different levels. I never should have stayed with her as long as I did. Now she was paying for it.

Camara, on the other hand, was both sexy and smart. What was my problem? As I stood in the shower, the truth about how messed up my life was right now hit me like a freight train.

My mother had been murdered a couple of months ago. Two of my favorite kids from the Wade Center had been kidnapped. I witnessed the rape and murder of a girl at Bluefield State, and a psychopathic killer was after me. I wasn't like Zeus. Sex didn't help me put things into perspective or relax me like it did him. I would've been all over Camara if I had met her at a different time in my life, which is probably why I hadn't.

I hoped Camara would stay around until all this craziness in my life was over, and then, maybe whatever we had between us could grow.

I toweled off and dressed in the clothes I had brought into the bathroom with me— a pair of jeans, no socks, and a red shirt that read F.A.V.O.R in black letters. When I came out, I saw Camara sitting on the couch playing God of War on my PS3.

"I wouldn't have pegged you for a gamer, girl."

"My brother used to let me play with him all the time. I remember when he got the first Resident Evil on PlayStation One. Watching him play that game scared the hell out of me. I remember watching him and his friends play Techno Bowl back in the day, too. They would really get into that."

Camara and I reminisced over classic games as I got dinner ready. Lasagna and baked catfish with steamed vegetables was on the menu. I had a couple of dishes I wanted to try, but I wasn't confident enough in my cooking to try something new. I got the pots and pans I needed out of the cabinets then got to work.

"It shouldn't take me more than forty-five minutes to an hour. Did you want to jump in the shower?"

"In a second," Camara said. I peeked in on her from the kitchen. She was getting in the game harder and faster than I thought she would. As I went back in the kitchen I heard Camara ask, "So what does that stand for?"

"What?"

"Your shirt. What does F.A.V.O.R stand for?"

"Faith's. Aggressive. Victory. Over. Reality."

"Cute." I heard her say after a slight pause. "Did you make that one up, too?" she finally asked.

"Nope. Old church saying. Just put it on a shirt. It's when God has a special blessing over your life. When things go your way and when obstacles you face start becoming opportunities."

"Soooo, God makes you lucky? Right?" Camara asked a bit unsure.

"Not exactly, but yeah. I guess that's the easiest way to explain it. I personally don't believe in luck though."

"Interesting." I heard Camara say as she got up from the couch and walked into the kitchen. "I just died so I'm gonna hop in the shower. That game's hard."

"Just the first fight. You'll get it."

"You did leave me some hot water, right?" she asked with a smile as warm as the sun.

"Take your time; there should be plenty left." I showed Camara where the towels and washcloths were and she took her bag and headed in the bathroom.

I had already seasoned the fish and the Stouffer's lasagna was in the oven when I heard the shower turn on. It occurred to me that when the time came, I would have to ask Camara about religion. It didn't bother me or turn me off to her that she wasn't very religious. But a relationship with her would only go so far if our beliefs and ideology were too different. We could still grow to be close friends, but I was hoping things might turn into more than that.

I pushed the thought to the corners of my mind. Today was a good day. One of the best I'd had in a long time, except for Eva's little visit. I wasn't about to mess it up with jumping the gun with stupid questions. Today I was going to enjoy Camara's company and have a good time come hell or high water.

Camara did take her time in the shower. By the time she came out, I had mostly everything finished and had managed not to burn anything. When Camara came into the kitchen, she had on black tights with a jean skirt and tight black shirt. The shoulders of the top exposed her bra straps. The out-fit made her look both feminine and athletic. When she sat down, she was still running a towel through her hair.

"Smells good. You can throw down in the kitchen," she said catching a whiff of the catfish.

"I can hold my own."

"Tell me about your trip to see your sister. What's she like?"

"Isis? It's hard to describe Isis. She's my older sister and in a lot of ways my best friend. She's smart as hell and never loses an argument. Not to me at least. Some people say we look a little alike, but I don't see it. She's very free spirited and can be impulsive. Real liberal."

"How much older than you is she? Two years? Three?"

I chuckled a bit at the question then answered her, "About four months."

"Four months!?" Camara said and looked a little embarrassed at how it had come out. I could tell she didn't mean to sound so shocked.

I couldn't help but laugh at the look on her face.

"I'm sorry, I didn't mean to say it like that."

"It's okay. I usually get a reaction similar to that when I tell people." I walked over to the refrigerator and pulled out a bowl of strawberries that were lightly frosted with sugar and placed them on the table in front of Camara.

"Snack on these. The main course should be done in a little bit."

"Have you been asking people about me? Are you reading my mind?" she said with a half grin. "How did you know I love strawberries?"

"I didn't."

"Well, you have to be getting information from somewhere 'cause you're doing too many things right."

"I'm observant. You looked hungry, like you wanted something to snack on. I guessed and just happened to guess right."

Camara took a bite of the strawberries.

"Too sugary?" I asked.

She shook her head with her eyes closed and said through a mouthful, "Perfect." Camara ate a couple more strawberries before she asked, "Explain that favor thing to me again."

"What do you want to know?" I asked while checking on the lasagna which was almost done.

"You said comparing it to luck was the 'easy way' to explain it. What's the not so easy way?"

"Well," I said trying to gather my thoughts. It was never easy to try and explain Biblical principals. The words of the Bible are like a sword, and my sword is long and sharp, but it still needed sharpening now and then. I had a pretty good knowledge of the Bible, but the last thing you want to do with someone who doesn't know much about it is to start spitting out verses.

"Well, the best way to explain it is that there is no such thing as luck. Favor is exactly like it sounds. God favors you because of your service to him, how you carry yourself, and live your life. It's like saying God works strongly in your life because you believe strongly in him. Does that make sense?"

"I think," she said rubbing a strawberry on the bottom of the bowl. She looked deep in thought. I hoped she would tell me what she was thinking.

"It sounds like your saying that God plays favorites," she finally said.

"That's not really it, either," I said checking on the vegetables. "It's more like—"

"What other games do you have for the PS3?" Camara asked cutting me off.

I looked at her and she was staring hard into her bowl of strawberries. Her body language was a little tense and I got the feeling the conversation was getting a little too heavy. Too serious for the lighthearted day we had. I don't believe in being a "pushy Christian" even though she did ask, so I let the change of topic fly.

We talked about video games, school, and friends until the food was ready. I was surprised at myself. The food came out better than any other time I had cooked this meal for myself and that was when I gave it my full attention. Maybe I should talk on the phone when I cooked from now on.

I served Camara a plate with a bottle of Lipton Green Tea and sat across from her. We talked easily and freely, but I knew religion would come up again sooner or later. It would have to if this was going to be more than friendship.

Halfway through our meal there was a knock on the door. I got up to see who it was. I had told myself I was going to have a good time with Camara today come hell or high water. When I saw the look on the face of the person on the other side of my door, my heart sank. Hell had come knocking.

# CHAPTER 43

I wasn't happy about Zeus showing up at my apartment. I could tell from the instant I saw him that he didn't have good news.

"We need to talk," he said then stormed in. He had on a leather jacket and black jeans with a gold shading that faded inward. He also had on new black and gold Air Force Ones and a black shirt that hugged him just enough to show the definition in the muscles he worked so hard on. His hair looked freshly cut. He looked like whatever got him so upset had interrupted him in the middle of a date. As put together as he looked on the outside, I could tell his emotional state was the polar opposite.

He didn't so much as look at me before he started pacing in my living room and spitting out the reason for his visit: "They found the bodies. About nine down in Jimmy Lewis Lake. Most of the people reported missing over the last couple of months were tied to the bottom of that lake. It's got AKA written all over it. They wouldn't have found those bodies unless he's planning something big. My contacts said something about a note, but they couldn't get me a copy of it yet. There's no way the police would have found those bodies unless the son of a bitch wanted them to."

Zeus rambled on for a couple of minutes. He had several stretches where he just cursed for a solid twenty to forty seconds. I tried to get a word or two in to calm him down, but he wasn't having it. He didn't stop talking until he finally noticed Camara. He looked shocked to see her at my kitchen table.

"Where the hell did she come from?" he asked me as though Camara had magically appeared at the table.

"She's been there the whole time, Zeus."

"Well, why didn't you say something? I'm spilling top secret information and shit here."

"You didn't give me much of a chance to say anything."

"I already knew about the bodies found at the lake," Camara interjected.

Zeus and I both turned to look at her. I could only imagine what the looks on our face portrayed, especially mine.

"You knew what?" Zeus and I asked in unison.

"I was going to tell you about it sooner, but we were having such a good time that I didn't want to bring it up." Camara's body language changed, she looked slightly nervous, almost like a child about to tell her parents some bad news. "I was the one who tipped the police about the location of the bodies."

"What?" Zeus and I asked again in unison.

Zeus rubbed his eyes and ran a hand over his head. "WHAT THE FUCK IS HE DOING!" he screamed to the ceiling at the top of his voice.

He looked more stressed than I had ever seen him: his breathing was getting heavier and he was rubbing the scorpion tattoo on his right arm. Zeus got that tat as soon as he was legal age to do so. Since then, every time he got angry, he would rub that thing as if it were alive. He told me once that the scorpion was always inside him and the tattoo was just a way of bringing it to the outside so he could control it better, something about the tat being a symbol of his anger. I'm still trying to get him to see professional help about that.

Camara looked concerned as if Zeus might start wildin' out any minute. I caught her eye and waved off her anxiety. Zeus always had a temper and sometimes he could Hulk out on people. He always managed to channel his rage in the right direction though. He just needed a few seconds to put his anger into words; he needed time to figure out the right questions.

I went to the table and sat to Camara's left. Zeus followed me and took the seat directly across from Camara. I knew he would want to sit there while he questioned her.

Zeus was usually easy going and had a way of setting the tempo of a room. When Zeus was in the room, people felt how he felt, people keyed in on his tone or emotion. I was able to stay calm, but I could tell Camara was somewhat uneasy under Zeus's intensity. She didn't back down. She looked him square in the eyes as he spoke.

"I'm sorry I reacted the way I did. You have no idea what I've been through the past couple of weeks. The scorpion has been trying to wake up," Zeus said rubbing his arm.

Camara shot me a look while trying to figure out what Zeus was talking about. I sent her one back to let her know not to ask.

Zeus looked back at Camara and asked, "Can you tell me everything you know about AKA?"

Camara looked authentically confused. "Who?"

"The killer. The one who's been doing all this. The guy who put all those people in the lake!"

"Zeus!" I said to calm my little brother down. "She said she tipped the police, not that she was working against them. Ask the right questions or I'll kick you out and ask them for you."

"Fine. Fine," he said taking off his jacket and hanging it on the back of his chair. He took a breath and was about to ask Camara a question when she beat him to it.

"Who, or what, is AKA?" Camara asked. The look on her face made it apparent that Zeus wasn't getting anything out of her unless he coughed up some information first.

I know Zeus was about to go into the "who the hell do you think you are" speech, so I cut him off.

"Tell her Zeus! If she knew about it already, the story would have been in the paper and on the news. Just give her your piece of the puzzle."

Zeus sighed hard, but relented. He told Camara the story about AKA. He even told her some stuff he hadn't told me. I think he wanted to make the story scarier—more real like a current danger. He wanted Camara to know what she was dealing with, what she was into. He laid it on thick, but I didn't doubt that he was telling the truth. Zeus wasn't the embellishing type.

When he was done, Camara sat back in her seat in shock. Zeus had shocked her with the details. He had thrown me for a loop, too, and I had heard a good bit of the story already.

Zeus let his story resonate for several seconds before he started questioning Camara again.

"Now that you know what type of person you're dealing with, why don't you tell me how you knew where those bodies were?" Zeus said with a calm intensity that only he could pull off.

Camara broke Zeus's gaze and looked off to the side. I could tell she was growing more and more uncomfortable. I reached out and held her hand in mine. She didn't say anything, but she gently squeezed my hand, letting me know the contact wasn't unwelcome. I wanted to tell her everything would be all right. I wanted to tell her how important it was for her to tell Zeus whatever she knew, so he could catch the maniac.

"I got a letter," Camara said before I got a word out.

"You got a letter from who?" Zeus asked.

"The killer, I would assume," Camara said looking slightly annoyed by the simple question.

"I mean who gave you the letter? Who delivered it?"

"The secretary at the paper Kim Kohls put it on my desk. She said a high-school age girl gave it to her to give to me. The girl said she was related to me, that she was my niece, but I don't have a niece. It's just me and my mom. I don't have any other family in West Virginia."

"Was the letter addressed to you?" Zeus asked. He didn't let up. He acted like he had been in this situation countless times before. Camara answered all his questions, but a hint of confusion hung from every word.

"Yes," Camara answered.

"Did it have a smell to it?"

"No."

"Any type of powder like substance come from the thing?"

"None that I can remember."

"Who else knows about the letter?"

"Just Miss Kohls, Melissa Cervantes, and two other editors at the paper."

"They all know what it says?"

"Yes."

"Where is the letter now?"

"I still have it. It's in my bag right now. I was going to give it to the police as evidence, but something told me to keep it."

"May I please read it?"

Camara was a little thrown by Zeus's seemingly gentle side. Despite his size and presence, Zeus can be one charming bastard when he wants to be. It's something he and I both inherited from our father.

Camara gently released my hand and went over to her bag for the letter. She took her seat and gave the letter to Zeus. When he finished reading he gave the letter to me.

"It's AK all right."

"How can you tell?" Camara asked.

"I've been chasing the guy for most of my adult life. Trust me, I know," Zeus said standing up and making his way to the kitchen.

I read the letter to myself then read it again. I wasn't sure what to think about it. I wasn't sure what to say.

"What's this?" I asked spotting another note under the one Camara intended me to read.

"That's a copy of the note found in the mouth of one of the murder victims."

"What?" Zeus barked. "How did you get that?"

"I had an associate of mine write down what it said. The police took the original. I don't think they know what this means yet."

"Let me see, Ezra," Zeus said as he took the letter. "No idea. I need a copy of this before I leave. Might give us a clue to whatever the hell he's planning next," he said and headed for the kitchen.

I read the note found at the murder scene when Zeus finished and then read it again. I knew exactly what it was and what it meant. The fact the Camara and Zeus didn't, the fact that none of the police knew bothered me a little. It read:

*And now, O our God what shall we say after this? For we have forsaken your commandments, which you have commanded by your servants the prophet, saying, The land, unto which you go to possess it, is an unclean land with the filthiness of the people of the lands, with their abominations, which have filled it from one end to another with their uncleanliness.*

My heart sank into my stomach as I read it a fourth time. I knew what it was. No doubt about it.

Zeus came back to the table carrying what I was positive was the rest of my lasagna and a bottle of beer.

"Help yourself," I said to Zeus.

"Don't mind if I do," Zeus said reaching for the pepper. "Is this the first contact you've had like this? Any other letters, calls, e-mails or anything?" Zeus asked Camara through a mouth full of lasagna.

She seemed to hesitate briefly. At first I thought she was thinking about the question, but it looked more like she was considering telling us something. I wanted to reach out and touch her hand again, but I didn't want to let on that I had noticed. Women don't like to feel like they can't hide anything, or be read too easily.

"Someone met with me and gave me information on the killer," Camara said evenly.

Zeus wasn't ready for that bit of information because he almost choked on his lasagna. He started coughing and his eyes watered up as he tried to get a chunk of lasagna down.

"What type of information?" Zeus said in a ragged voice.

"Everything. I probably know more about him now than you do. What towns he's been to. Who he's killed and where. Everything before he got to Bluefield."

I hated being speechless but it seemed to be happening a lot lately. Nobody said anything for several seconds that seemed like minutes.

"Where?" Zeus asked. His countenance became deadly serious. I almost didn't recognize him. Zeus's tone was rough and his energy became heavy and forceful.

Before I could say something to calm him down, Camara calmly got up and went to her bag again. She returned to the table with a brown folder and flopped it in front of Zeus.

Zeus slid his plate aside. Suddenly food was the last thing on his mind. Instead, he dug into the folder skimming pages and taking quick glances at the photographs. He didn't say anything or look at Camara or me for a minute or so. As franticly as he was going through the file, he was careful to keep everything in order, which was uncharacteristic of him. Zeus rarely treated anything with "kid gloves."

"Who else has seen these?" Zeus asked without looking up from the pages of the file.

"No one. I wasn't sure what to do with them. I wasn't sure who would believe me or take this seriously."

"Why are you giving this to me, now?" Zeus looked up asking the question as neutrally as he could, but I could tell he was suspicious.

"I don't know I just . . . you barged in here talking about the same mass murder I had just been given a huge case file on. It's obvious you know about this guy, so I just thought you should have my files. I didn't know what to do about it any way. I don't even know why it was given to me."

"Who gave it to you?" I asked.

"I don't know."

"You don't know. How do you not know?" Zeus cut in.

"I. Don't. Know." Camara said staring Zeus down. "I got a tip. I followed it. I got that."

"What did your tip look like, what'd he sound like?" I asked Camara.

"He stayed in the shadows as clichéd as that might sound. He had on some type of disguise. I'm pretty sure he was hunching over, I can't even tell you how tall he was."

"Why did you go alone? You could've called me?"

"Nathan went with me."

"Nathan? Nathan Goodman? He's scared of his own shadow. How did you get him to go with you?" I asked in astonishment.

"Nate was willing once I told him I would just go by myself. You seemed like you had other things going on, so I called Nate. He got through it okay."

"I don't know who Nathan is and I don't give a shit. What did the informant look like?" Zeus butted in.

"I already told you he wore a disguise. I'm not even sure if it was a man. The voice was muffled by some sort of electronic device. Whoever it was sounded like Soundwave from the old Transformer cartoons."

"All right, all right," Zeus said. He jumped from the table and walked into my living room and started pacing. "The informant isn't important right now—the information is. A good part of Bluefield may burn tomorrow night."

"You really think he can pull that off? I thought it was an empty threat, just something to scare us into printing that letter in the paper," Camara said.

Zeus held back a laugh that was aimed at her apparent ignorance. "You could've printed the letter on every page and the city would still burn tomorrow."

"Wait a minute. You mean this guy could possibly pull this off? How?" I demanded.

"I can't tell you how until after it's over. I might be about to stop some of it if the Pack were here. I can only react when I'm on my own and just finding out the day before, so I can only react. If I had more time, I might be able to do something, but not now."

"The entire Bluefield City Police is working on this. A friend of mind in the department told me that they have bomb squads from as far as Virginia coming in on this. What would you be able to do that they couldn't?"

Zeus stopped his pacing and locked eyes with Camara and smiled with an acidic laugh that dripped confidence in himself and his abilities. So much so that he didn't feel the need to justify the question with an answer.

Things were getting heated in more ways than one. I tried to keep the conversation moving.

"What can you do, Zeus? What does all this tell you?" I asked, anxious for my brother's response.

"Now that is a *useful* question," Zeus said as he continued to pace. "The only thing this tells us for certain is that AKA has his pawns with him. Even he couldn't pull off something like this completely alone."

"Why do you keep talking like this is a forgone conclusion? There's still time to stop this. How can you sound so . . . indifferent?" Camara asked.

Zeus paused for a minute. I could tell that his mind was racing. Skeletons peaking out of closets better left locked up tight. I know the look, that feeling.

"I've seen things like this too many times to count, Camara," Zeus said evenly. His shoulders were hunched and he looked like a man who spent too much time being an island unto himself.

"I'm not happy about it," he said, "but a chunk of Bluefield is going to burn tomorrow night."

The air in my apartment felt thick again as my eyes were drawn to the note found at the murder scene. I read it one more time and was sure I was right. It wasn't a note, it was a quote from a book of the Bible. The Book of Ezra.

# CHAPTER 44

## CAMARA

Camara wasn't sure how she felt about Ezra's brother. He was cocky and arrogant, but he had shown a slightly vulnerable side. He reminded her so much of Tarquan it made her sick. Ezra and Zeus were so different it was hard to believe that they were brothers.

Zeus's moment of solidarity quickly faded as he started doing push ups in the living room. He looked like he was getting amped up for a football game instead of thinking of how to catch a child abducting, homicidal, pyromaniac.

Zeus asked Camara a couple of times about her informant. Camara described the person she met in as much detail as possible.

"It could very well be AKA. Don't meet him again," Zeus said, and left it at that.

Camara couldn't understand how Zeus was willing to write off people. He talked about the possibility of people dying tomorrow in such an off-handed manner.

There wasn't much of anything left for the three of them to talk about and it was getting dark, so Camara left for McDowell. She drove with her music off, windows down and thought about her sorry excuse for a life. She wasn't sure why she gave Ezra and his brother the files. She wasn't sure why she hadn't given up all the files either.

The words of her "informant" came to her mind. She wasn't supposed to show the files to anyone. Would the informant know what she did? Would Zeus say or do anything that would implicate her? Camara realized there was a lot she didn't know, a lot she was unsure of.

The only thing that was an absolute to her was the fact that she enjoyed Ezra's company. She had told herself that she

238

wouldn't come on to him but wasn't surprised when she had failed miserably.

Camara pulled into her mother's driveway. Another car was parked on the street in front of the house. She was surprised because neither she nor her mother ever had visitors. As she pulled up closer to the house, Camara saw that the driver side and passenger side door of the car had been left open. Someone had gotten out in a hurry.

Camara's heart skipped a beat. *Tarquan* was the first person that rushed to her mind. She turned off her lights and stopped short of her usual spot in the driveway. Her windows were still down as she turned off the car and listened. Only the living room light was on in the house. The faint sound of screaming captured Camara's ear from all the way out in the driveway. Her heart was racing.

She could not remember her mother ever screaming, even when she should have. God knows she had plenty of reasons to lose her temper with her husband. Judging from the voices, it sounded like three people in the house. Camara grabbed her Glock from her purse. She slung her purse over her shoulder, more out of habit than any other reason, and crept up to the house. Her heart still raced. Her palms were sweaty, but balanced.

She had always liked guns. They were the great equalizer. Even if you're a five- foot seven, and a hundred and forty-five pound woman, the strongest man on the planet had to respect you if you could handle a gun.

After one more quick look at the car on the street, Camara was sure that she didn't recognize it. Camara tried to calm herself. She had the element of surprise on her side and wanted to know what was going on before barging in. She held the Glock firmly in her right hand and gently turned the door knob. She cracked the door enough to be able to hear more clearly what was being said in the house. She crouched down and listened.

"What do you think I'm doing here, Allison? I'm trying to make things right between us!"

"Well, it's too late for that, Nancy! Leave! Just leave!"

"I don't understand why you're so mad at Nancy, Allison. You should be mad at that piece of shit husband you had."

"Nobody is talking to you, Mable! Why are you even here?! I don't need you in *my* home talking to me about *my* husband!"

"She's here 'cause I asked her to give me a ride. You know my car isn't working."

"Now, Nancy, maybe if you don't have a way to get around on your own, then you should just keep your tail at home."

"This is the last time, and I mean the last time, I'm gonna try to make peace with you!"

"If you wanted to keep the peace, you would've buried your conscience and not told me what you did."

"It was killing me! I had to make it right between us. I thought you would want to know!"

"Oh, so now you feel better for telling me, but it's killing me to know. You're just selfish, Nancy. You just wanted to make yourself feel better. You just don't want Camara to know."

"Did you tell her?"

"Ha! That would just tear you apart, wouldn't it? She's the last to know how you are, isn't she? The last to know how low you really are."

"God, Allison, please tell me you didn't tell her."

"No. I didn't. I don't want to, but I can change my mind anytime."

"I would think you would respect the fact that she told you when she didn't have to."

"SHUT! UP! MABLE!

"Allison, all I'm saying is that . . ."

"One word! One more word out of you, Mable, and I'm going into my kitchen and grab a knife, and I'm not going to be cutting celery with it! Do you understand me?"

"You don't have to be nasty to her, Allison, this has nothing to do with her."

"And that's exactly why she shouldn't be here!"

"Mable, just come back in an hour and pick me up."

"Oh, no! Oh no. If she leaves you need to walk right out of here with her."

"Look, Nancy, I'm sorry but I don't have to be here and I don't even want to be. Let's just go. You're obviously not getting anywhere with this. Just let it go. She never was much of a friend or wife for that matter."

Camara jumped slightly at the sound of a sudden slap. Who had just hit whom? Camara couldn't tell. She couldn't imagine the Alley Cat unleashing her claws on anyone. Camara stood by the door and waited. The voices stopped and Camara assumed there was an intense stare-down taking place in the house.

After several seconds, Camara heard footsteps pounding in her direction. She quickly sidestepped around the corner just in time for Mable to miss her. Even in the dark, Mable looked flustered and discombobulated. She was mumbling under her breath and struggling to put her jacket on. She fumbled with her keys a few times, before she got in her car and slammed both doors then sped off.

Camara positioned herself back in the doorway. Her mother and Nancy were alone now. Camara waited and listened. She had to know what was going on and this might be her only chance to get the truth.

"You did not have to do that, Allison. I'm surprised at how you're behaving. It's deplorable."

"Deplorable! You have the nerve to speak to me like that? After what you did? After what you were doing for God knows how many years and you have the nerve to talk to me that way? Get out!"

"You just SLAPPED my ride out of your house, Allison, how am I suppose to leave?"

"You can walk just fine, and frankly it would do you some good. You only live five miles from here."

"I couldn't walk home now if I wanted to. It's dark outside."

"Then you better leave now. I have plenty of flashlights. I'll let you have one."

"For God's sake, Allison, I didn't have an affair with Melvin by myself all those years. It wasn't just me."

Camara's heart jumped into her throat. She couldn't swallow or breathe, she couldn't believe what she had just heard. Without even thinking, she slung open the door and confronted both her mother and Nancy where they stood in the living room.

They both turned and looked at her in shock. They couldn't have known just how much she had heard, but the look on Camara's face let them know that she had heard enough. Camara's eyes were fixed on Nancy. She had never felt more betrayed by anyone as she did now. Camara could only imagine what she might do if Nancy wasn't in her late fifties. She was blinded with rage. She couldn't think straight. The sound of her mother's voice brought her back to the here and now.

"Camie . . . what are you going to do with that?" Alley Cat said tentatively.

Camara was confused by the question for a second then she felt the weight of steel in her right hand. She had forgotten to put her Glock back in her purse. There was no point in trying to hide it now, so she kept it in view. Camara looked back at Nanny and saw genuine fear resonating in her features.

"Is it true?" Camara said evenly.

Nancy's eyes started to tear up almost immediately. Her breathing became labored as she struggled to find words to defend herself. The silence gave Camara the answer she wanted. Nancy tried to move toward Camara but was waved off.

Camara had her Nanny built up in her mind. She always imagined her to be kind, honest, and trustworthy at the core. Nancy had plenty of faults, but Camara always thought the good in her always broke through. Now all that Camara could see was Nancy's ugliness.

"Mom. I think you should find Nancy a flashlight."

Camara waited as her mother found a flashlight. Allison went to a nearby drawer, checked the flashlight to see if it worked, and handed it to Nancy. Nancy took the flashlight and walked toward the door. Camara thought she looked pitiful, but she didn't feel the least bit sorry for her. Nancy stopped beside Camara on her way out and still fought for words. "Camara, I'm sorry I . . ."

"Don't!" Camara said without looking at her. "Just . . . don't."

Camara looked straight ahead as the door shut behind her and she knew Nancy was gone. She hadn't seen Nancy's face as she left; she didn't want to look at her. At that moment Camara didn't care if she ever saw Nancy's face again.

****

Camara was so mad she forgot that the gun was in her hand and almost shot herself in the foot. She forced herself to loosen her grip and put the gun back in her purse, then focused on breathing. She was feeling too many things at once—confusion, disbelief, betrayal, but anger topped the list. Camara couldn't remember ever being this mad before in her life.

The fact that no one had told her made everything worse. She hated being out of the loop. She looked at her mother, locked eyes with her, but couldn't find the words to express what she was really feeling. The Alley Cat had something to say though. She was struggling for the words, but they were coming.

Camara could tell by the look on her mother's face that she was about to speak, but Camara's phone rang and cut through the silence before her mother got the chance. Camara avoided her mother's gaze and checked her phone. It was a text from her informant, the one who had given her the files.

He or she wanted to meet in Princeton in forty-five minutes. Coming from the county she knew she would have to push it but she could make it if she left now.

Camara left the house and slammed the door behind her before her mother could ask where she was going. She hopped in her car and was zooming across the mountain roads heading to Princeton before she knew what was happening. She played Jay-Z's Black Album to help her avoid spending too much time with her thoughts, but it couldn't block out how she felt. She thought about what Ezra's brother had told her, "It's probably AKA, so don't see him again."

She wondered how wise it was for her to not follow that advice, but her body just seemed to be on autopilot. She should have ignored the text and gone straight to bed, but she needed to be out of the house and this was a perfect excuse, although a dangerous one.

It was too late to turn back now. She had driven too far and too fast to just go home. She was taking the turns around the mountains of the county like a pro; she was shifting gears like she would've been more comfortable behind the wheel of a race car.

Driving had always been a release for her. She loved driving alone when she was a teenager. Nothing but her mind and the road to keep her company for miles and miles. She had always liked to go fast and she had the speeding tickets to prove it.

Camara was angrier than she had ever been in her life and it showed in her driving. She made it to Princeton in a little less than thirty minutes. She still hadn't thought about what she was doing when she pulled up to the meeting place—the old Princeton Post Office on Mercer Street at the corner of Center Street and Park Avenue. The building was going to be the site of a new, four-million-dollar library. Fund raising for the library had been an on-going effort for at least five years. They were finally close to having enough money to get started on construction. They had even bought some of the surrounding buildings in order to make room for parking.

Camara wondered why her informant would chose to meet here. It was practically out in the open.

The Saturn was parked across the street from the long-abandoned Post Office. Camara sat inside her car and wondered how smart this really was. She had been running on pure emotion until now. She had just wanted to get away and this was a good excuse. Now that she was here the chicken in her was starting to inch up her spine.

She examined the street and didn't see anyone else around. No people on the street, no cars passing by, nothing. Princeton was asleep, just as Camara knew she should have been. Coming here was dangerous and stupid, but something drove her forward; was it her own curiosity or her unwillingness to deal with the mess she left behind? All she knew was that she wasn't turning back. She had come this far and she was going to see it through.

Camara thought about calling Ezra, but for some reason she couldn't bring herself to do it. For some reason she didn't want him here even though she knew she might need backup. She considered calling Nate, but then remembered how spineless he had been last time and decided it was best if he didn't know anything about this.

The store her mother had been begging her to go in was directly to her left. An organic food store called Total Health and Healing where Alley Cat got a good chunk of her food. The club that Ezra had taken her to wasn't far down the street. Camara thought it weird how easily good memories could be overshadowed by bad experiences She knew she would never look at Mercer Street the same after this, no matter how things turned out. She took all of this in as she sat in the car and waited until she had five minutes left before the deadline for her meeting.

Camara reached for her shoulder holster in her glove box and carefully placed her Glock inside it after strapping it on. She threw on a jacket she had in the back seat along with her tennis shoes and grabbed a small flashlight from her purse. She needed to be ready to run or fight at a moment's notice.

The text she had gotten told her to walk to the back of the post office and find her way into the basement. She didn't like this set up at all. It was more closed off than the last meeting place. There would be less chance to escape and they would be in a much closer proximity to each other. *Why here?* Camara thought again to herself. The more she considered what the answer might be, the more confused she got. It didn't make sense.

Camara started her car and did a U-turn on Mercer Street and parked by the soon- to-be obsolete Princeton Public Library on Center Street and walked back to the abandoned post office. She wasn't sure if that was a good idea—as a matter of fact—she was almost certain, but she didn't want her car sitting across the street from the meeting place.

Camara knew all the risks and had calculated all the dangers and possible scenarios and everything pointed her to one conclusion.

Go home!

However, she still found herself walking across the street. She was committed ninety percent, might as well go the other ten. Camara was a lot of things but a quitter wasn't one of them.

A quick scan of the front door didn't look like a promising point of entry, so she made her way to the back like the text said. On the backside of the building, closest to Park Avenue, was a door. The hinges of the door looked like they may have been messed with recently. She saw glass on the ground by the doorframe and a gapping hole at the bottom left center of the door—a perfect place for someone to reach around and unlatch the lock on the door.

*Too easy.* She didn't want to go in that way unless she had to. It didn't feel right. She examined the back of the building again and found that several of the old windows were boarded up. Then she found one that had one loose board in front of another. When she moved the first board, she found a hole big enough to crawl through. Camara peaked her head through the window but she couldn't see anything. She pulled out her flashlight, surveyed the basement and went inside. She didn't like this. She was sure the informant wouldn't want to be cornered in a building that was so hard to get in and out of. There had to be more to this than it seemed. *How would they get out of here in a hurry if they needed to?* Did this mean that the informant trusted her? Did this mean that Camara was suppose to trust the informant?

The air in the basement was thick and dusty. It was obvious that no one had been down here for any extended period of time. Spider webs, dust and mold covered old dressers and cabinets. *Why here,* Camara thought. She felt like she was taking too big of a risk already, but she forced herself to explore more of the basement. Now she removed her Glock from its holster and held it in one hand and her flashlight in the other. The space was fairly empty. Whatever had been down here had been taken out to make ready for the upcoming construction.

The wood on the steps creaked and buckled slightly under Camara's weight as she walked to the upper levels to explore the rest of the building. She needed the light to see but was afraid to use it. She knew it could be seen from the street. Still, Camara explored her surroundings. She didn't want to be surprised. Her heart was already pounding in her throat. It was hard to breathe the stale dusty air, but Camara forced herself to inhale and exhale calmly through her nose. She was shaken to the core. Her heart and mind were racing, but her limbs were steady. Her hands were steadfast and her steps were confident. She moved as quietly as she could and listened intently into the darkness.

Camara didn't know why but her mind was all over the place. She thought about the Hunnicutt Foundation that donated a bulk of the money to fund the new library. Then, she thought about the day she and Ezra had survived the bombing at Hunnicutt Stadium and how scared she was that day. The same type of fear gripped her now; only now it was more like the nervous anticipation, like creeping up a rollercoaster gearing up for the fall. She didn't need to be thinking about other things now.

*Focus, Camara. Focus.* She reminded herself.

Something was going to happen. Camara could feel it and now more than ever— she wished she hadn't come alone.

What was she forgetting? Camara couldn't shake the feeling that something was missing or she didn't take all things into account when she made this trip to meet her informant. Something he had said to her when they first met. What was it?

She checked her watch. It had been exactly forty-five minutes since she got the text message to meet here. Was somebody playing games with her? Who would or could know how to mess with her like this? Camara was getting more antsy by the second. She cursed herself when her phone vibrated and she almost dropped her Glock. She looked around to make sure she was still alone, and promised herself she wouldn't be surprised like that again. Panic would get her killed. Of course, being stupid would get her killed, too, and it was definitely stupid coming here alone.

Camara checked her phone. It was another text—this one telling her to go back down to the basement. It told her to go back to the basement which meant whoever sent the text knew she had been in the basement and that she wasn't there any more. Someone was watching her from the street or were they in the building with her? Which was it? Caution began to turn into paranoia. Camara's mind was racing. She had forgotten something important that the nameless informant had told her. What was it?!

As quickly and as quietly as she could, Camara scurried down the steps to the basement. She checked her surroundings. Again no one was in the basement but she did find a small recorder sitting on a counter. She was sure it hadn't been there before.

Again, Camara took in everything around her. Everything looked to be in its place as when she went upstairs, only the recorder was a new addition. She was good at being stealthy, but she knew she had made noise when she entered the basement. Even though she went in through the boarded up window, which was quieter than using the door, it was possible that whoever had been in here would have heard her come in. How did someone get in to put this here without Camara hearing, then get out again?

Camara walked over to the recorder and found a small note lying beside it. The typed note read: Play me. So Camara did. The voice was different. It wasn't the same robotic voice of the informant she met in person. The voice was deep, disguised in a different way, and not very well.

"You always were predictable, baby, lazy too. Consider this a friendly reminder of the consequences if I don't start seeing some action on your part toward an outcome that would be in my favor. Dollars and cents. You should duck now."

Camara barely had time to register the voice coming from the recorder when a hail of bullets bombarded the boarded up windows of the basement. Camara threw herself to the ground and covered her head while ducking behind a support beam. The bullets exploded all around her sending dust and debris everywhere. The gunshots seemed to last forever. From the sound of the bullets and the rapid fire Camara guessed her attackers were wielding AK-47s.

The shooting finally stopped. Camara poked her head out just in time to see two shadows scurry from the new holes in the building. She tried to zero in on the sound of their footsteps, but her ears were ringing from the shooting. She was blinded by rage. She couldn't believe she had fallen for something this obvious. As soon as the shooting started, she remembered what the informant had told her. He said that he would contact her the same way as the first time. He didn't send a text the first time.

Camara almost hit herself for being so stupid, but she didn't. Snap's voice was on the recorder. He wanted to send a message; Camara would send one of her own. Against all rational thinking, Camara grabbed the recorder with her fingerprints on it and ran to the window she had come through. She looked for the direction her attackers had run. She stood with her Glock ready, running on pure adrenaline and hate. She saw one of Snap's cronies run up Park Avenue and she gave chase.

They didn't have much of a headstart on her, maybe five seconds and on the street that wasn't much. When Camara rounded the corner a blast from one of the AKs shattered the wall inches from her head. She avoided the bullets by ducking behind a car then quickly diving to the opposite side putting the car between herself and the shooter.

The shots were wild. Whoever he was, his mind was on escape not murder. Camara ran after them, her mind filled with murder not escape. Her Glock ready, she ran crouched down along a row of parked cars and followed the attackers as they ran onto Straley Avenue. The footchase continued until they got close to Straley Elementary where the two assailants jumped the small brick wall and made their way to the other side of the school. Camara lined one of them up. She steadied herself, aimed with deadly accuracy, then opened fire hitting her target in the leg.

Camara was about to close the gap between herself and her attacker when the uninjured one brought his AK around and let it loose in her direction. Camara's only cover was the small brick wall that led to the school grounds. She kept her head and didn't panic. Whoever Snap had sent, they were amateurs. They were burning through bullets and couldn't have reloaded. Camara listened to the gun to see if its explosions were getting any louder, to see if the rookie was doing the smart thing and advancing on her to protect his friend, but he wasn't. Camara began to make her move when she heard the clicks of the gun's chamber finally running out. Before she could do anything, she saw a small black object drop down from over the wall not five feet from where she was hiding.

Time stood still as Camara realized what had dropped in front of her. She moved in slow motion. She almost didn't have time to react. She jumped the brick wall and rolled away from the edge just in time to avoid being hit by the force of the grenade exploding. She expected to be shot by the rookies but they had hightailed it and were nowhere to be seen.

Camara took in her surroundings. Several house lights were starting to come on and people were starting to take notice of the gunshots and the explosion. Cars parked on the other side of Straley started to squeal in the night as their alarms went off full blast. When she made sure she was really alone and wouldn't be shot in the back of the head, Camara got up and cut across an ally to hit Mercer Street.

She didn't head directly back to her car. She circled around and waited to make sure she wasn't followed. Her heart was pounding, her head was throbbing, and her eyes darted at every sound. She made it back to her car after about ten minutes. As fast as she could, she threw her gun in her glove box and pulled out a screwdriver. She went to the back of her car and took off her license plate then placed it in the trunk.

Forcing herself to stay calm, she calmly drove out of Princeton. It took her longer than it should have because she took the side roads and avoided the streetlights. Not every streetlight in Princeton had a camera on it, but Camara wanted to play it safe taking every backroad and side street she knew until she hit Route 20 heading toward Bluewell. It was back to the county from there.

Why did they run? Why did she chase them? Why did she go in the first place? Why wasn't she dead? What type of game was Snap playing? Camara was bombarded with questions but didn't have a single answer. The only thing Camara felt she had the answer to was when all this would end. She had hoped to just leave him behind—that he would move on and forget her, but now she knew that wasn't going to happen. She wanted this to be peaceful, but Snap just didn't know how to let things go. This wouldn't end until Snap was dead.

# CHAPTER 45

He was excited. Things were going so well. He reflected over his plan as he drove to Welch. Everything was planned to perfection. He even knew where he would watch his masterpiece unfold. He felt like a child before Christmas, and tomorrow night was the night. The Bluefield Police would undoubtedly do their best to stop him from carrying out his threat, but it didn't matter. The town was already burning; only nobody knew it yet.

He was driving through different areas of McDowell County in his cab. His "death machine," as he liked to call it, was going to be his new way of terrorizing southern West Virginia until he moved onto the next city. It was how he liked to do things: show people something big, something mind blowing like setting a town on fire, then hit them with something more. And what was more mundane than a killer cab driver?

He was taking his time getting to know the areas he liked. Bluefield and Tazewell, Virginia; Bluefield, Princeton and Welch, West Virginia. Someone would die in each town. He had found the best places in each town and was confident he would have no trouble getting away with any of the murders. He didn't always commit pattern murders like this in every city he visited, but he felt as though he needed this. To him, it was like a runner cooling down after a good workout.

These types of kills were always risky. Everything that followed a pattern could be tracked and caught, which is exactly why he typically didn't do it. There was no way the local police and detectives could catch him, so he had to create a sense of danger. He had to perform on the edge. The only hard part was finding the best way to get started— finding the right victim to set the tone.

Tonight, he decided to drive down the backroads leading to Welch. He liked the drive. It was all narrow, two-lane curvy roads which gave him plenty of time to think. They were working on a highway to make this part of the state more accessible to the rest of the world, but it would be years before it was done. Until then, the road going through Bramwell was the only way in and out of the county.

The XM Radio in the cab was low, the fine melodies of Beethoven came through the speakers helping him collect his thoughts to guide his fantasies of killing. Classical music always helped him orchestrate his killings and plan ahead. Every kill was a piece of a puzzle, a move on a chess board.

He calmly and swiftly took the curves with one hand and held his lighter in the other. He took the turns confidently and efficiently, as though he had been driving these roads his whole life, which—to an extent—he had. He flicked his lighter open and shut, careful not to pay too much attention to its magnificence and veer off the road. Instead, he focused on the foosh sound from the lighter as the spark ignited, and then clank of the lighter closing. Each sound amped him up and took his mind to pleasurable thoughts of evil deeds. Each sound was the voice of the flame calling to him, guiding him.

*Tonight.* He wanted to kill someone tonight, but who? Should he kill tonight? He stopped thinking about the particulars of who and when and surrendered to the voice of the flame. It was never wrong. This was when his genius really shined. He was going to call it a night and return to his temporary house on Union Street, but the flame beckoned him to go further. *Why?*

It was getting late and he wasn't expecting to be out this long. He wasn't going this far into the county but the foosh of the fire starting and the clank of it dying had him engrossed and lusting for action. Something was going to happen tonight, he could feel it.

Foosh. Clank. Foosh. Clank.

Without warning, a light caught his attention on the side of the road. Immediately he slowed the cab down and flicked the lighter on. The only light in the cab was from the lighter and the dashboard. Mozart's "Death Mask" now gently echoed in the night as AKA looked though the flame at the light on the side of the road. The car had crept to a halt as it followed the light. It took a second for him to grasp that it was a flashlight. Why would someone be walking on these dark, windy roads at night?

The open flame danced and fluttered as he looked past it at the person walking on the side of the road. Another work of art had been presented to him, and the canvas was set perfectly. The flame had delivered. A smile crept across his face as he clanked the lighter shut and placed it in his breast pocket. Then he reached under the dash and switched the light on the roof of the cab. He eased up behind the person walking on the road until the car was parallel with his prey and rolled down the passenger side windows.

"Excuse me. Would you like a ride?" he asked in his friendliest voice.

An African-American lady who appeared to be in her mid-fifties bent down and looked into the cab. He didn't recognize her, but then again it wouldn't have mattered if he did. The outcome would be the same. Even in the sparse light he could see her cheeks were damp with tears. Her mouth and hands were shaking from the cold night air and the wind coming off the mountains.

"Boy, am I happy to see you," the woman said through chattering teeth.

"Then hop in ma'am," he said through a wide smile.

"It's so good to see a smiling face. You are a lifesaver."

"I haven't saved you yet. Hop in. I'll get you where you need to be." The irony of moments like these never escaped him. He always thought it was funny how people mistook a killing grin for a charming smile until it was too late.

"What are you doing out here this time of night?" she asked as she climbed into the back seat.

"Just driving around, ma'am. Guess it's your lucky night."

# CHAPTER 46

The cab driver looked in his rear view mirror as the woman climbed into the back seat. The woman flopped into the seat, a wave of relief washing over her. She looked calm and happy as though she knew everything would be all right. It took almost all of the driver's control to not burst out in laughter. *Out of the frying pan, into the fucking sun* he thought to himself.

"I was driving home after a long day. What's your excuse for walking in the darkness of these mountains?" he turned and said, grinning from ear to ear.

"It's a long story," the woman said.

"Fair enough," the driver said. "You're my last fare for the night so . . . where to?"

"I'm only about another four miles from here. I'm so happy you showed up when you did. I was sure this damn flashlight was going to give out on me."

"Then it is a good thing I showed up. You would've been walking blind," The driver locked eyes with the woman in the back seat and grinned at her. He held his best killing grin and stared at her just long enough to fill the cab with an awkward aura.

Before she could say anything, the driver turned, pulled off and started down the road. The doors automatically locked when the car was put in gear. The trap was sprung. She had no way out.

"So what's your name, stranger?" the driver said without taking his eyes off the road.

"Nancy. Nancy Hasley."

The driver looked back and noticed Nancy looking around and examining the back of the cab. He guessed she was looking for the ID that was suppose to be displayed in the cab for the passengers to see. She wouldn't find any.

"What's your name?" she asked. From her voice, the driver could tell she was just getting a vague understanding of her situation.

"Larnell," the driver said evenly. "I know you. I remember where I know you from now. You write the obituaries in the paper. Don't you?"

"Um, yeah. Yes, I do."

The driver hit his fist against the dashboard and screamed. "HEY! I knew. Sorry I stared at you the way I did. I knew your name sounded familiar. Hope I didn't creep you out."

"No. No. That's all right," Nancy said sounding a little relieved.

The driver noticed some of the anxiety leaving her body. He loved doing this— creating a rollercoaster ride of life and death.

"You do a such a good job illustrating my work. Some of the best I've heard in my travels, really."

"Thank you, I . . ."

*There it is.* The driver thought as he looked in the rear view, grinning with his back to his passenger. It took her a second to catch what he had said, but she did catch it.

"What do you mean?" she said unsure if she heard correctly.

"I like your work. You do a good job of making the dead seem alive in the hearts and minds of those they left behind. You never give just the facts. Your very good at it."

"What . . . what did you say your name was?"

"Larnell."

"Right, well my turn is just over there so if you could pull off on that street, I can walk the rest of the way."

The driver kept going. He passed the turn with no intention of pulling off the main road. He even picked up speed as he passed her street.

"Oops, not enough warning. Why leave now though, Nancy? We're just starting to get to know each other."

Nancy was starting to panic now. She struggled with the door handle and tried to push the door open. She wasn't thinking. At this speed, an old lady like her wouldn't survive jumping out.

This was also one of his favorite parts—when the mouse realized it was trapped in a cage with a hungry snake.

"What is this? Who are you?" Nancy screamed at the top of her lungs.

"You know me, Nancy. You've been writing up my work for months now."

Suddenly the driver slammed on the brakes and swerved off the side of the road. It was pitch black on the mountain except for the dome light in the cab. The driver turned to Nancy and pointed a 9mm pistol square at her right eye.

"I have many names, Nancy, but AKA is my favorite one to go by. Now I have a question for you. Did you ever take the time to write your own obituary?"

Nancy's eyes were flooded with tears and her hands trembled on the door handles as though she was waiting for them to open by some miracle.

"Answer me, Nancy. Answer me!" The driver screamed pointing the gun closer to her face, his voice deep and menacing, full of all his hate and anger.

She gasped and shook. She had to reach deep within herself to find any words to answer a simple yes or no question.

"Y-y-yes," she finally muttered.

"That's nice, Nancy. I'm happy you did that. I already know God has a special place in hell for me, but you can say a prayer now to try and secure your place in heaven if you like."

Nancy began to shake violently and weep as she closed her eyes tight. Her mouth moved in a silent prayer, and she was having trouble breathing. The driver couldn't make out the words. It all sounded jumbled together.

"On second thought, Nancy," he said interrupting her, "that shit takes too long, and it's not really going to help you anyway." His words caused Nancy's eyes to pop open wide with fear. She stared down the blackness of the gun's barrel. She locked eyes with the driver.

Then he pulled the trigger.

# CHAPTER 47

## CAMARA

The earsplitting buzz of a cheap alarm clock woke Camara at six in the morning. Instead of reaching over to turn the buzzing off, she grabbed the clock, flung it at the door and buried herself back under her covers. She was in no mood to get up. She had only stopped crying thirty minutes ago.

"At least you have plenty of energy to burn this morning," Camara heard coming from the direction she just sent her alarm clock flying. She tried to sit up in bed but was met with a rush of light as her mother flicked the light on. The sudden light drove her deeper under the covers.

"Where did you come from you old cat?" Camara asked without appearing above the covers.

"I may be old, but I'm still plenty graceful."

Camara felt the weight of her mother sit on the bed beside her. She stayed under the covers sensing what the topic of conversation would be. She wasn't ready to talk about it, but she couldn't run either.

"You gonna come up and talk to me, baby?"

"No," Camara said shaking her head and putting on her little girl voice.

"Camara, you're too old for this. Now get up!"

"I don't wanna," Camara said continuing her childish tone.

She heard a sigh come from her mother. She always thought her mom's aggravated sigh sounded like Marge Simpson when Homer did something stupid.

The Alley Cat stretched out on the bed beside her daughter and rubbed the section of the cover where Camara was.

"Are you okay, baby?" she said with a soft nurturing tone only a mother could manage.

Camara's emotions were still getting the best of her. She felt like everything in her life was pressing down and pulling

259

against her. She would have started to cry again if she had any more tears. She couldn't run and she wasn't doing a good job at hiding, so she chose to push her way though the situation.

"How long have you known?" Camara asked, still reluctant to leave her sanctuary of covers.

"That heifer told me a couple of weeks before you came home. She had no reason to tell me, mind you. She blurted it out so nonchalantly, almost as though she thought that because Melvin had been dead for a couple of years, I would just blow over it. Like it just wouldn't matter. Then she had the nerve to think that I was overreacting by being angry."

"Why didn't you tell me?"

Alley Cat paused as though wrestling for the truth before speaking. Allison Johnson had never been one to censor her words from anybody, especially her daughter. Camara didn't say anything but rather waited for her mother to talk. She knew what her mother said would be the truth. Her mother may leave out details, but she would never lie.

"I knew how you felt about Nancy. She helped raise you. Her daughter was your best friend, and I remember how close Nancy and you got once her daughter died."

Camara hadn't thought about Gail, Nancy's daughter and her best friend in a long time. They were always together as kids, which made Gail's death at fifteen so hard for Camara to take. Gail died in a drive-by shooting while visiting her aunt in Tiffany Manor, and Camara had been there to see it happen. She still had nightmares about it sometimes. She hadn't been back to Tiffany Manor since, and she had no plans of ever going back there no matter how 'reformed' people said it might be since the nineties. It was still hell to her.

"Is that when it started? Is that when Nancy started sleeping with daddy?"

Another pause from Alley Cat, Camara wasn't sure if this was a good or bad thing. Her mother had never acted like this before, so hesitant. Camara wasn't sure how to react to her.

"I do remember her and Melvin talking a little after Gail died, but I don't think that's when the affair started. That might very well be where it was rooted, when they started feeling close, but I don't think they were sleeping together then."

A wave of guilt rushed over Camara. Guilt that she had carried with her for years and was never able to fully let go of, even now. Her throat was dry and her mouth felt like cotton. She felt like she needed to swallow and couldn't; she had to remind herself that she could.

"This is all my fault, isn't it?" Camara said through a hoarse voice and dry sobs.

"Oh, stop that!" the Alley Cat hissed shaking Camara. "This has absolutely nothing to do with you."

"Mom, you don't . . . Gail died because of . . ."

"Gail died because you both were in the wrong place at the wrong time! It wasn't your fault, Camie. You've been putting that on yourself for too long now. Ten years is far too long to carry any burden."

Camara had no words to respond. She was sure she couldn't talk if she tried. It had been ten years since Gail was killed, and nobody knew the full truth of what had really happened. Nobody but Camara.

Camara felt like a fourteen-year-old girl again and didn't like it. It brought back pain and memories that were better left forgotten. Without warning, Alley Cat pulled away Camara's sanctuary of covers and exposed her to the light. Camara quickly covered her eyes and squinted. Being confronted by the light was like being confronted by the truth and Camara would have been much more comfortable hiding from both all day.

"You can't hide here all day. What will Mrs. Cervantes think?"

"That woman is the last person on my mind right now."

"Well, you need to get up and do your job all the same."

Camara sat up and fought to open her eyes. Her mother was sitting up too now. For some reason Camara expected her mom to look just as shipwrecked as she did, but she wasn't. Camara shouldn't have been surprised. She had rarely seen her mother cry and she had never seen her mother lose it even when she was down. When Camara was weak, her mom was strong. When her mom was weak, Camara was strong. That's just the way it went.

"You look like hell," Camara's mother said rubbing away dried tears. "Hurry up and jump in the shower or you'll be late."

"She'll be there you know. She sits right beside me every day."

"Just because she sits beside you don't mean you have to say anything to her. She may not have cared what I think, but your opinion means a lot to her."

"I don't think I can find anything good to say to her. I'm not going to sit there and be fake with her all day. I'm not going to pretend like everything's fine when it isn't."

"I'm not telling you how to act, but you still have a job to do. You still haven't told me about all that drama that went down yesterday at the paper. We can talk about this later tonight. I'll tell you everything you want to know and we can talk about whatever you like. Now hop in the shower and I'll fix you some breakfast."

Alley Cat got up from the bed and made her way to the door. She moved with a grace that shouldn't belong to a woman of her years and had a spring in her step as though they just finished having a casual conversation.

"And I'm sure you can find some reason to want to go to work today," she said with a smile as she disappeared through the door.

Camara chuckled and managed a smile at the irony of that statement. She was going to a job where she had to sit beside a woman who she just learned had been having an extensive affair with her father. She was expected to write an article outing a serial killer's presence in Bluefield for a mysterious androgynous robot. Her boss was going to look at her sideways unless she was working some angle of the bodies found in Jimmy Lewis Lake. The city might burn tonight killing God knows how many people and it could all be her fault, and her crazed ex may be planning to kill her for money she didn't have in some insane effort to get her back.

All this ran through Camara's head and she flung the covers over herself and flopped back in the bed. Getting up just wasn't worth it.

"GET UP CAMARA!" She heard coming from downstairs.

*Damn! When did she get psychic powers?* Camara thought from under the covers.

"NOW!"

"Jeez," Camara said to herself and got out of bed.

She took off her clothes and headed for the bathroom. As she got in the shower, she struggled to think of something that would get her through the day, something that wouldn't make the day drag by, something to make it bearable to leave for work. She just needed to think of something that would bring a smile to her face. Then she remembered.

Ezra would be there.

# CHAPTER 48

I was still being followed. When I got in Dirty Vegas to head for work I saw Ren and Stimpy across the parking lot staring at me. Now they had stopped trying to be sneaky and sat right in the open. The fat one even waved at me from the passenger seat. I almost went over and talked to them. I felt like giving them a piece of my mind, but I let it go.

I drove to the Telegraph and wondered why I still did this job. I only had a few people who liked me there now and it wasn't like they were paying me a lot. I didn't have anything holding me in West Virginia, but I still hadn't left. I wasn't scared to go like some people; I just never had any real motivation. The past couple of months had provided me with plenty of reasons, but I was still here.

The lush green of the Appalachian Mountains surrounded me as I hit 460 heading to Bluefield. The mountains were low and rolling and seemed to extend from East River Mountain that dominated the horizon. Specks of yellow and red were in the trees and the sky was clear and vibrant. The East River Mountain Range ran along a section of Bluefield, West Virginia into Virginia. A tunnel ran through the mountain leading straight to Virginia and North Carolina. As I took in the scenery, I remembered why I had stayed as long as I had in West Virginia. I loved it here—plain and simple. It had a lot of problems. There weren't many jobs, with fewer well paying ones. Depending on how you looked at the area, not a lot to do and not a lot of variety.

I knew plenty of people who'd see this area through those eyes, but I saw potential. I was in love with what I knew southern West Virginia could be, what I prayed it would be one day. There's a lot of room for growth here, but someone just had to step in and take advantage of it.

Still, I could leave if I wanted. Maybe put my social work degree to use. I've thought about it several times but never followed through. A change of pace could be good for me.

I pulled into the Telegraph and walked inside. A temp was working for Kim today. She must have taken what happened yesterday pretty hard. It's not like her to miss work. I made my way to the staircase and ran into Lois about halfway up.

"It's good to see you still want to come to work from time to time," Lois said.

"I'm sorry I haven't been around lately."

"Don't worry about it, Ezra, I'm just messing with you," she said placing a hand on my shoulder. "Still I would like to actually *see* you from time to time. How are you?"

"I'm good, really. After almost being blown up a couple of days ago, I've really been able to put things into perspective."

"You know that's just what it takes sometimes," Lois said through a laugh.

"What's up with Kim?"

"She's all torn up about not being able to remember what the girl looked like that delivered that letter from the serial killer."

"You know about that?" I asked.

"You know about that?" Lois shot back. She was over the production department, so it makes sense that the gossip would trickle down to her.

"I just thought everybody was supposed to be tightlipped about it."

"Well, it can't be too big a secret if you knew. I'm guessing Miss Johnson filled you in. Am I right?"

Lois gave the serious look. I wondered if I had just gotten Camara in trouble.

"Um, well . . ."

Lois couldn't hold her poker face and started laughing at me before I could come close to thinking up some pathetic lie.

"Sorry I had to. You're so easy."

"That's not funny," I said very unamused.

"All the heads of the departments know, but you're right, we are being tightlipped about all this. At least for now. We're waiting for all the bodies to be ID'd and the families alerted. We'll run the story in a day or two."

"All right. I'll keep my mouth shut until then."

"Have you heard anything about Nancy?"

"Nancy? No why?"

"She's not here today. She's never missed a day of work for as long as I've been here. She always here early and gets the coffee started. She hasn't called in or anything."

"That is weird. On the other hand, Nancy hasn't been sick in like two years, so she's overdue for a cold or something. I'm sure she's okay."

I played it off as best I could, but I was a little worried about Nancy. She had always been a horse. I couldn't see her being too sick to come to work, let alone too sick to call in.

"Is anyone else missing I should know about?"

"Camara is working hard at her desk if that's what you're asking."

"It wasn't, but thanks for the info anyway. What's on the schedule for today?"

"I'll double check for you when I get back up, but it's nothing exciting. All the sports in Mercer County have been shut down indefinitely."

"What? Serious? When did that happen?"

"In about five hours. Mayor Hill decided it would be good to put a hold on the football season until we can find out what's going on around here. Basketball season might get the axe too, unless some progress is made."

"How did she manage to do that?"

"Help from the governor, of course! He came down and had a meeting with Hill. People are scared and the story about the bodies found in Jimmy Lewis Lake isn't going to make it any better."

"This is going to cost the high schools and colleges a bit of money. What's Concord University going to do? I know they just put in that new technology center."

"Concord will be okay as long as they get to have basketball. They never made a lot off football anyway, and they can always raise tuition again. They never really seem to have a problem with that. I'm more worried about Bluefield Beavers' football. They go upstate just about every year."

"I'm going to need a second job, aren't I?"

"Probably," Lois said patting me on the chest. "Head upstairs. I'll give you what I got when I get back."

I scaled the hallway steps and went into the newsroom. I had been smart with my money over the past several months and had a nice cushion in the bank, but I was going to need a consistent check. No sports meant less work. I didn't like to depend on freelance graphic design—this area just wasn't great for that—but I might not have an option. I had some out-of-state work lined up, but that's never a sure thing. I thought again about my social work degree collecting dust. As sad as it was there's always work in that field. Some child is always being mistreated somewhere.

Camara was to my right. She didn't see me come into the newsroom, so I snuck up behind her and covered her eyes with my hands.

"Guess who?" I said.

Camara's hand gently reached up to touch mine and I felt a smile form across her lips. Her hands were soft and sent shock waves through me. It's funny how a simple touch from the right person can make everything else disappear.

"Uuumm. Strong manly hands. Sweet masculine cologne. It has to beeee. . . ." Camara teased then said, "Morris Chestnut!"

"What?"

"Taye Diggs?"

"Nope."

"Borus Kojo?"

"Not even close."

"Mr. Marcus!"

"Oh, hell no!"

"Oh, my God! Denzel!"

"Better."

"Better than Denzel?" Camara said, sounding disappointed. "I don't think it can get any better than Denzel."

I turned Camara around in her chair so that she faced me. As I turned her, she kept her hand gently on mine.

"Are you sure about that?" I asked.

"Hmmm," Camara said looking me up and down. "You're making me think twice about it. Are you going to be here long?"

"I doubt it. Lois said she found some stuff for me to do in town. I'm going to need the work since it looks like there's no more sports in Mercer County for a while."

"I heard about that. Or rather, I heard the sports writer's reaction to that."

"Dan. What did he do?" I said sitting on Camara's desk breaking our hand contact. I didn't want her to let go, but we were at work.

"Well, he threw the papers on his desk after he kicked his computer, but that was before he paced around the newsroom cursing the mayor. Then, I think he quit."

"Dan threatens to quit every year after basketball season. He'll be back. Have you heard from Nancy?" I said looking over to the empty desk beside Camara.

"I'm not sure where she is. I'm sure she'll show up somewhere sooner or later."

There was something about Camara's tone that bothered me. The way she dismissed any concern for Nancy bothered me. However she had known Nancy longer than me, so, if she wasn't worried, I didn't think I should be.

"What are you doing tonight?" Camara asked.

"Praying for rain," I said reaching for a laugh. I felt relieved when I got one. Camara seemed to understand my weird sense of humor. "You?" I asked.

"I was hoping you would take me out."

"I can do that. Where did you have in mind?"

"Somewhere nice to eat that isn't so close to Bluefield."

I had just gotten back in town, but I had to admit, I wouldn't mind leaving again— even if only for a few hours.

"I know of a couple of good places to eat in Beckley. I know a few places in Wytheville, too."

"Either is fine with me. I just. . . . I don't want to just be waiting around for something to happen, you know."

I nodded to Camara and an understanding passed between us. I knew exactly what she meant and she knew I felt the same. A pyrotechnic lunatic had threatened Bluefield. He said the city would burn tonight. Camara and I wouldn't say it aloud, but we both thought that the killer might be able to pull it off. Zeus had convinced us of that much.

Lois walked into the newsroom and gestured for me to follow her into her office for my assignment.

"Meet me at my place at five?" I asked.

"That's fine. I would like to leave before dark if possible."

Again a silent understanding passed between us. I reached out and touched her hand again, and looked into her chestnut eyes.

"Five," I said.

"Five," Camara replied

As I walked away, I knew I was in trouble. A sadness came over me as I left Camara's side. I didn't want to be away from her, but I was excited about seeing her tonight. I tried to think of another explanation for how I felt, but I knew what it was. I had only known her for a month, but I was falling for Camara Johnson.

# CHAPTER 49

**EZRA**

I didn't have much to do today. Lois gave me some events she wanted captured on film at Princeton City Hall and the Chamber of Commerce. Lois also wanted pictures of the Bluefield Virginia Board meeting as well as pictures of the buildings in downtown Bluefield, West Virginia, that were overdue to be torn down.

I didn't stay long in Princeton. Nothing very interesting was being said, so I got the shots I needed and went on to Bluefield, Virginia. The ongoing topic for a long time had been the new mall that was supposed to go up in the area. The mall had agreed to come, but when they found out that the Super Wal-Mart in that same area had been given free water by the state they wanted free water, too. The super Wal-Mart at one point had been the biggest on the East Coast, so the state was happy to give them the free water at the time to generate business. Now the deal the state made seemed like they had shot themselves in the foot.

I got some pictures at the city hall meeting then headed to downtown Bluefield, West Virginia. I also took some pictures of the rundown buildings and empty retail spaces. At one point, downtown Bluefield would have buzzed with life and possibilities, but it was so long ago you could only find proof in history books.

Seeing the buildings made me remember that night at Bluefield State. I remembered Isabelle Sparks and wondered how long the regret of that night would follow me. I've only seen her in pictures, but her face still haunted my dreams. I could see her asking for help, asking me not to stand there and watch her struggle and be raped and killed. I sometimes thought about what her ambitions were, what she would have done with her life.

Isabelle's death was a dark cloud over my head; it was a direct consequence of my choice. All I could do was pray for a chance to redeem myself one day.

I finished early and called Camara to see if we could meet for lunch. Melissa had her running around the city checking in with possible leads, so I was on my own. She told me that she was on Union Street checking on a missing girl. She assured me that she would finish in time to meet me at five for our excursion out of Bluefield.

With nothing to do, I headed to Applebee's to grab a bite to eat, then headed to my favorite spot in Bluefield, the East River Mountain Scenic Overlook. The overlook was the perfect spot to get a good view of the whole town. You could see sections of Bluewell in one direction and see past Bluefield, Virginia in the other. You could also see some of the best sunsets in the state from up here. I parked Dirty Vegas at the top of the mountain and stood on the wooden terrace.

The trees were still different shades and hues of green that blended into the blue atmospheric haze and the sun was blending into a flurry of orange, blues, and purple clouds. The smell of wildflowers hit me from a sudden updraft and brought back memories of a simpler time. I thought of my mother for the first time without feeling a gaping hole in my heart.

I was a firm believer that you didn't get over the loss of a loved one. The best you could do was put their memory inside you so that it no longer caused you pain. I think I was finally starting to get there, and I think Camara was helping.

I walked back to my car and grabbed my acoustic guitar. I looked for Ren and Stimpy as I got to the car, but I didn't see them. I was sure they were around so they must have decided to hang back. Whatever their reason, I appreciated it. I was in a good mood and didn't need to see them off in a corner somewhere staring at me.

I sat on the edge of the terrace and played some Carlos Santana, Jim Morrison and a few of my own personal tracks. I let myself go and played like the town was my own stage and everyone could hear me. Nothing cleared my head like music. Nothing took me away like my guitar. I got so into my own groove that I didn't notice anyone was around until I heard clapping after I finished an original tune.

I turned around and saw a guy wearing a wife beater and baggy jeans so low you could see his boxers. The poor guy couldn't run if you paid him to. He was light-skinned, not very tall, and not a very muscular build. He had tattoos covering both arms, a couple I recognized as jailhouse tats.

"That shit was tight," he said and continued to clap.

"Thanks. I didn't know I really had an audience."

"I just rolled up. Ain't been here but a couple of minutes. Waz yo name?"

"Ezra." I could tell from the way he talked that he wasn't from West Virginia.

"Ezra. That's a hot name. Sounds biblical n' some shit ya know. You from around here?"

"Born and raised. I can tell by your accent you're from up north, right?"

"Southside Chicago."

"What are you doing in Bluefield?"

"Getting married, son. My girl's from around here so we came here to tie the knot. Soon as that's over I'm getting her up out of here and I'm not looking back, ya feel me?"

"I hear you, but this isn't a bad place if you get used to it. Doesn't cost much to live here."

"I bet. Where you stay out?"

"Some apartments in GreenValley. Not a bad place to raise a family."

"If you say so. I've been here two weeks n' shit, yo, I've already had enough."

The guy walked over to the edge of the terrace and spit over the mountain. Something was off about him. He seemed cordial enough, but the energy he put off was all wrong.

"You look like a man of the streets," he said. "Where can a guy find some action around here?"

"Second thoughts about getting married?"

"Nah, nah, that's gonna happen. Just try'n to get my dick wet with a few different bitches before I'm on lock down, ya know what I mean?"

"Sorry, not sure I can help you there," I said picking up my guitar getting ready to leave. This guy was creeping me out. He hadn't said anything too weird, but something about him made me uncomfortable.

"You out, Ezra?"

Something about the way he said my name bothered me, but I wasn't sure what.

"Yeah, got somewhere to be. I didn't get your name."

The guy pulled out a joint and lit it up before answering my question. "Larrnell." He said through a cloud of smoke. "Larrnell Odom."

"Nice meeting you, Larrnell," I said as I turned to leave.

"See you around, Ezra."

I walked to Dirty Vegas, put my guitar in the back and started the drive down the mountain. Something about that guy bothered me. He reminded me of the drug dealers that my brother used to run with. Something about the way he said my name. The way he said it, like he knew me.

# CHAPTER 50

*Right here.* Ezra Walker was right here in front of him. It would have been so easy to kill him on this mountain. Twenty . . . He counted twenty different ways that he could have done it and less than half involved the gun he was carrying.

Ezra had no idea how close he just came to death. It took an extreme amount of control to not cut his throat after his affront at Bluefield State. However, patience had paid off. It wouldn't be hard to find where Ezra lived now. It would have been easy to follow him from the paper anytime, but he knew he would have another opportunity like this. The fire told him so, and fire had never lied to him.

The only thing that stopped him was that his god had already determined how Ezra should die and demanded to be present when it was time. He reached in his jeans and pulled out his lighter and flicked it open. He held the lighter out over the town of Bluefield and a rush of excitement came over him.

Foosh. The city was engulfed in flames.

Clank. Everything was normal.

Foosh. Hundreds died as the fire spread and raged out of control.

Clank. Back to the present.

It was all set. The plan was in motion. Bluefield was already burning but no one was smart enough to see it yet.

He imagined how it would look before it happened. He wondered which direction the winds would blow the fire. He imagined the blaze in all its fullness and glory. Tonight was his night. His coming out. The beginning of his legend. Bluefield should feel privileged that he had picked them for this honor.

He had killed countless people in countless towns in America, but he had never caused damage on this scale before. He wondered how Zeus would react to what he would do tonight. What would he say?

But there would be time for Zeus later. Ezra was the new target for now.

Foosh.

*And the streets ran red with blood,* he thought to himself looking through the flame. The lighter flicked closed as he stood alone on the edge of the East River Mountain Overlook.

He closed his eyes and was so anxious that he could almost hear his favorite sound in the coming night sky. The sound was an orgasmic bliss like it always was. He couldn't wait to hear his favorite screams. The screams of fire trucks.

# CHAPTER 51

## CAMARA

Camara was ready to get out of Bluefield. Everything in her life was fighting against her. She had too much to think about before all the mess that went down last night; she had already felt like she was falling off the edge. It wasn't surprising that Nancy didn't show up to work today. On some level, Camara felt good that Nancy was ashamed enough not to show her face. It was surprising, however, that Nancy didn't call in.

Camara pulled up to Ezra's apartment in Pauli Heights right at five and checked her make up. Her hair was down and crinkly without looking frizzy. She wore black pants that hugged her around the hips and thighs then flowed as they went down. She had on a solid pink short-sleeve shirt with a lightweight black jacket and matching shoes to set everything off. She also had on her favorite Victoria Secret push up bra and perfume. It had been a long time since she felt sexy so she pulled out all the stops tonight.

She took more time than she usually did to get ready because she wanted this to be special. It had to be—she needed to get her mind off everything. One night. Just one night with no problems, no interruption was all she asked for. No murders to investigate, no leads to follow, one night out with a hot guy was all she asked for. She felt she deserved it.

Camara sent Ezra a text and he came right out. He had on a black, gray and white button up with black jeans and black New Balances. His black leather jacket highlighted the width of his shoulders; his walk was confident and masculine. He didn't try to do the gangster limp, but still had plenty of swagger in his step.

Camara was so excited to see him she couldn't hold back her smile. Camara felt a jolt when he smiled back at her. She

276

noticed everything when he smiled, from the look in his eyes, to the curl in his lips and his white straight teeth. It was perfect.

"Right on time," he said.

"I'm never late," Camara said confident in herself.

"You sure you don't want me to drive?"

"It's fine. I like driving. Ever since I was sixteen, I would sometimes take my car and just drive to Bluefield then back to the county. I don't mind."

"If you're sure."

"Where are we going? I don't care how far just a long as it's out of Bluefield. I'm working with a full tank."

"Is Beckley far enough?"

"Perfect, Beckley it is."

It didn't take long for Camara to hit I -77 North toward Beckley. It was only about a forty-minute trip, but it seemed to go by much faster. Ezra and Camara talked the whole way. They shared their political views for the first time. Ezra was every bit of a conservative as Camara thought he would be. Normally she would only be attracted to someone as liberal as her, but Ezra had a way of sharing his conservative views in a liberal way. He challenged her at every turn and on every issue. If someone had been riding with them they might have thought the conversation was getting heated, but they both just enjoyed arguing.

They got to the movies and Camara told Ezra to pick. She wanted to see if she could guess which movie he would pick.

"How about the new Bond flick? I've been meaning to go see it."

"Perfect, I love Daniel Craig," Camara said and smiled at herself for guessing right. She liked that she was starting to know him as well as she was.

After the movie, they went out to eat at a Chinese restaurant. The restaurant was mostly empty and the lights were dim. It reminded Camara of their first date at the Mayflower but with an Asian flare. She wasn't sure if it was the nicest all-you-can-eat Chinese place she'd ever been in or if it just seemed that way because she was with Ezra.

What was it about him that had her so twisted? What was it about him that had her ignoring common sense? He was different. He was safe, a nice guy. Camara almost laughed out loud—she was falling for a nice guy. She was certain she would have laughed in Ezra's face five years ago. She thought she really was growing up.

The night was going so fast. Camara looked at her watch and it was already twelve.

Ezra must have noticed, "You thinking about Bluefield?"

"Is it that obvious?"

"Yes. You shouldn't worry though. Lois or Melissa will be calling us the second something happens. No use in worrying until then."

Camara rubbed her head and looked away playfully. "Uuumm, I kinda turned my phone off."

"Really? Me, too," Ezra said and they both laughed. They knew they were running from their jobs but didn't care. Tonight was going to be their night and they weren't in any hurry. They continued to sit and talk after they finished their food.

"What time does this place close?" Ezra asked one of the waiters cleaning tables. The waiter didn't say anything, just pointed to the sign on the wall. The sign said the restaurant closed at twelve.

"What time is it?" Ezra asked Camara.

"Ten till one," Camara said checking her watch. For the first time they took their attention off each other and noticed the annoyed look of all the workers. The buffet had been closed and the back houselights were off. Several of the workers were staring at Camara and Ezra, one in particular. The shortest of the crew stood meat cleaver in hand looking more comical than frightening.

"I think it's time to go," Ezra said as he got up from the table and Camara followed suit. Camara noticed that Ezra left a hefty tip on the table for them staying too long.

Camara was the first to laugh as they got into the parking lot. They took about two steps out the door before they heard the door slamming behind them. The lights flicked off.

"Well, we over stayed our welcome," Camara said taking hold of Ezra's hand.

"They looked like they were about to Kung-Fu Hustle us out of there. They were looking crazy," Ezra said laughing.

"I think we could've taken them."

"Did you see the short guy? He was ready to go to war. He looked like Tetsuo."

Camara burst out laughing at the Akiria reference.

"You've seen that movie?" Ezra asked.

"My brother liked Anime. I got a little nerd in me."

"Really," Ezra said pulling Camara closer.

"I've got a lot in me that you don't know about yet," Camara said leaning in closer. Camara lightly placed her hand on Ezra's chest and held his hand with the other. As safe and temperate as Ezra was, he still felt electric up close. Every time Camara got near him, she felt soft. It was his confidence without being cocky, his abundance of knowledge without being smug, and his sense of self that made him sexy. His looks didn't hurt either.

Camara leaned in and kissed him gently. She felt shock waves. She felt bad for thinking it because she knew he wanted to go slow, but she wanted to know what Ezra would be like in bed. One of her favorite singer's songs sprung to mind, Jill Scott's "Crown Royal." She thought the song fit what it would be like to make love to Ezra. *Is that what Ezra would be like?* Camara thought. *Crown Royal on Ice.* She hummed in her head.

She didn't think she would find out tonight, but it was ok. The kiss was sweet and tender, exactly what Camara needed.

Camara rested her head on Ezra's chest and he put his arms around her. She felt grateful that he was so tall and that she had decided to wear flats tonight. She didn't get to feel small often, and she was enjoying every second because she knew it couldn't last.

"We need to get back?" Ezra finally asked.

"Nooo," Camara said protesting like a child being told they had to leave the playground before she was ready.

"It's getting late and we got a drive ahead of us. I-77 will take you out if you give it the chance. I don't want you to pass out."

"I've got you to talk to me on the way, I'll be fine."

"I don't know I ate a lot. I think I'm starting to get the Idis."

"Well, you better wake up. That wasn't soul food we just had, so you can shake it off," Camara said tapping Ezra on the shoulder.

"Come on," Ezra said moving to get into the car. "You ready to get back to Bluefield?"

Camara answered honestly, "No."

# CHAPTER 52

## CAMARA

The drive back to Bluefield seemed much longer than the trip to Beckley, but Camara didn't mind. Ezra was hanging in there, but he had started yawning before they even hit 77. Camara was going to try to wake him up but he looked so cute trying to fight sleep. She finally decided to let him lean back and drift off.

Tonight had been a good night. Camara was scared to check her phone so she didn't. It was irresponsible and might get her fired but she couldn't face what she might find. She knew she would be responsible if anything happened. She wasn't sure if she could handle the guilt. If it was a viable option, Camara would have gladly hightailed it to Charlotte or Washington, D.C. just to get away.

It had been proven time and time again that people who wait for the long-term solutions over instant gratification do better and are happier with their lives. Camara believed this completely—she just didn't have any patience. Too many times in her life she had gone for what worked in the moment, thinking that moving from one situation to another was getting her somewhere. She was moving after all. But, as she looked back and really thought about it, there was a lot in her life she had never moved on from. Now Camara could only wonder where her life would be if she had tackled some of her issues dead on instead of running.

She wondered which Ezra was to her. Was he just Mr. Right now, or was he the real thing? It felt real. She had never had a man make her wait to be physical the way Ezra had. Why did that make her want him more? How did he have her so confused? They had both gone through a lot over the past several months and Camara was scared that she and Ezra would only last for as long as their individual hurt brought them together.

What was Ezra's real story? Camara still didn't know and doubted she ever would. Another sad truth to Camara's life was that she had always been a sucker for the mysterious. Ezra intrigued her more than anything. The whole town of Blue-field had an opinion of him, be it good or bad, and Camara wanted a firsthand look. With everything that happened with Snap so fresh in her mind, it didn't make sense for her to get involved with someone so fast, or even at all. So why was she doing this to herself? Why was she doing this to Ezra?

Camara was so lost in thought she didn't notice a figure hanging out of the car in front of her pointing something in her direction. Flashes came from the person hanging from the car window and holes burst through Camara's front wind-shield. The windshield cracked loudly as two bullets flew into the passenger side of the car where Ezra's head would have been if he hadn't been leaning back asleep in his seat.

Camara wasn't sure if the gunshots or her swerving across the highway had caused Ezra to spring up, but he was wide awake now.

"What the . . .!" he screamed while trying to get his bearing in the swerving car.

"Stay down!" Camara screamed trying to regain control.

More shots rang out in the night hitting the windshield and the front of the car. Camara reached into the back, pulled out her purse, and released her Glock from its hiding place. She clicked the button on her door to roll down her window, pointed her Glock out and opened fire on her assailants empting a full clip into the car. She got a small amount of pleasure seeing their car swerve in the open highway. They weren't expecting her to return fire.

"You got a gun!" Ezra said in shock. "Why do you have a gun!?"

"Switch me sides."

"What?"

"Take the wheel, I can't shoot with my left hand."

"What!?"

"Hurry up before they start shooting again!"

**"What!?"**

"Take the fucking wheel, Ezra!" Camara said hitting the button to roll Ezra's window down and activating the cruise control at the same time.

Ezra grabbed the wheel as Camara climbed over him, then reached for her spare clip in her purse. Camara put both hands on her Glock like she had been trained to do and took her time. The only reason she had emptied her first clip so fast was because she wanted the element of surprise. She wanted them rattled and off balance. Now she was in control and could take her time.

She fired one shot in the back window of the car and kept the driver off balance. The car kept swerving almost hitting a ditch on the shoulder of the road. The driver was jumpy, so was the shooter. Camara had counted twelve flashes and pops coming from the attacker's gun since they first opened fire. Driver and shooter were both out of control and too busy reacting when they should be thinking.

"Turn the lights off," Camara said keeping her eyes on the car. They were speeding up now. They wanted to put some distance between them and Camara's bullets. They were starting to gain some composure.

"Do what?" Ezra asked looking at Camara like she was crazy.

"Trust me. Just follow their lights and stay behind them. They won't be able to see us."

"Can't we just stop and let them go?"

"No! We don't know how many of them there are. They could be setting us up for an ambush or more could be coming. We can't just sit on the side of the road and wait for the cops. We need them out of our way. Turn off the lights."

Ezra did as he was told, but Camara could tell he didn't like it. He was just starting to pull everything together. He had been sound asleep when this started so Camara could only imagine how fast everything must be moving for him. Hell, they were moving too fast for her. She had faith though that he wouldn't choke when she needed him.

Ezra got into the lane on the left and sped up. It was pitch black in the car now but Camara felt Ezra shift and pick up even more speed. He had gotten his head in the fight now. He knew what Camara wanted before she told him.

Ezra was pulling up beside the car. The punks in it must not have seen them because three guys leaned out of the windows and opened fire right where they were seconds ago. Two in the back and one on the passenger side—Camara listened to the shots. A semiautomatic, an Uzi and a shotgun were the weapons of choice for the idiots in the car. At least that's what they sounded like to her. With that kind of hardware, Camara knew this wasn't random.

"Whatever you're going to do, you better do it now. I'm just about driving blind here."

Camara used the flashes from the guns in the other car to pinpoint the back tire and used the headlights to find the front.

"When I count to three, punch it. We want to be in front of them if I do this right."

"And if you don't?"

"Then it won't matter. Ready?"

"No."

"One, two, three—" Camara took her time and focused on her targets then squeezed the trigger twice in succession. The first shot hit the back tire. Camara wasn't sure about the other, but she got the effect she wanted.

The driver swerved to the right and the tire blew. The driver also did the worst thing he could have done and slammed on the brakes causing the car to roll and flip over before resting in a ditch on the side of the highway. Camara wasn't sure, but she thought she saw at least two of the thugs thrown from the car.

She leaned out of the window, looked back as the car disappeared in the distance, then screamed and beat the side of the car in triumph.

"Tell Snap he'll have to do better than that! Fuck him! Do you hear me!? Tell him I said, 'Fuck him!'"

Camara sat back in the car and rolled her window up. Ezra had already turned the lights back on and was only doing seventy. Camara looked over at him. He was looking at her like she was the craziest person he had ever seen.

"You might want to keep you eyes on the road," Camara said checking the clip in her Glock.

Ezra slowed down and pulled off to the side of the road.

"What are you doing? We can't stop," Camara said.

Ezra didn't respond. He stopped the car in front of a sign that read, *Bluefield* 15 miles and turned the lights off.

They sat in silence for a moment. Camara wanted to give him time to collect his thoughts; she needed time to collect her own. Stopping like this wasn't smart.

Camara waited as long as she could but she couldn't take it any longer. Snap might have sent more pawns after her. They needed to move.

"Ezra, I know you're shook up. So am I. But we really need to move."

Ezra reached for the roof and pushed the dome light on. Camara didn't recognize him for a second. His face was empty—devoid of any real expression. All Camara could go on was the hint of anger in his eyes. He was struggling with his emotions, trying to find the right way to express them.

"How long have you been carrying a gun?" Ezra asked. His voice was colder than Camara had ever heard it before. His gaze was deep and unblinking.

"What?" Camara said in earnest shock. "What does that have to do with anything?"

"What was all that about? What are you into that you need to carry a gun?"

"This is not the time to discuss this, Ezra. We need to go."

"It's now or never."

Camara leaned back and folded her arm. "Oh, really. That's how it's going to be now? Your way or no way?"

"I just want an answer. Can't you see how I would have some questions after all that?" Ezra said, his voice sounding harder, angry.

"We don't have time for this! Move. I'll drive from here on out."

"Will you just give me an answer, please?"

"Damn it, Ezra, what the hell is wrong with you? He might have more people following us! We need to get off the damn highway."

"Who are you talking about? What do you think is going on here?" Ezra said in an accusing tone.

"What does it matter?" Camara shot back.

Camara keyed on Ezra's eyes and clinched her fist. She couldn't believe he was being so stupid. Didn't he understand what she was saying? Didn't he understand the danger they could still be in? It was taking all of Camara's control not to hit him. Her blood was boiling.

Ezra finally seemed to get the message on his own. He reached up and turned off the dome light and started the car. They were back on the highway heading to Bluefield in silence. Camara couldn't remember the last time she had known someone for such a short time that she was able to get this mad at. Her left foot was tapping the floor of the car. She couldn't keep her hands still. Her heart was about to pound its way out of her chest.

Then, Ezra did what she least expected. He reached out and cupped Camara's hand. His grip was firm and gentle. She almost hit him because she wasn't in the mood to be touched now.

"I thought they were after me," he said, his voice reclaiming the tenderness Camara was used to hearing. She didn't pull away, but she still wanted to hit him.

"What do you mean?" Camara said trying to hold on to the anger she felt.

"You remember Zeus telling you about AKA? Well, the reason Zeus knows so much about him is because they've had a type of war going on between the two of them. It's kinda like a cat and mouse thing, each of them taking turns being the mouse. Something changed though. AKA wanted to change the rules. He wanted it to end and Zeus thinks he'll try to take me out to get to him. I thought those guys were a

part of his gang. I thought you were going to get killed because of me. Just like my . . . like my . . ."

Camara heard the pain in Ezra's voice as it trailed off. He
sounded on the verge of tears, but what she could see of his
face didn't even show he was upset. At first Camara was a little put off by it. She thought he was being weak, a momma's
boy. Then she remembered the articles she read about his
mother. About what happened to her, how most of Bluefield
thought he was involved. Camara put two and two together
and her heart sank. She could only imagine what he must be
feeling. The survivor's guilt must be unbearable. Camara had
a similar feeling about her friend Gail.

She didn't know what to say, but somewhere in her heart
she decided on the truth. She felt Ezra deserved it.

"I'm pretty sure they were after me," Camara said then
took a deep breath. "My ex is a man name Tarquan Tate. He
has different sides to him. On one hand, he can be gentle
and sweet. The type of man you want to take home and who
could charm your grandmother into falling in love with him.
On the other hand, he is a stone-cold bastard with a small
army at his disposal. They call him Snap because of how
quick he can switch from one persona to the other."

Camara paused and looked away from Ezra. She didn't
want to hurt him, but he needed to hear the truth. He deserved at least that much from her.

"I won't lie and say I didn't love the man, but that was
before I found out about the other side of him. He was very
good at keeping that side from me for a long time. I should
have known. All the signs were there, I just chose to ignore
them. I keep looking the other way until there was nowhere
else to look.

"A part of me never really trusted him. I never told him
where I was from. That alone should have been enough,
right? The fact that I wouldn't open up enough to the man I
thought I was in love with to tell him where I was from was
a huge red light. I didn't ask a lot of questions about his past,

so he didn't ask about mine. I think we each just saw each other the way we wanted.

"I didn't want to believe that I could be that wrong about someone. I finally wised up and ran, but he followed me. Snap has a huge ego. He has this like . . . grandiose sense of self-importance. He couldn't take me leaving, so he's using his army of cronies to intimidate me into coming back to him. Of course, his pride won't let him admit that, so he's going about it in a very round about way.

"I don't even think he genuinely wants me back. He just doesn't want anyone else to have me. He even went to the trouble of making up a story about how I stole money from him and that's why he's doing all this. He doesn't want his boys to know how pathetic he is."

Camara's hand never left Ezra's. That was the first time she told that story to anyone. She had been carrying it inside for so long, and it felt good to be able to share that with Ezra, even if she couldn't bring herself to give him the whole truth.

"So we both have killers after us and they each have a small army of killers that they can use to get at us at anytime, anywhere?"

"It looks that way," Camara said. She looked over at Ezra and saw a slight smile as he started to chuckle. Camara looked confused. "What?" she had to ask.

"You don't . . . you don't find that funny?"

"What? That we both have killers after us?" Camara asked clearly not seeing the funny side in all this while Ezra burst out in laughter. "Did I miss something? How is that funny?"

"We are so screwed!" Ezra said somehow finding it funnier once he said the words aloud. "What else is there to do but laugh?"

Ezra laughed himself to tears; Camara still didn't quite find the funny side in all this. She let Ezra get all the laughs out. She had to admit that as weird as his reaction was, it somehow made the situation easier to deal with right now. She finally started to laugh too, more so at Ezra, than the reality they were facing.

When Ezra stopped laughing, he reached into his pocket, pulled out his phone and turned it on.

"What are you doing?" Camara asked.

"I'm calling the police."

"Why?"

"Why not?"

"It's too late for that now. What are we going to say? We were in a shootout on 77 going about ninety miles an hour and then drove off from the scene. How's that going to look to the police?"

"This is a toll road Camara. They'll know you were on the highway from the pictures. We haven't seen any other cars since the toll and none at all since the shootout. We need to at least call it in. If not, it'll look worse. Why do you people never want to call the police?"

"What do you mean you people?" Camara said feeling very behind the curb.

"Sorry, I was talking about you and my brother. Forget it. I'm calling the police though."

Camara didn't have to think about it long to realize Ezra was right. She looked up and saw that they were about four or five miles out of Bluefield now.

"Oh, crap," Ezra said looking at his phone.

"What? What is it?"

"I turned my phone on and I've got a butt load of missed calls and a texts. The text is from Lois."

"What does it say?" Camara asked, but knew exactly what it said. Camara was pulled back into her other reality—one unbelievably worse than the insane world of Tarquain's hit-men. It was too much. It was all her fault. It was as if she had entered a dream, one where everything moved in slow motion. Five syllables hammered like thunder claps in Camara's ears as Ezra read the text.

"Bluefield is burning."

# CHAPTER 53

I couldn't believe my eyes. I took the Bluefield exit and was heading west on 460. It was two a.m, but the horizon was full of oranges and reds like the sun was just setting. My heart broke because I knew it wasn't the sun but a fire, a big fire.

I was just winding down from the shootout I had just been involved in and now I was confronted with what I had hoped to run away from . . . What I had prayed I wouldn't see when I got back. I checked my phone again. I had two missed calls from T, five missed calls from Isis and three from Zeus. Lois was the only one who left me a voicemail and sent me a text.

I looked over at Camara and got a little worried about her. She was staring at the colors off in the distance like she was in some kind of trance. I wasn't sure what she was thinking, but I could see she was off in her own world. She had handled the shootout like it was nothing, like she had been there before. She had no problem taking charge when the chips hit the fan in that situation. The guilt at possibly being responsible for what was happening now was too much for her though. Still, she couldn't turn away.

It was my turn to take charge now.

I gave Zeus a call back to see if he had any info on what was going on. He picked up on the first ring.

"Where the fuck are you?!"

"Just got back in Bluefield. I'm heading for south side."

"What?! Why?"

I thought about it and realized I really didn't have a reason. I knew I couldn't help.

"I wanted to make sure some people were okay," I said truly enough.

"Let me handle that. You're not a firemen or a policeman. You need to go home. This has AKA's stink all over it. I know it's him. Go home and wait for me. It's not as bad as it looks."

"Are you looking at what I'm looking at?"

"He got some houses but mostly tress and shrubs. It's only about thirty houses spread around Bluefield. I think every fireman and volunteer from Beckley to Tazewell is here, along with most of the police. They're doing a damn good job, too. Surprised the hell out of me. Go home, you'll just be in the way here. I'll be there when I can to fill you in on what happened."

"Fine. Camara's with me though. I'm not sure how she would feel about us leaving. She's in la la land."

"She's with you? Good. I need to talk to her about those files. Keep her with you." There was a brief pause like Zeus just caught what I had said. "She's what?"

"Later. I'll see if she's okay with this," I said looking over at Camara. She was still gone. I started to think leaving might be a good idea.

"I don't care if she's okay with it or not—keep her with you, and go home. You have no idea how important this is," Zeus said. I could tell he was getting impatient.

"Okay, okay. I still might go to East River Mountain right quick."

"Why?"

"I can get a good view of Bluefield from up there. I need a picture for the paper."

"WHAT!? Nigga go home. Shit!"

"It's my job, Zeus."

"What the hell is wrong with you?"

"It's not like I want to, I'm just say'n."

"Listen, there's already a news crew from News Channel 6 on the way up there, and News Channel 59 crews are already on this. I'm sure your boss will have plenty of pictures to use tomorrow. Now. Go. Home," Zeus said then hung up on me. That's how he was sometimes when he reached a certain point of frustration. Argument over. Case closed. I win.

I took a deep sigh. I hated it when my little brother tried to boss me around. I hated it more when he was right. It was my job to get pictures for the paper, but it didn't seem that important right now. I got to the intersection of K-mart and Holiday Inn and did a u-turn. The fire in the sky shone like the dawn of a new day. It was beautiful and horrible all at once.

I looked over at Camara again and her facial expression hadn't changed, she still hadn't said a word. We drove away from the inferno in silence. The farther away we got, the darker it got. It was like coming out of a nightmare. Like coming out of hell.

In the sky I could see the moon. It was full and looked like a pale red ball in the sky. It reminded me of the color of dried blood. The moon didn't turn that color very often but it had to tonight of all nights. I knew it was only dust in the atmosphere that made it look that way, but it still left me with a bad feeling about what else was to come. My dad's dream came back to my mind. Something told me the fire was only the beginning. Things would get worse before the sun came up. I turned my focus back to the road and prayed I was wrong. I looked back up at the pale red moon. I wasn't feeling very optimistic.

# CHAPTER 54

He stood on top of the East River Mountain Scenic Overlook with his arms stretched out to the sky and looked out to God. His god was glorious and powerful. It was all consuming and unstoppable. It would only stop when it was ready. The efforts of the trivial flesh bags in the city were useless. His plan was as perfect as the fire he created. He left clues for Zeus, breadcrumbs for him to follow. He wondered how long it would take for Zeus to catch up.

The flame had stretched to different areas of north side, and the east end of Bluefield, and it was slowly gaining momentum. The south and west areas of the town were almost engulfed.

Standing on the edge of the overlook, he felt his adrenaline pumping. He felt every one of his five senses heighten with the excitement. His vision became more focused allowing him to see the carnage in detail from distances that he shouldn't be able to see. His ears picked up both the blaring sirens and the faint screams of people trapped in their homes and on the streets. His nose inhaled the scent of the charred foliage and burning flesh. The smell of blood and gasoline were so thick he could taste them in his mouth. His hands felt like they were burning as he held them out toward the fire, that plus the culmination of all his other senses, sent a blistering tingle sensation up and down his spine. It was absolutely orgasmic. Nirvana.

Every small town he did this in, the feeling was the same. He could never figure out if his heightened level of awareness was real or not. It probably wasn't. He was a psychopath after all. He was proud to say that he was the worst kind, the greatest of all.

He took in a deep breath and inhaled the smells of the fire again. He thought about Zeus. He wondered just where Zeus was in all this. What was Zeus feeling? What was Zeus thinking? Did Zeus know his brother was going to die tonight? He hoped so. He hoped Zeus knew, so that it would hurt him even more to know that he was too late . . . That he should have done something different. Every cop within a hundred mile radius is here, not even a ten minute drive from where Ezra Walker would die, and none of them would be able to save him.

He looked into the fires as they spread and could see into the future. He saw Ezra lying in front of him. He saw the fear in Ezra's eyes as he moved to deliver the killing blow with his favorite weapon. He envisioned killing Ezra with his beloved instrument to play the ballad of slaughter, his favorite brush to paint on the canvas of butchery. He hadn't killed with it for some time. He wasn't sure why the fire wanted him to use it, but he would and would enjoy every second of it.

He saw Zeus crying over his dead brother's casket barely able to recognize the mutilated body. He saw Zeus swearing his name and the day he was born, swearing vengeance that he would never have.

He pulled a cell phone out from his pocket and read a text message. Ezra had just gotten home and he had the newspaper bitch with him. His plan would have continued even if she would have printed his letter, but it would have added to the mystique about what he had accomplished tonight. He had been meaning to pay Miss Johnson a visit. Two birds, one stone. It wasn't a coincidence. He stopped believing in coincidences a long time ago.

*Good,* he thought. *The more the merrier.*

Ezra would be given time to settle in, time to get comfortable before death came pounding at his door. Maybe Ezra will be lucky and get some before he died.

Tonight would be his grand exit from Bluefield and it wouldn't do any good to go out without a bang. He reached into his other pocket and pushed a button on a remote control device, then waited. Two explosions rocked the north side and southern sections of Bluefield. He could see the flash of the explosions, feel the force of them even though he was miles away, he heard the thunder in his ears. Glorious. Beautiful.

"That should keep them busy," he said to no one in particular.

He was in his car and driving down the backside of East River Mountain as a news van came up the front side. He had left just in time. There were no coincidences.

"Shit!" he said to himself as he disappeared down the mountain. He had done everything perfect except one thing. He had made only one mistake. He overlooked one important detail that the van rolling to a stop where he had been only moments before made him remember. He forgot to set his DVR to record the news.

# CHAPTER 55

**EZRA**

Camara was lying on my bed with her head buried in one of my pillows. It took me a while to give up on getting her to move, so I ended up just carrying her into my apartment. I took her shoes off and went outside to get her purse out of her car. It made my head hurt to look at the car.

The front of the car was riddled with bullet holes. I doubted it had much life left in it. The glass on the headlights was shattered. It was a miracle the lights worked long enough for us to get to my apartment. The front windshield had holes in it right where my head would have been if I had been sitting up in my seat. The whole windshield was cracked on the passenger side.

I opened the door and grabbed Camara's purse and her gun fell out. I stopped and looked at it. I still didn't know what to think about the shootout. I hated guns. Always have. I didn't want to be around it and I certainly didn't want it in my home, so I put it in Camara's glove box.

I shut the door and noticed a car backing into a space right across from where I stood. It was Ren and Stimpy. I had forgotten all about them! Things were going so well, then so bad that I hadn't given them a thought. Were they there for the gunfight? They had to be. I didn't remember seeing them, but I don't remember looking back either.

The car pulled into its space when the lights flashed twice. I got the message. They wanted me to know they were there and they wanted me to stay put. I was number one priority for Chief Wilson as soon as the fires were out. I didn't know what to do, so I went back into my apartment and locked the door.

I held my hand over the lock and imagined that I was locking out everything. This was my home. This was my castle. I was locking out the cops that I knew would be coming for me. Wilson will try to pin something on me even though he still didn't have anything. I was locking out a serial killer that had a vendetta against my brother and was trying to kill me just to hurt him. I locked out gangsters that wanted to kill me for being around the woman I *thought* I was falling for. I locked out a town that thought I was capable of killing my mother. I was locking out my whole life.

I rubbed my head and threw Camara's purse on the kitchen table then kicked off my shoes. I went into the bedroom to check on her, expecting to find her in the same state I left her in, but she was sitting up in the bed waiting for me.

"Thank you for bringing me here," she said in a soft vulnerable voice. "I don't think I would have done too well being around all that."

I wasn't sure what I needed to say. This was the first time Camara had spoken since we got back in Bluefield. I wasn't sure how she needed to be handled in situations like this. Did she want me to talk or just listen? My only guess was that she was feeling guilty even though nothing that happened tonight was her fault.

"Well, we're not dressed for warm weather, so I decided to bring us somewhere cooler," I said without really knowing why. My sense of humor tended to kick in at times where most people wouldn't find anything funny. I still got a slight smile from Camara that followed a 'you must be off your rocker look.'

"How do you do that?" Camara asked.

"What?"

"You know. Make the most fucked-up-terrible situations not so bad."

"I think that depends on who you ask. Most people would say I make them worse."

"No. You make things easier to deal with," she said then laid back down on the bed.

"Are you okay?" I asked hoping she would want to answer.

"No. I'm not. Was all that my fault Ezra? Really? Tell me the truth."

"Of course not. This psycho would have done this regardless if you printed that article or not. I can't see why even a crazy person would go to all the trouble of planning how to do something like this unless, they were going to do it. That would've been a lot of effort gone to waste."

"I guess that makes sense," Camara said hugging the pillow. "Do you want to talk about what happened earlier? You know, the other thing."

"Do you have anything to say?"

I sat on the edge of the bed and waited for Camara to think. She almost started a couple times, but I could tell she was having a hard time finding the words. The only light in the room was from the streetlight shining through the blinds in the window, but I could still see tears starting to flow in Camara's eyes.

I lay beside her and took her in my arms. I wanted to protect her, but I wasn't sure if I could protect myself at this point. If this maniac could really pull off burning a city, how could I stop him if he came after me? The sunrise would only bring more problems for me. I wouldn't be able to lock out everything forever. I only had tonight, and tonight I only had Camara.

We lay there and let the silence speak for us. There was plenty we had to talk about later, but for now I didn't feel like pushing the issues.

"I'm scared," she said softly in my ear. "I don't know what to do."

I turned to face Camara and rubbed my hand along her hair, then her cheeks. Her skin was soft as silk, her body was sleek and toned. Everything about us being together seemed perfect; everything except for the mess our lives were outside these walls. As much as we were drawn together, everything was stacked against us.

"I'm not going anywhere. We'll figure this out," I said.

"Promise?" Camara asked taking my hand in hers.

"Promise."

Camara kissed me softly on the lips. It was the sweetest kiss I ever had, somehow even better than our first. That kiss was more healing than any medicine could ever be. It fanned away the clouds in my mind and became a light that cut through the darkness in my soul. It quelled the anger in my heart and gave me relief from the weight I had been carrying for months. It was my red kryptonite.

Camara moved my hand slowly down until it rested on her backside. I wasn't thinking. There wasn't any room for thinking. I didn't know what the sunrise would bring. My room was my fortress and Camara was a queen that made me feel like the king of my own Wakanda. Nothing was promised to me beyond these walls. All we were guaranteed was tonight.

# CHAPTER 56

## CAMARA

Gentle hands rubbed across arm and chest muscles that were as smooth and hard as marble. Camara removed Ezra's shirt then lightly kissed his neck and chest. Powerful hands cupped her behind; Camara could feel Ezra's hardness press against her. She rubbed back on him until she found a nice rhythm.

She wanted this. She needed this.

Ezra didn't rush like every other man she had been with. He knew how to take his time, how to make this special. He was gentle in all the ways she needed. He was powerful in all the ways she wanted.

Camara took off her shirt and unsnapped her bra. She kissed Ezra and gave him her tongue. Her breast rose and fell on Ezra's chest as her breathing became heavier. The rhythm they created was igniting a fire in Camara like sticks to dry leaves. Camara moaned and called Ezra's name. He felt so good against her. She wanted him inside her.

What they were doing didn't altogether make sense. They were just involved in a gunfight and a town was burning less than fifteen miles away. Camara didn't know if Snap knew where Ezra lived. It would have been easy enough to have him followed. Snap had promised her six months, but it looked like he would renig on his promise, and Camara didn't know what he would do next. There would be a lot for the both of them to deal with in the morning, but tonight caution was blown to the wind. Ezra finally gave in to her and not a word was said between them.

Ezra got up and stood on his knees on the bed. Camara positioned herself in front of him, giving him her back. His hardness was pressed against her and Camara danced in slow motions like she was dancing on a crowded club dance floor.

There was no music in the room, but there didn't need to be. Camara had her own in her head and Ezra was right on pace.

His hand gripped her waist and squeezed powerful and strong. A hand cupped Camara's breast and beaconed her closer. Ezra moved her hair to one side and her neck and bit at her shoulder. Camara reached back, placed a hand on the back of his head, her breathing slow and deep while Ezra's hands glided over her breast and played with her nipples.

"I want you," Camara whispered in his ear. She didn't mean to but she couldn't help it. He was driving her crazy. "I want you inside me," she said so softly she wasn't sure if he heard.

Five fingers found their way down Camara's stomach. Fingers explored her body, sliding over every inch of her. Camara moaned a sweet song to Ezra and her tongue played in his ear; Camara felt him shiver.

Camara was on her back again as Ezra removed her black pants with ease, then the pink thong she had been wearing. He came closer to her, supported his weight above her on arms of stone. They kissed as Camara unbuttoned his pants and fished for his penis, then she took her thumb and middle finger and measured its circumference. No need to rush.

She pulled it out and shamelessly looked down at it. She bit her bottom lip, as she gripped it with both hands.

"Do you like what you see?" Ezra asked.

A moan and a nod was all Camara could muster at first. "Have you measured this thing lately?" she finally asked

"Not since I was a teenager."

"It's been a while. I might not be able to handle the likes of you."

"That mean you want to stop?"

Camara shook her head. "Not even. The only way to get used to riding the horse again is to jump back on the saddle. Just means start slow."

"I planned on taking my time."

Camara looked into Ezra's eyes and lightly stroked with both hands taking one hand from shaft to tip then the other.

She placed her feet on his hips and pulled down his pants with her toes.

They were both naked now, neither ashamed of their bodies as they looked at each other in the pale blue light that shined through the cracks in the curtains. Their skin was burning; their bodies pulsing. Surging with anticipation.

Ezra still took his time. He didn't rush or give her what he knew she wanted. She was going insane, but she didn't want him to stop. She wanted penetration, wanted to take all he had, but he teased her instead.

She both hated and loved what he was doing to her. Again they rubbed up against each other and found a rhythm that fit them both. It felt like he was already insider her. She rolled her hips and caught his thrust and delivered her own in return. His thickness pulsed between her legs. She felt every inch of him glide across her. Six inches. Seven. Eight. Then six. Then nine. Ten.

Camara called on the lord again and again. "Now. Do it now," Camara said through labored breaths.

"There's nobody here, Camara," he said kissing her brow and cheeks. "Not yet. This is going to last until the sun comes up."

Ezra was more than she could handle. He exceeded her expectations. He was so thick, so in control. He was a diesel engine. A song came back to Camara's mind that she had thought of early. She thought it would sum up Ezra flawlessly, but now she thought it didn't do him justice. Still she hummed her best Jill Scott impression to herself. Camara thought he was all the song said and more; she licked her lip then breathed deeply. *Crown Royal on ice.*

# CHAPTER 57

AKA stood outside Ezra Walker's apartment with his back to the door holding a twenty-pound battleaxe. His head was hung low and the axe was firmly clutched in both hands. He shut his eyes and role played in his head how he was going to kill Ezra and the bitch that was with him. Would he kill the bitch first, then Ezra? Would he keep her alive long enough to know that Ezra couldn't save himself and surely couldn't save her?

What weapons would Ezra have at his disposal? Not that it mattered. Ezra could barely hold his own against him when he was wearing stilts and tired from raping a teenage whore. There was no disguise this time, no distractions. He was going to take his time and enjoy this.

He opened his mind and became aware of everything around him. He absorbed everything with all five senses like he had on East River Mountain. The sounds of the crickets and other insects in the night, the feel of the floorboards under his feet. The comfortable and familiar weight of his weapon, the sight of the two cops to his left that were now dead in their vehicle, no one would be interrupting this moment for him. He smelled the gasoline that he placed in the field of flowers to his left. His heart leaped with anticipation of seeing it ignited.

He thought about all the people in the apartment complex, as they lay asleep in their beds or watching the news coverage of the conflagration happening not ten minutes away. He bet that they all thought they were safe. That the fires couldn't possibly reach them. But he was here, fire came with him everywhere he went. Fire never left him, it was him. If he was there, no one was safe, they just didn't know it yet. Nobody ever knew the worst could possibly happen to them until it happened.

He took deep breaths letting himself get a little buzz from the gasoline. He got prepared to give the signal to his men. Any minute he would know. He would feel when the time was right.

He thought about what Ezra was doing right now. Did he know he was moments from death and clinging desperately to his last seconds of life? Was he in a corner balled up with fear, or was he completely oblivious?

The axe was spinning in his hands. He could feel the energy coming from the weapon; it was ready for blood.

Almost. Almost time.

Ezra. He would kill Ezra first then have sex with the bitch before stomping her brains out. He wanted someone to be there to witness his victory over Walker.

His mind elapsed to one of his favorite movies, The Shining with Jack Nicklaus. He remembered watching the DVD commentary of the best scene in the film. Jack was standing there with the axe about to bust his way into the bathroom to kill his ugly inane sack of shit wife. He was getting himself pumped to act out the scene. He rallied a crazed look in his eye and he said, "Axe murderer. Axe murderer." Jack repeated that like a mantra over and over before doing the scene.

He did the same before his first killings and it seemed appropriate now.

*Axe murderer.* He thought to himself. He felt himself slipping into the persona.

*Axe murderer!* He thought again lightly tossing the head of the axe in his right hand. The axe got lighter with each toss, with each repetition of his mantra.

*Axe murderer!*

**Axe murderer!**

He was ready. It was time. He would remember every sight, every sound, every smell of this night. He would kill Ezra and his bitch and get away free to terrorize Zeus another day. He had seen it by looking to God. He had seen it in the future.

*Axe murderer!*

He raised the axe above his head and the signal was given. The sky above Pauli Heights apartment busted into a fire of blistering heat. Flame arrows, grenades, sprays from flame throwers covered the tops of the buildings and busted open windows.

He wondered how safe everyone was feeling now.

Axe held high. His hands were steady and had a firm grip, the axe light as a feather. "Axe murderer!" he said aloud this time. It didn't matter if anyone heard him now. His lips formed into a killing grin, his chin up proud and strong.

Then, he turned and faced the door.

# CHAPTER 58

### EZRA

"Did you hear that?" I asked Camara.

"No," She said. Both her hands were around my butt pulling me toward her gateway to heaven, but I stopped short.

I had just finished teasing, licking and sucking every inch of her and was about to give her all I had. I had just about pierced her walls and was about to penetrate her like a bunker buster when I heard a bang come from somewhere in my apartment.

"Don't stop. Please, don't stop," Camara said through heavy breathing. I didn't want to, but I knew I heard something.

"You had to have heard that," I said and tried to climb off her but she wouldn't let me.

"It'll go away," she said and tightened her legs around me and pulled me in closer still. She used her hips to thrust against me and my eyes rolled back. She felt so good I couldn't think. I couldn't fight her. I didn't want to. Maybe I had imagined it. Maybe my subconscious was playing tricks on me, trying to tell me this wasn't a good idea. But I had stopped myself from doing what I wanted to many times. Tonight was all I might have. I didn't want to ruin it. I gave her all I had, all at once, and her fingers scratched into me and she screamed with pleasure and sweet agony.

Then I heard the thumping again. Louder this time.

I hated to, but I jumped off Camara, rolled off the bed and started putting my pants on. I definitely heard something and it wasn't going away.

"What are you doing!?" Camara screamed in protest.

"You didn't hear that?"

"Hear what, Ezra? Shit! Are you seriously going to get me hot like this then just . . ."

Camara jumped as the pounding came again, this time accompanied by the sound of splintering wood.

"What the fuck was that?" Camara asked.

"Now you hear it, huh?"

Again something pounded the door and Camara again jumped then pulled the cover from the bed over herself.

"Oh, my God, what is that?" Camara said in a whisper.

"Stay here."

"Okay."

All I had on was a pair of pants as I crept my way into my living room. The banging had stopped, or was it pausing? I couldn't wrap my mind around the obvious. Who does this? Who breaks into someone's home like this?

There wasn't much light in my apartment. Only single beams of light from the hallway came through the gapping hole in my front door to accompany the strains of light that came from the blinds.

I took a few steps toward the door. My heart was beating harder with every step. I passed the kitchen, but as I got closer to the door, I felt a chill run up my spine. I picked up a steak knife from the counter and held it in a downward position in my left hand ready to attack or defend.

I could hear screams coming from the hallway. People were running and slamming doors. I caught the faint smell of smoke.

"Ezra. Ezra, are you there? Say something," Camara said in a mousey voice from my bedroom doorway. I could tell she was still naked from the faint light coming from my room. She had the sheets from the bed loosely wrapped around her.

I turned to her, but before I could speak something came hammering through the hole in my door. My heart pumped into overdrive and Camara screamed. Whatever came through the door assaulted me like a Juggernaut. I couldn't get my balance; it was all I could do just to hold on to the knife in my hand. I was slammed into the wall and all the air was knocked out of my lungs. Light from the hallway was shining in my eyes. I didn't have time to adjust as I felt what I was sure was a foot connect with my jaw.

"Come, Walker! Don't make this too easy on me! You saw how I like to fight for it. Come on!"

That voice. I know that voice! It was the same one I heard at Bluefield State. That voice belonged to Isabelle Sparks' killer. It belonged to AKA. I couldn't see straight, but was able to place a kick in the center of his chest. It felt good to connect a blow with all my momentum.

"Camara! Go in my room and lock the door. I'll handle him!" I screamed as loud as I could which was nothing more than me coughing up the words. My voice was weak. I still hadn't gotten enough air back in my lungs.

"Who are you!?" Camara screamed. "GET OUT OF HERE! LEAVE US ALONE!"

"Don't worry bitch, you'll get your turn," the figure said in the darkness. Then I heard the crunch of fist on bone and saw Camara fall to the ground. How did he recover from that kick so fast?

"No!" I yelled as adrenaline surged in my body pushing me forward.

One swift motion from the figure and I scarcely saw the gleam of something metal sailing towards my face. I saw it just in time to lean back and do a lifesaving Matrix impression. What was that in his hand? How did I miss it when he came through the door?

I was on my back and almost before I could move, silver flashes came down and destroyed the floor where my head had been seconds before.

"Good Walker, you're making this interesting! Keep it up!" The voice taunted me from the blackness in my living room.

I moved to get up. I tried to go on the attack but was met with a lightning kick to my stomach. An iron grip captured my left wrist and pinned it against the wall. Before I could react, a foot hit my hand like a sledgehammer causing me to drop the knife. I felt an explosion of pain as at least three of my five fingers broke. I might have heard the crunch of the bones snapping if it wasn't for my howling in pain.

An iron fist delivered an uppercut to my face. I was disoriented. I needed a second to regroup; I couldn't form anything remotely resembling a defense.

Sparks!

I saw the silver sparks in a blur rushing towards my head. What was that? Whatever it was, it was sharp. I saw what it did to my floor. I ducked just in time for it to cut the blinds on my window. I took mental notes as I avoided death. Whoever this was, he was impatient. Every strike was a killing one. He was anxious.

I needed to fight back. I needed to go on the offense. My room. I could fight back if I could get to my room, but he was too fast. He would kill me if I gave him my back and made a break for it. I needed to get him off balance.

I crouched low, rolled in the direction of my TV and struggled to get my eyes in focus. I could see the source of the silver sparks more clearly in the new light created from the destroyed blinds. It was an axe. He was trying to kill me with a freaking axe!

He came at me again as impatient as before. I clutched the PS3 from my entertainment center and chucked it. I hit him square in the face. I heard a satisfying yell of pain that let me know I had hit my target then bolted for my room.

I tried to find Camara somewhere on the way, but she was nowhere to be found. I got to my room and grabbed my sword from the mantle by its sheathe. The gold designs sparkled in the sparse light in the room and the black finish glistened. The sword was about twelve pounds, but it never felt heavier. This was the first time I picked it up to seriously defend myself.

"KYAA!" I heard screamed from the living room.

Camara!

I ran back into the living room and saw Camara deliver a tiger's claw to AKA. She was still butt-naked, but she didn't let that slow her down. I rushed in to press the advantage that Camara created. Before I could get there, AKA struck Camara then grabbed her by the throat with a fluid motion of one hand and threw her in my direction. Then lightning flashed across her abdomen exposing glimmers of crimson.

"No!" I shouted at the top of my lungs.

Camara was unconscious and bleeding. I couldn't tell how deep it was, but I knew she was hurt. She needed a hospital.

I looked up at AKA. The nameless bastard stood seven feet in front of me. His stance was erect with confidence. His body language was smug and condescending. The axe in his hand leaked scarlet drops on the floor.

"Do you know why you can't beat me, Walker? It's because you can't kill me. You can't get angry enough to kill me. You're scared of the rage in your heart. You don't have it in you. I'm going to kill you both and you can't do anything to stop me."

I moved Camara out of the way. Not far, because I didn't want to risk opening the cut at her stomach any farther than it was. I didn't pay attention to his words. He wasn't going to psyche me out. I stood up, placing myself between Camara and AKA. I wouldn't let him hurt her again.

AKA looked at the sword in my hand. I swore I saw a smile form across his lips.

"Perfect," he said.

Perfect? What the hell was he talking about? Ignore it, Ezra. Don't let him psyche you out.

It hurt, but I put the sheathe in my left hand so I was free to draw it with my right. I've been around swords all my life. I knew how to use them. I could beat him! I knew I could! Just ignore what he's saying.

"Even better," he said.

*Ignore him.* He's trying to make me angry. Make me careless as he is. I can beat him.

"Where did you find your mother's head?"

One question. That question stopped my breathing and turned my heart into a useless lump in my throat. I couldn't move. Blood covered his nose and mouth. I wasn't sure if that was from the game system I threw at him or Camara's blow, but he was covered with his own blood. I looked into his eyes as he stepped closer and could see the devil in his features. He was a demon.

"Where did you find her head when you walked into the house, Walker?"

Red! All I could see was red! My skin was burning, my eyes wide and unblinking. Something else. His voice. Where had I heard that voice? Then I remembered my trip to East River Mountain. I remembered the name of someone I meet there.

"Larnell?" I said in shock. He had been right in front of me, not eight hours ago and I had no idea. I wasn't sure he heard me say the name until I saw him wink at me and laugh at me in amusement.

"Where was Sherri's head?" he said in a heartless voice with a cold grin. The axe was still in his hands, but that question cut through everything that I was.

He said my mother's name. It felt like the worst insult imaginable and all he did was say her name. How dare he speak her name! I couldn't hold myself any longer. I screamed a war cry and charged at him in reckless abandonment of all common sense and strategy. I still hadn't even pulled out my sword.

"There's the rage I'm looking for!" AKA screamed then slammed his axe in the floor. He grabbed me with both hands and used my own momentum against me, spun on his heel and threw me through my living room window.

Glass shattered and twinkled in the moonlight as I felt the sting of dozens of fragments imbedding themselves into my skin. In that instant everything moved in slow motion. My descent to the ground lasted a lifetime. My father's warning was in the forefront of my mind. *You got beat because you got stupid, you got angry. You're not your brother, don't fight like him. Cage and focus your anger or it'll kill you.* I replayed it as best as I could remember, tightened my grip on the swords sheathe, and made it ready to adsorb the hit with the ground.

I'm not going to let him psyche me out. He's not that much stronger than me. He used leverage that's all. He used my mother. He wouldn't get me like that again.

My sword was still safe in its sheathe. I swore to myself that when I pulled it out, it would be to deliver a killing strike. I would win the fight or lose with the first swing of my blade.

Camara.

He was in there alone with Camara. I had been thrown a good five feet through the window and had rolled another eight. I ran back to my apartment window as fast as I could. Adrenaline and renewed focus fueled every step of my bare feet across the grass and glass fragments. Before I got to the broken window, AKA was already jumping through it to meet me. He looked like a goblin coming at me. He looked crazed flying through the air, axe held high; lust for blood lined every feature. He looked something more than human.

Damn it! He kept putting me on the defensive every time I tried to mount an attack. I was pushed back but had control as I dodged the anxious swings of the axe. A field of flowers under a pale red moon was our battleground. This is where one of us would die.

Camara.

My sense of time was out of whack. How long was he in there with her alone? Was it long enough for him to finish her? What had he done to Camara?

# CHAPTER 59

## CAMARA

Camara's head was throbbing. She felt like she was hit twice in the head with a cement block. Her body was so stiff that it was hard to move. She felt an intense pain radiate across her stomach. What was that? Why did her stomach hurt? She felt warm liquid drip on her hands. She held the section of her injured stomach. A putrid smell hit her but she couldn't place it.

BLOOD. Her hands were coated with her own blood. Memories came rushing back to her, but she couldn't believe it. That psycho cut her with that fucking axe. Who was he? Where was he? Where was Ezra? Camara looked around the room. She was alone. The window in the room was shattered. Was it like that before she was knocked out? She couldn't remember. Her head hurt so bad.

What was that smell? Sweat? Blood? Smoke? What was that? Why was it so familiar?

She rubbed a hand through her hair and tried to pull herself together. As she tried to get up, pain shot through her stomach and pulsated through her entire body. She made it to her feet after an exhausted effort. She realized she was still naked, but it didn't matter.

Camara was too pissed to care. That bastard cut her. He tried to kill her with a fucking axe! An axe! Like this was the damn middle ages or something.

She could hear something in the distance, but couldn't focus on it.

Her gun. Where was her gun? She would show that freak how to kill somebody in the 21st century. She just had to get her hands on her Glock. Where was it?

*Think, Camara. Think! Where is it?*

Then Camara saw her purse on the kitchen table. Her adrenaline pumped at the thought of vengeance. Revenge pushed her forward.

That sound. What is that sound?

She reached for her purse and poured its contents on the table. No gun. Where was it? Where was it?

Screaming. Did she hear screaming or was it just her head pounding? She felt like her head was going to split in two.

*Car.* It had to be in her car.

Camara held her stomach and stumbled to what was left of the door. As she walked through it, she couldn't believe what she was seeing. People were screaming and running franticly around the parking lot. All the buildings in the complex were engulfed in flames. It seemed like everything around her was burning. Buildings. Cars. People. Then Camara remembered the smell. It reminded her of that night on Stadium Drive when she watched someone burn alive.

The smell of smoke and burning flesh caused Camara to vomit blood and Chinese food onto the sidewalk. People screamed for help trying to save their loved ones still trapped inside the apartments. Screams filled the air as people ran like human torches in the night. Small powerful explosions ignited all around her.

Camara pushed the pain and everything around her out of her mind. She blocked it all out and focused on her objective.

*Gun. Find the gun. Kill the bastard.*

Thankfully, the door to her car was unlocked. She wouldn't have had the strength to go back inside and get her keys. Camara searched the car as fast as she could.

Where did he put it? She checked under the front seats then the back. The bending and stretching made the pain in her stomach unbearable.

"DAMN IT!" she shrieked in frustration hitting her fist on the dashboard.

*Glove box. Check the glove box.*

As soon as Camara opened the glove box the gun fell into her hand. She had never been so happy to see anything in her life.

Now she just had to find him. Where was the motherfucker hiding? Where was Ezra?

Camara hobbled back to the apartment as fast as she could. Before she got through the door, she thought she saw two figures in the field at the back of the apartments. The only light came from the buildings on fire and the sparse moonlight, so she wasn't sure of what she saw. She moved closer and squinted her eyes. It was Ezra. He was okay; still fighting like she knew he would.

Camara, Glock in hand, was about to make her way onto the field when she heard something metallic scrape the ground and roll past her feet.

*Grenade!* She jumped with all her strength and made it through Ezra's doorway just in time. The explosion was loud and rocked the walls in Ezra's living room.

*This is insane. This is insane!*

Camara pulled herself to her feet again. The excessive adrenaline blocked out most of the pain. On her feet, Camara looked out the shattered window and was struck with horror at what she saw. The field was on fire! Ezra was still out there!

Camara ran to the bedroom and acted without really thinking. She placed the gun on the table and grabbed the blankets from the bed. The sheets still smelled like Ezra and were damp from their sweat—a reminder of a love interrupted. Another thing that fueled her anger, tonight was supposed to be their night and it was ruined. They were escaping hell and creating their own heaven in this room, on these sheets.

*Push it out! Focus! Don't get emotional. Not now!*

Camara gathered all the sheets into a ball, threw them into the bathtub, and turned the water on full blast. She kneeled in front of the tub and soaked all the sheets fast as she could.

It was times like these when she wished she didn't have D-cup breasts. Damn things got in the way.

*Focus, Camara! Focus damnit!*

Camara stopped thinking about her body and worked as fast as she could. Her thoughts went to Ezra. She prayed she wouldn't be too late.

Ezra would be okay.

She believed in him. He might not even need her help.

# CHAPTER 60

I really needed some help. I couldn't gain any ground. I could take this guy. I had the skill, but I was kept off balance from the jump. AKA's defense had gaping holes in it and his movements were spastic. He expected blood with every swing and became more berserk once the field burst into flames around us. It took me a second to catch a whiff of the gasoline that encased the perimeter of the field entrapping us in a ring of death.

This had to end fast or we both would burn alive.

I dodged several strikes from the axe and blocked others with the sword's sheath. The sheath chipped and cracked from the force of the axe. I still hadn't drawn the sword, and I wouldn't until the right opportunity presented itself. I had regained control of my emotions and my mind. He made me lose myself for an instant; my father's words brought me back. I blocked out the pain I felt and placed my whole concentration on stopping the man in front of me. I was going to kill him before he killed me.

"You're not your brother, Walker!" AKA yelled through heavy breath. "I'm going to kill you, then that bitch of yours! Stand still! You're only stalling!"

His weapon had to weigh twenty or twenty-five pounds and he was swinging it like a madman. Real sword fights don't last as long as they do in the movies. This wasn't a dance. To fight at a high intensity for a solid two minutes you have to be in superman shape—add to the equation swinging a battle axe. He had to be getting tired, even if he was too crazy to know it.

I dodged a downward attack that was slower than the ones before. I saw an opportunity and jumped at it. Literally.

I jumped on the axe's long handle, just below the blunt end, forcing it into the ground, sent a knee to AKA's already bloody nose, took the bottom of my sword's sheath and connected with his jaw all in one fluid motion.

Promise would've been proud.

I rolled away from AKA and gave myself plenty of room to either defend or attack. He had underestimated me and tired himself out. This fight was over. I was going to win. He just didn't know it yet.

"You think your slick, Walker? You think you can win?"

The fire was starting to spread closer to the center of the field where we were. Flames rose ten feet on all four sides of the field. Neither one of us would be able to make it out of the field without suffering at least third degree burns or worse unless we got out soon.

It was hard to breathe from the blistering heat and gasoline fumes. I wasn't sure why we both hadn't suffocated. I heard screams echoing in the backdrop past the flames. Sweat was running down my chest and back, and I felt the stiffness of the grass under my bare feet. I had to constantly squint to see through the brightness of the flames around us.

A slight chuckle bubbled up from somewhere deep in my soul. Somehow I found irony in the fact that I had admired this field and the flowers that grew here. The view of the field was one of the reasons I picked the place, and now I was fighting for my life in it. I could very well burn to death here, but it was okay. I wouldn't be dying alone.

AKA struggled to pick his axe up from the ground. I could tell by the look in his eyes that he expected me to charge after him while he was seemingly defenseless. I stood still and watched him. I waited until he finally pried the axe loose, then listened to the most evil, most joy-filled cackle I ever heard in my life. He laughed like the villain from a Saturday morning cartoon. I was ready to put a stop to that laugh forever.

"You know this is over for you, Walker. Have you given up? Ready to put your head on the chopping block?"

I didn't say a word. I would let him taunt me as much as he wanted. I had his number now. The outcome would be the same no matter what he said.

"I told you why you couldn't beat me. You're not willing to kill me. You blew the only chance you're gonna get. You're not willing to win."

I took hold of the sheath in my left and the hilt of my blade in my right. I was sure that my left hand was broken, but I blocked it out and was proud of the grip I managed on the sheath. I was hot and it was getting harder to breathe. I readied my stance. I felt the grass between my toes and dug them in the dirt to give myself solid footing. No more dodging. I wouldn't go back on the defensive again. I was going to take a page out of my brother's playbook: "Only move forward."

"The sad thing is that this is the end for you, but only the beginning for everyone else. Did you know I could see in the future? A portal to the future is all around us. Can you see it? I was going to leave Bluefield after I killed you, but God wants me to stay. And it was you who was the incentive that inspired the change. The future looks bright for me in Blue-field. It's a shame you won't be here to see it!"

He lifted his axe above his head and charged at me, just as I knew he would. Silver and red descended on me from above. I planted my feet more firmly in the ground and got ready to adsorb as much of the blow as needed. I lifted the sheath to block and released the fury of my sword again in a fluid motion. The sheath shattered under the impact with the axe, but I still managed to divert the blow enough to miss. I side-stepped and created my own silver sparks across AKA's abdomen. The sword cut deep into his gut. It was the most satisfying feeling I ever felt in my life. There was no remorse in my strike. I took vengeance for little Nick Cooper and Charles Dwight, for Isabelle Sparks, for my mother and countless others.

AKA fell to his knees and his axe imbedded itself into the ground beside him. It was over. I did it. I killed the monster.

I started looking for any possible way to escape the fire alive. I didn't have time to celebrate my victory. The fire looked the weakest toward my apartment, but I knew there was a small creek that ran parallel with the road in the opposite direction.

The fire was blinding. I could feel the heat steaming the sweat off my skin. My throat was dry as cotton. The rush from victory started to subside as the possibility of burning alive was settling in. It didn't even bother me as long as he was dead. The world is better off without a monster like that breathing.

I felt it was worth the self-sacrifice, but I had to at least try to stay alive. I took one last look at AKA dead on his knees huddled over himself in the dirt. This was him. This was the man who killed my mother and haunted my dreams all these months. I had killed my boogieman. He had killed God knows how many people and I had put him down. He looked pathetic kneeling over in a pool of his own blood. It somehow felt peculiar. Dying like this was better than he deserved.

I wanted to taunt him the way he taunted me. I wanted to know what he thought of himself now, but I turned in the direction of the creek without saying a word. My only chance was to gain enough speed and hope the fire wouldn't do much damage. I might make it! Maybe there was a chance to survive. It would hurt like hell, but I would be alive.

I only got five steps away when I heard a bang that sounded like the planet cracked in half. I didn't know what it was at first, but I felt the cold numbness spread through my lower body. I looked down and saw a waterfall of blood coming from my stomach.

I feel to my knees and struggled to breathe. My vision was already cloudy and the numbness spread though my whole body. I coughed up blood from somewhere deep inside me. I felt a presence hovering over me. It was AKA holding a .45 to my forehead. The son of a bitch was still alive! How was that possible?

"Next time you kill someone, Walker, make sure their dead," he said through contrived breathing. His stomach was cut open. I could see bits of his intestines hanging out. He could only be alive by some incredible force of will. My vision was a mix of bright reds and oranges. My eyes went in and out of focus. I could see past the gun in his hand then straight into AKA's eyes. Did he have the gun the whole time? He guessed what I was thinking.

"Just because I didn't show one, didn't mean I didn't have one," he said full of pride in himself for having the strength to finish me off, to see me die first.

"You're not a killer, Walker. You always confirm the kill." His voice was weak and broken. Blood bubbles formed with every word he spoke. His legs were shaky, but somehow his hand was steady.

"Any last words, Walker?"

My vision was switching from clear to fuzzy. Bright reds and oranges faded in and out to blacks. A high pitched buzzing was in my head, but I still heard him. I was dying. I knew there were fires all round me, but all I felt was ice spreading from my torso, blood pouring out from my stomach. He had killed me, but I knew I'd killed him, too. Any last words, he asked.

"Don't miss," I said with as much strength and defiance in my tone as I could summon staring into his dark soulless eyes.

That evil laugh pierced the buzzing in my ear, but it wasn't full of as much arrogance as it had been before.

"You have more of your brother in you than I thought."

Those were the last words I heard. The last words I would ever hear spoken. As I faded into blackness, all the strength left my body. My last thought was of Camara. I prayed she was okay.

The shots rang out in the night.

BANG.

BANG.

BANG.

I heard cannons go off one after the other before I felt cold consume my entire body.

Strange . . . it didn't hurt.

Then, I fell into blackness and waited to see the light at the end of the tunnel.

# CHAPTER 61

## CAMARA

Camara was wrapped from head to toe in four soaking wet sheets and she still barely made it through the blaze. It only took her three steps to get to the other side of the fire, but still the heat was incredible. She wasn't sure if she could do that a second time. It might have helped to put on some clothes but desperation overshadowed common sense.

Once she came through the fire, Camara dropped to her knees and pried her eyes open. She had managed to put some distance between her and the wall of flames.

Everything around her was so bright, burning. The fumes from the burning gas assaulted her senses. Her eyes watered. Breathing was difficult.

*Focus girl. Focus! Where is he? Focus.*

Camara had a bundle of about nine or more soaking sheets in one hand and her Glock in the other.

Camara turned to see Ezra running out of the fire when he was shot in the back. Ezra fell to his knees and the monster wielding the axe struggled to get to its feet. Camara's Glock was tangled in the wet sheets. She was still fighting to free it when the monster stood in front of Ezra.

*No! Hurry damnit! He still hasn't noticed me.*

An insane laugh full of pain and triumph pierced Camara's ears. The bastard thought he had won. He thought this was over for Ezra, but he was dead wrong. Camara finally set the Glock free from the sheets and without thinking took aim.

She fired three perfect shots, all hitting her target center mast in the chest. Snap would've been proud.

The monster and Ezra both fell. Did the monster manage to fire off a shot before he died? Camara couldn't be sure. The only shots she heard were her own. She picked up the sheets and ran to Ezra's side.

Ezra's blood caked the ground and stained the grass. Camara could feel its warmth under her bare feet as she stood over Ezra. Camara had limited medical knowledge, but she knew Ezra must be going into shock. His pulse was weak.

Camara glanced to her side. The monster's eyes were wide open and a smile was frozen on his lips. He looked insane, like a wild man, even in a pool of his own blood. His blood and Ezra's were mixing together on the ground and it made Camara sick. The monster's eyes were staring at her. Cold and lifeless. Taunting her even in death. Camara pointed her gun at those eyes and fired two shots at them. The monster's face exploded inward and chucks of brain burst through his skull. Those eyes would never stare at anyone else.

Camara turned her attention to Ezra. He was semiconscious. There was no way Camara would be able to lift his dead weight even if she was in perfect health, let alone when she had a painful gash in her stomach. Camara took the sheets and wrapped Ezra in them as best she could.

"Come on, Ezra. We've got to move. The fire still isn't that high on this end of the field. We still got a chance. Just need your help, baby. Come on. Get up."

Ezra was still out of it. He looked like he was alert enough to know what was going on, but was too paralyzed to do anything about it. If nothing else, Camara thought he would die from blood loss. She could possibly drag him through the fire but they would be severely burned before they got halfway across the firewall.

Suddenly, Camara remembered her dream. She remembered her mother telling her that God would catch her. Would God pull her out of the fire? No. God helped those who helped themselves. Faith without actions is worthless.

Camara might survive if she left Ezra. If she turned and ran and left him to burn alive, nobody would know. Ezra was the only truly good thing to come into her life in years. Leaving him wasn't an option.

Camara did the only thing she could think to do . . . She prayed.

She was never one to put much stock in prayer before but she prayed with all her might. She prayed for forgiveness. She prayed for courage. Camara prayed for God to give her strength. She wasn't going to sit here and watch Ezra die. She had to try no matter how impossible it seemed.

She was once told that faith was the substance of things hoped for, the evidence of things unseen. Camara was definitely "hoping" for Ezra and her to live to see tomorrow and it was "unseen" to her how that could happen.

Flashes of lightening lit the sky. Thunderclaps echoed and shook the ground. Camara looked up. She could barely see the sky from the smoke, but out of nowhere clouds were filling the sky. Maybe it would rain. Maybe she had a chance.

Camara wrapped herself back into her sheets and grabbed the others that Ezra was covered in. She remembered Alley Cat telling her in times like these God carries you. That he sends you a guardian angel.

Camara tugged on Ezra's dead weight. He might as well weigh a ton. Camara put all her faith in God and asked again for strength. She closed her eyes and prepared herself to try again. Now more than every Camara needed a protector. God may not come when you want him, but he was always right on time. That was how the saying went, right? What better time was there than now?

Believing with all her heart, Camara tightened her grip and tried again. A protector would come—an angel, a champion.

# CHAPTER 62

## ZEUS

I was fucking pissed. I've always had a bit of a temper, but I can't remember the last time I was this mad. The worst part, I was mostly mad at myself. I always try to do too much. I always have to be the hero. I stayed in Bluefield and helped firemen do their job. I stayed and helped the cops get people to safety. I tried to help as many people as I could and even managed to save a few lives. I risked my life to keep perfect strangers alive. Now my own brother could be dead because I wasn't there to help him.

Things were just starting to settle down. The fire was more or less under control thanks to the rain that sprang up by some miracle. People died but not as many as could have. I felt good for doing my part. Then I heard one of the nearby police officers report a call that had just come in: A fire had broken out at Pauli Heights Apartments in Green Valley.

I ran to my car and hit highway 460 at a hundred and ten miles an hour. Driving on a wet highway at this speed was like playing Russian roulette; you never knew when you might hydroplane. In the distance, I could see two police cars, two ambulances and a firetruck following me. I felt like there should have been a cavalry of emergency personnel coming with me but things weren't that stable in Bluefield. I was actually lucky to get as much help as I did.

I clutched the steering wheel so hard my knuckles turned purple. I had gone over my mistake at least twenty times before I got out of Bluefield. AKA knew where my brother lived. I told Ezra to be careful, but I knew it was only a matter of time before AKA went after him. I should have moved him somewhere. I shouldn't have told him to go home now. He should have been kept closer.

At first, I justified my lack of action by telling myself it was the only way to draw AKA out of hiding. I knew he wouldn't come after me directly. He never does. Still I shouldn't have used my brother like a pawn. I was playing a chess game. I thought I could see the whole board. As I got to the Blue Prince Road exit, I saw the smoke coming from Ezra's apartment complex and anger filled my core. I pounded the dash of my car cursing as loud as I could. I could see the fire in the field behind Ezra's place from the highway. The fire looked like it completely enveloped the field

AKA and I had been doing this back and forth game for years. It was a big game that I was losing. I hate to lose. AK knows that.

"He's alive," I said to myself. "Damn it, Ezra, you better be alive."

I wanted to say I couldn't believe what I was seeing when I pulled up to the apartments, but that would have been a lie. The tops of all the buildings were on fire, but thankfully, it looked like the rain had kept the fire from spreading. All the apartments still had a chance of standing in the morning. The rain wasn't much, but it slowed down the fire long enough for the other firemen to get here. The police finally pulled up not too far behind me.

I pulled my car into the old Blue Prince Dollar Theater so it would be out of the way, then sprinted the distance of the apartment complex to get to my brother's place. People were screaming all around me, some running around like chickens with their heads cut off. They had no idea what to do. Several charred bodies lay on the ground and several people were bleeding and in need of medical attention. Everyone needed help but I ignored them all and let the cops work crowd control. I was only here to help one person. I was here to save one life.

The first thing I saw was the last thing I hoped for. Ezra's door was smashed inward. Chips of wood were all over the ground and chunks had fallen into the apartment. I stepped gingerly through what was left of the door, ready to kill.

I pulled out a small flashlight that I had been carrying and freed my Desert Eagle from its nest. The weight of the Eagle felt at ease in my hand like it always did. I was ready for anything. I honestly wanted to shoot someone, but I doubted AK would still be here. I thought a fight might help relieve my nerves and tension. I entered Ezra's apartment feeling nervous excitement mixed with terrified anticipation.

All the lights were off in the apartment. Beams of gold and ruby from the fire shined through cracks in the drapes. My small flashlight and the glimmers were all I had to guide me as I searched the apartment. I could feel the heat seep from the broken window and permeate the room.

The Eagle was held at bay. I scanned the inside of the apartment carefully. It was a crime scene and I didn't want to touch anything. My adrenaline pumped at thoughts of the unknown.

Where was Ezra? Was AK still here? Ezra said that Camera chick, or whatever the hell her name is, was with him. Where was she? AK couldn't have done all this alone. Where were his cronies?

There was a big dent in the wall in front of me. Whoever came through the door did so with a lot of power. The dent was high up telling me someone must have been picked up several inches when he hit the wall. A lot of people take my size for granted; they don't take time to see the brains behind the muscle. I could read a crime scene better than most yuppies with forensic science degrees. I took my time, soaked in the details and kept my eyes open for anyone who may still be in the apartment. I needed to know what happened here, but I couldn't take long. I gave myself sixty seconds to find the answers. The best way was to follow the blood trail.

Blood never lies.

There was blood on the floor in the living room, blood in the hallway. I used the evidence at the scene to follow the pattern of the fight. From the kitchen to the hallway, from the hallway to the living room, blood was everywhere. Someone had been cut bad, but could still be alive. Not enough blood for them to have died.

I followed the drops of DNA with my eyes and found a trail that lead from the bathroom to the front door, or was it the front door to the bathroom? I heard the sound of running water and followed it to the tub. Bloody handprints were on the ground and wall of the bathroom. They had to be a woman's judging from the size and shape.

Damn, it was hot. What type of fire can burn like that? I thought I could smell the scent of gasoline fumes but I couldn't tell with all the sweat and drying blood, with cologne and perfume permeating the air in the apartment. All the smells infused together making the air hard to breathe.

I peered into Ezra's bedroom and spare room. Ezra's sword and bed sheets were missing, but other than that there was no sign of blood or a struggle. After making sure the apartment was empty, I focused my attention on the living room.

Why would Ezra grab his sword? The fact that he did told me a few things: One- he had time to get to it, and two- AK busted in here and probably didn't have a gun on him or didn't use it. He wanted to play with Ezra. I bet he didn't know what he was in for especially if Easy got a hold of his sword. My brother might be alive after all.

I had been in the apartment all but thirty seconds and I was already starting to sweat up a storm. It was fucking hot in here. The air was getting thicker. Some of the smoke was starting to blow in. It was harder to breathe. Where the hell were the firemen?

I checked the living room quickly again, picking up every detail. Blood on the wall—someone was hit hard. Probably in the nose or mouth. A huge crack in the floor: looked like some type of weapon caused it, but the shape wasn't right for a sword. Maybe an axe. Ezra's PlayStation 3 was smashed on the floor and had drops of blood on all the pieces.

An impromptu weapon? Used by who?

The floor was indented. Someone pivoted on their heels.

Why?

To deliver a kick? No. Two indentions on the ground swirled slightly in blood. A punch? No, the angles of the feet were wrong. A throw? Throw where?

I stood beside the spot where the throw had originated, careful not to mess with anything. I preformed the throw in my head. I imagined the angle and strength of the thrower, the position of the person thrown. Someone had walked right into this. I followed the path of flight, and then I saw the shattered glass fragments sparkle under my flashlight. I looked up and saw the busted window and the fire on the other side of it. I saw blood lined footprints moving toward the window in running strides. A bloody handprint was on the window seal. Whoever got thrown out the window was followed. Everything lead to the inferno outside the apartment!

"Shit! Are you fucking serious?"

****

I put the Eagle back in its nest and ran out the door.

Again I was sprinting with everything I had. My legs pumped hard and my stride was long. At that moment, I could have given Usain Bolt a run for his money.

I ran along the edge of the apartments and tried to find a weak spot in the fire. I squinted my eyes and searched the fire for anything resembling a person trapped inside, any life in the blaze. I felt a little stupid running around the fire with only a sixty-second diagnosis of the crime scene, but I knew I was right. I was always right—whether I liked it or not. Somebody was thrown in this field. Was it Ezra or AK? Were they in the field when it was set on fire? I had no way to know so I searched and held on to hope.

I screamed my big brother's name. I got no response for all my effort. Sirens wailed in the background as I searched through the fire, its light blinding me as I tried to look though. The fire truck and the ambulances had finally caught up.

"HELP!" I heard a hoarse voice call out from behind me.

"Shit." I wasn't ready for what I saw, but I was overjoyed all the same.

Two people were making their way up the side of the fire in my direction. I ran to meet them and recognized Ezra's lifeless body draped over a woman's. The woman was practically carrying him on her back. They collapsed just before I made it to them and fell in a heap on top of one another. Blood was everywhere.

I remembered Camara's name when I saw her. She didn't look built enough to move Ezra, let alone carry him, but somehow she had done it. They were both soaking wet and caked in blood and mud from somewhere. Camara was completely naked and Ezra had on nothing but jeans with scorch marks on them. I looked closer at Camara's skin and saw burn marks all over her as well. Mostly second with a few third degree burns I thought, but couldn't be sure.

I checked them both for pulses but I could only find one on Camara.

"Damn it!" I barked in frustration.

I refused to believe my brother was dead. I refused to believe I wasn't in time to make a difference. I checked him again. This time I calmed myself first, tried to get a grip on my own heart rate.

Yes. A pulse. It's faint and weak as shit, but it's a pulse. Thank God.

"Hang on, Easy. You're going to be okay."

I moved to run and intercept the ambulances when a hand grabbed me by the ankle. I looked down and saw Camara looking up at me. She was delirious. Trapped somewhere on the edge of reality and a nightmare of whatever hell she had just been through. I could only imagine what was going through her head.

"Don't let . . . don't let . . . him die," she managed to say through a hoarse voice and dry, cracked lips. Then, she faded into darkness.

Camara may have given her life to save Ezra's and I had barely remembered her name. I swore I would pay her back if I got the chance. I ran to the ambulances as fast as I could and promised that I wouldn't let either of them die. In all my life, I haven't made many promises. I can honestly say I've never made a promise that I hadn't kept. I wasn't about to stop now.

# CHAPTER 63

## ZEUS

I managed to get the ambulances to pick up Ezra and Camara and cart them off to Princeton hospital. Bluefield Regional and Tazewell Hospital were almost full so we had no choice but to go there, which was fine by me. If push came to shove, I would call in the family healer to take care of Ezra, but I would rather avoid the headache if possible.

I told the EMT that no one else had been as badly hurt as them. If that was true or not, I didn't know. I didn't care.

I rode in the back of the ambulance with my brother. I did my best to stay out of the way while he was getting patched up. He had lost a lot of blood. Luckily, I remembered Ezra's blood type so the EMT could start the infusion right away. I was surprised that he had plasma with him at all.

Ezra had a broken hand and a bullet hole through his stomach. His body also had scrapes and cuts all over, likely from being thrown through his window. I didn't get a good look at the wound, but I'd wager he was shot in the back. Knowing how AK works it wouldn't surprise me.

We got to Princeton Hospital pretty quick. The ambulance Camara was in was close behind. As soon as we arrived she and Ezra were wheeled into the emergency room. I followed, but kept my distance. Nurses surrounded them—poked, probed and checked them top to bottom. Not a lot of people from Bluefield had been brought to Princeton yet so they got a hefty dose of attention.

I found a spot in the corner of the emergency room and watched the medical staff work. It was everything I could do to not scream: I was so fucking mad. I could feel my anger boiling inside me waiting to be set loose. I don't have a lot of medical knowledge, but I could tell Ezra was in worse shape than Camara. I couldn't take it any more so I walked out into the lobby and waited. I couldn't bear to stare at a situation that I couldn't fix. I couldn't stand feeling so powerless.

I paced for what felt like an eternity. I hated waiting. I hated not being able to do anything. I hated the fact that this was my fault. I should have thought more ahead. How does AK do it? He's always ahead of me. Every fucking time!

After about thirty minutes, a tall white-haired doctor came out to talk to me. I didn't bother to get his name. Wasn't important. His face was somber and carved with apprehension. He had news that he didn't want to tell me. News I didn't want to hear.

"Are you related to either of the people you brought in?" he asked. I could tell this wasn't easy for him. The doctor walked as if a ten ton weight was sitting on his shoulders. His face was weathered and worried. It was going to be a very long night, and he knew this was the first of many heart-wrenching moments he might have to deliver.

"Just give me the news. How bad is it?" I asked bracing myself for the worst.

The doctor took a deep sigh then began to speak, each word hitting me like a brick to the face.

"The woman has a chance. She has a wound to the abdomen that was our main concern. It's nasty but not very deep, but she lost a lot of blood. We managed to close the wound. She also took a blow to the head and experienced some slight head trauma. As of now, we haven't found any signs of internal bleeding so we're optimistic. Only time will tell how bad it really is though. The next forty-eight hours are important for her. She was also severely dehydrated. We gave her a blood transfusion and she's stable. I think she'll make it." The doctor's voice trailed off after that.

At that instant I realized how young he looked. He looked legit enough, but I could tell he hadn't had to give the "*There's nothing I can do*" speech very often. He would get plenty of practice tonight.

"Is he dead?" I asked point blank looking the doctor square in the eye.

"No. Not yet. There's not much that can be done for him, I'm sorry."

I held up a hand and stopped the doctor from talking. I needed a second to figure out what I was going to do. I wanted to punch him in the face for what he was saying, but I knew he was just giving me the truth. If you go around punishing the messenger; nobody would ever tell you anything. He was just doing his job, but that didn't stop me from wanting to hear what I wanted to hear.

"How bad?" I asked clearing my throat. "How bad is it? Just give me the facts."

The doctor swallowed hard before he began. He made a feeble attempt to hide it. He stood tall and regained his professionalism. I think I intimidated him; I had that effect on people.

"His injuries are too severe. His left hand is crushed but that is the least of his problems. He's lost too much blood. We've got him stable but he's bleeding internally and we can't stop it. He wouldn't even have made it to the hospital if they hadn't infused him in the ambulance. Both his kidneys are failing. His right lung has collapsed. I'm very sorry, but I don't think he'll make it through the night."

The ground opened up and a pit of despair tried to claim me as its own. The words hit me hard and cut me deep. I had never felt like this before. Not when my only real father figure, the man who taught me everything I knew about catching criminals, died. Not when my own mother died in a crack house in Baltimore. I had never felt like this when someone was about to die. I'd seen a lot of death in my life to be a young as I am.

I paced back and forth in front of the doctor. He didn't move or talk. Just waited to see if I had any questions. He didn't just bail when things got rough. I appreciated that. I respected him for that.

"What's your name?" I asked.

"Dr. Geoff Kolins," he said a little surprised by the question.

"My name is Zeus Champion. Dr. Kolins that man in there is my older brother. He's the only man I've ever loved. He's my best friend. I can't let him die."

I almost wished I hadn't said that when I saw the look on Doc Kolins's face. He looked like I crushed his world. I could tell he felt helpless. He began to speak but I cut him off.

"Do you think he could survive a helicopter ride to Charleston?" Again I caught the doc by surprise. "Yes or no, Doc. Could he make it to Charleston?"

"I believe so, yes. But there is considerable amount of risk involved. His other lung could collapse, and he could go into cardiac arrest, or he could simply bleed out, just to name a few possibilities. I understand how you must feel, Mr. Champion, but there wouldn't be anymore they could do for him in Charleston, not with the extent of his injuries, and that's if he survived the flight. The bullet wrecked havoc on his internal organs."

"He's going to die if he stays here, right?" Desperation laced my voice and I felt a lonely sorrow wash over my face. Ezra wasn't going to die tonight. I wouldn't let him, no matter how much of my own pride I would have to swallow to make it happen. I locked eyes with the doctor. He knew what I wanted to know.

Again Doc Kolins cleared his thought. "Yes, I'm afraid it's possible."

"Then start up a helicopter. My brother is going to Charleston."

"I'm not sure I can allow that, Mr. Champion."

A flash of red flashed in my eyes and I thought I heard a click in the back of my head. Anger boiled hot, and almost burst from the well inside urging me to crush Doc Kolins' face, but I held it in, only because I knew I must not have heard what he really said.

"Excuse me, what did you say?"

Doc Kolins tried to stand firm but took two steps back as I approached him. I could only imagine how imposing my frame was to the doctor. I had a good five inches or more on him.

"I can't in good conscience authorize a flight to Charleston for your brother. A lot of people are coming here tonight. Calls are already coming in about how full Bluefield Regional and Tazewell are. We can expect to be at our max in less than an hour. I'm sorry, but I don't see how your brother can survive the night let alone survive that flight. That trip might actually save someone else's life.

"We only have so many helicopters available and they take time to load and refuel. Every trip counts. I'm sorry but I just can't sanction a trip when I don't believe it will warrant any results."

It took every ounce of my strength not to free the scorpion on Doc Kolins. I felt a stinging sensation like a thousand needles poking my right arm where my scorpion tat was, settling into a ball of fire in my fist. Only the crunch of Doc Kolins's bones on my knuckles would remedy the burning.

It was hard, but I held the scorpion in check. He didn't understand. He was just trying to do his job, but he didn't understand. He didn't know what I knew. The problem was I didn't know how to explain what I knew. The scorpion was still in its cage but barely. It was hungry and ready to attack. I looked at Doc Kolins in such a way that he knew he had to listen to what I was going to say.

I started to explain my reasoning as calmly as I could to Doc Kolins when I got a surprise that I wasn't at all ready to deal with.

"WHERE IS EZRA WALKER!?" I heard the barking voice of Police Chief Wilson from the main entrance to the emergency room. He stormed in with two other officers as though he owned the place.

Chief Wilson scanned the room and it was only seconds before his beady eyes found me. He and his tin cops walked up to me. Their chests out, stride pompous and arrogant, they strode in like sentinels of law and order and demanded respect. I labeled them as soon as they stepped to me, trying to shove their authority down my throat. They were just in my way. They were scorpion food.

"Where is he?" Wilson barked in my direction.

"He's in intensive care. You can't question him 'cause he can't talk . . . so leave," I said.

"I don't need to question him. I already know he's guilty. I'm here to bring him in!" Wilson said his face already red.

"And how is that? What proof do you have that a man that was beaten and shot in Green Valley had anything to do with what's going down in Bluefield?"

"He killed two of my officers!"

"What? Says who?"

"Says me, that's who. I've had Walker followed for weeks. My officers told me he was involved in a gunfight right before the fires started."

"Bullshit!"

"Oh, it's true all right. Maybe you don't know your brother as well as you think."

"Even if it is true, how could he be involved in the fires if he was in a gunfight?"

"I don't know if he's the clown or the ring leader. He could be the guppy or the big fish. I frankly don't care! All I know is that he's a part of this and I'm taking him in and getting some answers. "

"He's dying, you asshole! You're not taking him anywhere."

Wilson turned to his two cohorts and spat out orders.

"Find him! Now! Search every room in this damn hospital if you have to. If he's really dying, then we'll wait. Hope he gets sent to whatever level of hell he deserves."

The officers ran off and started to search the emergency rooms leaving me alone with Chief Wilson and Doc Kolins.

"Watch your mouth, Wilson," I said my voice a low rumble.

"What's wrong, Zeus? Can't handle the truth?" he said inching toward me. He was challenging me, daring me. He didn't know the scorpion was already awake.

"I don't know what bug crawled up your ass, but you got five seconds to back up off me."

Wilson got even closer. His face was red and his breath was hot. Both his hands were cupped behind his back, which let me know he didn't consider me a threat. He thought he was untouchable. That pissed me off.

"Your brother is going to burn for what he did, Zeus, and there's nothing you can do about it. He dumped those bodies in Jimmy Lewis Lake, he killed Isabelle Sparks, he killed my officers and he killed his own fucking mother. If that sick fuck makes it though whatever the hell happened to him, I can promise you he'll wish he would've died tonight."

Wilson was close—too close. His voice was so low I doubted Doc Kolins could hear him. I couldn't take it any longer. Too many buttons had been hit at once. The scorpion was set loose. I reached out with my right arm and grabbed Wilson by his uniform. I could tell by his expression I caught him by surprise. He hadn't thought I would do anything with witnesses around. He didn't know me very well. If he did, he would know I didn't give a shit who he was or who was around. You don't threaten my family.

My strength threw him off balance and he wasn't ready for what I did to him. I picked Wilson up with one hand and slammed him against the nearest wall. Hard. I put everything into it. The walls shook and a painting fell to the ground causing the frame to shatter.

I wasn't going to take this from him. I wasn't going to take this from anyone. Everyone was trying to kill my brother. They were trying to stop me from saving him and I wasn't about to let that happen. I would bitch-slap the devil himself if he got in my way. No punk ass police chief or bitch ass doctor was going to stop me.

Wilson began to speak, but before he could get out a word, I put both hands on him and lifted him a solid five inches from the floor. Then I slammed him harder against the wall.

Then, again.

The walls of the hospital shook. I was willing to bet that everyone on this floor would have heard the booms Wilson's back made against the dry wall.

All my anger was in what I did. It was anger at myself, at Ezra for being beaten, but most of all anger against AKA. He was doing it again! He was a step ahead of me, but this time he had changed the rules. He had gone after my family. I was losing, and I hate to lose.

I let go of Wilson and let him fall in a heap at my feet. I had taken the wind out of him, but other than that the only thing I had really hurt was his pride. His two officers came around the corner, hands on their guns ready to react to whatever they found. What they found was me looming over Chief Wilson like a shadow of death and punishment.

"Get on your knees right now!" one of them yelled drawing out his pistol.

I turned to look at them both. They were both shaky on the triggers. Rookies. The scorpion on my right arm tingled and anger pulsed through my whole body. I was calm and steady and the two officers could see that. I was bigger than both of them by at least twenty pounds. My calmness must've had them ready to shit bricks. They didn't know who they were messing with. I just didn't give a fuck anymore. I was willing to take this as far as I needed to save Ezra. They wouldn't stop me. My brother was going to Charleston if I had to fly the goddamn helicopter myself.

"Stop," Wilson said weakly from the floor. He was struggling to catch his breath. He was coughing and his eyes were watering. "Where's Walker?" He somehow managed to get out.

Both Officers were shaking. The one that had told me to freeze was the one that answered Wilson's question.

"He's here. He's plugged up to all these machines. He looks in bad shape, Sir."

I turned to Doc Kolins who had fallen back into the corner of the waiting room. I knew the look on his face all too well. He wanted to leave, but like a bad car wreck, he couldn't look away. I had that look too many times at the murder scenes I'd visited when I first started.

"Put Ezra on a helicopter to Charleston, or do you need some further persuading?" I said not bothering to disguise my tone as anything other than a threat.

"Mr. Champion, I can't. Even if he survives the flight I seriously doubt that they can do anything to help him."

"Do it," Wilson said collecting himself from the floor.

"What?" Dr. Kolins said.

"Do it. Put Walker on a flight to Charleston. If he dies, he dies. If he lives, he's mine. Put him on a helicopter."

Wilson signaled his officers to lower their weapons then locked eyes with me. Wilson was flustered, still trying to catch his breath. "Try to get your brother fixed. I think it will be better if you try and find out there's nothing you can do . . . that God's going to send him right where he belongs and you did everything you could and it wasn't enough. I'll deal with you later, Mr. Champion."

That almost got him a broken jaw, but I held the scorpion in check. My brother was more important than the level of satisfaction the punch would bring. I had to get him to Charleston. He would be all right if I could just get him there. I had to believe that. If Wilson wanted to help, even if he was just getting off on whatever sick game he was playing, that was fine with me.

Wilson turn toward Dr. Kolins. "Get that man to Charleston, Doctor." Wilson then turned and left with his officers in tow. He flashed me a cocky smile and winked at me before he left.

Reluctantly, Dr. Kolins starting giving orders to staff to make ready to move Ezra. Before he disappeared around the corner, he glanced at me. I didn't know if it was a look of pity or sorrow. I didn't care. He didn't know what I knew. None of them did.

I reached into my pocket and dug out my phone. Only one person could save Ezra now. I only had one hope. I hadn't talked to this person in a long time and our last conversation wasn't a good one. I wasn't even sure if she would answer the phone. I was relieved when she picked up after the third ring.

"Unless this starts with an apology you're just wasting your breath, Zeus."

"I'm sorry."

There was a pause on the other line. "Huh, really?"

"No, I just didn't want you to hang up. I need you to meet me at Charleston Hospital."

"I don't have time for this, Zeus."

"It's Ezra." Silence echoed on the other end. Questions were on the tip of her tongue. I could feel it. I hope she would save them for later.

"When?"

"Twenty minutes or thirty minutes. Depends on how fast they can load him up."

"This better not be any bullshit, Zeus."

"Just be there. You're his last chance." I got the last word in then hung up the phone.

This was Ezra's best chance but I didn't have as much faith in it as I would have liked. I was desperate. I knew I was grasping at straws, but I had to try. I wasn't going to let my brother die. This would work. It had to.

# CHAPTER 64

## ZEUS

It wasn't long before I was sitting outside the emergency room in Charleston Hospital. Ezra had almost died three times on the way. Prayer and his will to live was all that kept him alive. I wasn't used to feeling so helpless. I couldn't take it.

They put Ezra in the intensive care unit and had him stable. Both his lungs had collapsed, and a kidney had failed. The machines he was plugged up to were the only thing keeping him alive. They had stopped most of the internal bleeding, but he was still in bad shape. One flip of the switch and it was all over. The doctors had all pretty much given up. There just wasn't anything to be done. No surgeries could fix him, no procedures to try, that was just how it was.

We had arrived at the hospital a couple of hours ago and she still hadn't shown up. I couldn't believe she wasn't here yet. What the hell was she doing? Ezra had been moved out of intensive care to a room to clear space for people that actually had a chance. The doctors were just waiting for me to turn the machines off. I demanded three second opinions and had gotten the same answer. Everyone was ready to write Ezra off.

I pressed my forehead against the cold glass of the window in the room. I saw the sun start to crest over the horizon and rage boiled in my heart. It didn't bother me. The thing that was getting me was I had nothing to punch, I had no one in front of me to shoot. I had nowhere to direct my feelings so they turned inward. The regrets of my life assaulted me like a bazooka. All I could think about was my mistakes, everything I had done wrong.

Ezra should have known exactly what he was dealing with. I didn't tell him about all the evidence I had dug up

343

because this wasn't his life. This wasn't his cross to carry, but it ended up falling on him anyway.

AK wasn't working alone. He had help to pull this shit off. He had used more help here than he ever had before. Everything was on a much grander scale than it had been before. Why was that? Why so much help? It didn't matter right now. I swore to myself that I would kill AK for this. I would kill him and everyone that helped him. I swore that if I could find his parents still alive I would kill them too for giving birth to the sick motherfucker.

I looked back at Ezra lying unconscious in bed. My brother was practically dead and AK was all I could think about. He had driven my brother to the brink of death and had managed to leave it to me to usher him to the grim reaper's waiting arms.

An apology was all I could muster as I stood over Ezra's body. All I could hear was the sound of the machines forcing air into his lungs, the beep of the monitor keeping his heart beating. Tubes and wires and needles were everywhere. I knew he wouldn't want to stay like this. I knew if he could talk he would want me to end it, but I wasn't sure if I could. I could bench press a solid three fifty but I wasn't sure if I was strong enough to flip a switch.

Then something happened that hadn't happened to me in years. A chill came over me, my hands shook slightly and a tear ran down my cheek. I was sad and pissed all at once; I wasn't sure which caused the tear. I looked at the main power switch of Ezra's lifeline. I tried to get myself ready to do the hardest thing I would ever do in my life.

"So you're human after all," I heard a voice say from the doorway.

I looked up and saw my older sister walk toward the bed and stand across from me on the other side of Ezra. She was wearing sandals, brown sweat pants and a black hoody.

"Where the fuck have you been, Isis?"

"I don't need your shit right now, Zeus," she said as she walked towards Ezra. "I wasn't ready to be here. I wasn't ready to deal with this."

"Well, you're too late."

"He's not dead."

"Why did you even bother showing up?"

"For the reason you called me here."

"What are you waiting for then? Do your thing."

"You and Ezra always believed in this divine ability stuff, not me. I don't know what you expect me to do."

"Well, you need to start believing. Why do you always have to run from what you can do? I wish I had your gift."

"Whatever," Isis said. After all these years she'd never really come to grips with what she was capable of. I can't say I blame her. I could understand how it would be unsettling.

"What's wrong with him? How bad is it?" Isis said clearly wanting to change the subject. There were more important things on my mind so I let her condescending tone slide.

"You tell me."

"I just got here, Zeus. Where's his chart?"

"Look him over. You tell me what's wrong with him."

"This is stupid."

"This is your gift. Why are you afraid to help our brother?"

"Because this is stupid. I don't believe in this crap. I'm an atheist for crying out loud."

"No you're not! You just say shit like that to piss me off."

"Why didn't you just call dad?"

"I haven't talked to Promise since mom died."

"You haven't talked to me since mom died. What's your point?"

"This isn't what he does. This is your soup."

"This is bullshit! Why would you call me here and put all this on me? Now if Ezra doesn't make it, it's all my fault, right?"

"See, that's your problem. You think this is all about you."

"Me! You're the one who has to make everything about you, Zeus. You have to be in control! You have to feel important! You have to have people feel grateful to you. You always have to be the hero."

"God, you're so fucking selfish!"

"How am I selfish?! Where do you get off calling me that?"

"You're standing there with the ability to save Ezra's life and you're more concerned about how you would feel if you fail before you even try. You don't want to feel responsible if he dies and you're scared you won't be able to deny your God-given abilities if you succeed 'cause you never did something this intense. Well, let me tell you something, sister, if Ezra dies, it's because of me. It's my fault that he's here and I take full responsibly for that. If he lives, then it's because God worked through you to make it happen. This has very little to do with you. So make it happen."

"You're such a hypocrite, you know that? You talk a big game about God and Jesus when chips are down and you're desperate, but you'll be back on the street fucking whores and shooting drug dealers no matter what happens to Ezra."

"I got my vices. Pussy is one of them. But, at least I acknowledge my shit instead of running from it."

"Well, how many more people have to die before you quit doing what you're doing?"

I hung my head and looked off a little. She was right. This had happened once too often. The weight of my past pressed down on my neck and shoulders.

"We all are called to do something. I'm not perfect but I believe that. There are sick people in the world, Isis. Killers, rapist, someone has to catch these bastards. I don't know why I'm good at it, but I am. You haven't seen what I've seen. I can't let stuff like what I've seen slide. I just can't. I'm not gonna let a murderer run lose if I can stop'em."

"If you believe in God so much, why don't you just do this yourself? God can work miracles through anyone, right?" Isis's tone had changed. She spoke less defensively and sounded a bit softer. I knew somewhere deep down she was more scared to succeed than fail.

"Not my soup, Isis," I said and lowered the railing on the side of Ezra's bed. "Just tell me what's wrong with him. Then

I'll leave you alone. I'll drop the whole thing. Just . . . just tell me what's wrong with him," I said and moved to the corner of the room by the window.

I watched Isis for a moment. She stood still and took several deep breaths before walking over to the other side of the bed. From the angle where I stood I could see her face as she sat on the bed and looked at Ezra.

Her eyes were watering but she didn't shed a single tear. She placed her hand on Ezra's chest. She kept her hand there and something moved into the room. Something I couldn't explain. The best I could liken it to was the calm inside the storm.

Isis ran her hand over Ezra's left hand and squeezed it. She rubbed his legs then his shoulders before resting her hand on his forehead. The whole time she sat beside him her hand never broke contact with Ezra. She placed her hand over his gunshot wound and rubbed it gently. She mumbled softly to herself, but her words increased the intensity of the presence in the air.

Emotion filled the room and overcame both of us. We each handled it in our own ways. Isis never took her eyes off Ezra. I wanted to ask what she was thinking but I kept my mouth shut. If she looked my way, she would have seen my eyes running like a kitchen sink.

She bent down and kissed Ezra on the cheek, took his hand in hers and reached for the power switch of his lifeline with her other. Her jaw tightened and then she did the last thing I expected her to do. She flipped the switch.

"Nothing," she said with her back to me still holding Ezra's hand. She turned to look at me and I couldn't read the expression on her face. I couldn't tell what she was saying. I couldn't make sense of what she had just done, until a tear finally ran down her cheek and she uttered five words that would send shockwaves through my whole body and open up the waterworks.

Isis smiled and said, "Nothing is wrong with him."

# CHAPTER 65

**EZRA**

I tried to open my eyes, but light burned my retinas forcing them closed. I lifted my hand and shielded my eyes, but it didn't seem to help. I stretched out my legs and arms and tried to adjust to my surrounding.

"Look who's finally awake," I heard a familiar baritone voice say from the corner of the room. "How are you feeling?"

"Great. Stiff, but great," I said twisting and stretching again. I squinted and Zeus came into focus. He looked terrible, like he hadn't showered or shaved in a days. I could slightly smell him from the other side of the room.

I sprung up in my bed and folded my legs. I felt so energized that it took me a minute to realize that I wasn't in my apartment. I looked around and saw the curtains around the bed and monitors to my left. I was in a hospital. Why would I be in a hospital? I shot Zeus a confused looked and he returned my gaze.

"It'll come back to you in a second," he said looking like he was waiting for something.

I moved to scratch my head with my left hand, and then it came back. I remembered my hand being crushed, the same hand that now worked perfectly fine. I remembered the struggle in my apartment, the fire. The pain of being shot in the back, seeing blood flow out of me like a waterfall was fresh in my mind. I thought I was dead. How did I get out of the fire? How am I still alive?

"Camara!" I said suddenly remembering she was with me.

"She's okay," Zeus said raising a hand. "She's still in Princeton Hospital."

I looked around again. Nothing made sense. I remembered passing out in the field outside my apartment. I was dead, wasn't I? I should be dead.

"Where am I?"

"Charleston."

"And, I'm alive because of . . ."

"Isis. Well, God really, but you know how all that works better than me."

"Oh," I said starting to piece the puzzle together. "You got Isis to come?"

"That's a story in itself. Let's just not get into that."

"Ok. Camara's in Princeton?"

"She wasn't as bad off as you. She had a nasty cut and some bruises, but I talked to a friend of hers, a Michonne I think, she told me that she was okay. She was passed out until yesterday, dehydration and exhaustion were the big things with her. You, on the other hand, almost didn't survive the trip here."

"So, she's okay?"

"I called and checked in again yesterday evening. I think she saved your life, so the least I could do was see how she was. I'm going to have to pay her back some way."

"What happened?"

"You tell me."

Hesitation gripped me. I remembered what I had done, but I wasn't sure how I felt about it. "I think I killed him, but that was after he killed me, so I'm not sure."

"We'll talk about that a little later."

"How did I get here? How bad was it?"

"Bad. You're really feeling okay? How do you really feel, right now?"

"Hungry."

"Stop playing."

I rubbed my shoulders, "Who's playing? Give me a steak and watch me work."

Zeus got up from his chair and started pacing back and forth in my room. "Unbelievable. Unfreak'n believable."

"How long was I out?" I asked.

"Two days."

"Huh, feels like it."

Zeus stopped at the foot of my bed and looked me straight in the eye with a type of intensity that I wasn't used to seeing from him. "We really need to talk."

"Find me some food, and I'm all ears," I said with a smile that my brother returned.

"It's good to have you back, Ezra," Zeus said as he moved to leave the room.

\*\*\*\*

"I never left."

"Yes, you did," Zeus said looking back at me, then exited the room.

Zeus came back fifteen minutes later with a full course meal. It was hospital food, but I didn't care. I would've eaten food from Sonic at this point, and I hate their food. As I inhaled my food, Zeus filled me in on the extent of my injuries. If half of what he was saying was true, which I had no reason to think it wasn't, I should have been six feet under by now.

He told me about the damage done to Bluefield in the fires. It wasn't as bad as it could've been. About thirty people died and a lot more were injured. Those numbers also could've been a lot worse.

Isis had stayed in the room as long as she could before Zeus started to piss her off. Once the doctors stopped gawking at me over the miracle of my recovery, they gave me a clean bill of health. When Isis saw I was really okay, she felt it was safe to leave. My younger sister and brother, Val and Israel, had even managed to come to Charleston to see me along with Promise, which was a bit surprising. Zeus also told me that Tamra had come to see me, and then he went into the heavy stuff.

I should've known it was coming. Zeus was never much of a talker, but he was chatting up a storm. He started to tell me about Chief Wilson and his vendetta against me, but I had him skip that part for now. I would deal with Wilson's craziness later. He told me more about AKA. He told me things

I didn't know, and things I didn't want to know. Things that almost had me throwing up all the food I had just gulped down.

"He's not dead. You didn't kill him."

"And you're positive about that . . . how?"

"No body at the scene."

"Could've burned. Nothing left but ash."

"That fire wasn't hot enough to burn every trace of a body, and you know it. Some bones would have been left behind. That carcass was moved."

"Who could do that without the cops noticing?" I asked through a mouthful of mashed potatoes.

"Had to have been moved while the field was still on fire. That, or someone on the police force is on AKA's team."

"That possible?" I asked.

Zeus stared at me with his infamous "are you serious" expression, and I had my answer.

"So, how does this guy work?" I began after downing some greens. "How many people do you think AK has with him at one time?"

"It's hard to say. He needed at least eight to pull off that stunt at Hunnicutt. Beyond that, it's hard to say. Things are different this time. I think he wants to end our game of cat and mouse, but you surprised him by staying alive. You messed up his gambit. I seriously have no idea what's going to happen now. You have no idea how bad that pisses me off.

"All I know is, you're in this deeper than ever. I'm going to stay in West Virginia for a while. I should be able to get my pack down here eventually. We're going to need their help."

"This isn't going to end, is it?" I said moving back to my potatoes.

"It'll end. I'm going to kill him, Ezra. I swear on everything I am, that I'm going to kill him, and every one of his psycho henchmen. This is going to end in Bluefield, just like he wants it to. One way or another," Zeus's voice was full of an infectious determination.

"How are you so sure the person I fought wasn't AK?"

"I'm not so sure. I'm just going off one assumption and one fact."

"What's the fact?"

"If it wasn't him, he'll let us know. He wouldn't let us think we've won for too long. He should, of course. It would be the smart thing to do, but his ego is too big for that."

"What's the assumption?" I said chewing on the baked chicken breast.

"If it really had been AKA you would've been dead before I got there."

"Well, thanks for believing in me."

"Has nothing to do with you. I know how he works. This is serious now. AK or me, one of us doesn't have much longer to live. This has been building for years, and you have no idea how sorry I am you're so involved, but I promise you, Ezra, that if I go, I sure as hell am going to take him with me."

A silent understanding passed between Zeus and myself. I knew exactly how far he was willing to go to stop who he must've felt was the devil incarnate. It both worried and scared me to see my brother so hellbent on the murder of another person. Not that I could find a reason not to want him dead, but it was the way he approached it. He was obsessed.

"Something else bothers me."

"What's that?" I asked.

"AK has been using his cronies more than he has in the past. I think there's a reason for that."

"What?"

"I think he might be training an apprentice. Someone to take over for him if he loses, or someone to compete with."

I didn't know what to say to that. I couldn't imagine a mass serial killer training a "mini-me" version of himself. The quiet in the room was broken by the sound of the phone beside my bed ringing.

"Who has this number?" I asked.

"Isis, Promise, your friend Tamra. That's about all I gave it to," Zeus said with a dark expression. I could tell he was barely in the room with me.

I picked up the phone and the voice on the line froze me to the bone. It was a voice I could have gone a lifetime without hearing again.

"Hello, Ezra. Congratulations on your speedy recovery. I'm very impressed." The voice was cold and taunting. Zeus's attention was still off in his own world.

"Though you cut off one head another grows more fierce ready to take its place. No one you care for is safe. I will destroy your mind, body, and soul for what you've done to my master. We'll meet soon." he said then hung up.

I could feel my heart sinking in my chest and my mouth tasted like I had been eating cardboard. I felt sick and wanted to throw up. It took me a second to start breathing again. I reached over and placed the phone on the hook, my mind racing a million miles a second. A feeling like hands about to grasp my throat came over me.

I looked at Zeus and sighed deeply. "It's going to get worse, before it gets better, isn't it?"

Zeus finally looked up, knocked out of his self-imposed exile from reality. "Who the fuck was that?"

# EPILOGUE

## SNAP

Snap stepped out of his black BMW and walked over to the new recruits lined up on the end of the parking lot in front of him. The initiation of his new soldiers would take place in the parking lot right outside Bowen Field in Bluefield. After the fires that destroyed a good chunk of the area, he had to pay a lump sum to the patrolmen that covered this section of town, but it was a worthwhile investment. Snap didn't show it, but he was excited. He always enjoyed the initiation part of what it took to be a member of his Set. Tonight wouldn't be any different.

Thoughts of Camara ran through his mind. Sometimes it seemed like she was all he thought about. He thought about what she did to him. What she stole from him. What she took was more valuable than money, but no one would understand that, not even those in his inner circle. He hated Camara most of all for that. He hated that she reduced him to a man who had to keep secrets from the people he most trusted.

His second in command, Dice, had the recruits weeded down to ten from a group of about forty. He had them ready to meet in less than a week. Ten in all remained, maybe five would become members. Snap confidently walked over to his right-hand-man and commanded the attention of all his soldiers without saying a word. Snap's presence was unmistakable, no matter where he was. He knew it and he loved it. He demanded respect, and people usually gave it to him or didn't live long enough to regret it. He was going to take his time. This was the next generation. They deserved his full attention.

The ten rookies were lined up and faced several cars with their headlights pointed at them. They couldn't have been able to see the details in Snap's face or the faces of any of the other members of his set. Snap had always kept his core network small, as surreptitious as possible. They were rarely in the same place at the same time, but they were always present at the initiations. For most of these first timers, this would be the only time they would see his "brain trust" all together. There were six in all, including himself. They worked in pairs of two and controlled different aspects of business. They all answered to Snap, but they all had their own territory and resources.

Sergeant worked with Black Tie, a mountain of a man at six-nine. He wore black slacks with a gray shirt and his trademark black tie. He wore glasses that he didn't really need but wore to intellectualize his appearance. Snap always thought it was silly for him to do that. Put spectacles on the Incredible Hulk, and he's still the big-ass motherfucker in the room.

Then there was Quicks. He wore all white on his five-eight frame. He was mixed, half black, half Italian. His hair was slicked back in a tight ponytail and a cigarette edged his lips. Quicks was as smooth as they came. His every movement was controlled and calculated. Despite his name, Quicks, rarely rushed anything he did or said, and if he ever did, you can believe it was to kill someone. Quicks had established himself as the most ruthless killer of The Set. Of everyone in his brain trust, Snap admired his style the most.

Quicks worked with Biggs. Being the only white guy in The Set, he was the only one who looked out of place. He wore a black suit with white pin stripes and matching black and white shoes. He looked like a dark-hair green-eyed Brad Pitt. He could have been right at home in some Abercrombie and Fitch runway show. None of the ten rookies would see any of them again until they proved themselves.

Snap wore a black-on-black three-piece suit with matching shoes. His head was freshly shaved bald and he wore one-sided sunglasses that allowed him to see out clearly but kept others from seeing in. He walked the line of recruits, looking them all up and down for several seconds each. They had listened to what they were told. None of them eyeballed him or even looked directly at him. They were all dressed business casual. Shirts tucked in. Pants around their waist. Some even wore ties.

"All these boys local, Sergeant?" Snap asked his main recruiter. Drill Sergeant had been working with Snap for about five years now. Every major city or backdoor town they went to, he was always able to find a drop or two of young blood for The Set. He had on a cream suit with a red shirt and tie.

"More or less, sir. Three from McDowell, three from Princeton and the rest from Bluefield," Sergeant said while sitting on the hood of his dark gray Lexus holding a semiautomatic rifle. He was a large man with a baby face. He was well into his thirties, but he barely looked out of his teens despite his bulk. The bastard still got carded when buying alcohol. His look was why Snap gave him his job, why he was so good at it. It was easy for him to get in with the younger crowd no matter where they were. Sergeant just belonged, no matter what hood he was in.

Snap continued to inspect his new soldiers. He sized them all up. He had always considered himself a good judge of character. He had to be to get where he was now in life. He had learned long ago that the best way to take what you want from people, who would otherwise not give you anything, was to know what they were capable of. All men had limits. All men could be broken. "These boys know what they're getting into?" Snap asked.

"Yes sir," Sergeant replied.

"Do you think they're ready?"

"I wouldn't have brought them in front of Dice if I didn't."

Snap finished inspecting all ten soldiers and walked back over to Dice.

"Is it just me, or are they getting younger?" Snap said starting a silent conversation with his right-hand man, making sure to keep his back to the rookies. Snap often wondered what he would do without him. Dice was the only person he trusted completely; the only one he would trust with his life.

"Nope. We just getting older, dawg."

"Right, I keep forgetting that," Snap scanned the line one more time. "Who's the kid in the middle?"

"I didn't get any names from Sergeant. Just met these pups. What you thinkin'?"

"He's the only one that looks real hesitant to me."

"Wanna cap'm. Make a good example. Set the tone ya know."

"We can't start killing people to set an example right off the bat, Dice. It's hard to maintain control over people if all you have is fear. They have to respect us first before any of them can really last."

"It's quicker."

"My way is more fun."

"If you say so."

Snap unbuttoned his suit and loosened his tie, then walked over to the rookie in the middle of the pack. He was tall, thin, maybe six- one, couldn't be more than sixteen.

"You know why you're here, son?" Snap asked plainly. The rookie was calmer than he expected. His voice was strong. If he really was as nervous as he looked, his voice didn't betray it. Snap respected that.

"Yes, sir. I know why I'm here."

"Do you know what we do? You ready to put in work?"

"Yes, sir," the youth said.

There was something in the boy that Snap liked instantly, and that almost never happened. He saw himself in the boy. The initiation would be hard on him. Snap wanted to see how much he could take.

"That's one of the boys I sent to deliver your message to that bitch of yours," Sergeant said from the side. "That one you talkin' to handled himself like a pro. His partner didn't make the cut. One bullet in the leg and ready to squeal like a bitch."

Snap turned from Sergeant and looked back at the youth in front of him. Some people just aren't shooters. Each soldier has their own talent, their own way to help the cause.

This boy didn't look like he would be good with a gun, which made him more valuable. Snap was impressed.

"Where are you from?"

"Bluefield, sir."

"What's your name, son?" Snap asked staring deep into the boy's eyes knowing the boy could only see his reflection in Snap's dark glasses.

"Israel."

Snap chuckled. That wasn't the name he would've been able to guess in a million years. The kid didn't look like an Israel. Snap gave the signal to his team, letting them know where they were to start.

"Well, Israel, get ready to be a part of The Set."

# ACKNOWLEDGMENTS

And so it begins. Hopefully this is the first of many novels to come. I want to take the time to thank all the people who were patient with me, and all the people who knew I was writing a book for about a year and a half and kept asking me when it would be out. I hope this was worth the wait. I want to also thank all the people who at one point told me I couldn't write a book, it's because of you that I found the drive to start and see it through to the end. Thanks to my mother for praying for me. Thanks to Ronnie, Stephen, Tamra, and Sarah for the support in the beginning. Most of all thank you,

Loren—never would've gotten started without you.
C.R. Ward

Makes his home in Southern West Virginia where he studied both graphic design and studio art at Concord University.

LaVergne, TN USA
17 January 2011
212724LV00001B/76/P